GO AHEAD . . .
MAKE HER DAY

Laura never knew what hit her. One minute she was walking, and the next he was grabbing her wrist, slapping on a handcuff, lifting her off her feet.

"Forget it," he said as he strode across the room. "You're not going anywhere yet." He dumped her on the bed and cuffed her to the headboard. Then he left.

She looked at the cuffs, picturing herself at a locksmith's with a brass headboard attached to her wrist. And then she remembered who she was with and smiled. The man had a multitude of talents, she had to give him that. He could pick locks, charm you senseless, debug rooms, scare you half to death, and probably talk you out of your first-born child.

And could he kiss.

Lord, could he ever.

DEBORAH GORDON

BEATING the ODDS

HarperPaperbacks
A Division of HarperCollinsPublishers

This is a work of fiction. The characters, incidents, and dialogues are products of the author's imagination and are not to be construed as real. Any resemblance to actual events or persons, living or dead, is entirely coincidental.

HarperPaperbacks   *A Division of* HarperCollins*Publishers*
10 East 53rd Street, New York, N.Y. 10022

Cover photography by Herman Estevez

First printing: May 1992

Printed in the United States of America

HarperPaperbacks and colophon are trademarks of HarperCollins*Publishers*

❖ 10 9 8 7 6 5 4 3 2

For my parents, Bob and Lillian Hannes,
who have all of Dottie Greenbaum's good qualities,
and, thank God, none of her bad ones.

ACKNOWLEDGMENTS

Sacramento is a wonderful place for a writer to live because so many resources are so close at hand. Elisabeth Kersten, director of the Senate Office of Research, provided a wealth of general background information. Special Agent Dell Rowley of the FBI answered many of my questions (and, alas, declined to answer many others). Information on horse racing came from Roy Minami, Chief of Administration of the California Horse Racing Board; Kathi Wisner and her colleagues at the Hartford answered my questions about the insurance business; a brief education in firearms was provided by the guys at Zeke's Guns and Ammo; and my friend Larry Ward, a computer expert with the legislature, explained numerous details about computers. For information on the legislature, I spoke with Bill Whiteneck, the consultant to the Senate Education Committee; Gina Pandelopoulos, the committee's secretary; Mary-Alice Morr, Senator Henry Mello's scheduling secretary;

and Louise Sears, personal secretary to Senator Gary K. Hart. (Senator Hart, not to be confused with Gary Hart of Colorado, is one of California's finest legislators.) My thanks to all of them for taking the time to help me get my facts straight. Any errors are mine, not theirs.

Finally, my heartfelt thanks to my editor, Carolyn Marino, whose excellent insights and suggestions helped me make the transition from my Brooke Hastings romance novels to *Beating the Odds*, the first book to appear under my own name.

BEATING the ODDS

ONE

reddie Phelps, the Sacramento general agent for the Columbia Life Insurance Company, was fast asleep in the passenger seat of his Mercedes-Benz, emitting a remarkable cacophony of wheezes, mutters, and snores. Laura Miller, who was driving, had been his secretary for a year and a half now and recognized the pattern. He'd had too many scotches at lunch. It was possible that he'd overindulged out of grief and shock over the murder of his client and close friend, U.S. District Judge James C. Hollister, whose funeral they were about to attend, but Laura doubted it. The truth was, Freddie got blitzed at least twice a week, and the fact that he'd sold tons of insurance over the years and had clients die on him with dismaying regularity had nothing to do with it.

Despite a six-figure income and a slew of prominent friends, he was a hick with simple tastes, a Midwestern good ol' boy who focused on the bright side of life. He liked fancy cars, boozy lunches with his cronies, and long sessions at the poker table with his pals. He disliked hard work, funerals—an unfortunate aversion given his choice of occupation—and being alone. He especially disliked being alone at funerals. Luckily, his wife Mary Beth, last year's Hospice Volunteer of the Year, was a real brick when it came to final farewells.

The brick, alas, was in Europe with her elderly parents and wouldn't be back till Sunday, so Freddie had asked Laura to keep him company. She hadn't minded going; she finished her work early most days and was always on the lookout for ways to keep busy. She did more of Freddie's job than he did by now, from sorting and answering his mail to writing his agency's weekly in-house newsletter.

Even more to the point, she found Hollister's death fascinating. More than once, she'd pictured herself solving the crime, then handing the whys and hows to the FBI. Her best friend, Vicki Stonehouse, teased that it was the frustrated reporter in her.

Laura couldn't deny it. Years ago, when her soon-to-be ex-husband had been in grad school, she'd worked as a researcher for a Boston-area newspaper, a job she'd absolutely loved. Even as a child, she'd been the type who dug for the story behind the story—and usually found it. Now, deep down, she hoped Hollister's funeral would give her some clue as to who had killed him.

He'd been dead since early Tuesday, when a passing motorist had discovered him slumped over the wheel of his car on a quiet country road off the interstate, about fifteen miles south of the city. There had been a pair of bullets in his brain but no gun in sight. Ever since, Laura, Freddie and everyone else in the office had talked nonstop about who might have done it. There was no shortage of suspects. Anyone who'd been a judge for sixteen years was bound to have made some enemies.

Laura turned into the driveway of the Capital Presbyterian Church in Carmichael. As she pulled into a parking space, Freddie twitched violently and gave a taurine snort. "Michelle . . . " he said.

She turned off the engine and peered at him, hoping he was coming around. He could be tough to wake up when he got drunk and passed out. His head slid downward, then jerked up again. "The hell with it," he muttered.

He was evidently dreaming about Michelle Buckley, his former girlfriend. His job was mostly a sinecure, but he did have one crucial duty—to recruit people to peddle Columbia's policies. Until recently, Michelle had been one of them. She'd come on board about the same time as Laura and had promptly started sleeping with the boss.

She'd been a star from the start, in part because Freddie had steered so many prospects her way, taking life easy while she'd nailed down business. He'd bought her a glitzy new piece of jewelry after every big sale, but he could well afford to. As the general agent, he'd received a cut of the commission on every policy she'd sold.

Then, about a month ago, in late February, she'd dumped him for a broker in San Francisco and moved west. Less than a week later, after a long and liquid lunch, Freddie had called Laura into his office and told her about his vasectomy in great detail. He'd been drunk enough to extol the size of her breasts, the shape of her backside, and the color of her eyes and hair, both of them an ordinary brown. His compliments—and his inability to get her pregnant—were presumably meant to beguile her into offering herself as a repository for his favorite bodily fluid.

It wasn't a happy thought. With his pointed nose, pronounced overbite, and beady eyes, he reminded her of her son Seth's pet rat Gummie, except that Gummie had better hair. Freddie had been pestering her ever since, but it was nothing blatant, just an occasional drunken confidence, careless endearment or light pat on her back or shoulders.

She'd responded by ignoring his behavior, telling herself he would give up and look for someone else once he realized she wasn't interested. She was afraid to be any more direct; his ego was fragile to begin with, and he'd been stung by Michelle's rejection. She couldn't afford to get fired on some trumped-up pretext. She was in the middle of a divorce she hadn't wanted—her husband had left her for another woman—and she needed every paycheck she could earn.

Besides, with two young children to care for and emotions that were as erratic as the old station wagon she drove, her chief goal was just to make it through each week. Her job was enjoyable if not challenging, she liked her coworkers, and her office was only a short drive from her house. Those were real pluses right now.

Freddie shifted in his seat, then opened his eyes and blinked blearily. "We're here?" Yawning, he slowly straightened, lurching his way up the back of his seat like a drugged rodent. "Already? I just closed my eyes."

The trip had taken the usual half hour, but there was nothing to be gained by pointing that out. Freddie never admitted to passing out or even to sleeping soundly, only to resting his eyes while he thought Deep Thoughts. "I had good luck with the lights," Laura said.

"Yeah, I noticed. Still, you made great time, especially for a Friday afternoon." He patted her shoulder. "You're a good little driver. Wouldn't trust just anyone with my Benz."

He'd only let her drive because she'd told him she wouldn't keep him company otherwise, and even then, he'd argued about it for a full five minutes. He was the type who could belt back a six-pack and then insist he was sober enough to drive a school bus. "I know," she said, annoyed by the way he'd patronized her but trying not to show it.

She paused, thinking about his reaction to Hollister's death. While he'd gone through the appropriate motions, the loss had barely seemed to touch him. Probing for information, she continued, "It's a good thing I drove, though. You seemed to be lost in thought the whole way here. It's Judge Hollister, I guess. You were such good friends. His death really hit you hard."

He frowned in confusion. "Uh, yeah." Thanks to the scotch or maybe the nap, he was a little slow on the uptake. "Jimmy was a great guy. Hell of a lot of fun at the poker table. Smartest guy I knew, too, but he never showed off about it." He looked devastated by the tragedy of it all. "God, I'll miss him. He was one of a kind. A real prince."

"It's been a hard year for you. First you lost Mr. Albright and then the judge. . . . "

"Yeah, it's been hell, all right. It was so damn sudden with both of them. One day they were here, and the next they were gone. When I think about Artie's body, floating out there in the Pacific till nothing was left but bones . . . It gives me nightmares, did I ever tell you that?"

Arthur Albright, another client and friend of Freddie's, had died in a boating accident the previous August, and his body had never been recovered. Freddie had gone to Lake Tahoe immediately after the funeral, saying he needed to be alone. By some strange coincidence, Michelle had been out with the flu for the next four days.

"No, you never did," Laura said. "And now you have to speak at another good friend's funeral. Will you be able to get through it?"

"I wish I didn't have to. I'm afraid I'll break down."

Actually, he loved making speeches and would have eulogized Hollister from his deathbed. People would have gathered around to listen, too. He was a good storyteller, in great demand at funerals, fund-raisers and testimonial dinners. "It's not too late to beg off. I'm sure Mrs. Hollister would understand—"

"No, no. I couldn't do that. I promised. Don't worry, though. I'll be fine. I'll concentrate on the good times. Try to block the tragedy out."

Laura checked the time. It was two-thirty, and the service wasn't till three. "It's early yet. Do you want to sit a while longer and collect your thoughts?"

"No. Let's take a walk." He opened the door. "Stretch our legs. Get some fresh air. It'll calm me down."

Not to mention sober him up. But a walk was fine with Laura. She didn't want him to deliver his eulogy like a zombie reanimated by Chivas on the rocks. Having lost her own father the previous June, she empathized with Hollister's family too much.

Besides, she had a habit of worrying about people who didn't deserve it, like Freddie and her almost-ex-husband Allan. She blamed it on biology. She'd obviously inherited the dreaded Jewish-mother gene from one of the champs of the species, her own mother Dottie, and it was running amok inside her body.

She and Freddie got out of the car. People were arriving relatively slowly, but she expected a big turnout in the end. Hollister had been a consummate political fund-raiser during his days as a corporate lawyer, and his wife, like Freddie's, was from a prominent local family.

They started walking, Freddie waving to people he knew as they circled the parking lot. Laura recognized an auto dealer, a developer, and a professional athlete.

All three were Freddie's personal clients. She knew that because she'd taken over the job of making sure big policy holders paid their premiums on time.

The athlete, a starting forward on the Sacramento Kings, checked her out and smiled. She was flattered. He was the flashiest, best-looking member of the team, and also the owner of one of the best names in the game.

She smiled back, then asked Freddie, "What's Royal Paine doing here?" Most of the mourners were middle-aged, rich, and white. Paine was young, rich, and black.

"He and Jimmy were friends from the Capital Athletic Club," Freddie said. "Royal hangs out there a lot, playing ball and shooting the breeze. Hell of a nice guy."

The Capital Athletic Club was in midtown Sacramento, about ten minutes from Freddie's agency. He went there two or three times a week, but since he showed no signs of engaging in physical exercise, she assumed it was to watch, schmooze, and hustle easy business. The club wasn't restricted—Allan belonged there, too—but it had its share of wealthy and prominent members.

"You mean Judge Hollister used to play basketball with Royal Paine?" she asked. Hollister had been tall and strong, but in his middle fifties.

"Just pickup games, when they needed another body on the floor. Both of 'em were nuts about college sports. They both went to Duke. Both played hoops there." Freddie waved to someone getting out of a silver Porsche a few yards away. "Hey, Mike! How's it going?"

The man turned around. "Can't complain, Freddie. It's a damn shame about Jimmy, though. We were playing basketball just last week. He was fifteen years older than me and he almost shut me down. He was as tough as they came. I can't believe he's gone."

"Me, neither." Freddie shook his head sadly. "He wasn't like me, Mike. He took care of himself. Should have lived to be a hundred. I'll tell you something. I'm going to miss him every day of my life."

Mike nodded. "I know. A couple of guys at the club mentioned how close you two were. I'm sorry."

"Thanks. I just hope . . . " Freddie paused, his face tight with emotion. "I hope they nail the bastard who killed him, that's all."

Laura glanced at him in surprise, thinking he was more upset than she'd given him credit for.

"You remember Laura," he added. "My secretary."

Mike smiled at her as they shook hands. "Of course. It's nice to see you again, Mrs. Miller."

She tried to place him. Nothing clicked, but it probably should have. Most men she met just didn't look like Mike Whoever-he-was. Tall and handsome, he had crisp, dark hair, light blue eyes, and perfect teeth. He had money, too, judging by the Porsche and the way he was dressed, in a white shirt, paisley tie, and Italian suit. He was L.A. sharp, not Sacramento dull.

"Same here," she said. "I'm just sorry about the circumstances."

The smile got broader, the eyes warmer, the voice more teasing. "You're wondering who the hell I am, aren't you?"

All that and charm, too, she thought. A few months ago she wouldn't have noticed, but she was slowly coming to life. She smiled back. "Now that you mention it . . . "

"My name is Mike Clemente. We met at Pavilions." Pavilions was Sacramento's fanciest shopping center. "You were with Freddie, walking through the courtyard. It was about a month before Christmas. You showed me some T-shirts you'd bought for your kids, from Banana Republic. I wound up getting one for my son."

Laura remembered the day he was talking about. It had been the Monday before Thanksgiving, the day she was filing for divorce, and she'd been a wreck just thinking about the future. She'd dreaded the holidays—that vacant spot at the table. She'd been worried about how the kids would adjust. She'd been sure the emptiness and pain would last forever.

Freddie had found her crying in his office and insisted on taking her to Pavilions to cheer her up. He'd been genuinely kind that day, buying her an expensive lunch at Mace's that she'd barely touched and telling her funny stories that she'd barely smiled at. Then he'd coaxed her into a couple of stores, gradually getting her involved in picking out Christmas gifts for his family. The T-shirts had been on sale, so she'd bought a pair for Seth and Sarah, for Hanukkah.

Along the way, they'd run into several people he knew, and Mike had obviously been one of them. "I remember now," she said. "It was a bad day. Freddie was trying to take my mind off my problems. I was walking around in a fog back then."

Mike smiled as if he knew exactly what sort of problem she meant. "I've had days like that myself, most of them during my divorce."

"We all have," Freddie agreed. "We have to help each other through the tough times, or what good are we?" He started toward the church, and Laura and Mike fell into step on either side of him. The front entrance was down a walkway through a rectangular courtyard. "The thing is, at least we're alive. At least we have a future. Not like Jimmy. The nicest guy in the world, and someone shoots him. Who can figure it?"

"You knew him as well as anyone did," Mike said. "What do *you* think?"

"That it was someone he sent to jail. Someone who decided to get even when he got out."

"Maybe, but we lawyers have a saying. Beware of your own clients. They don't get mad at the D.A. He's only doing his job. Same with the judge. But the defense attorney had better watch his back if his clients don't get off, because he's the one they blame."

So Clemente was a lawyer, Laura thought. "Even if they're guilty?" she asked.

"*Especially* if they're guilty. If they were innocent, they wouldn't need him. They expect results. What else are they paying him good money for?"

Freddie looked fascinated. "No kidding, Mike. Did any angry clients ever come after you?"

"No, but I wasn't a criminal lawyer. I did corporate work. All I had to do was word contracts the right way and my boss thought I was Clarence Darrow."

Laura liked men who had a sense of humor about themselves. "Was?" she asked, warming to him. "You mean you don't practice law anymore?"

"Yes and no. I'm a lobbyist now. I did technical and legal work at first, but I'm around the capitol much more now. My firm represents some large corporations." He named a few—big agriculture and medicine, big liquor and tobacco.

She felt a stab of disappointment. Talk about representing special interests . . . In her book, lobbyists like Clemente were nothing but shills who said whatever they were paid to and handed out bribes more politely termed campaign contributions.

They came to the end of the walkway and looked around. The semicircular driveway in front of the church was choked with cars by now. The main entrance was to their left, at the top of several deep, wide steps. A man was standing by the door, somberly greeting people.

Laura recognized him from the parties she'd been to at the Phelpses. He was Hollister's son Charles, a student at McGeorge Law School in Sacramento. Below him, at the bottom of the steps, two men in sunglasses and ill-fitting blue suits watched impassively as mourners slowly filed by.

She nodded toward the two men. "Those guys wear the worst suits," she said to Freddie. "It must be some sort of uniform. They can't all have bad taste."

He rolled his eyes. "Jesus, what bozos. What do they think? That whoever killed Jimmy is going to drop in to pay his last respects?"

"Then you figure they're federal agents?" Mike asked.

"Sure. One of 'em came by the office on Wednesday. Grimmest guy in the world. I told him some great stories about Jimmy, but he never even cracked a smile."

The agent had spoken to Laura, too, but only to ask for Freddie. "In fact," she said, "if he'd been any stiffer, he could have questioned Jimmy directly."

Mike looked amused. "You can't blame him. They're under a lot of pressure on this one. The government can't let people go around murdering federal judges. What did he ask? If Jimmy had any enemies? That sort of thing?"

Freddie loved telling people about his meeting with the FBI. "What *didn't* he ask? He wanted the story of Jimmy's life. Who his friends were, whether he had any business deals going, how he spent his time. And then he started asking about insurance, looking for some kind of angle there, but that was crazy. I handled all that for Jimmy. Sold him two policies, one whole life and one term, but Maggie, his widow, is the sole beneficiary of both. We talked for over two hours, but whether I gave him any leads . . ." He sighed. "I don't know, Mike. Jimmy and I were friends for twenty years, but everyone has secrets. I'm afraid I overlooked something important. Something that could break this thing wide open. I'm too involved in it, I guess. I keep going over and over what I—" He stopped abruptly, frowning at a stretch limo that had pulled up to the church a few seconds before.

A platinum blond got out—Hollister's former mistress, Bonita Franks. She wore a black veiled cloche, a black dress, and diamond-and-onyx antique jewelry. Reaching into her purse, she pulled out a black lace handkerchief and dabbed at her eyes. Laura thought the handkerchief was an especially nice touch. She'd never seen one that color in a store. Maybe Bonita sewed.

"Oh, hell," Freddie muttered. "That's all we need."

"Interesting dress," Mike said. It was long sleeved, high necked, and halfway up to her crotch. "Who is she?"

Freddie sidled closer to him. "A friend of Jimmy's. The kind who shouldn't have come, if you know what I mean."

Bonita closed the door, sniffling loudly as the limo pulled away. "Laura, honey, go over there and shut her up," Freddie said. "Make sure she behaves herself." He paused, then added to Mike, "Laura's good at calming people down. Jewish girls usually are. You ever notice that?"

"Can't say that I have," Mike answered. "Good luck, Mrs. Miller. It looks like you're going to need it."

"You're right, there." Freddie patted Laura's backside. "Run along, before she gets to the steps."

She gave him a dirty look, then walked stiffly away, wondering when he was going to get the message and leave her alone.

TWO

Freddie had lied to Mike Clemente. There had been a third policy on Hollister's life, a very large policy, and Laura wondered why he hadn't said so. After all, he'd volunteered the details of the other two policies readily enough. And since he'd sold the third one himself just two years before, he couldn't have forgotten it existed.

The omission couldn't have been a welcome display of discretion on his part, either. The purchaser and beneficiary, Bonita Franks, was weeping prodigiously as she wove her way toward the steps, and Freddie hadn't been remotely discreet about who she was. On the contrary, he couldn't have been any more blatant if he'd poked Mike in the ribs and winked broadly. It had been vintage Freddie Phelps.

The lady's histrionics were vintage Bonita Franks, too. A singer and pianist in South Lake Tahoe, she'd never met a situation she couldn't overdramatize. Theatrical to begin with, she laid it on with a trowel whenever men were around. Laura wasn't sure if there was any higher intelligence beneath the girlish pouts and breathy gossip, only that Bonita was either very

13

shrewd or very lucky. She'd bet on her lover's death and was now a cool million richer.

Laura knew about the policy because the home office in Ohio had sent Freddie a notice the previous January saying the premium was overdue. She'd offered to call Bonita with a reminder, but he'd told her it wasn't necessary. He'd seen Bonita over Christmas, he'd explained, when he'd taken his family skiing. She'd given him the money in cash, about thirty-five hundred dollars, but in the excitement of the holidays he'd forgotten to make the payment. He'd written a check on the spot and Laura had promptly mailed it.

Watching Bonita now, she wondered where all that cash had come from. Tips? Gambling? Something shadier? Was that how she satisfied her passion for antique jewelry?

Bonita moved to the steps and took a deep, quivery breath. She looked as if she'd wandered away from the set of a B movie from the forties about a hard-edged mob moll.

Laura hurried to intercept her, her sympathies with Maggie Hollister. It was bad enough that Maggie had lost her husband. She shouldn't have to cope with the sight of some bleached-blond bimbo carrying on like a cross between Blanche DuBois and Connie Corleone in front of her family and closest friends. Besides, as the betrayed wife in her own domestic drama, Laura had very little use for girlfriends.

"You must be in shock," she said, putting her arm around Bonita's waist. The woman's Giorgio perfume was strong enough to drop a camel in its tracks and deodorize it at the same time. "Is there anything I can do?"

Bonita sneezed into the black handkerchief. "It's so awful, Laura. I loved him so much. I lived to make him happy."

"I know you did. You're so flushed, I'm afraid

you're going to faint." Laura maneuvered Bonita toward the walkway that led to the parking lot. "There's a water fountain in the courtyard. Come on."

Bonita grabbed her arm with enough force to send her halfway to her knees. The woman was a head taller than Laura and downright robust. "I don't know how to thank you," she said. "I felt so alone in the car, coming here to say good-bye to Jimmy. You have no idea what it means—to see a friendly face, to hear a caring voice. . . ."

Bonita had seen her friendly face and heard her caring voice about twice a month, whenever Jimmy had brought her by the agency to have lunch with Freddie and Michelle. Laura's desk was in an alcove outside Freddie's office, opposite his private door from the back parking lot, so she'd been hard to overlook. Bonita had usually asked her how she was, then spent the next five minutes talking about herself.

Jimmy had been discreet, Laura had to give him that. He'd always brought in cold cuts that they'd eaten in Freddie's office. They'd never made much of an effort to be quiet, though, so she'd listened in whenever the conversation got interesting or her work got especially boring. She hadn't been able to resist. Bonita, whose real last name was Frangelico, had been much too prime a source of entertaining gossip.

Thanks to Bonita's job, she was always seeing celebrities, often with people they weren't married to. She was also a fount of good Mafia stories, not that Laura had believed them all. Bonita claimed the local wiseguys were great fans of hers, but Laura figured she would have been headlining in Vegas if that were true, instead of singing five nights a week in the Alpine Room, a posh restaurant in the Monte Carlo Hotel. Unless she had a lousy voice, that is, and then the Alpine Room would have been the most she could reasonably ask for.

Laura got her to the water fountain and held up her

veil so she could drink. Afterward, Bonita leaned against the wall and stared absently into space, seemingly numb with pain. Laura didn't buy all that grief, but she didn't think it was a complete sham, either. Bonita was simply immersed in her current role, that of the late, great man's bereaved mistress, who had selflessly devoted herself to brightening the last dreary days of his life.

Laura checked her watch. Another minute dragged by. She leaned close to Bonita and said quietly, "It's getting late. We should go into the church now." Preferably into the darkest corner of the very last pew.

"Yes," Bonita said. "We should." But she didn't budge.

Laura backed up a step. Discretion was a fine thing, but the scented air around Bonita was a toxic wasteland. "If it's too much for you . . . I've got the keys to Freddie's car. We could skip the service—go for a ride."

She shook her head. "No. I have to say good-bye."

Apparently she planned to shout it into the church from the walkway, because she remained rooted to the cement, her eyes watery and vacant. Laura pondered her options. There might be a last-ditch way to snap her out of her trance, but it was awfully crass. Then again, so was Bonita.

"I know you must be worried about the future," she said, trying to be tactful. "*I* would be in your place. Freddie can be so slow sometimes—there are all those papers to collect. You know how insurance companies are. I'll help as much as I can."

There was no reaction. So much for tact. "See that you get your check as soon as possible," she added.

Check was the magic word. Bonita blinked, then gazed at her soulfully. "That's very kind of you, not that I care about the money. But Jimmy loved me. And he was so insistent on protecting me. . . . "

"Of course. I understand." But Laura didn't understand at all. If Jimmy had loved her so much, why hadn't *he* paid the premiums?

Bonita straightened. "I'll be all right. It was just—seeing the church. Realizing the horrible finality of it all." Her eyes welled up. "I'm not going to look at him, Laura. I couldn't bear it."

"Actually, Freddie told me he was—"

"His dear face so pale and cold. His noble head torn so cruelly asunder." She lowered her eyes. "He deserves gentler memories than those."

She'd meandered into a Shakespearean tragedy now. Given Laura's fascination with Hollister's murder, it was too good an opening to pass up. Solving the case was probably just a crazy fantasy, but asking questions and sifting evidence was a lot more fun than real life had been lately.

She took Bonita's arm and coaxed her toward the church. "Yes. He does. Especially from the people who loved him. You and Jimmy . . . You were star-crossed, Bonita. Like Romeo and Juliet."

"Star-crossed." She brightened, obviously taken with the description. "Yes. Our paths crossed at the wrong moment in time. If only he'd been younger. Less important."

Less married, Laura thought. "Still, you had many precious hours together before—That is, your love for him was so pure. I'm sure he trusted you. Confided in you."

"Yes," Bonita agreed. "He did."

"And being so close to him—so involved in everything he felt and did—you must have asked yourself again and again. . . . Who could have attacked him that night?"

"Yes. I can't stop thinking about it."

"And?"

Bonita looked around warily, as if the murderer might be lurking behind a doorway at that very moment, waiting to pounce out and silence her forever if his name should chance to pass her lips. "It might be dangerous to speculate."

Laura simply waited. It was obvious she wasn't done.

Her voice dropped to a murmur. "I had a fan up at the lake, Laura. His name was—Let's call him Johnny. He liked to shoot craps."

She'd segued into *The Gambler* now, although what her story had to do with Hollister . . .

"So what happened?"

"He kept losing. On credit. He couldn't pay, so they let him work off his debt smuggling in dope from Mexico. He got caught. Rumor had it he'd made a deal with the Feds. He disappeared last winter. Everyone figured he was in a protected witness program."

She stopped at the end of the walkway, clutching Laura's shoulder in a death grip. Three TV trucks were parked in front of the church now, blocking most of the roadway and snarling traffic completely.

"They just found him," Bonita continued. "He was trapped under the ice in the lake, and when it thawed . . . " She noticed the trucks and let Laura go. "His hands were gone," she hissed, smoothing her dress and veil. "Do you know what that means?"

"Whacked," Laura whispered back. A mob hit. She'd read all about them. She loved mystery novels and true-crime books.

"Yes." Bonita started forward. "That's what they do when you snitch. They cut off your hands. Sometimes even your head."

So far as Laura knew, Jimmy's head and hands had been in their usual spots, attached securely to his neck and wrists. "I don't understand. Do you think Jimmy was mixed up with—"

"No. Of course not. But they're killers, Laura. Cold-blooded killers. And when you make them mad . . . When you send them to jail . . . "

It was the revenge theory again, and, Mike Clemente's comments to the contrary, it made a lot of sense. There was only one problem with it.

"I see your point, but what was Jimmy doing on a deserted back road in the middle of the night? Are you saying he agreed to meet someone he'd sent to jail?"

"Yes. Obviously he was tricked. They convinced him it was someone who needed his help, or someone who had important information about some crime. And then—and then . . . " She swallowed hard. Laura was afraid the weeping and wailing would erupt all over again. "If only he'd called the police! He would still be alive."

They'd reached the steps in front of the church. Jimmy's son was talking to a pair of elderly women now. "I shouldn't have brought it up," Laura said, hoping she could slip Bonita past them. "It's too painful for you to talk about. You're all flushed again. You need to sit down."

Ignoring her, Bonita strode straight up the steps, right to Charles Hollister. He looked startled for a moment, but then smiled and held out his hand. Laura followed helplessly. To her amazement, they obviously knew each other.

Bonita took his hand in both of hers. The two elderly women stared at her in pinch-faced disapproval, then marched inside.

"Oh, Charlie!" she said. "I'm so terribly, terribly sorry about your father. He was a wonderful man. I'm going to miss performing for him."

If Charlie knew how intimate those performances had

been, it didn't show. "You were a real favorite of his, Miss Franks. It was nice of you to make the trip down. I just hope you get back to the lake in time for work."

"Even if I'm a little late, I still had to come. A girl doesn't have many fans like the judge. He was always so enthusiastic about my singing."

Charlie nodded. "I know. You gave him a lot of pleasure over the years."

Bonita looked deeply touched. "Why, thank you, Charlie. It's sweet of you to say so." She glanced furtively at the federal agents. "I was a little worried. . . . Those men down there . . . I know cops when I see them. Is everything okay?"

"Everything's fine." Charlie's tone was crisp, almost dismissive.

"Then why are they here?"

He withdrew his hand. It was obvious he didn't want to discuss the subject. "It's just routine."

She looked annoyed, but only for a second. "Oh. That's a relief. I was concerned about your family."

"We're fine."

"Then you don't expect trouble or—"

"Not at all, Miss Franks." He looked at Laura. "Thank you for coming, Mrs. Miller. It's nearly three. You should probably find some seats."

Laura murmured the appropriate condolences and hustled Bonita inside. Although she didn't resist, Bonita seemed irritated or upset, as if Charlie had slighted her somehow. They signed the guest book in the vestibule, accepted programs from a sober young man by the door, and went into the sanctuary. Three cameramen were lounging against the back wall, waiting with bored expressions for the service to begin. Laura was surprised the family had let them in. Old-line Sacramentans were usually more private.

Most of the pews were full, but there was space at

the far ends of the last several rows. She started toward a side aisle, but Bonita went straight ahead. Sighing, Laura followed.

Bonita walked halfway up the center aisle, then stopped. "I don't see Jimmy. I thought he'd be right up front."

"He's at the funeral home," Laura said softly. "That's the custom here. Freddie told me about it on the way over." To be exact, he'd grumbled that it was hard for a man to do his best work when the subject of his efforts wasn't even there to hear him.

Bonita looked crushed. "I wish I'd known. I would have left earlier—gone over to see him. Now I won't have time. I have to be back by six-thirty."

A commitment for which they could all be devoutly grateful, since it would keep her away from his family. It wouldn't have done any good to remind her about his pale face and shattered head. Consistency wasn't her strong suit. Melodrama was.

"You shouldn't blame yourself," Laura said. "Believe me, Jimmy will understand. We should sit down now."

Bonita nodded and headed for a tiny space a few rows up. They wound up wedged in so tightly that Laura resigned herself to reeking of Giorgio by the time the service ended.

The pastor walked in at three-fifteen and delivered a glowing eulogy. Bonita raised her handkerchief to her eyes and sobbed, fairly softly, fortunately.

The congregation sang a hymn next. Bonita joined in enthusiastically, in such a pure, rich soprano that people looked around to see who was singing. With a voice like that, she couldn't have been in tight with the mob. She would have been a star by now.

The pastor read a psalm after that, and then Charlie spoke briefly but emotionally about what a wonderful father the judge had been. Freddie was next. Bonita checked her watch as he made his way to the front, obviously worried about the time. The traffic on Highway 50 was heavy on Fridays, especially after four or five o'clock. If she didn't leave soon, she might be late for work.

"My mother passed away four years ago," Freddie began. "A few hours after I got the news, the judge called me up, saying he had a feeling something was wrong. I told him about my mother, and he said he'd take over my charitable commitments while I was back in Ohio. He didn't just offer, he insisted."

Freddie's voice was hoarse with tears, but he bravely carried on. "That was the judge. He had a million friends, and he kept up with all of us. He knew everything that was happening in this town and he was always trying to make it a better place. He noticed things—little things the rest of us missed—and he remembered things the rest of us forgot. And we all got the benefit." He smiled. "Except for the lawyers in his courtroom. They couldn't slip a thing past him."

There was soft laughter from the congregation. "But it wasn't just a keen eye and a good memory. He had a sixth sense about things. Once we were watching a ballgame, and the pitcher, Rick McNally—Terry and Sue's boy—got hit in the head with a line drive. He had a slight headache, but otherwise he felt okay. He wanted to stick around, but the judge nagged Terry into taking him to the hospital."

Freddie paused. "Turned out he had a brain hemorrhage and needed surgery. If they'd waited too much longer—But they didn't thanks to the judge, and Rick was fine in the end. The judge was modest about it afterward. He always was when it came to his hunches, but he never ignored them. He was lucky, maybe even clairvoyant, and he knew it. He could have made a fortune at the track, but we all know how he felt about gambling, about the way it could destroy people's lives. A dinner on the World Series was as much as he'd ever wager."

Freddie continued with several anecdotes, painting a verbal picture of Hollister's life. There was his tenacity on the basketball court and the injuries he'd suffered as a result. His concern for kids had prompted him to chair a project to combat the spread of gangs in the area. He'd been an avid fisherman and skier, going to Lake Tahoe regularly, and an enthusiastic traveler, visiting Europe or Asia every year with his beloved Maggie.

The eulogy was a long one, but so funny and heartwarming that no one got bored. Laura had always thought of Hollister as a slick big shot with a flashy mistress and a large bank account, but even she was moved.

So was Bonita, but only for the first twenty minutes. Then she stopped sniffling and started fidgeting. It was past four by the time the pastor returned to the pulpit. He announced that a reception would be held in the social hall following the service, offered some final words of comfort to the family, and closed with a brief prayer.

"This lasted a lot longer than I expected," Bonita said as she and Laura got up. "I thought I'd have time to go downtown, but now . . . " She hesitated. "Laura, I have a huge favor to ask you. You know Jimmy's apartment? The one I used to stay in when I came here?"

Laura nodded. It was across from the capitol, a combination love nest and professional retreat. "I know the building, but I've never actually been in the apartment."

"It's 4C. I kept some of my things there." They made their way to the aisle. "I was going to get them after the service, but there isn't time now. The landlord could throw them out before I get back to pick them up, you know? I mean, he'll probably want to rent it again starting on the first. Could you go there for me? Pick up my things and send them to the lake? I know it's an inconvenience, but I'd just be so grateful. . . . "

"It's not an inconvenience at all," Laura said. "My house is only ten minutes away. I'd be glad to help out."

And she genuinely was, but as much due to curiosity as altruism. She'd been hearing about that apartment for at least a year. Freddie had used it too, along with God only knew how many other friends of Hollister's. She was dying to get a look inside. Was there a mirrored ceiling in the bedroom? A four-poster suitable for bondage?

"You're a doll," Bonita said as they walked out of the church. "Come sit in the car. I'll write out a list of everything I left and give you the keys."

The limo was waiting by the front steps, parked where the TV trucks had been. Laura slid in after Bonita, leaving the door open to let some fresh air inside. The interior smelled like a bordello.

Bonita jotted down the items and their locations, filling both sides of her program. She seemed so eager to have everything back that Laura offered to send the items UPS Overnight and accepted some money to cover the cost.

Bonita hugged her like a long-lost relation afterward. "Thanks for everything, Laura. I never would have made it through the funeral without you. Promise me you'll come see me sing. Bring a friend if you want. I'll buy you both dinner."

"Thanks. I'll try my best." And for a free dinner in a classy restaurant, she really would. Vicki had a place near the lake and was always offering to let her use it.

She got out of the car. One of the federal agents watched her stolidly. Maybe it was routine—they seemed to watch everyone and everything—but more likely, it was her proximity to Bonita. Flashy blonds in limos tended to attract attention, and she'd just spent the past hour and a half by Bonita's side.

She suddenly wondered if they knew who Bonita was. Jimmy's close friends could have told them, but maybe they'd decided that details like mistresses were best kept private. Laura might have agreed, but anyone who stood to profit by Jimmy's death to the tune of a million bucks had to be considered a murder suspect, even someone as flaky as Bonita.

Freddie wasn't outside the church, so she headed for the reception, passing Mike Clemente in the courtyard. He was talking to a slick assemblyman who chaired a prime juice committee—a committee whose members received fat campaign contributions from the interests they were supposed to regulate.

Mike saw her and smiled, but his attention was clearly on the assemblyman. She smiled back, but no more sincerely than he had. He represented pond scum for a living. He was bound to have gotten infected.

The social hall was packed. Laura helped herself to coffee, then looked for Freddie. She found him in a back corner, talking to Maggie Hollister and Alice Albright, the woman whose husband had drowned the previous summer. At the time, the Albrights had lived in an expensive area of Sacramento called the Fabulous Forties, on the same block as the Hollisters and the Phelpses. Alice had since moved, settling in a small town in the foothills. Her son owned and ran the family business, Albright Investments, now.

Alice had changed since the last time they'd met. She was thinner, and a living testimony to the wonders of plastic surgery. Somewhere in her midsixties, she didn't look a day over fifty. Laura wrote to her regularly on Freddie's behalf, composing warm little notes that he skimmed and signed. He was a great believer in staying in touch with his friends and relatives; he sold more insurance that way.

She extended her condolences to Maggie Hollister, reminding her that they'd met at several of the Phelpses' parties, then said to Alice, "Freddie talks about you so often. I know he's worried about how you're getting along."

"I've managed." Alice turned to Maggie. "Things slowly get better, Maggie. Moving helped. Getting away from all the memories, you know."

"But my life is here," Maggie replied. "My children, my work for the hospital and symphony. And, of course, I'll want to continue Jimmy's fight against gang violence."

"Are you sure that's a good idea? I mean, in view of—"

"Yes, Alice. I'm not going to be intimidated."

"Well, try to keep an open mind about moving. It's lovely up in Pollock Pines, and much more civilized than people think. I never have a problem finding work, and you know me and my jobs." She'd had a parade of them since her husband's death, all part-time. "If I start missing my family and friends, I'm only an hour away."

"Yeah, she's down here all the time," Freddie said. "I keep finding her in my living room, yakking with Mary Beth."

Alice smiled. "Every month or two, anyway. Why don't you come spend a week with me, Maggie? Try it out?"

Maggie shook her head. "Thanks, but I'm not the back-to-nature type. If I move anywhere, it will be to San Francisco. I'd love being able to hop in a cab and be at the opera or symphony ten minutes later."

"If you should change your mind—"

"I'll invite myself. I promise. I should circulate now." She touched Freddie's arm. "Thank you, Freddie. It was a wonderful talk. Jimmy would have loved it."

"It was an honor to be asked." He paused, then added softly, "Now don't you worry about that letter, Maggie. It was probably some creep's idea of a joke."

"I'm not worried. Charlie is—and the FBI, too, I suppose. It was lovely to see you again, Laura. Alice, be sure to call me the next time you're in town. We'll have lunch."

She pecked Alice on the cheek, then walked away. Laura was amazed by her composure.

"She's doing wonderfully well," Alice remarked, "especially in view of that awful letter. Much better than I did, really." She noticed a man waving at her from a few yards away. "There's Arthur. I'd better get on my way. We have big plans for tonight."

She joined her son, who smiled at Freddie but didn't acknowledge Laura at all, even though they'd met last fall at one of Freddie's parties. He was thirtyish and cute, like a younger, shorter-haired version of the comedian Richard Lewis.

The two of them disappeared into the crowd, and Laura turned back to Freddie. "What was all that about a letter? Did Maggie receive some sort of threat in the mail?"

"Yeah. Come on. Let's go." He took her arm. "I'll tell you about it in the car."

Mike Clemente was still in the courtyard when they got outside, talking with a distinguished-looking man of about fifty. Freddie said good-bye, and Mike answered with an absent smile and a quick wave. His companion called out, "Nice job, Freddie," then turned back to Mike. The two men resumed their conversation, talking to each other in an animated but intimate way.

"Who was that?" Laura asked when they were out of earshot.

"His name's Craig Tomlinson. He's from L.A."

"He must have been a good friend of the judge's, to come all the way to Sacramento for the funeral."

"Yeah, a very good friend, but he probably combined it with business. He's up here all the time. The guy's loaded. Runs a couple of corporations. Gives a lot of money to the Republican Party. That's how Jimmy met him. Brought him to our poker games all the time. Hell of a nice guy. A terrific hunter—he brought me some ducks once. I guess he's one of Mike's clients."

He was a rich corporate executive, so it was a logical assumption. Laura unlocked the car. "Why don't I drive? You've had a rough afternoon."

"You're right, there. You want to drive, go right ahead." They got inside and put on their seat belts. "By the way, you did a great job with Bonita. You girls really know how to talk to each other. I still can't believe she showed up. You'd think she'd have some respect."

"Then Maggie didn't know about her?"

"Maggie? Are you crazy?" He laughed. "Not unless you told her."

"Not me." Laura backed the car out. "I didn't tell the FBI, either, but maybe I should have, given that big insurance policy. Did you?"

"Tell the FBI?" He fiddled with the air conditioning. "To be honest, it was a tough call. A man is entitled to some privacy, you know what I mean? But then I thought about the insurance policy, and I decided it made her a suspect. I had to mention it. They're the experts, not me. They have to decide what's important."

"You're right. You had to level with them." She made sure she sounded admiring. Freddie would tell her more that way. "That letter Maggie got . . . Is that why they came today?"

He nodded. "Partly, and it wasn't just the two guys out front. They were all over the place, watching everyone."

"My God, what did the letter say? Did Maggie tell you?"

"Sure. It was something like, 'Mrs. Hollister—what happened to your husband could happen to you. Don't make the mistake of sticking your nose where it doesn't belong.' She got it yesterday. It was mailed from South Lake Tahoe on Wednesday, but that doesn't prove anything. Someone could have driven up there to send it."

Or Bonita could have dropped it at the local post office. "I've heard the FBI can do amazing things with letters. Trace the typewriter and the paper, pick up latent fingerprints . . . "

"They sent it to the lab back in Washington, but Maggie thinks it was done on a laser printer. Even the envelope. They might not be able to tell much."

"Do they have any theories about who wrote it?"

"Who knows? The Feds are like clams. Maggie figures they're getting nowhere fast. That's why she let the media in. She thought the publicity might help— that someone might see the story and decide to talk. I'll tell you what, honey. Swing by Mace's. I'll buy you a drink and tell you what I know."

Intrigued by the murder or not, Laura wasn't having cocktails with Freddie Phelps. He wanted to make a pass, not talk. "No, thanks. You know me. I hate to keep my kids waiting at day-care." That was true. Bonita's errand would have to hold till tomorrow morning, when Allan fetched the kids for the weekend.

"Then how about lunch on Monday?" Freddie paused. "My treat. It's the least I can do, to thank you for keeping me company today."

Laura was noncommittal. Freddie cajoled her for a minute longer, then fell back asleep.

THREE

Seth, Laura's nine-year-old, was watching TV in his baby-sitter's living room when Laura arrived to fetch him and his five-year-old sister Sarah. He glanced up as she approached the couch. "Hi, Mom. I was watching for you on the news, but they didn't show you. Man, there were a lot of people at the funeral. They showed Royal Paine walking in. Did you see him?"

"As a matter of fact, I did. Mr. Phelps waved to him in the parking lot. Mr. Paine smiled at me."

"Wow. He's the freshest guy they have." Seth paused, fidgeting a little on the couch. "Tim was telling me about this funeral he went to." Tim was one of his friends. "They left the coffin open and people could look inside if they wanted—right at the dead person's face. Did you look at the judge? Could you see the bullet holes in his head? Were his brains oozing out?"

Laura had learned over the years that failing to satisfy Seth's sometimes lurid sense of curiosity only intensified it. She explained that the casket hadn't been present, much less open, then added, "But if it had been, there are people who fix things like that—who make the person who died look as nice as possible."

Seth screwed up his face. "You mean they touch rotting dead people?"

"They're not rotting yet, it's too soon for that, but they couldn't do their jobs without touching them. They consider themselves artists, sort of like Hollywood makeup people. So if someone dies in a bad accident, for example, they think of it as a challenge to make that person look just like he did before it happened, or even better."

"What a sick job." Seth clicked off the TV with the remote, his curiosity apparently satisfied. "I'm hungry, Mom. What are we having for dinner?"

"It's been a long day. I don't feel like cooking. How about some Chinese take-out?"

"Yeah, great! We were gonna have that on Wednesday, with Dad and Carolyn, but we didn't. Tina didn't want to." Tina, a one-foot-tall fairy, was Sarah's imaginary friend. "Sarah said Tina was sick of Chinese food and wouldn't eat it, and that if Tina wouldn't eat it, she wouldn't, either. So Dad asked what Tina *would* eat, and Carolyn got really mad, because Chinese food was her idea in the first place. She said Sarah was a spoiled brat and Tina wasn't even real, but Dad stuck up for Sarah. Carolyn got even madder—she said Dad was stupid to give in to us all the time, and that she didn't care what we ate but she wasn't going to get it. Then she went to her friend's house for dinner and Dad took us to Taco Bell."

Carolyn Seeley was Allan's girlfriend, a beautiful and successful public relations executive. The two had met while she was helping his employer, the local school district, pass a bond issue. They lived together in Carolyn's house in nearby Land Park now.

Laura had learned about the affair the previous July, after it had been going on for six months. Allan had promised to cut things off, but waffled back and forth instead, until, two months later, Laura had told him to move out. If it had been just the two of them, she might have waited longer, because she still loved him and saw him as weak, torn, and confused, rather than monstrous. But the turmoil in the house was having a negative effect on the kids, making Seth act out at school and Sarah withdraw, and that was something she *couldn't* wait out.

Seth and Sarah were her first concern, so much so that she'd wanted to stay home with them while they were young. She'd gone back to work solely for financial reasons, and only after Allan, a child-development expert, had sworn that a good day-care program wouldn't harm them. He'd undoubtedly been right, but she still found it hard to let someone other than herself look after them.

She reminded Seth that Carolyn wasn't used to children and sometimes got a little impatient, then went to find Sarah. The little girl was climbing on the jungle gym in the backyard while the baby-sitter, Mrs. Fujimoto, watched and clapped. Though physically fearless, Sarah was quieter than Seth and more high strung; Seth tended to talk a blue streak while Sarah kept things inside. Laura got her down, gave Mrs. Fujimoto a check and collected Seth. Then she drove the three of them—or four of them, if one counted Tina—to the take-out place, where they picked out dinner with the full cooperation of everyone concerned, both real and imaginary.

Laura checked her answering machine when she got home—there were no messages—and then called the kids to the table. Seth began describing a science experiment he'd done and would have chattered about it indefinitely if Laura hadn't gently cut him off in order to give Sarah a chance to talk. Her daughter, it turned out, had had a substitute that day.

"Was she nice?" Laura asked.

"She was okay, I guess," Sarah said.

"What did she do with the class? Anything special?"

"She polished her nails."

"Right at her desk? During class time?"

"Yup. Bright red."

"And what was the class doing while she was polishing her nails bright red?"

"Drawing pictures."

"Of what?"

"Anything we wanted."

Conversing with Sarah could be like pulling teeth. "What did *you* draw?" Laura asked.

"Our house."

"Did you bring the picture home?"

"Yes." Sarah paused. "It's in my backpack. Should I get it?"

"Yes. Get the masking tape, too."

Sarah went off to her room, returning with a large piece of paper folded into quarters. Laura's throat tightened as she opened it up. It wasn't only of the house, but of the family, too—and not the family as it was, but the family as Sarah wished it to be. All four of them were standing in front of the door, the children between their parents. Tina was on one side and Sam, their corpulent gray cat, was on the other, looking covetously at Seth's pet rat Gummie.

Laura hugged Sarah and told her she was a wonderful artist, then taped the picture to the front of the refrigerator.

They finished eating and cleared the table. At six-thirty, as Laura was loading the dishwasher, the phone rang. It was her mother Dottie, who called her every Friday at six-thirty to ask her to go to religious services.

The death of Laura's father the previous June, which had left Dottie alone in New York, had plunged her into a numbing depression. The gloom had begun to lift only after Laura had finally confided that her marriage was falling apart. The news had given Dottie a whole new lease on life. Her only child needed her. There was a reason to go on. Last fall, she'd sold her house in Queens and moved to a retirement community in Roseville, about half an hour from Laura.

At first, she'd dropped in constantly with everything from chicken soup to nut cake, staying to scrub and polish like a demented dervish. But to Laura's great relief, she'd soon grown too busy organizing activities at her apartment complex and running around with her new friends to waste time cooking and cleaning.

She visited once or twice a week now, which was just about right, and called almost daily with gossip and advice. The downside was the men she dug up—the sons, nephews, and cousins of every Jewish senior in sight, some within shouting distance of Medicare themselves. "Dottie's dates from hell," Laura called them, although the details did have a certain after-the-fact entertainment value when she related them to Vicki.

Dottie passed on some family news, then launched into her pitch about services. They belonged to the same reform temple, but Dottie was a tireless volunteer, while Laura generally went only on Sundays, when it was her turn to take the kids to religious school. "Religion can be a great comfort, Laura. It saved my sanity when your father died, I don't mind telling you that. Besides, it would do you good to get out. Mix with your own kind."

"Maybe next week, Mom." It was what Laura always said. "I'm kind of tired tonight."

"You should take vitamins, Laura. Get more exercise. At your age, you shouldn't be so tired." Dottie paused. "You remember my neighbor Rose Lefkowitz? Her son is visiting from Los Angeles. He's divorced.

Forty-eight but very youthful-looking. Not so tall, but he has a good head of hair for a man his age, and he's thin. She's bringing him to services. I want you to meet him. He was lovely to me. He has wonderful manners."

"I'm sure he's very nice, but—"

"A professional man, Laura. A dentist like your father. Rose says he has a busy practice. A house in Beverly Hills. His children are in college and his ex is remarried, so there are no complications there. A man like that would take good care of you."

"I've told you, Mom, I don't need a man to—"

"I know you don't, but there's nothing so wrong with it, either. What's the matter? A dentist isn't fancy enough for you? Your father didn't make me a good enough husband?"

Laura had heard all this before. "Actually, I'm holding out for a surgeon," she teased.

"A surgeon I could probably find you," Dottie said with a laugh, "but *you* want someone who makes a living saving the world. I'll tell you, Laura, you married that type once already and it didn't turn out so well. Take my advice. Go for the dough next time."

Laura smiled. It was one of Dottie's favorite refrains, but she didn't mean it. Between her mother's donations to charity and her father's free treatment of the poor, the family had never had extra money. "Okay, Mom. I'll do that."

"I should be so lucky, but it's my own fault. We should have raised you to be more mercenary. Listen, darling, I'll give Dr. Lefkowitz your number. Have dinner with him some night. Or take in a movie. What do you have to lose?"

A few hours of peace and quiet, thought Laura, but she agreed. It was easier to go out with her mother's prospects than to argue. Dottie always grumbled a bit when things didn't work out, but her irritation never lasted. There was always another find on the horizon, a fellow who would prove such a paragon of Jewish manhood that even Laura would see the light.

She said good-bye, then finished cleaning the kitchen. The kids asked to play Monopoly afterward. She would have preferred to relax with a magazine or call Vicki to gossip about the funeral, but Seth and Sarah would be with Allan all weekend and she knew she would miss them after they'd left.

She set up the board in Seth's room, on a bridge table. She had such bad luck that she figured she would have been better off at services with Dr. Lefkowitz. She'd just wound up in jail for the second time in three circuits when the phone rang.

"Roll for me," she said as she got up. "If I get out, buy me whatever I land on."

The call was from Mike Clemente, who told her he'd enjoyed seeing her and was sorry they hadn't talked again during the reception. She thought that was an odd thing to say. Far from seeking her out, he'd been so busy with movers and shakers that he'd barely noticed she was there.

"I thought it was a nice service," she answered, making polite small talk. "Very moving."

"Yes. It was. Freddie's a good speaker. I didn't know the judge as well as I would have liked to, and Freddie gave me a feeling for what sort of man he was." He paused. "You seem to have done well with the judge's friend. Freddie told me she's a professional singer. I figured she'd take one look at the cameras and faint dead away. She could have gotten some great publicity out of it."

"She probably would have if she'd thought of it, but they weren't taping when we walked into the church."

"So how did you calm her down?"

"Just listened, mostly. She likes to talk."

"In that case, I'd like to offer you a job with my firm. If you can head off hysterics just by listening, you must be incredibly persuasive."

"Not really," Laura said, enjoying the compliment all the same. "Listen, I'm in the middle of a Monopoly game with my kids and they'll rob me blind if I don't get back to it. What can I do for you, Mike?"

"Go out to dinner with me tomorrow night," he said.

She was astonished. He'd been charming that afternoon, but she'd gotten the feeling he was charming to everyone. He'd smiled a few times, but she could have been sixteen or sixty and he would have smiled the same way.

She frowned, wondering if there had been a signal she'd somehow missed. She was out of practice when it came to men. Then again, even if there had been, he wasn't her type. As her mother kept pointing out, she went for the idealists, men like Allan who worked in the public sector for far less money than they were worth because they wanted to make the world a better place.

"Thanks for asking," she said, "but no."

"That's it? Just 'no'? You're not going to spare my feelings by claiming that you're busy, or going out of town, or even that you have to wash your hair?"

"No. I'm sorry."

"Involved with someone else, then. Or not ready yet to get involved with anyone. Give me a little hope here, Laura. Please."

She smiled to herself. He sounded more amused than desperate, but she was still flattered. "Sorry, Mike. I can't."

There was a short silence. "Can I talk you into lunch? That's a smaller commitment."

"I'm afraid not."

"A cup of coffee at Java City, then. That's hardly any commitment at all."

"No. I'm sorry."

"Me, too. I don't meet many women like you." He was quietly serious now. "Smart, sexy, and funny. If you change your mind, give me a call at the office. I'm with Burke/Maravich. I'll let you get back to your Monopoly game. You should probably count your money."

Laura said she would do that, then hung up. She couldn't believe how slick the man was. He'd handed her the best lines since Euclid and she knew it, but she still felt as desirable as Michelle Pfeiffer. He was probably a depressingly effective lobbyist.

She returned to Seth's room and studied the board. Her position had improved miraculously during her absence and the kids were stifling giggles. Either they'd taken pity on her or they were trying to prolong the game.

They continued playing, with no end in sight when bedtime came around. The kids begged to keep going, but Laura said no. Allan kept them busier than she did and let them stay up later, so they would need a good night's sleep.

She got them to bed and settled down in the living room with the latest issue of *Discover*. She was rescued from a science article so abstruse that it might as well have been written in Urdu by a knock on the door. She turned on the outside light and peered through the peephole. It was Allan.

Her first thought was that they'd gotten their signals crossed about when he was coming for the kids. He picked them up on Friday nights occasionally, but that hadn't been their arrangement this weekend.

Then she got a better look at his face. Something was wrong—so wrong that even the phone wouldn't have done. This wasn't about the kids. He'd come to see *her*.

Alarmed, she opened the door. In truth, their divorce-in-progress was a lot friendlier than the last few years of their marriage had been. Allan, a workaholic who'd spent time with the kids only on weekends even B.C.—before Carolyn—had rediscovered fatherhood once he'd been faced with losing it, and never missed a weekend or midweek night, even when it meant rearranging his schedule. Laura's lawyer had warned her that he was laying the groundwork for a custody fight, but she didn't buy that for a moment.

His newfound devotion wasn't an act—a struggle for the children's hearts, or a crusade for fathers' rights. He loved the kids and was trying to show it. His attentiveness and affection had made the divorce as easy on them as such things could be. And for that alone, Laura would have forgiven him the world.

FOUR

He walked inside and kissed her on the cheek. He always kissed her when he saw her. He thought of himself as her friend.

She didn't turn away, because in truth, he was. He fixed things around the house, phoned her regularly to see how she was doing, and helped her during minor crises. He'd even given her a birthday present the month before.

Vicki said he was keeping his options open, but Laura knew it was more complicated than that. For one thing, he felt guilty about how he'd behaved and wanted to make amends. For another, nobody had known him longer than Laura or understood him better. No one had been more loyal or trustworthy. He couldn't give those things up, not even now.

"Hi," he said. "I like the dress. It's new, right?"

"It's Vicki's. I borrowed it for Judge Hollister's funeral." It was navy with white piping and made her look taller and thinner. She was considering refusing to return it. "I didn't have anything right. You know, dark but not black. I didn't know him well enough for black."

"You should have bought yourself something new. I would have given you some extra money."

He'd been generous financially, more so than she'd expected or the court had required. "I wouldn't waste your hard-earned money when I could borrow something for free, but thanks anyway." She closed the door. "You don't look so good, Allan. You want something to eat? Or a cup of coffee?"

"Not food. I'm not hungry. But coffee sounds good." He paused. "To be honest, I don't feel so good. I was hoping we could talk."

Laura might have told him to take his problems to his girlfriend, but she didn't. Maybe she was masochistic or stupid, but she still cared about Allan. They'd spent fifteen years together, most of them fairly happy, and he'd given her two children she loved fiercely. The fact that he'd left her didn't erase those years, or negate his simple decency since.

"Sure," she said. "There's some coffee on the stove. Come get yourself a cup."

He followed her into the kitchen. His appetite returned when he spotted the homemade chocolate chip cookies on the counter. "Carolyn never makes these anymore," he said as he grabbed a handful and put them on a plate. "She did when I first moved in, when the kids started coming for weekends, but it didn't last."

Of course not, Laura thought. She'd gotten what she wanted, so why would she keep exerting herself? "Carolyn has a demanding career and a big house to look after," she said. She wasn't going to disparage the woman who'd replaced her—not to Allan, anyway. "You can't blame her for not having the energy to bake."

"She has the energy to go to the club three or four times a week to work out. Anyway, a maid does the cleaning, not her." He poured himself some coffee. "She's not . . . domestic. She won't even sew my buttons on. I have to pay the cleaner to do it."

"So sew them on yourself. And if you want chocolate chip cookies, learn to make them. The kids will help you. They know how."

He stared at her, the mug in one hand and the plate in the other. "I'm not going to get any sympathy from you, am I?"

"No."

"You're not even going to say 'I told you so'?"

"Nope. I have a lot of empathy for her, Allan. I mean, if you're as little help at her place as you were here—"

"I'm not. I'm a lot better."

Laura doubted it. "Oh? Really?"

"Yes. Really. Look—I know I should have done more when I was with you. I just didn't want to. I mean, nobody in his right mind volunteers to clean toilets and pay bills. You shouldn't have let me get away with dumping everything on you."

He didn't seem to realize he was still trying to do it. "Don't put it off on *me*. You yelled at me every time I mentioned it. I thought I could keep our marriage together if I shut my mouth and stopped hassling you."

"Yeah. I guess you're right about that, too." He looked uncomfortable now. "I really did a number on you—running around with Carolyn and claiming I was swamped with work. And the crazy thing is, I convinced myself it was true—that you were the one who was being unreasonable. I can't believe what a jerk I was. I'm sorry."

"So you've told me before." He hadn't been so explicit, but his regrets were hardly new territory. "It's over and done with. Please—stop feeling so guilty about the past. I'm not angry anymore, or even racked with pain. I'll be fine. Let's just get on with our lives, okay?"

"I can't." He grimaced and looked at the floor. "I've fucked it up too badly, Laurie. I thought Carolyn was so perfect—everything I ever wanted in a woman. That was stupid. *I* was stupid. She's not."

Laura stared at him in amazement. This *was* new territory. She knew from Seth that he and Carolyn squabbled occasionally, but every couple did. Far from complaining about her, he was always talking about how much he admired her and about what fun they had together. It was incredible, really. Reality had set in after only six scant months of living together.

"If you have problems with Carolyn," she said more gently, "you should talk to *her* about them."

"I've tried. It's hopeless. I don't know what I want. What I should do."

He sounded so forlorn that she took pity on him. "Go on into the living room. We'll talk."

"Okay. Thanks." He wandered off.

She poured herself some coffee, then joined him on the couch. He was staring dejectedly into his mug, looking lost in thought. "So tell me. What's so wrong with Carolyn?" she asked.

"In twenty words or less? Everything you said in September—the day I moved in with her."

She'd said a lot of things that day, starting with the fact that, for all Allan's complaints, he wouldn't have married her if, twelve years before, she'd been like Carolyn was now. He'd wanted someone stable and responsible back then, someone who would put her family first and provide him with a comfortable, well-run home. Now he wanted spontaneity and excitement. He was starstruck by the idea of having a successful, high-powered wife. He didn't just want a different woman; he wanted a different life.

He would get one, too, she'd told him that morning. Carolyn was a swell playmate, but she'd never be much of a wife and mother. If that was what he wanted, fine—as long as the kids didn't get lost in the shuffle. Personally, though, she thought he was kidding himself. He'd start missing the things he'd had with *her* and want them again. And if he expected Carolyn to provide them, he was out of his mind.

She sipped her coffee, enjoying the fact that she'd been right. She'd been angry and upset that day, and the lecture had been mostly bravado. "She was better girlfriend material than wife material, hmm?"

"Yeah." He put down his mug. "Before I left you, I'd walk into her house and she'd be dressed in cellophane. Or I'd leave work and she'd be waiting in a limo, ready to take me out of town for the night."

"And she stopped doing those things once you started living with her." Illicit affairs were conducive to romance; putting the toilet seat down four times a day wasn't. "She expected you to help with the cooking, unload the dishwasher, take out the garbage—"

"I told you, I didn't mind that. At least give me credit for learning something."

"So what was the problem, other than her refusal to sew on buttons and bake cookies and her failure to keep greeting you wrapped in cellophane?"

"But she did. It was just that she picked the damnedest times. . . . " He actually blushed. "I opened the door one Friday—the kids couldn't see her, thank God—and there she was, waiting in the hall in nothing but a G-string and—"

"Spare me the details. I hope you closed the door very quickly."

"Of course I did. I told her to put on some clothes before she opened it again. She said she'd forgotten the kids were even coming, but she didn't see why they should spoil things. She wanted me to park them in front of the TV while she took me upstairs and, uh . . . Well, you know."

Indeed, she did. Allan had told her about Carolyn's erotic prowess back in August, when she'd still been trying to compete. She was a genius with rope, a magician with her mouth, and a marvel with body paint—the Michelangelo of the mistress set. Laura had felt inadequate ever since.

"Yes." She nibbled on a cookie. "I trust you declined."

"You're damn right I did." He looked disgruntled. "She got mad at me, can you believe that? She said I was repressed. And boring."

"Let me get this straight. You're unhappy because she craved your body so desperately that she couldn't wait to pleasure it." That wasn't entirely unreasonable. Allan had thick dark hair, sexy brown eyes, and a rangy build. "That wouldn't seem to be grounds for complaint, Allan."

"Then try this one. About a month ago, she decided we should go away for the weekend—she tells me this at ten on Saturday morning—but I had the kids and she didn't want them along. She expected me to dump them on some neighbor she said she could get, some woman I didn't know. Naturally, I refused. She went anyway, with one of her friends. I stayed home with the kids."

"Umm. Seth mentioned something about that. He said it was a sudden business trip."

"Because that's what I told him and Sarah. I didn't want them to feel they were in the way, or that they'd stopped me from doing something I wanted to." He slumped down a little. "Not that I did. I see the kids too little as it is. I wasn't going to give up one of my weekends with them when Carolyn and I could go away some other time. She resented that. She says I put them first—that I'm a lot less fun than I used to be. For over six months, she nagged me to leave you, but now she says it was better when I lived with you and cheated."

Laura had heard tons of stories about divorced fathers and their children, and most of them went the same way. The fathers found new women and the children got short shrift. Support checks started coming late or not at all; visits were constantly canceled. Allan had always been different and Laura had always been grateful—even more so now, after learning about the price he'd paid.

She shifted to face him, feeling closer to him than she had in months. "So that's the problem? She's jealous of the kids because they take your attention away from her?"

He nodded. "I never realized how self-centered she was till I moved in with her. If I don't give her what she wants, she sulks. Or picks a fight. Or storms away. She says the kids are spoiled, that I indulge them too much. There's no appreciation for how hard this has been on them—and on you and me, too."

"And if there were? If she were better with the kids? Would you still be here right now?"

"Maybe not, but there's not a chance in hell she'll change." He sighed. "It's incredible, Laurie. She talks about us having a child together, but it's some crazy, romantic notion that has no connection to reality. It's the attention she wants—everyone asking about her pregnancy, everyone admiring her baby. And her house . . . It's just a house. It's not a home. It's not like here." He reached for her. "Oh, hell. I was crazy to ever leave you."

He put his arm around her, kneading her breast in just the way she liked. She didn't touch him back, but she didn't move away, either. He was terrific in bed.

She'd loved sleeping with him before Carolyn had entered the picture—the raw sex as well as the emotional closeness—and had missed it ever since.

He unbuttoned her dress. It had been so damn long and he was so damn good. . . . There was no real harm in it, she thought. One last tumble, for old time's sake.

Unless it stirred up feelings she preferred to forget. She hesitated, then pushed away his hand.

He unhooked her bra. "Why not, honey? I'm not going back to Carolyn. It's over."

"You know how many times I've heard that before?"

He began to caress her. "No. I lost count. But this is the *last* time. I promise."

"But nothing's changed." All the same, he was turning her on—a lot. "You didn't know you were leaving her when you first walked in. And the moment you walk out—"

"Who's walking out? I had to talk about things before I realized what I wanted, that's all."

She shook her head. "Be honest with yourself. You'd still be with Carolyn if it weren't for the kids. You know you would. And stop feeling me up."

He dropped his hand. "Okay, but I love your breasts. They were beautiful when you were eighteen and they still are. Remember when you were nursing the kids? How your nipples got sore and I rubbed them for you?"

She remembered. He'd been gentle and playful, and they'd usually wound up in bed. He'd been so sweet back then, so passionate and tender. "About Carolyn . . . "

"Okay. Maybe I *would* still be there, but it wouldn't last. It couldn't, because the kids aren't the only problem. I don't love her. I convinced myself I did because it was the only way I could justify having an affair, but she's too cold. Too selfish."

"But great in bed. It'll pull you back."

"Why? So are you." He moved closer. "I want to come home, Laurie. My whole life is here. You. The kids. Please. Just one more chance."

She weakened a little. After all, he'd finally seen the light and noticed Carolyn's faults. "I don't know, Allan. You had a fight with Carolyn, so you ran from her to me."

"Because you're the one I want to be with. Carolyn and I have had fights before and I haven't come over. This one was different. I was totally fed up. It's over, Laurie."

She weakened still more. "Even if it is, we can't just pick up where we left off. There were problems—"

"I know. I'll do whatever you want. Anything to be with you and the kids. Come on, honey." He put her hand on his belt. "I still love you. You know I do."

He'd pushed all the right buttons, both physically and emotionally. Maybe, finally, they could start again. Make it work this time. Become a family again.

She unbuckled his belt, unfastened his slacks, and slid her hand under his briefs. He was already hard. That was reassuring. Last summer, she'd had to work like crazy just to get him interested enough to have sex.

He kissed her, the sort of erotic, passionate kiss he'd given her when they'd first begun dating. After a few minutes, he mumbled something about going into the bedroom, and they got up. The kids were fast asleep, but they'd been known to wake during the night. The bedroom door could be locked.

She couldn't remember the last time they'd undressed each other, but they did it now, then got into bed. He bent over her, his mouth on her breasts, his hand on her belly. He excited her slowly and thoroughly, making her forget everything but her own pleasure.

Finally he thrust himself inside her and started moving. Her orgasm was long and sensational. She couldn't have asked for a better time in bed. But afterward . . .

Afterward, there should have been feelings of tenderness and love, of renewed closeness. There weren't. No regrets or guilt, either. She simply felt . . . empty inside. And the emptiness was confusing and a little frightening.

Allan started moving again. He wasn't finished yet. She did all the things he liked, trying to speed him up. She wanted this over as soon as possible. He kept pumping away on top of her, faster, wilder, and to no obvious avail, until both of them were panting with exertion.

She wondered what was taking him so long. After all, he'd started this, not she. Then again, he'd been having great sex all these months, maybe even as recently as tonight. She hadn't.

He finally climaxed, then rolled onto his back and pulled her against his chest. He seemed happy and satisfied. From his point of view, things had gone well.

She lay with her head on his shoulder, put off by the hot, wet feel of his skin, feeling manipulated and resentful. He hadn't wanted her, not nearly as much as she'd wanted him, and it clawed at her self-esteem. "That took you an awfully long time," she said. "Did you sleep with Carolyn tonight?"

"No. I wouldn't have come here if I had." He sounded offended. "Anyway, it wasn't *that* long."

"Yes, it was. What was the problem? My body? Is it a turn-off after hers?" Carolyn was a blond goddess, four years younger, five inches taller, and disgustingly firm and thin. Skinny, actually—she had no breasts or hips to speak of—but Allan had seemed to prefer it that way.

"No," he said. "It wasn't you. I was distracted, that's all. I have a lot on my mind."

"We haven't slept together since August, Allan. I'd sort of hoped *I* would be on your mind." But she hadn't been, not in the way he'd led her to expect. He'd given a great performance, but it had been all technique, no passion.

"You were," he insisted. "But so were some other things. There's still no progress on a contract with the teachers and the union's been talking about a strike. Try to understand. . . . " He massaged her back, silently placating her. "I had a two-hour meeting with Ned Brown this afternoon. You know what a pain in the ass he is. I couldn't just shut it out. I'm sorry."

Allan was the school district's chief negotiator and Brown was the head of the teachers' union. He was always on TV, attacking, complaining, and demanding. Two hours in the same room with him wasn't a meeting. It was cruel and unusual punishment.

She softened. "Oh. How did it go?"

"Not well," he said, and sighed heavily.

He spent the next fifteen minutes explaining. He'd always been obsessed with his work, and she'd always listened attentively to the details. It was only after he'd left that she'd realized how rarely he'd listened back. He'd gone through the motions at times, but his mind had obviously been elsewhere. On *important* things. On *male* things.

He finished telling her about the meeting, then yawned and stretched. "God, I'm tired. I hate to fall asleep on you, honey, but . . . " He rolled onto his side. "Umm. Nice. I'd forgotten what a great bed this is."

She moved away from him. "You can't spend the night here, Allan."

He frowned. "Why not?"

"Because the kids would find you here tomorrow morning."

"So?"

"So they'd assume you were coming home."

"I thought I was. What else was tonight all about?"

"Not that." She'd been through too much—tried again and again, got lied to again and again, felt stupid again and again. And worthless. And humiliated. "I told you before—we can't just pick up as though Carolyn never happened. All the problems that existed before—"

"What problems? I went crazy for a while, but it's over now. There are no problems."

She thought about the times he'd "worked late" or "gone out of town," the times she'd driven to Land Park and spotted his car on one of the streets near Carolyn's house. "Without some changes, some real communication, I can't go back to the way things were. We'd have to go for counseling. Then we could see."

He was silent for several seconds. "You're not giving me credit for learning anything," he finally answered. "For the changes I've made. I do a lot more around the house now. Spend a lot more time with the kids. That was your main complaint, right? That I didn't help out enough?"

It had been once. She knew better now. "Maybe, but it was never the real problem. Our whole relationship was. You were the sun and I was a minor planet. I won't go back to that. I want to be thought of—and treated—like an equal."

"When did I say you weren't?" There was an exasperated edge to his tone.

"You didn't have to say it. It was obvious from the way you behaved. Deep down, you thought your work, and your concerns, were much more important than mine."

"Maybe my work, but not anything else." He rolled onto his back and stared at the ceiling. "How can you think I don't listen to you? That I don't value your opinions and care about your feelings? Anything you want, I've tried to give you. It hasn't always been easy."

He sounded confused and a little hurt. Guilt washed through her. He *had* been good to her during the past six months.

"I appreciate everything you've done, Allan. You've been great with the kids and terrific about money. It's just—if we're going to get back together, I need some things to be different. And I don't see how that's going to happen without counseling."

"But it already has. Why can't you see that? I have a hundred things to deal with, including a possible strike, and to waste time and money on something we don't need . . ."

It was the same old story. She turned away, saying nothing, feeling defeated and very tired.

He sighed. "If it's so important to you—"

"It is."

"Then we'll go. I don't have a big philosophical problem with it. I'm just busy, that's all." He stroked her hair. "Come on, Laurie, don't be mad. I'll do whatever you want. I owe you at least that much, after all I've put you through. You want to find someone and make an appointment, or should I?"

"I will," she said, partially mollified.

"Okay." He yawned and closed his eyes. "My briefcase is in the trunk. I'll check my schedule in the morning, tell you when I have some free time."

She couldn't believe what she'd heard. He thought everything had been settled. "Allan, I still want you to leave—to get your own apartment."

"Now?" He smiled. "Isn't it a little late at night?"

"You can look around this weekend. In the meantime, you can stay at a motel, or go to Phil's." Phil was his best friend. "I don't want the kids to find you here.

It would get their hopes up, and if things don't work out—"

"They will. I promise."

"Fine." She tossed aside the covers. "*I'll* leave. You stay."

"Okay, okay." He opened his eyes and sat up. "This is crazy, though. We'll be spending the weekend together—"

"No, we won't. I don't think we should make any changes, at least not so soon. It's your weekend, so you should do what the kids expect and take care of them. It'll be easier on them that way."

"Easier for them to spend the weekend in a motel room? Or on the floor of Phil's spare bedroom?"

He had a point. "Okay. You can stay here. I'll go away."

"Where to?"

She thought for a moment. "Vicki's place at the lake."

"That's what you really want? To go off somewhere by yourself instead of staying with me and the kids?"

"Yes." She did want to get away—away from Allan, away from her problems, away from the hassles of daily life. She still had the birthday money her mother had given her; it would cover the costs.

"But we talked. We made love." He ran his hand through his hair, visibly rattled. "Doesn't that matter? Didn't you like it?"

"It was fine," she said, and got out of bed.

"Only fine?"

She didn't reply, just grabbed her robe and pulled it on. She couldn't meet his eyes.

He stood up. "I thought we were going to be a family again—that you wanted us to be together. That can't happen if you're a hundred miles away."

Her throat got tight. "It's not that easy, Allan. I

want to be happy, not just to . . . settle." Settle for security, for predictability, for tepid affection. "I want love—"

"I do love you."

"And commitment. And emotion."

He stared at her. "It's you, not me, isn't it? You don't want me to come back. You don't love me anymore."

He was right. She didn't, not in the same powerful way, but she couldn't bring herself to say so. It was too cold, too final. She hoped her feelings would change.

"I don't know," she said. The words left a dull ache in her gut. "I still care, though. Let's take things one step at a time, okay? I'll see you tomorrow morning."

"Yeah, okay." He started to dress. "I'll be over around nine."

The cat scratched at the back door, and Laura let him in. He rubbed against her legs, and she picked him up and cuddled him against her face, finding more comfort in his cool, soft fur than in Allan's promises or arms.

FIVE

Vicki Stonehouse was six years older than Laura and almost the same size—five feet five if you stretched things, and a hundred twenty-five on a thin day. She'd moved in across the street in August and immediately sought Laura out. They'd hit it off over their first cup of coffee and begun trading confidences over their second.

In addition to championing a staggering array of good causes, Vicki kept the books for the family business—two drugstores she and her husband Frank, a pharmacist, had bought in Sacramento after selling their home and business in Los Angeles. They'd moved up north because they were tired of the L.A. congestion and could get so much more bang for their money here, not only the drugstores and the biggest house on Laura's street, but also the condo at Tahoe and enough cash to put their daughters, now fourteen and sixteen, through college.

One of the things Laura liked best about Vicki was that nothing fazed her. You could confide that you'd been seduced by a Martian and she would nod calmly and ask if he'd been any good. You could even admit

55

you'd been seduced by your soon-to-be ex-husband, as Laura did later that evening when Vicki called, and know that she wouldn't pry, wouldn't offer unsolicited advice, and certainly wouldn't tell you what a fool you'd been. She didn't ask if he'd been any good; in the case of Allan Miller, she already knew the answer.

Laura explained about Allan's staying in the house, then asked to use Vicki's place at the lake. Vicki said yes, no questions asked. Except one: "Do you want some company?"

Laura did. Vicki offered to drive, and Laura accepted. Vicki's Bronco was better in the snow than Laura's wagon and had a rack on top for their skis, not to mention being newer and more reliable.

They left as soon as Allan showed up, at nine-fifteen in the morning. Laura waved good-bye to Seth and Sarah, who'd positioned themselves by the front door to watch her drive away, then settled back in her seat. "You have no idea how good it feels to get away," she said. "No kids, no ex-husband, no mother, no house. Just two whole days of doing what I want. I feel like I've been in a room where the walls were slowly closing in, squeezing me tighter and tighter, and suddenly they've started moving the other way."

"An interesting metaphor," Vicki said. "Interpersonal relationships and home ownership as a form of torture."

"Self-inflicted," Laura admitted. "If I weren't so damn obsessive . . . You know what I was thinking when I hugged the kids good-bye? After I got through feeling guilty about leaving them, that is?"

"Nope. They looked fine, by the way. They didn't even frown, much less throw themselves on the ground and scream."

"They *are* fine. They were thrilled that Allan had left Carolyn. I guess they didn't want to push their luck by nagging me to stay home."

"Umm. They're saving that for the next time. So what were you thinking when you hugged them good-bye?"

"That I should garden. That was my original project for this weekend—to clean up the garden if the weather was nice."

"You damn well should," Vicki said. "Your rosebed's a disgrace. It's lowering property values in the entire neighborhood. I hear a delegation from the city council is coming on Monday to demand that you prune and weed."

"Then it's a good thing they can't see the tiles in my shower. They're supporting life. I'm afraid that nothing short of garlic and crosses will eradicate it by now."

Vicki smiled. "Maybe yesterday, Laura. Not today. I happen to know that your house is spotless, that you got up early and cleaned."

"You're right." She hadn't had time for spotless, but she'd sprayed enough Tilex in the shower to asphyxiate an asthmatic. In truth, the mold hadn't stood a chance. "How did you know? And why are you smiling that way?"

"You smell of Comet and Clorox."

Laura sniffed her hands. "No, I don't. I showered afterward. Really, Vick, how did you know?"

"Other than the fact that you clean most every Saturday, and that you're too compulsive to leave a mess behind when someone is coming over, even your ex-husband?"

"It was Mom, not Allan. I called to tell her I'd be at Tahoe, and she insisted on stopping by the house to check on the kids. All I needed was for her to find crumbs all over the kitchen and swing into action. It would have driven Allan crazy. Now, stop changing the subject and explain what that smile was all about."

"I was reveling in my astonishing powers of observation. For example, I know that you didn't look at your paper this morning, because it was still on your driveway when we left." Vicki stopped for a light and signaled a left turn. "You didn't watch the news last night, either."

That was true. She'd gone straight to sleep after she and Vicki had spoken. "Incredible. Not since Sherlock Holmes . . . I have a stop to make downtown. Eleventh and N. You might want to go straight up Land Park Drive."

"Okay." Vicki turned off her blinker. "What's at Eleventh and N, other than the capitol?"

"The late Judge Hollister's love nest. I ran into his mistress at the funeral. She was in rare form—dressed in black from head to toe and revving up for a major bout of hysterics. I went over to calm her down and wound up sitting next to her during the service. She gave me the keys to the apartment and asked me to pick up some of her things. I told her I'd UPS them, but since we're going up to the lake . . . " The full impact of Vicki's words suddenly hit her. "Wait a minute. Was there something interesting on the news and in the paper? Something you expected me to mention?"

"Talk about Sherlock Holmes." Vicki grinned at her. "The story was on Channel 3. I was shocked. Really, Laura, I couldn't believe it. I couldn't wait till this morning to see what you'd say. The *Bee* picked it up and ran it on page three. I guess when it's someone else's scoop, they don't feature it as prominently."

"Stop milking this for all it's worth, and tell me what shocking news I managed to sleep through."

"It concerned the late Judge Hollister. Given how interested you are in his—"

"Right," Laura said, smiling now. Her problems seemed a lot less serious when Vicki was around. She was the best antidepressant since Prozac. "Get on with it, already."

"The Feds were investigating him for conspiracy, racketeering, and obstruction of justice. He allegedly had ties to organized crime interests in Nevada and California. The FBI wouldn't comment on the story, but Channel 3 claimed it had confirmation—an anonymous government source."

Laura stared out the window, seeing only a blur of green. "I'll be damned. Hollister a crook." At least according to the FBI, he was. She assumed that was where the anonymous government source labored and leaked from. "Were there any details?"

"Only that the investigation was in the preliminary stages, meaning, I suppose, that they were still trying to nail him when he died."

The news slowly sank in, and along with it, a dozen thoughts and questions. "In a way, it all adds up. He had a mistress who claimed she had fans in the mob. He was the target of what looked like a gangland hit. But still, why would he get mixed up with organized crime? It couldn't have been for money. According to Freddie's eulogy, he and his wife went to Europe every year. I've seen his car—it was a new Cadillac—and I've passed by his house. It's huge. His wife was from a wealthy family, and he must have made investments when he was a corporate lawyer. Financially, he should have been set for life."

"But suppose his investments went bad? Or suppose he spent every dime the minute he earned it? He was still living the way he did when he was a lawyer, but he couldn't have been making even a third as much money. Returning to private practice wouldn't have been an option, not as long as a Republican president was in office. Not with his political connections and his wife's social pull. He was on the short list for the Court of Appeals. He had a shot at a Supreme Court nomination, with every likelihood of a vacancy within the next few years."

"Okay. We agree he wouldn't have left the bench, no matter what sort of trouble he was in. He was too ambitious. He even taught for the past few years in order to strengthen his scholarly credentials. But if you're saying he got mixed up with loan sharks and did them favors when he couldn't pay them back . . . If he needed money, why not borrow it from his family and friends?"

"Because he needed it for something he couldn't tell them about," Vicki suggested, "like a drug habit."

"Then he would have lied. He could have come up with a convincing excuse. He was supposedly a brilliant man, although his relationship with Bonita does make one question that." Laura paused, trying to think of another motive. "What about blackmail? Suppose he had skeletons in his closet from his days as a corporate attorney? Shady deals he'd engineered or evidence he'd planted or suppressed to keep rich but guilty clients out of jail? And suppose the mob found out about it? They might have threatened to expose him unless he did them an occasional favor."

Vicki pulled into a parking space on Eleventh Street, right around the corner from the entrance to Hollister's building. "I like that theory. It appeals to my liberal paranoia about big business."

In Vicki's world view, big businessmen were venal unless proven otherwise, as were their bankers, their lawyers, and any elected representatives who voted their way when she and her fellow liberals took the opposite position. "What paranoia?" Laura teased as they got out of the car. "He was a Republican. He was rich. He was a big-time lawyer with clients to match. He had to have been a crook."

"Upstanding citizens don't usually wind up with bullets in their brains. And he *was* being investigated—"

"By that hotbed of fascist oppression, the FBI."

Vicki laughed. "They're only fascist oppressors when they hassle civil rights protesters and environmental activists. When they go after the Ku Klux Klan, corrupt savings and loan executives, and judges who run errands for the mob, then they're the finest law enforcement officers on the face of the earth."

"How about when they watch innocent people at funerals?" In retrospect, Laura found that distasteful. Was her picture in some file now, her name in some computer?

"Then they're just doing their job," Vicki replied, "unless they're watching me or one of my friends, in which case it's a flagrant abuse of authority that can't be tolerated in a free society. Never trust the cops unless you need them desperately, Laura. That's what I always say."

Laura said she agreed, digging into her purse for Bonita's keys as they walked around the corner. They were climbing up the steps when a pretty young blond leaving the building noticed them approaching and stopped.

She grabbed the door before it could close and wedged her foot against it to keep it open. "Mrs. Stonehouse! It's great to see you again. How have you been?"

"Just fine." Vicki hugged her, then held her at arm's length to inspect her. "You look beautiful, Heather, as always. How's your job going? Do you like it?"

"I love it. I thought Sacramento might be boring after San Diego, but it's great. It's so exciting—being right in the middle of things, I mean."

"She means politics," Vicki explained to Laura. "This is Heather Martin, Ken Carlsen's stepdaughter. She got her masters from U.C. San Diego last June. She's working as an analyst on the assembly side now. Heather, this is my neighbor and good friend, Laura Miller."

Laura shook Heather's hand. "I'll be honest, Heather. Vicki's told me only a little about you—all of it good, by the way—but a ton about your stepfather." Carlsen, a state senator, was currently running for governor. "All of it wonderful. She thinks he walks on water."

"But he does," Heather said. "This state wouldn't have half as many problems if more politicians were like Ken. He's smart and dedicated, and he can't be bought."

On the contrary, he had enough money at his disposal to buy a few people himself, Laura thought. Heather's mother Jane had been a wealthy widow when she'd married Carlsen twelve years before, thirty-eight to his thirty-three.

"That's exactly what I keep telling her," Vicki said. "I want her to work on the campaign, but she claims she doesn't have time. I can't imagine why a single mother with two young children and a full-time job could possibly be short of time, can you?"

Heather smiled. "Actually, I can, but knowing you, Mrs. Stonehouse, you'll manage to talk her into it." She looked at Laura. "I don't know if Mrs. Stonehouse ever mentioned that we were neighbors in Bel-Air."

"Yes. She did."

"Well, I wasn't around very much—I was fourteen when the Stonehouses moved in, and already in boarding school—but whenever I was, Mrs. Stonehouse would try to recruit me and my brother for one of her causes. You know, collecting cans and bottles to recycle, or getting our friends to donate clothes they'd outgrown to a homeless shelter. She always succeeded. She won't take no for an answer. I'm glad she's on *our* side."

"You have your mother's beauty and your father's charm," Vicki said. "Ken should put you in a commercial. You'd be dynamite."

Heather looked pleased. "Thanks. I'll tell him you

said so. By the way, if you're here to see him, he's not around. He and Mom are campaigning down south this weekend."

"Actually, we came by the building to do a favor for a friend. Give my regards to your mother next time you speak to her, would you? Remind her that she owes me a letter. And tell Ken to get more rest. I saw him last week at a hearing, and he looked tired and tense. He'll never make it past the primary at this rate."

Heather stiffened. "Running for governor is hard work, especially when you're determined not to let your responsibilities as a senator slide even a fraction."

"I wasn't being critical," Vicki said gently. "I'm just worried about him, that's all. Old friends should have that right."

"You do. I'm sorry I snapped. It's just, I'm worried about him, too." She added that she would remind her mother to write, then walked briskly down the steps and disappeared around the corner.

"She's very protective of him, isn't she?" Laura said.

Vicki nodded. "According to Jane, she adored him right from the start. She was about twelve then. She always used to talk about working with him, and now she more or less does." They walked inside and rang for the elevator. "Jane thinks it's great for both of them. They look after each other—keep each other out of trouble."

"Trouble? As in?"

"Drugs. The capitol is full of them. Men who are after Heather's money and women who are after Ken's body. Not that he's ever looked at any of them," Vicki added quickly, "but they certainly look at him."

"I'll bet they do. There's no shortage of Carolyn Seeleys in the world." Or Allan Millers, either. It took two. "I take it he has an apartment here."

"Umm. Number 5C. He's had the place for years, since before he married Jane."

Vicki had once mentioned that Jane had decided to stay in Los Angeles after she'd married Ken, living the same life she always had. He flew south most weekends to be with her but always paid his own way, holding himself to a high ethical standard even in the freewheeling days when lawmakers had routinely accepted expensive gifts like free rides on corporate jets. The abuses of those years, and the fact that the FBI had sent formerly powerful people to jail on charges like extortion and money laundering, had led to a tightening of the rules about what gifts public officials could accept.

The two women stepped into the elevator and rode to the fourth floor. Apartment 4C was to their left. Laura rang the bell and waited. There was no answer.

"I'm glad no one's here," she said as she unlocked the door. "It'll give us a chance to look around. According to Freddie, this apartment sees a lot of action. Some of the state's most prominent citizens fornicate regularly inside."

"Which makes one wonder how they avoid running into each other."

"Good question. Maybe there's a calendar or appointment book. I've always pictured the place as really kinky. A cross between the Casbah and a leather bar in the Castro district." She opened the door. The foyer was furnished with a hooked scatter rug and what looked to be Gold Rush-era antiques. "God, how disappointing. I'll be crushed if it's all this tasteful."

It was. The apartment contained a walk-through kitchen, an L-shaped living room with a fair-sized dining area, and a bathroom and two bedrooms. One of them was locked, but Bonita had given her the key. The room was furnished as an office—Hollister's professional retreat, obviously.

At first glance, the only items of even remotely prurient interest were the queen-sized bed with its brass headboard, tangled black comforter and red satin sheets, and the glass-fronted gun case in the office. The case, which was mounted on a side wall, was designed to hold four rifles or shotguns but contained only two.

There was a double light switch by the office door. Wanting a better look at the guns, Laura absently flipped both levers. Not only did every light in the room go on, so did the computer on the oak desk and the printer on the hutch above it.

She peered at the guns. "That's odd. Freddie told some stories yesterday about what an avid hiker and fisherman Hollister was, but he never mentioned hunting. And even if he did hunt, why would he keep his rifles here instead of at home?"

"Maybe he used them for something other than hunting," Vicki said.

"Maybe, but I can't picture him as either a vigilante or a mass murderer."

Laura walked over to the bookcase, which took up the top half of the back wall. She checked out the titles, most of them novels and recent nonfiction, then walked to the desk. In addition to the computer equipment and a fax machine, it held expensive leather office accessories and a sleek, black answering machine with a dozen high-tech features built in, including a two-line phone. The only other item of interest was the leather portfolio on the floor, wedged between the office chair and the left side of the desk's kneehole.

She frowned, puzzled by the set-up. "It doesn't add up. The towels in the bathroom are still damp, but Hollister's been dead for nearly a week. True, other people use this apartment from time to time, but there's a gun case when Hollister didn't hunt, and that bookcase over there . . . Look at the titles. There are no law books except for a guide to California law and some yearly supplements, a law dictionary, and an old directory of California lawyers. There are hardly even any reference books." A dictionary, an almanac, an atlas. . . . "No legal knickknacks, either—a scale of justice, a gavel, that sort of thing. There's a computer, so obviously someone worked here, but it isn't the sort of office a judge would have."

"You're saying it wasn't Hollister's apartment?"

"Or that he shared it with someone else—someone who still uses it, and not just for sex. Maybe he's the one who's been working at this desk . . . the one who showered here this morning." If so, he could return at any time and find them here. "I want to look through the portfolio, see if I can tell who it belongs to. Do me a favor. Go to the front door and put the chain on."

"You're impossible," Vicki said with a laugh. "What on earth were you weaned on? Nancy Drew? Brenda Starr?"

"Superman comics. Mom disapproved, so I had to sneak them in and read them under my covers with a flashlight. I wanted to be Clark, not Lois. I thought it was dumb, the way she always had to be rescued."

"You would have been smarter, I suppose."

"Absolutely."

"Well, far be it from me to hinder your rich fantasy life." Vicki left the room, still smiling.

Laura unzipped the portfolio and took out the file folders inside, three of them. The first contained a typed schedule of the sort a secretary would prepare for her boss's business trip.

The day before, he—or she—had flown from Los Angeles to Sacramento, attended Hollister's funeral, and dined with someone named Jerry Burke. The owner of the portfolio was scheduled to go hunting this weekend with Ed Lefferts, meeting him at his home at eleven this morning. There were four more appointments on Monday: meetings with Carolyn Seeley at nine, Mike Clemente at ten and Jack Bessell at eleven, and a speech to deliver at the Sutter Club at twelve-thirty. His flight back to Los Angeles was at three-twenty.

Laura was startled to see so many names she recognized—not only Carolyn and Mike, but also Ed Lefferts, a local bank president, and Jack Bessell, the Machiavellian Speaker of the Assembly, whose principality was the state Democratic Party. She checked the two folders beneath. The first contained copies of correspondence between Craig Tomlinson and Carolyn Seeley, pertaining to PR campaigns for two of Tomlinson's businesses, the Tahoe Monte Carlo Hotel and ACX Enterprises. The second contained some legislative bills and correspondence analyzing and discussing them, between Tomlinson and Jerry Burke, the president of the lobbying firm of Burke/Maravich.

"So?" Vicki said.

Laura nearly dropped the folders. "You scared the hell out of me. I didn't even hear you come in. Take a look at this stuff."

Vicki skimmed everything, then said, "These obviously belong to Craig Tomlinson. He seems to be our hunter, too. Do you know who he is?"

"The president of something called ACX Enterprises."

"It's an umbrella corporation. Their main holding is an agricultural and industrial chemical company."

"And the part-owner of a casino."

"He also has an interest in a racetrack, Murieta Park in Riverside County. Pollutes the environment with one hand and empties people's pockets with the other. My kind of guy, Laura."

Laura smiled at Vicki's acrid tone. It was a toss-up as to which she disliked more, the gaming industry or toxics manufacturers. "I saw him at Hollister's funeral. He was talking to Mike Clemente."

"You've met Mike Clemente?"

"I have now. Freddie knows him from the Capital Athletic Club. We ran into him on our way into the church. Mike mentioned that he was a lawyer and lobbyist—a high-powered one, I gather."

"Very high-powered. He's fairly new around the capitol, but damn effective. He's smart, likable, and he really knows his stuff. That has a way of getting a lobbyist great access." Vicki sighed and shook her head. "He's so cute, too. What a waste."

"Yeah, well, even if he lobbied for the Boy Scouts, I doubt you'd want to introduce him to your friends. He hits on women at funerals, Vick. He—"

"He *what?*"

"It was poetic license. We made small talk at the funeral, but he called me a few hours later to ask me out." Laura gave Vicki the details, then added, "I thought it was odd that he would call me. He wasn't particularly interested in me at the funeral. Like I told you, he practically ignored me afterward."

Vicki looked amused. "When it comes to Hollister's murder, you see conspiracies under every rock and bush. Maybe Clemente's attracted to you. Maybe he didn't show it at the funeral because he was thinking about Hollister or wrapped up in business. Did that ever occur to you?"

"Only briefly. The man wants something from me, Vicki. I just don't know what it is."

"Your body, you dope."

"Much as I would like to think so . . . " She slipped the folders back in the portfolio and set it on the floor. "I should have said yes. I might have learned something that way. I mean, how much do we really know about him, other than the fact that he works for the scum of the earth?"

"A fair amount, actually. Jerry Burke hired him

about a year ago. Stole him from some company down south, I think. He specializes in financial stuff—securities, banking, that sort of thing."

Laura walked to the bookcase. "Let's look him up," she said. "See if he's listed."

She pulled out the *Directory of California Lawyers* and turned to the section on Southern California. There were lawyers with the last names Clement and Clements, but no Clementes. She rechecked the first names, thinking there might have been a typographical error, but found no Michael under any similar last name. And Michael Clemente was definitely the name he went by; the Burke/Maravich stationery in Tomlinson's portfolio had listed Michael V. Clemente as one of the associates.

"Interesting," she said, smiling in a superior way.

"So I made a mistake." Vicki flipped to the section on Northern California. "The firm he used to work for must be up north."

Laura turned to the C's. There was no Mike Clemente. No name even reasonably close. "You were saying?"

"The book is over two years old. Maybe he was working in another state at the time, or still in law school. Or maybe he was inadvertently left out. If you ask me, the fact that he's not listed doesn't prove a thing."

One of those things was certainly possible, but all the evidence pointed the other way.

SIX

The fact was, Clemente's statements at the funeral didn't jibe with any of Vicki's theories except the last one, an accidental omission, a mistake that was highly unlikely in a directory put together from lists of members of the bar. He'd acted like an old pro when it came to the law, Laura told Vicki. As if he'd seen and done it all. As if his lobbying firm had hired him precisely because of his knowledge and experience.

"That doesn't sound like a brand-new lawyer to me, or even like a lawyer who came here from another state. Admit it, Vick. The man is mysterious. Maybe even shady."

"Or a fast study who talks a good line. The best lobbyists always do."

Laura reshelved the book. "Doesn't it strike you as odd that he's had a meteoric rise from out of nowhere?"

"Not from nowhere, from Southern California, and his sort of talent goes a long way in a short time in this town."

"But he lobbies for a gambler. He was friends with a judge who had dealings with the mob."

Vicki rolled her eyes. "I'm on the other side of issues from Burke/Maravich all the time, but I've never caught them doing anything illegal. They don't have to. They're too damn good at working the system."

Laura put on the brakes. Vicki was right. Her imagination had run away with her, and she even knew why. Clemente was handsome, charming, and slick—as quick with his tongue as a chameleon snaring a fly. He even worked for the bad guys. In a way, she'd *wanted* him to be mixed up in Hollister's murder. He was a much more interesting suspect than a run-of-the-mill mobster or an angry ex-con.

She smiled sheepishly. "So I got carried away."

"Just a little. Let's get Bonita's things and get out of here. Tomlinson could still show up." Vicki checked her watch. "It's only ten, and he doesn't have to be at Lefferts's house till eleven."

"So he'll find us here. So what? We have a legitimate reason—" The phone suddenly rang, interrupting her. She and Vicki looked at the answering machine.

A light was on, indicating that the call had come in on line one. They heard three notes of the sort made by a touch-tone phone—*do, re, mi*—and then a man's voice, curt and deep: "Friday, March 27th at two P.M. through Monday, March 30th at noon. Out."

"That was a recording," Laura whispered. "From the machine's tape. It's playing back." She could tell by the tone quality and the low volume of the voice. Vicki nodded in agreement.

There was a beep. Another *do, re, mi*. And then a different male voice, with a pronounced twang: "Monday, March 30th. Six till ten P.M. Out." *Beep! Do, re, mi.* The second voice again: "Cancel the previous message. Tuesday, March 31st, noon till two P.M. Out." The machine beeped twice, the three notes sounded, and yet a third man spoke—but live this time, not on the tape. "Thursday, April 2nd, four till seven P.M. Out." Then the tape rewound.

"That's how the men who use this place avoid running into each other," Vicki said. "They listen to the tape, then add their own plans. The three notes must be a code that instructs the machine to record whatever follows and play it back later for callers. There's a beep between messages and two beeps after the final one, so a caller knows when to talk."

Laura was torn between disgust and fascination. "High technology in the service of promiscuity. The first voice was obviously Tomlinson's. Did you recognize the others?"

"Not the third, but the second sounded like Norm Daley."

Daley was an assemblyman, a rifle-toting, flag-waving gay basher who Vicki swore was secretly unsure of his masculinity.

"Umm. He fits right in with this crowd. I wonder what they use line two for? Business calls, maybe?"

"Makes sense," Vicki said. "After all, this *is* an office."

Laura flipped open the lid of the compartment containing the two microcassette tapes. There were a daunting number of lights, switches, and buttons inside, along with a set of impenetrable directions full of indecipherable abbreviations. "Geez, will you look at this thing? Mirisaki must have hired a Buddhist monk to write the instructions." She peered at its innards. "There's apparently a tape for each phone line. Maybe we could call line two from line one. Listen to the outgoing message."

The second number, like the first, was on the front of the machine. Laura made the call. Vicki leaned close so she could hear the recording.

The phone rang twice, then was picked up. "This is

555-7711," a breathy female voice said. "We're out of the office right now, but please leave a message, and we'll get back to you just as soon as we can. Please wait for the beep before you speak."

Laura quickly hung up. "My God, that was Bonita Franks."

"You think she's running a business from this apartment?" Vicki asked.

"She can't even keep track of what she said five minutes ago, so I doubt it. It must be Tomlinson's."

"She would have met him through the judge, I suppose."

Laura thought about the papers in Tomlinson's portfolio. "No. She probably already knew him. She sings in the Alpine Room. That's in his hotel."

She studied the machine for another few seconds. There were two playback buttons, one for each line. Her finger began to itch. Within moments, she was tapping one.

Nothing happened. She pressed it more firmly, but once again, nothing happened. She tried the other button. The machine played the tape they'd already heard, then rewound. "You think the playback for line two is broken?" she asked.

Vicki shook her head. "There's probably an extra security mechanism programmed in, a code you have to enter before it will play back any business messages."

More intrigued than ever, Laura said, "Let's take a quick look around. See if we can figure out what the office is used for."

She opened the top left drawer of the desk. It contained a compartmentalized plastic tray filled with office supplies. The next drawer down held stationery, including letterheads for three of Tomlinson's businesses. There were local phone books in the bottom drawer, along with directories to elected officials, the state bureaucracy, and registered lobbyists.

She opened the top drawer on the right. It held more office equipment—a stapler, a calculator, a tape dispenser. . . . Her eyes widened. In the very back, tucked behind a large box of pens, was a blue-black revolver with a wooden handle. The gun was at least nine inches long.

"I don't know much about guns," she said, "but this thing looks like it could disable a charging tank with a single shot."

Vicki studied it but didn't touch it. "You can't prove anything by me. Of course, if you want statistics about how many lives we could save with better gun-control laws . . . "

"You've already quoted them to me, Vick. Several times, in fact." Laura closed the drawer. "It must be Tomlinson's. He seems to have a fondness for firearms. Besides, you can never tell when a Mafia turf war will break out over who gets what percentage of the casino and racing profits."

Vicki said she couldn't picture a Godfather-style gang war being fought in Sacramento, and checked the final two drawers of the desk. They contained documentation for the office equipment.

Laura looked at the computer. A C-prompt was on the screen, glowing invitingly, all but beckoning her in. Vicki noticed the longing expression in her eyes and sighed. "You wouldn't, Laura!"

"But this is obviously Tomlinson's office, and he's one of the bad guys. Anyway, what harm can it do?" She grinned. "Just three little letters, Vick. 'DIR.'"

"They'd drum me out of the ACLU for this," Vicki said resignedly, "but all right, since it makes you so happy."

Laura sat down and brought up a list of directories. When she tried to access one of them, though, the phrase ENTER PASSWORD appeared. She tried a few possibilities—Tomlinson, CT, ACX, Murieta, and so forth—but each time, the computer flashed back INVALID PASSWORD. Only games and DOS files were accessible, not directories containing files created by users.

Tomlinson was obviously something of a security bug. In view of that, it was interesting that he'd given Bonita the key to his office. Laura wondered if she did more for him than sing and make recordings for his answering machine.

They continued to look around, but found only office supplies and more books. They locked the door and returned to the foyer, checking the secretary desk and closet there, but once again, found nothing out of the ordinary.

The kitchen was next. Laura noticed the phone on the wall and checked the number. It was yet another line.

She took out Bonita's list. The first item was a blue fondue pot with six forks, and the second, a blue and white teapot. Both were where she'd said they would be, in a cabinet beside the stove. Expecting to find nothing of any great interest, Laura checked the drawers. She saw cutlery, kitchen gadgets, spices, aprons, pot holders. . . .

And then she spotted another gun, smack on top of a stack of dish towels in the drawer next to the sink. It was small and silver with a wooden handle, a Lady Smith, according to the writing on the barrel. "What was that you said about not having any gang wars in Sacramento?" she asked Vicki.

"Maybe Tomlinson was paranoid about being robbed."

"What a boring theory. If they can't be part of a Mafia stash, they should definitely be connected to sex." She closed the drawer. "Picture it, Vick. Norm Daley on his hands and knees, dressed in a garter belt and stockings, being used by some brawny guy who's buck naked except for a holster, a ten-gallon hat, and cowboy boots."

"What? No riding crop?"

"That's a different fantasy. The English prep school one."

Vicki looked inside a cabinet, then closed it. "You've been watching the porn channel on cable too much."

"Religiously. That *is* the one that shows us what our lawmakers are up to, isn't it?"

The rest of the drawers and cabinets contained cleaning products, kitchenware, and paper and plastic goods. They took some grocery bags to hold Bonita's belongings, then walked into the dining area. It was furnished with an antique credenza and breakfront in addition to the table and chairs, but the pieces held only dishes and linens.

The next few items on Bonita's list were in the living room—bottles of Amaretto and Tia Maria, which were in a chest that served as a liquor cabinet, and some audiotapes and CDs, which were in an armoire that had been converted into an entertainment center. Given the types of songs pianists in restaurants usually sang, Laura wasn't surprised by most of the titles on the list—albums by legends like Sinatra, Broadway shows, and CDs by recent stars like Whitney Houston and Mandy Patinkin. But several rap albums were included as well, and that did surprise her, or at least amuse her. Most adults she knew considered the phrase rap music to be an oxymoron. She wondered whether Bonita liked the stuff or was simply trying to keep up with the times.

The drawer holding the tapes and CDs was crammed full, so it took a while to locate the ones Bonita wanted. The only other items of interest in the living room were the pornographic videos in the next drawer down, tucked in among such popular movies as *Raiders of the Lost Ark* and *Tootsie*. The films had titles like *Insatiable Vampiress* and *Love Slaves from the Orient*, indicating, if nothing else, that the people who came here had a variety of erotic tastes.

The only rooms left were the bedroom and bathroom. Bonita had left a black negligee and a green-and-white caftan in the bedroom closet. As Laura pulled them out, she noticed that someone else had left a large, body-hugging jumpsuit made of soft black leather trimmed with silver studs and buckles. The outfit featured a detachable executioner-style hood and a stud-rimmed circular cutout at the crotch, apparently meant to glorify the male sex organ.

She held it up. For all her jokes about the apartment, she hadn't expected anything quite this quirky. "A guy would get awfully hot in this, don't you think?"

"How can you look at it and think about how hot it would be?" Vicki fingered the cutout. "Actually, I was picturing Frank in it."

"Just Frank? After eighteen years of marriage?"

"Okay. Maybe Kevin Costner, too, chasing me around the bedroom at full mast. No hood, though. You wouldn't want to hide a face like that."

"If Kevin Costner were wearing this in my bedroom, he definitely wouldn't have to chase me," Laura said. "Of course, he wouldn't have to chase me even if he were dressed in a chicken suit complete with beak."

"And Allan? Suppose he were wearing this?"

Laura hung it back up. "The truth? I'd laugh." And that told her something about her feelings, something she didn't want to analyze.

In addition to clothing and shoes, the closet contained a large cardboard carton on the shelf above the rod. There was more black leather inside—thongs, collars, leashes, and blindfolds—along with handcuffs and shackles made of metal, vibrators of every conceivable type, and numerous objects indicating that some of the men who came here enjoyed receiving or inflicting pain. Objects with gruesome spikes and clamps. Suggestively shaped objects too big not to hurt. Objects meant to lash and sting. And finally—it was hardly a surprise by now—yet another revolver.

A shiny silver pistol with a very long barrel, it was perhaps a foot long. Laura slipped her index finger through the trigger guard and picked it up. The Ruger Super Redhawk, it was called. It looked like a real gun and not a toy, but its location indicated it was used for sick, sadistic games.

She'd read about things like these but never actually seen them, and touching them put a queasy knot in the pit of her stomach. She put the gun back. "Bonita and Hollister . . . I wonder if they used any of this stuff?"

"And if they did, who did what to whom?"

"Bonita had a big insurance policy on Hollister—a million dollars," Laura said thoughtfully, "but she paid for it herself. I know she liked the prestige of dating a judge, but he didn't seem to support her or give her expensive gifts. My guess is, if there was S&M going on, he was the one who got beaten. She would have expected a lot more from him if it had been the other way around."

"Unless she enjoys that sort of thing."

"I suppose, but I always wondered what he saw in her other than her looks."

"You don't think youth and beauty are enough to a man his age?"

"He could have had more. He was handsome and successful. There must have been plenty of attractive, intelligent women who wanted to sleep with him. It would help explain the relationship if he liked to be dominated and Bonita was especially good at . . . " Laura groped for words. "Doing whatever it is men like that get off on."

"Not every guy *wants* intelligence, but maybe you're right. After that bust in Elk Grove a few years back—"

"Exactly." The cops had raided a self-styled "mistress of discipline," finding her little black book in the process. Although the names had never been made public, being listed in a book like that could be embarrassing to someone in Hollister's position. It could even destroy his career. A mistress was a lot safer.

Laura returned the box to the shelf. Vicki, meanwhile, was checking out the phone, remarking that the number was the same as the one in the kitchen. Laura jotted all three numbers down. She had no immediate plans for them, but one never knew what the future might hold.

"Are you thinking about reserving the place?" Vicki asked. "Coming back here some evening with a date and dressing him in the leather jumpsuit?"

Laura shook her head a little sadly. "Nope. Not a single man I know could do justice to it."

They continued looking around, finding provocative underwear in the dresser, some for men and some for women; a lethal-looking black pistol in the night table, nestled in a sea of condoms; and exotic lotions and creams in the medicine chest in the bathroom. They packed up the rest of the items on Bonita's list—an electric toothbrush and bottles of various hair-care products sold only through beauty salons—and left the apartment, locking it behind them.

Back in the car, Laura slid Bonita's Whitney Houston album into Vicki's CD player and began talking about the funeral and its aftermath. Bonita had claimed she was in a hurry to get her belongings because the landlord would want to rerent the apartment now that Hollister was dead, but it almost certainly belonged to Craig Tomlinson, not to the late judge. Laura could understand the lie—a judge might not want it known that he was using an apartment belonging to a casino-and-track owner—but not the hurry. Even more to the point, if Bonita had wanted her things so badly, why hadn't she driven to Sacramento sooner and gotten them herself?

Next, Freddie had implied in his eulogy that Hollister had opposed gambling vehemently. If so, why had he accepted Tomlinson's hospitality? Had he simply been a hypocrite—he'd taken part in a regular poker game, after all—or had something more sinister been going on?

Then there was the way those closest to him had reacted to his death. His dear friend Freddie had barely noticed he was gone, much less cared. His mistress had given a performance that was as unconvincing as it was melodramatic. His widow had been gracious and talkative, hardly the picture of wild bereavement. Had none of these people grieved? Had none of them loved him? And if not, why not?

"Maybe it's like that Agatha Christie book, *Murder on the Orient Express*," Vicki said. "Maybe they all did it. Are you sure there were only two bullets in his head?"

"I only know what I read in the papers. The Feds could have changed the real details. You know, so they could spot a phony confession."

"So add up all the suspects, then go to the cops and tell them you know there were actually that same number of bullets in Hollister's body. See what they say."

"Thanks, Vick, but I have enough problems without getting myself arrested for murder."

Vicki glanced at her, serious now. "Oh? What problems do you mean?"

It was an invitation to talk, but Laura didn't accept it. She was having too good a time to think about Allan and ruin the rest of her day. "My mother, for one. These men she comes up with . . . The latest is some dentist from Beverly Hills. 'Not so tall,' she says. That means he's five feet four, tops. 'A good head of hair for a man his age.' He's as bald as Willard Scott. "And 'thin.' He's probably a dwarf with Marfan's Syndrome."

"But only very tall people have Marfan's. Like basketball players and Abraham Lincoln."

"So Lefkowitz is the first short person. A medical marvel. He's also forty-eight years old, but what do I expect? I'm thirty-four. Divorced with two kids. Not much money. I have as much chance of remarrying as Yasir Arafat has of being given a testimonial dinner by B'nai B'rith."

Vicki laughed. "That's if you're *forty*-four. Believe me, you won't be single for the rest of your life, not if you don't want to be."

"You sound like my mother. Of course, she's assuming I'll see the light and get smitten by one of her finds. She thinks I'm too choosy. Do *you* think I'm too choosy?"

"I think you've got too much going on in your life right now to have the energy for men. There's more out there than you think. When you're ready, you'll start noticing."

"I've heard that before. It's not when you're ready, it's when you're desperate. That's when men who are fifty and live with their mothers start looking sensitive and caring. When men who talk about themselves nonstop seem open and honest. When men who expect to sleep with you because they've bought you dinner sud-

denly seem generous." Laura screwed up her face.
"God, what a depressing thought. You think I'll ever
sink that low?"

"In the past twenty-four hours, you've said no to
two men, Allan and Mike Clemente, so I doubt it."

"But I said yes to Allan." And, more and more,
wished that she hadn't.

"You said yes to sex, but he wanted more. You put
him off. That counts as a no."

Laura appreciated how generously Vicki defined
things. "In that case, it was actually three. Freddie
asked me out for a drink after the funeral. You'd think
he'd be afraid someone would see us and tell his wife,
but it never seemed to cross his mind."

"Because he knows people won't tell her, or if they
do, that she'll assume it was strictly business. Or knows
he fools around and doesn't care." Vicki sounded disgusted. "I assume that wasn't all. What else happened?"

Laura provided the details, but not without a certain
amount of embarrassment. Vicki had taken Freddie's
recent behavior more seriously than she had, and she
was beginning to think Vicki was right.

"It doesn't make sense," she finally mumbled. "I do
more than half his work. I even write to his friends and
relatives. You'd think he would value me for how easy
I make his life. It's obvious I'm not interested, so why
doesn't he find someone else to sleep with and leave me
alone?"

"Because he lost Michelle Buckley and he's decided
you should replace her. His self-esteem is at stake.
Besides, you've catered to him for a year and a half
now, and that's enough to convince a man like Freddie
that you're secretly dying for it." Vicki's voice had a
hard edge that Laura wasn't used to. "Face it, Laura.
He barely sees you as human, much less equal. He
doesn't value the job you do because first and foremost,

he wants two or three places to stick his penis while he hears how wonderful and important he is. If you won't go along, he'll find some excuse to get rid of you and hire someone who will. Maybe she won't do everything in the office that you do, but she'll do enough to keep things going, and that's all he wants. That and his own gratification."

Vicki was flushed with emotion now. "You're either a fool or a masochist if you stay there a moment longer than you have to. Given all you've been through lately, I know you're in no shape to fight him—both of us have seen what can happen to women who file grievances or law suits—but I do expect you to face reality and get out. And soon."

Laura sat there, speechless and stunned. Vicki had never spoken to her that way before, it wasn't her style, but every word had rung true. She was nothing to Freddie Phelps and there wasn't a damn thing she could do about it. The outcome was inevitable.

She felt humiliated, then angry. What was it with men, anyway?

She clicked off the CD player. "I'll update my résumé. I'll start job hunting next week, but I can't afford to quit yet, not with Allan moving into his own apartment." He hadn't paid any rent at Carolyn's. Her father, who'd founded Seeley and Associates and worked out of Palm Springs now, owned the house she lived in and had paid off the mortgage years ago.

"I'd offer to lend you enough to tide you over so you could quit *now*—"

"No, Vick. I'd only feel more pressured."

"—if there were the remotest chance you'd accept it, but since there isn't, at least let me ask around for you. I know a lot of people. I could probably find you something more interesting and better paid than what you're doing now, if you're ready to work harder."

Whether she was or wasn't, she knew she should be. The kids were older now, more self-sufficient. Her life had changed radically, but she should be used to that by now. "Okay," she said. "Thanks. And, uh, thanks for the push. I obviously needed it."

"You're welcome." Vicki ejected the Whitney Houston album. "Get out one of Bonita's rap tapes, would you? I'm curious about what she likes. According to my kids, the worst of it's violent, sexist filth, and the rest is boring and annoying."

Laura fished them out. "Which do you want to listen to first? The artists—and I use the term loosely—are named L.L. Cool J, Young M.C., and D.J. Jazzy Jeff & The Fresh Prince."

"I'll leave that to you," Vicki said. "You sound as if you're familiar with their respective oeuvres."

"Not really. Seth plays rap on the radio sometimes. It all sounds the same to me. Bad." She inserted the L.L. Cool J album into Vicki's tape player.

She'd heard enough within the first eight bars, but Vicki insisted on listening to the whole song—in the interest of objective criticism, she said. Afterward, as the tape rewound, she asked incredulously, "How can Bonita like both Sinatra and *that*? They aren't even in the same universe. Play the next one, Laura."

Laura inserted the Young M.C. tape, and once again they listened to the first song. Vicki was baffled to the point of fascination by then, while Laura simply felt a headache coming on. "And third and last," she said, and thought silently, *Thank God,* "we have D.J. Jazzy Jeff and the Fresh Prince."

As she took out the tape, she noticed that it wasn't the original album, but a copy recorded onto a blank Memorex cassette. Bonita hadn't bothered to stick on a label listing the songs, maybe because they were printed on a paper insert folded into the plastic cassette holder.

Laura slid the tape into place, then pressed the play button.

The music, if that was the proper term, wasn't better, only weirder. She was doing her best to tune it out when the lyrics stopped and a woman began moaning heatedly. Laura could make out only part of what she said: "Oh, God. Yes. Yes! . . . baby. . . . harder." She caught the word "more" spoken by a man, and then the woman's "I love you." An assortment of masculine grunts and feminine groans came next, uttered against a background of impressive thumping and creaking.

The thrashing stopped. A period of silence followed. Then a man said something in a voice even more muffled than the woman's, and the woman responded and laughed. Although Laura and Vicki listened to it twice more, they could make out fewer than a dozen words—"no good" and "not fair" from the man, and "won't hurt her" and "someone else" from the woman.

"Somehow," Vicki drawled, "I don't think that was part of the song."

"If it was," Laura said, "the tone quality was sure lousy. It wasn't recorded over the original, by the way. The tape was a blank Memorex."

Suddenly the woman spoke, purring something in a thick French accent. Once again, they listened to it several times but could make out only part of what she said: "But you asked . . . *monsieur*. And now . . . with you."

"No," the man groaned. "Don't start in. . . . " But if he actually meant to stop her, he didn't succeed. Indeed, it was obvious from what little they could make out that after the first minute or so, he no longer wanted to.

They continued to listen. The only words they heard were muffled exclamations of passion, but the nature of the activity couldn't have been clearer. The woman was suckling noisily and the man was panting violently. Every now and then she paused, and he gasped some version of "Don't stop." Finally there was silence—dead silence.

"Jesus," Laura said in awe. "I think she might have killed him."

She hadn't, though, because she eventually spoke again, murmuring something including "my turn," "nice and hard again," and "real good." Then the love-making resumed and continued for several minutes more. There was nothing more on the tape. The other side was blank.

Laura pressed the eject button. "What do you suppose that was all about?"

Vicki shrugged. "I don't know. Bonita and Hollister, maybe? A tape they made to turn each other on with?"

"Maybe, but why disguise it as something else? Compared to the rest of what was in that apartment, the tape is Bambi Meets Mary Poppins."

"Unless she was blackmailing him with it."

"Then why not keep it in her home? Besides, the quality is too poor to recognize his voice—assuming that *was* his voice."

"And if it wasn't?"

"Maybe it was a couple who used the apartment and could be damaged if their affair became public knowledge. Maybe Bonita made the tape to blackmail them with. All I know is, it's the only interesting thing she wanted back."

But the theory had a couple of holes ten times the size of the one in the jumpsuit. First—once again—why would Bonita leave a blackmail tape in Tomlinson's apartment? And second, no reporter they knew would have revealed a man's sexual peccadilloes unless he was a public figure who'd surpassed the merely sordid and ventured into the truly outrageous, like the congressman who'd had wives and children in both California and Washington. This muffled tape had no apparent value as an instrument of blackmail.

Laura didn't have any answers. She only knew that the tape intrigued her. That it might even provide a clue to Hollister's murder. And that there was no need to return it to Bonita.

SEVEN

Vicki was horrified. "What do you mean, you're going to keep it? Don't you think she'll notice, for God's sake?"

"Sure she will, but so what? I'll tell her I couldn't find it. She'll assume someone realized what was on it and swiped it before I got there."

"And suppose it really is a blackmail tape? Suppose her friends in the mob know about it and own a piece of the action? Don't you think they'll suspect you? They could visit your house and leave it looking like Dorothy's place after the tornado."

Vicki had a point. "I guess I was a little rash. How's this? I'll make a copy. I'll keep the original because the quality will be slightly better, and an expert might be able to retrieve what we couldn't make out, but that shouldn't present a problem. How hard could it be to find a blank Memorex tape like this one?"

"I love the assumption you're making—that there's a high-quality double tape deck in my rustic little cabin."

Laura had seen pictures of Vicki's place at the lake. It was anything but small and rustic. "Of course there is, just like the one in your house. Your husband is a sound freak. If he shells out for a three-bedroom condo, he's damn well going to put the best equipment money can buy in there."

"Okay. You're right." Vicki sighed, much too heavily for Laura to take seriously. "I don't have the heart to ask you where this is going. I haven't seen you this cheerful since Stanley Gluckman came out of the closet and you didn't have to keep your second date with him."

Stanley had been another of Dottie's finds, a freeway materials engineer who'd thought paving mixtures was the most fascinating topic on earth. "I don't know," Laura said. "It's a close call."

She looked out the window. They were crossing the summit now. Lake Tahoe, a sky blue gem sparkling in the sunshine, was surrounded by tree-covered mountains whitewashed by recent spring snows. It was a scene of such breathtaking beauty that it seemed unreal, and so sweeping and vast that Laura could never come here without feeling small. It was a comforting sort of smallness, though, a profound awareness that she was a tiny part of something majestic and even transcendent.

They arrived at Vicki's condo forty minutes later. It was located near the Heavenly Valley ski area, about fifteen minutes from the casinos at the state line. After carrying their luggage inside, they turned up the heat and went out for lunch. They picked up some groceries afterward, locating the right Memorex tapes in the same supermarket.

It was past two by then, but such a perfect day that they decided to ski for as long as the light lasted and the snow held up. Laura didn't care that it was more slush than powder, especially at the lower elevations, or that she was too rusty to ski the hardest, most enjoyable trails. She had good company, magnificent scenery, and exhilarating speed. She enjoyed working her body, enjoyed feeling it respond.

She was relaxed but full of energy when they got home, one of those benefits of exercise that the women's magazines are always touting but that scrubbing floors never seems to provide. She and Vicki started talking about dinner, trying to decide whether to cook or go out. They finally settled on picking up a pizza.

Then Laura remembered Bonita's invitation. "On the other hand, we could go to the Alpine Room and eat for free. Bonita invited me to watch her sing. She said to bring a friend along—that she'd comp the dinners. We could return her things at the same time."

Vicki was agreeable, but pointed out that the Alpine Room was one of the most popular places in town. "You can't call at six on a Saturday night and get a reservation, and unless you have a reservation, you won't get in."

Laura picked up the phone. "Let's find out how much pull Bonita has."

The answer was, more than enough. The restaurant was booked solid until Laura mentioned that Bonita had invited her. Then the reservation clerk said he'd see what he could do and put her on hold, presumably to check out her story. When he returned, an opening had materialized.

"I really appreciate your finding a table for us," Laura said. "We live in Sacramento. It would have been disappointing to come all the way up here and not hear Bonita perform."

"Sacramento?" The clerk sounded harassed, but also amused. "You're the second one in the past hour. Leave it to Bonita and the boss to pick the busiest night in weeks to invite their friends from out of town."

"Well, thanks again. If you have a free moment, could you tell her I'm looking forward to seeing her, and that

I'll bring along the things from the apartment?"

The clerk said he would pass on the message and excused himself to take another call. "We're eating at nine-thirty," Laura said to Vicki, "but why don't we go early? I'm saving whatever dinner would have cost us, so I figure I'm entitled to spend a few hours at the casino."

"You'll lose the price of a pizza in half an hour, but actually, *I* was going to pay for dinner. You're my guest."

"You paid for the groceries. *I* was going to pay, but I'll treat you to brunch tomorrow instead, with my winnings. I feel lucky tonight."

"And I feel tired. That's what happens when you reach forty. How about resting for a while before we go out?"

"Only if you help me copy the tape," Laura said. "If anything interesting turns up, I'll give it to the police. I promise."

"Okay. You win. If I can't talk you out of it, I want it to be as good as possible. We live on a nice, quiet street and I'd like to keep it that way."

In truth, Laura couldn't have managed without Vicki's help, because the equipment was a total mystery to her. It took some adjusting, but in the end, they wound up with a copy that, to Laura's ear, was indistinguishable from the original. Vicki went in to nap while Laura called her kids and then her mother, entertaining Dottie with a description of the N Street apartment.

Afterward, too wired to sleep or even to read, she took out the rest of Bonita's tapes and skipped methodically through each one to see if anything had been recorded over the original songs. Nothing had.

They arrived at the Monte Carlo Hotel at eight-thirty, Laura carrying Bonita's belongings in a Nordstrom shopping bag that was a masterpiece of efficient packing. They checked it at the desk, then went into the casino. Laura chose blackjack because she'd heard the odds were better at cards than at the slots. She'd never played before, but she'd watched Allan and understood the basics. She found a quiet table, acted as if she knew what she was doing, and slipped into a smooth, comfortable rhythm.

With the third hand, she began to win. By the seventh, she felt she couldn't lose. Vicki stood and watched, saying nothing.

Her bets got larger, her play more reckless. The moves she made defied all logic at times, but they usually paid off. It was like being in the zone, that mystical state of consciousness she'd experienced a few times while skiing, when you succeed at almost everything you try, effortlessly and without deliberate thought.

Forty-five minutes and a hundred dollars later, Vicki dragged her out of the casino and over to the desk. They picked up the shopping bag, then walked to the elevator. Laura was dazed by how easy it had been to win—and how exciting. "I'm going back after dinner," she said. "It's obviously my night."

"If you believe that, Tomlinson has a bridge he wants to sell you. He loves people like you. They wind up losing every dime they've won."

"Easy come, easy go," Laura said. But deep down, she knew she'd keep winning.

The Alpine Room was a dark, romantic restaurant on the top floor of the hotel. They were seated immediately, at a window table with a view of a moonlit mountain. It was a desirable location, not too far from the dance floor but isolated enough to talk privately.

Bonita was on a small stage in an alcove cut into one of the walls, diagonally across from them beyond a sea of tables. She was singing "I Dreamed a Dream" from *Les Misérables*, accompanying herself on the piano with grace and skill. Many of the people in the room had stopped talking in order to listen.

There was a moment of hushed appreciation when she finished, then a burst of applause. Laura put aside her menu and picked up the shopping bag. "I'm going to say hello to Bonita. If the waiter shows up, order me the scampi, would you? No appetizer or soup, oil and vinegar on my salad, and if you're having a glass of wine, I'll have one, too."

"I'll get us a half carafe. Is white okay?"

"Sure." Laura thanked her and left the table, walking parallel to the wall rather than zigzagging through the congestion. She'd almost reached the corner when she heard her name, spoken in a questioning male voice. "Laura?"

She stopped and looked around. Someone was getting to his feet at a small table halfway between the stage and the corner. She squinted at him. Mike Clemente. He certainly got around.

Intrigued, she smiled and walked over to him, holding out her hand. He'd been here longer than she had; he'd finished a salad and half a cocktail. "Mike! How are you?"

Rather than shake her hand, he took it in both of his and held it for several seconds. He smiled back at her very warmly. The smile affected her in the oddest way. Part of what she felt was sexual, because he was so damned good-looking. Part was sudden anxiety, because she didn't know who or what he was. And part—the strangest part—was the same sense of recklessness she'd felt downstairs, when the right cards had come up again and again.

"That depends," he said. "Are you alone?"

She shook her head. "No. I'm with a friend."

"Then I'm only fair. Your friend—is it anyone I know?"

She wondered if he thought she was with Freddie Phelps. "Maybe. She seems to know you—by reputation, at least."

"She?"

"Vicki Stonehouse."

The smile got broader. "A formidable opponent. I was going to ask you both to join me, but now I'm willing to beg."

Laura considered putting him off, but it was too good an opportunity to ask him some pointed questions. And if Vicki turned ten shades of green, so be it. "Oh? Why is that?"

"Because she has some extremely paranoid theories about a horseracing bill we're working on. This is a perfect opportunity to educate her."

"Far be it from me to interfere with the workings of our great state legislature. You should join *us*, though. We have a table for four by the window." She pointed to where Vicki was sitting, then held up the shopping bag. "Go on over. I have some things to give Bonita."

"If you don't mind, I'll wait till you're finished. Given your friend's low opinion of me, I'm not brave enough to show up at your table without you." He fingered the necklace she was wearing, a small gold nugget surrounded by tiny rubies. "This is pretty. Very unusual."

"Thank you. I shouldn't be long." She turned away, puzzled by everything he'd said and done. He was too confident to worry about Vicki's reaction, so why had he stalled? And that line about the necklace . . . He'd used it as a pretext to touch her, to establish a more personal relationship. It had worked, too, if the sexual jolt she'd felt was anything to go by. In other words, he'd put some fancy moves on her just now, and she wondered why.

Bonita was finishing up a song when Laura reached

her. She rose to acknowledge the applause, then threw out her arms and gave Laura a hug. She was wearing a green sequinned gown and her signature antique jewelry—earrings and a matching necklace made of emeralds and diamonds.

"You're a doll," she said, taking the shopping bag and setting it aside. "An absolute doll. To come all this way just to bring me my things."

Laura didn't correct her. She was a mystery in her own right. It wouldn't hurt to find out more about her. "Things are a little crazy with my ex-husband right now. I was—"

"Tell me about it!" Bonita rolled her eyes. "God! Men! The way they act sometimes, I think we should give them up."

"The judge, you mean?"

Bonita looked offended. "Of course not. Not Jimmy. He was a saint."

Not unless the FBI had developed a sudden interest in hagiography, he wasn't, but Laura backed off. She should have been more subtle. "I'm sorry. I don't know what I was thinking."

"I understand. You're down on men right now. Because of your ex, I mean."

Laura nodded. "I guess you're right. I was glad to have a reason to get away. That's some apartment, by the way. All those antiques . . . Are they real, do you think?"

"Oh, definitely. Good ones, too." Bonita fingered her necklace. "Antiques are one of my little hobbies, you know."

Laura wondered if Bonita would slip up—admit that the apartment wasn't Hollister's. "What do you suppose will become of them now that the judge is gone?"

Bonita looked uncomfortable, or at least preoccupied. "Uh, I have no idea. The landlord can't give them to Maggie because she didn't know about the place. I guess he'll have to sell them." She brightened. "Or rent the place furnished. I even know someone who might be interested. My boss, Mr. Tomlinson."

She was quicker than Laura had given her credit for. "Oh? Does he visit Sacramento often?"

"All the time. On business, you know. It would be awfully convenient for him." She paused. "I hope you didn't have trouble finding any of my things."

"None at all. We were in and out" —Laura snapped her fingers— "just like that. My girlfriend Vicki and I, that is. She's keeping me company this weekend. We're staying in her condo. It's near Heavenly Valley."

"Yes, I know. That is, they told me you wanted a reservation for two. I was thrilled you were coming. I'm so pleased to be able to repay you for all your trouble by having you and your friend as my guests."

"You're a wonderful singer. I wish I'd come sooner."

Bonita's eyes filled with tears. "To cheer people up when times are hard—I live for that, Laura. It's my calling. I only hope I'll be able to make your world a little brighter tonight."

"You already have," Laura said. "Maybe you'll be able to join us later. I ran across another friend—"

"Yes. I saw you talking. Isn't he a hunk?"

"I didn't realize you two knew each other." Judging by Clemente's reaction at the funeral, they'd never met.

Bonita winked. "We didn't till earlier tonight, but we sure do now. I'll be over during my next break."

Clemente had obviously charmed Bonita senseless. Laura smiled and excused herself, then returned to his table. "You made a big hit with Bonita," she said. "Is that why you came to the lake? To meet her?"

"Sure. You were my first choice, but when you turned me down . . . " He put his hand on her waist and started forward. "I was trying to reassemble my shattered ego when I thought of Bonita. There's a woman, I said to myself, who knows how to treat a guy. Not like Laura Miller. So I hopped into my car and drove to the lake."

He was pulling her leg. Very hard. She couldn't help laughing. "I doubt your ego is that fragile. Really, what are you doing here?"

"The truth? I had some business to take care of."

"Oh? What sort of business?"

"I had a meeting with a client."

"Did you? Who?"

His hand tightened on her waist, bringing her to a stop. "I'm not going to answer that. It's confidential."

He didn't sound annoyed so much as firm, as if he was warning her to mind her own business. It was only prudent to retreat. "I'm sorry. That was unforgivably nosy."

"You're not sorry at all," he said, "but I don't mind. I'm flattered you're so interested in my activities. Not that I don't wonder why. You weren't last night, when you wouldn't even have coffee with me."

There was nothing she could say to explain, so she changed the subject. "So you came for a meeting and stayed to hear Bonita?"

They started walking again. "Right. Freddie mentioned she worked here. I realized how good she was when I heard her at the funeral, so I decided to stick around and catch her tonight at dinner."

Laura suddenly recalled her conversation with the reservation clerk. "But when you called for a table, the place was completely booked, so you said you were a friend of Craig Tomlinson's. That he'd invited you to come tonight."

"So she told you about that, did she?" He smiled. "It wasn't true, but it could have been."

"She didn't say a word about it."

"Oh? Then who did?"

Laura couldn't resist. "You really want to know? Who's the client you came to see?"

"Tell me something. Why *are* you so interested in me?"

"Why are you so interested in *me*?"

They'd reached the table now, but neither of them sat down. "I don't think I can answer that honestly without sounding either sexist or crude," he said.

"So lie." She grinned at him. "You're a lobbyist. You should be good at that."

Vicki looked at her with an I-can't-believe-you-just-said-that expression on her face, but Mike never missed a beat. "True, but I've found that lies are usually counterproductive. The truth—properly framed—gets you a lot farther."

He turned to Vicki. "Mrs. Stonehouse, we've crossed swords a few times at the capitol. I'm Mike Clemente."

"I found him at a table near Bonita, sitting all by himself, and invited him to join us," Laura explained. "Think of it as taking in a stray dog. A bloodhound."

Vicki made a quick recovery. Even the bloodhound line didn't faze her. "And to think I despaired of getting you involved in the animal-rights movement, Laura! It's interesting to finally meet you, Mr. Clemente."

"Mike."

"Mike, then. Please, sit down."

He held out Laura's chair for her—the salads and wine had come—and sat down beside her. The waiter had brought a third setting by then, but placed it next to Vicki. Mike moved it across the table.

"We were talking about you just this morning," Laura said to him. "I mentioned to Vicki that we'd met, and she said she'd seen you around the capitol. That you were very effective, especially given how new you were. I believe you said you were in corporate law before you came to Sacramento?"

He lazed back in his chair. "That's right."

"You specialized in securities and banking."

"Yes, in Los Angeles, but that's something I never said. Not to you."

"Vicki did." Laura sipped her wine. "So what made you decide to join a lobbying firm? After all those years in Los Angeles, I mean?"

"It wasn't 'all those years,' at least not in L.A. I practiced there for about a year. Then I got an offer from Burke/Maravich and decided to accept it."

"So you were originally with a firm somewhere else?"

He nodded. "In Chicago, but that was a million years ago. I got bored with it after a while, wanted to try something different. I've practiced on and off ever since."

"How fascinating," Laura said. "Why don't you tell us your entire life story? We wouldn't want you to skip a single detail."

He shrugged and then obliged, telling her a lengthy tale of frequent moves, jobs in law, management and banking, and a marriage broken up by his extreme restlessness. His ex-wife and son lived in her hometown of Seattle now. His story matched the facts—what few of them Laura knew—but that only proved he was glib, not honest.

"You certainly move around a lot," she finally said.

"Like I said, I'm restless. I used to tell myself I'd settle down when I was forty, but that was ten years ago, when forty seemed like a lifetime away. Fifty or even sixty is probably more realistic."

"But isn't that awfully hard on your son? Having a father hundreds of miles away, never knowing where he's going to run off to next?"

He turned in his chair, staring at her with a leashed intensity that all but pinned her to her seat. "When I said

I was restless, I meant in the sense of enjoying new challenges. It's not where I live. It's what I do. I miss my son. I see him about twice a month and wish it were much more often. I hate being seven hundred miles away."

Laura felt a sense of connection then, as if she'd seen through the layers of smooth charm to the emotions beneath. "So why not go back to Seattle? You can do the same thing in Washington as you do down here."

"My ex-wife remarried last year. Her husband is the news director of a local TV station. That's a position with as much job security as managing the Yankees when Steinbrenner is in charge. Four years ago he was in Orlando. Eighteen months ago he was in Houston. It's pointless to go back to Seattle when a year or two from now, my son could be somewhere else."

"If you miss him so much, why don't you file for increased physical custody?" Laura asked. "You're a lawyer. It would be easy for you."

"Because my ex-wife is a decent person. A good mother. If we talk and she agrees, that's one thing, but to go into court . . . I'd have to be a bastard to put her through something like that." He paused. "How would you feel if your ex-husband dragged you into court and tried to take your kids away from you?"

It was her worst nightmare. She paled and looked away. "I'd hate him for it. I'd want to kill him."

"Exactly. There's enough strain between Nancy and me without my doing anything to add to it. It would only hurt my son. I figure she'll come around eventually, but it takes time."

Clemente had answers for everything, Laura thought, answers that sounded reasonable and sincere. He was either a nice guy in a cheesy line of work, or the best bullshit artist she'd ever met.

EIGHT

The waiter showed up with their entrees and a bottle of wine—for Mr. Clemente, he explained, compliments of the management. The label was French, and Laura figured the wine was expensive.

"I'm impressed," she said once the waiter had served it and left the table. "The Tomlinson connection again?"

"Probably, but he's a client, not a personal friend. We're following a few bills for him. I mentioned it to the manager when I first came in." He looked at Vicki. "One of those bills is AB 2962. I'd like to talk to you about it, if you don't mind."

Vicki sipped her wine. "For something this good, it's the least I can do. Actually, I enjoy hearing you talk. You do it so well. But nothing you can say will convince me that off-track betting is good public policy."

The two of them started to argue, Mike stressing fiscal benefits, and Vicki, social liabilities. "Given the moral weakness of your position," she finally said, "you make the best case that can probably be made, but it will be moot in the end. You'll never get the bill out of Ken's committee. I mean, the whole reason he was given Governmental Organization in the first place was because the public considered the legislature such a cesspool. The leadership wanted someone they could work with in that position, but they also needed a knight on a white horse."

"And Ken Carlsen has the shiniest armor in town. I know that, but like you said, Carlsen is a guy we can work with. He might have said no in the past, but he realizes the state needs money badly. He knows this bill will provide it."

"Not when the price tag includes opening the door wider to the mob and taking food out of the mouths of hungry children," Vicki insisted. "I'd be amazed if Ken is even willing to discuss this bill with you, much less support it."

"He's running for governor. The prospect of taking office and having to deal with a huge deficit—"

"Have you talked to him about it?"

"No," Mike admitted. "Jerry Burke was lobbying the bill till very recently. Ken had Jack Waltzer meet with him."

"Ken's chief of staff," Vicki said to Laura. "He meets with the heavy hitters that Ken can't or won't see. So, Mike, how did Jerry do?"

"Jack listened politely. That was it. But it's only March, and I've heard rumors that if things look bad now, they're going to look even worse after April 15th, when the tax revenues are added up."

"And you're concerned about the shortfall," Laura said. "As a public-spirited citizen, that is."

He studied her for a moment. "Why do I have the feeling that you're about to launch a dart straight at my head?"

"I can't imagine. I was simply going to suggest that raising the tax on alcoholic beverages might be a better way to generate money, even though your buddies in the liquor industry fight like deranged ninjas every time an increase is even mentioned."

He smiled. "Have some more wine, Laura. Your glass seems to be empty. And just as a point of information, have you done any gambling tonight?"

"A little. Why?"

"So you disapprove of gambling and drinking—and by extension, of me, because I represent those industries—but you do both."

She reddened. He had her. "In moderation. Your clients would go broke if they had to rely on people like me. Their profits depend on their products being abused."

"All the same, I could hardly drag her out of the casino," Vicki said. "She won a hundred bucks, all of which she'll probably blow later on."

"Whose side are you on, anyway?" Laura asked.

"Yours, of course, but he's right. After all your mother's efforts to raise a nice Jewish girl, you've still got a taste for vice. Blackjack, French wine, *sheygetses* . . . "

The word meant non-Jewish men—as in Mike Clemente, obviously. "I never should have taught you any Yiddish," Laura grumbled.

"I'm a quarter Jewish," Mike said, "and you take life too seriously, Laura. Drink up. A little vice won't kill you."

"I think you *want* me to get drunk."

"You're right. I wish it had occurred to me sooner." He noticed Bonita approaching and stood up. "You'd be a lot less trouble that way."

Bonita sashayed up to him, put her arms around his neck and kissed him on the mouth. For a pair that had just met, they were awfully friendly.

"You're a damn good singer," he said as he helped her into a seat. "Good enough to be headlining downstairs. Good enough to be performing on Broadway."

"Keep telling me things like that," she answered

with a giggle, "and I'll give you a private show."

Just as she had for the judge—whips, handcuffs and all, presumably. Her bereavement hadn't lasted long. As for her fidelity, Laura doubted it had existed in the first place.

Mike sat down. "Good enough to be going on world tours. Good enough to be cutting albums that go platinum. How about later tonight?"

"I'm sorry, sweetie, but I can't," she said. "I've got special company coming. How about tomorrow afternoon?"

"I'll be at a meeting in Sacramento. Why don't you tell your *company* to come tomorrow afternoon?"

"I wish I could, but it's too late. He's already on his way. We'll do it some other time, though, I promise." She patted his hand. "But give a girl more than a few hours notice, okay?"

"I'll do that. Are you listed in the phone book?"

Bonita took a gold business-card case out of her purse. "Here, take a card. You can have one, too, Laura. Maybe you could show it around."

Laura looked at the card. It was pink with black writing. "Bonita Franks," it read, "*Chanteuse et Pianiste*. Weddings, Charity Events, Private Parties."

"Thanks. I'll be sure and do that." She put the card in her purse. "Bonita, this is the friend I was telling you about, Vicki Stonehouse."

Bonita handed Vicki a card. "It's nice to meet you. I hope you're taking good care of Laura."

"I'm doing my best. Thanks for everything, Bonita. I'm enjoying your singing enormously. Mike is right. You should be playing in one of the big showrooms."

She beamed. "Aren't you nice to say so! Tell it to my boss, would you?"

"No, really," Laura said. "You should be. Why aren't you?"

"I'm only twenty-six—"

"Madonna was a star by then," Vicki pointed out, "and you're a much better singer than she is."

Bonita looked at the table, visibly embarrassed by the topic. "Thanks, but the songs I sing—the music I love . . . " She fidgeted with her card case. "Besides, I'm no Madonna. She's so uninhibited. So outrageous. I could never do that on stage. I'll never attract the kind of following that gets you gigs in the big rooms."

Laura was amazed. There was a rational human being in there after all, hiding under the flirting and ditziness. "Not even as a warmup act? It would be a start, anyway."

"I tried that once," Bonita said. "It was a disaster. I, uh, I had to force myself to even go on, and then . . . " She hesitated. "It's just—there were so many people out there, all of them staring straight at me."

"And?" Vicki asked gently.

"I was terrible. These scratchy sounds came out of my mouth, all off-pitch. I kept thinking I was going to throw up." She squared her shoulders and raised her chin. "But I'm a fighter, Vicki. I won't give up. I'm working on my problem with someone very special right now."

"You mean a therapist of some sort?"

Bonita looked insulted. "Of course not. I'm not crazy. She's a hypnotist and astrologer."

So much for rationality, Laura thought. "How interesting," she said. "What does she do?"

"Well, my basic problem is, I'm an Aries, and Mercury was in Leo when I was born. That means I'm talented but very sensitive. The aura is right for me in a dark restaurant, but anywhere else, I freak out. Madame Zubia told me I could overcome that with hypnosis, but it takes time. Every week, she plants positive energy in my mind, and eventually it will neutralize the negative energy and take over. I'm making progress already. You know my business cards? I just had them printed. It's an exciting new venture for me."

"You can't miss," Mike said. "Not with your talent. I can't say I like it, though. Once you're a huge success, you won't have time to give me private shows anymore."

Laura slid him an amused look. If he'd been any cuter, Jim Fowler could have put him in a cage and displayed him on "The Tonight Show."

They ordered dessert, then made small talk. An effusive compliment to Bonita's jewelry elicited the claim that she'd saved long and hard for it, but otherwise Laura could have napped for the next ten minutes and not missed anything. She was dying to bring up the judge but didn't dare, not without a good opening. Bonita was too touchy about the subject.

And then, as Bonita nibbled on a piece of cheesecake, she brought him up herself. "Life is so strange, don't you think? Yesterday I was just devastated, and today, here I am with you wonderful people, really enjoying myself. And I owe a lot of it to you, Laura. You were such a comfort to me at the funeral, and so nice to run my little errand so I wouldn't have to sit up here and worry."

"I was glad to help. I knew how upset you were. Under the circumstances, you're doing wonderfully."

She nodded thoughtfully. "Mere mortals like you and I are helpless when the Grim Reaper comes calling. We can only accept it and go on. I'm grateful for how Jimmy enriched my life. I'll carry him in my heart forever."

"Well, I think you're remarkable. Very strong. I mean, after that news report last night—"

"It was a vicious lie." Bonita gestured almost imperceptibly, but at what, Laura couldn't tell. "Don't turn around," she whispered, "but there's a man named

Joseph Cassani sitting in the corner. Joey the Bowie, they call him. After the way he . . . " She drew her finger across her throat.

Laura had heard of him. He owned a snow-removal service in town, among other businesses. "Isn't he the local—"

"Yes. He and his friends come in here to see me sing, you know? I talk to them all the time. You have to, with men like that. Anyway, they never asked after Jimmy, or told me to pass on messages. They never even spoke to him when he was in here watching me sing."

Her nostrils flared. *"He didn't know them!"* she cried. "I'm sure of it! He was an honorable man, struck down in the prime of his life for trying to help someone. The FBI . . . They're scum, dragging his name through the mud when he's not even here to defend himself. They should be ashamed. *Ashamed!"*

"You should go and see them," Laura said. "Set them straight."

She shuddered. "I can't. Joey might find out. He has spies everywhere."

Suddenly, in the quickest mood shift Laura had ever seen, Bonita smiled and stood up. "Will you look at the time? It's back to work for this girl. It was lovely to talk to you all." She winked. "Stick around if you want to. The later it gets, the hotter *I* get."

Mike watched her wiggle away, then shook his head in bemusement. "She's a real original. Astrology and the Mafia. Heck of a combination."

"But you like her," Laura said.

He shrugged. "Sure. What's not to like?"

"I mean, you find her attractive. You want to . . ." She hesitated, then went ahead and said it. "You want to sleep with her, don't you?"

"A gentleman doesn't respond to questions like that."

Laura rolled her eyes. "You've got to be kidding. You propositioned her right in front of us."

"That wasn't a proposition. It was flirting. It made her happy." He stroked Laura's cheek, lightly and seductively. She felt it in all the standard erogenous zones. "Like that. You should try it some time."

She moved her chair closer to the wall. "I did, fifteen years ago in Boston. All it got me was an early marriage and a wandering husband. Why would you want to make Bonita happy? Is it some sort of humanitarian thing?"

"Absolutely. A personal commitment to make every woman I meet as blissful as possible. How am I doing?"

Laura laughed. Clemente was bulletproof. It was a waste of ammunition to take potshots at him, but the ricochets were so funny that she never minded missing the target.

"Not bad," she said. "About Bonita—"

"Hey, listen, I know how you women operate. She's a friend of yours. Whatever I say will go straight back to her."

"She's not my friend. She's a casual acquaintance."

"You babysit her at funerals—"

"She would have made a scene. I was concerned about Maggie Hollister."

"And pick up her purchases from Nordstrom—"

"Not purchases from Nordstrom. Some things from an apartment in Sacramento where she stayed every now and then. It was right on my way."

"Okay. So you're a casual acquaintance. For a casual acquaintance, you're a pretty good friend."

"Laura has a neurotic need to look after people," Vicki said, "even when she barely knows them. People a lot like you, come to think of it. If you play your cards right—"

"You'll make a bundle downstairs," Laura interrupted. "What are you afraid will get back to Bonita?"

"That I'm much more interested in *you.*"

"Do you ever give a straight answer?" she asked in exasperation.

He pondered the question. "Okay. The truth is, Tomlinson's an important client. My boss just added me to the account and I want to stay there. I didn't realize Tomlinson and Bonita were personal friends until I met her, and then . . . " He sipped his coffee. "I make it a rule to be nice to my clients' friends. If that means feeding Bonita's ego, I'm happy to do it. It's as simple as that."

"In that case," Laura teased, "Joey the Bowie Cassani is sitting just a few tables away. Why don't you go over and proposition *him?*"

"Because he's dancing with a flashy redhead in an orange dress at the moment. I doubt he'd be interested in me."

Laura looked at the dance floor. The man with the redhead was tall and burly with a shock of salt-and-pepper hair. She found it interesting that Mike had recognized him. "You've met him, then?"

"Nope. Seen his picture in the paper. By the way, didn't anyone ever tell you that you wait for an invitation with guys like Cassani? And that you never speak until you're spoken to?"

Laura had read about mob etiquette. He was right. "How do you know? Personal experience?"

He smiled. "I'm an Italian from Jersey City. I learned it in the womb."

She gave up. She couldn't get the better of him, not after a two-hour trip, three hours of skiing, and three glasses of wine. She noticed their waiter at the next table and called him over, asking for more coffee. If you sipped pensively enough, you didn't have to talk, especially if you pretended to be transfixed by the entertainment.

Mike and Vicki kept up the conversation, discussing politics. Laura listened absently, looking at Cassani and the redhead every now and then. They went over to talk to Bonita when she finished her ballad, returning to the dance floor a few bars into the next song. Cassani was obviously enjoying himself. He was smiling, dancing the tango with enthusiasm but no particular grace. Watching him, it was hard to believe he was anything but a middle-aged man out for a night on the town, probably with a paid companion.

Then the song ended, and he headed straight toward Laura. He was even bigger than she'd realized, big enough that his size alone would have made her uneasy even if his reputation hadn't. She watched him approach out of the corner of her eye. You didn't stare at a Mafia boss.

He stopped about ten feet short of the table and said something to the redhead, who left him and headed for the corner. Then he continued forward, looking at Mike. Mike was on his feet by then, reaching for the hand that Cassani was holding out.

"Mr. Clemente. I understand we have several friends in common. I wanted to stop by. Pay my respects."

"It's an honor, sir. I appreciate your consideration." Mike paused. "If there's ever anything I can do for you . . . "

"You can introduce me to your two very beautiful companions," Cassani said.

"Of course. This is Mrs. Miller" —he nodded toward Laura— "and Mrs. Stonehouse. Ladies, Mr. Cassani."

"A pleasure." Cassani gave a courtly little bow. "Enjoy the rest of your evening, ladies. Mr. Clemente, I'll look forward to seeing you again."

Mike nodded deferentially. "Thank you, sir. It was very gracious of you to come over."

Cassani turned and walked away. Laura sat in stunned silence, picturing him with a knife in his hand, slitting God only knew whose throat. And Mike Clemente . . . She would have understood if he'd simply been polite, but his response had gone far beyond that. He'd fawned. Maybe he wasn't on chummy terms with Cassani and his circle yet, but he obviously hoped to be.

He'd probably succeed, too. Mafia dons usually summoned the people they wanted to meet to smoky back rooms. They didn't stop in full view of the public and introduce themselves. Clemente was obviously someone important. Someone who merited special treatment.

She finished her coffee, amazed that her hand didn't shake. "Speaking of the rest of our evening, I have a date with a blackjack table. Vicki? Are you ready to leave?"

"No, but since you insist on returning everything you've won. . . ."

Mike was still standing. "I'll walk you to the elevator," he said.

Her heart began to race. She didn't want him anywhere near her. "No. That is, I wouldn't want you to go to all that trouble."

"It's no trouble." He put his hand on her shoulder, and she stiffened. "About Mr. Cassani, Laura . . . There's a certain way you speak to men like that, especially if they go out of their way to say hello to you. Let's call it extreme deference. That's another thing I learned in Jersey City. He and I understand each other very well. He knows I work the legal side of the street, possibly, I admit, to his benefit at times. I know better than to cross him. I won't hear from him."

Laura didn't answer. It was obvious that if Cassani did ask Mike for a favor, he would do it. Maybe he wouldn't have much choice, but he was the one who'd put himself in that position, by working for people who'd cozied up to the mob.

"You're appalled," he said. "You think I'm a crook, if not legally, then at least morally. But I'm not. I'm just a realist who'd like to make enough money to give my son everything I had to do without."

She stood, then moved away from his hand. A lot of people grew up poor. Most of them tried to do well by their kids. But very few kowtowed to the likes of Joseph Cassani as part of their jobs. "I have to be going," she said. "Vicki?"

They started away from the table. To her relief, Mike didn't follow. He simply wished her good luck, then sat down again.

At first, Laura did as well as before, winning sixty dollars more in the next half hour. Vicki finally left to try the slots, saying she'd be back in an hour. Laura's luck faded after that, but only a little. Although she lost more often, she always recouped and wound up ahead. In her mind, money she hadn't even won yet was already spent. Brunch for her and Vicki, clothes for Seth and Sarah, a purse her mother had admired at Macy's . . . Winning was preordained. She was invincible. Infallible.

Maybe that was why she refused to accept it when the odds caught up with her and her luck turned sour. She kept waiting to win, to recover what she'd lost and more, but the cards only teased her. A king when she'd needed a nine. An eight when she'd needed a seven. She told herself to be patient. The cards would come her way again.

But they didn't. By the time Vicki returned, she was down to less than forty dollars in winnings. She was anxious and a little desperate now. She'd been up almost two hundred dollars. She couldn't have been stupid enough to throw it away. She had to get it back.

Vicki touched her arm, but her eyes never left the table. There was no need to explain. Vicki could see her chips—what was left of them.

"Let's go," Vicki said.

Laura shook her head. "Just a little longer."

"Here. Take my keys." Vicki held them out. "I feel sick, Laura. I'll take a cab home."

The casino faded—the table, the chips, the cards. Laura felt as if she were drifting from a bright, throbbing fantasy land into someplace dim and hazy. "It's okay. I'll drive you." Disoriented, she gathered up her chips.

Her head cleared a little as they walked outside into the moonlit night, and a gust of cold wind sliced through her. "Go back inside," she said to Vicki. "Wait in the lobby where it's warm. I'll bring the car around."

"I'm fine," Vicki said, and kept on walking.

"You feel better now?"

"I never felt sick."

Laura finally understood. "You wanted to get me out of the casino before I lost everything. Thanks." She shook her head. "I don't know what happened to me in there. It was weird. Scary." She shivered. "Maybe I should avoid casinos in the future. You're always telling me how obsessive I am. Do you think I'm a compulsive gambler?"

Vicki unlocked the Bronco and they climbed inside. "You've been to the lake before. Did you gamble any?"

"Just the slots. Not blackjack."

"And nothing like this happened?"

"No. Not even close."

Vicki started the car and backed it out. "Then it was

probably just some crazy reaction to stress. Don't worry about it."

"You're telling *me* not to worry?" Laura demanded. "The champ of angst? I'm terrified I'll go bonkers in the South Hills shopping center, withdraw my entire life savings from the Golden West Bank and blow it on lottery tickets in Land Park Liquor and Deli."

"How prosaic. Your nightmares are usually more creative than that."

"Abandon my kids and move to Nevada. Feed my gambling habit by specializing in bizarre sex acts at the Mustang Ranch."

"An improvement," Vicki said. "If it would make you feel better, just stay away from temptation."

Laura leaned back in her seat. She couldn't blame Vicki for laughing at her. She *had* sort of jackknifed off the deep end. "Easy for you to say. Temptation is all around me. The local bingo hall. The temple's Las Vegas nights. Lottery tickets in every supermarket and drugstore." She sighed. "You're right about off-track betting. It's a terrible idea. Addicts like me would never be able to resist it."

"Speaking of which, tonight was an interesting evening, wouldn't you say?"

"Very interesting. Tell me again how Clemente is your typical lawyer-turned-lobbyist."

"I know how it looked, but I also heard his explanation. Where the truth lies . . . " Vicki shrugged. "Where there's shady money, there are usually wiseguys, and given the interests Mike represents, he's bound to run into them. But whether he works with them or tries to steer clear of them, who knows? Obviously he'd never met Cassani before tonight. Personally, I thought he looked flattered by the recognition. I also thought he sounded convincing afterward, when he tried to explain his behavior. But the only thing I'm sure of is, the guy is a good actor."

"You've got that one right," Laura said. "And Bonita? After tonight, I think she knows Cassani better than she admits. Maybe Hollister did, too. I'd love to see the 302s on the case, wouldn't you?"

"The 302s?"

"At the FBI. The agents' reports."

"Oh. What in hell are you reading these days? FBI procedurals?"

"Nonfiction about how the Feds are trying to break up the mob. I wonder if Joey the Bowie ever uses a gun?"

"Don't ask me. I'm busy defending the First Amendment this month. I don't have time to solve murders."

"Come on, Vick. Don't you wonder about Hollister and Bonita? I mean, could anyone really be that flaky?" Laura turned on the overhead light and opened her purse.

"What are you doing?" Vicki asked.

"Finding Bonita's business card. I'm curious about her house. If it's one of those showplaces down by the lake, she probably has another source of income besides her job. A rich lover in the mob, for example."

"Or a rich legitimate businessman," Vicki said.

But skeptical or not, she listened to the address. The street was between Highway 50 and Heavenly Valley, she said, so she passed it all the time. The houses in the area were nicer than average, but not opulent.

Laura talked her into taking a quick look. She figured they'd have to squint at the place in the moonlight, but the outside lights were on, illuminating the driveway and front yard as well as the house itself, giving them a clear view of both from their vantage point in the middle of the street.

A two-and-a-half story building with a pitched roof, the house was expensive but not opulent. Bonita worked in a first-class restaurant and no doubt made good money, at least a couple of hundred a night in wages, plus tips. She had nobody to spend it on but herself, so she could probably afford a place like this.

Two cars were parked by the house, one in the driveway and one in front. The first was a white Cadillac, the second a silver Porsche. Jimmy Hollister's Cadillac. Mike Clemente's Porsche. She didn't know which surprised her more—or what to make of either. She only knew that being here was exciting in a unique, almost sexual way.

She was about to identify the cars for Vicki when the front door of the house swung open. Vicki noticed it too. Before Laura could see who was coming out—or be seen, given how dark the street was—Vicki put the car in gear and gunned down the street.

NINE

During the past year or so, Laura had gotten very, very good at blocking out subjects that pained her. But as much as she tried to block out Allan, she couldn't, because he was waiting at home with the kids and wanted to come back for good. She couldn't pretend that didn't exist, not indefinitely.

She poured out her heart to Vicki as they drove home, finally murmuring, "I don't know what to do. One moment I tell myself that he's really trying to change. That with counseling, it could be okay. A reasonably smooth life with a man I care about. Getting back together would be better for the kids, there's no doubt about that. And the next . . . " She sighed. "The next, I want more out of life than smooth. After last night . . . I'd forgotten what it felt like—that irrational physical attraction. How exciting it can be. Hell. Chemistry. I sure do pick 'em, don't I!"

"What can I say? The guy is a perfect ten. The fact that he lobbies for sludge and plays footsie with the mob doesn't erase the looks, the charm, the wit, and the brains. Maybe you should have an affair with him and get it out of your system."

Laura shuddered. "No. The thought of him touching me—it makes my skin crawl. I've reached new neurotic heights here. He turns me on and makes me nauseous, all at the same time."

"Makes you nauseous or scares you?" Vicki asked.

"Both, probably." Laura massaged her temples. "I'm too damn tired to deal with stuff like this. Why did Allan have to come back and complicate my life, anyway? I was getting used to things the way they were. I wasn't happy, but at least I was . . . settled."

Vicki patted her shoulder. "You agonize too much. Both of us know what you're going to do. For Seth and Sarah's sake, if not for your own."

"Yes. Go to counseling. Try to work things out." Given her love for the kids, what choice did she have?

Allan wasn't home when she got back. Vicki's sixteen-year-old daughter Becky was taking care of the kids, watching them while they played in the backyard. Allan had left three hours before, Becky said, at three o'clock, to "clean up some work at his office."

Laura's first thought was that the work was Carolyn, and the office, Carolyn's house in Land Park. Her heart started pounding. She stared at the phone. In the end, she couldn't stop herself from calling and checking. But he was really in his office, taking care of paperwork that had piled up while he was arguing with Ned Brown.

She hated being so suspicious. The lack of trust was like acid eating at her gut. Even worse, she was disappointed and resentful. The moment he'd come home, even for a weekend, he'd fallen into the same old habits, working when he'd promised to spend time with the kids.

She fed them dinner and got them ready for bed, then finished the Monopoly game. Seth won. He and Sarah had napped and weren't tired, so she let them stay up and watch TV so they could say good night to their father.

She was so caught up in her problems that it was nine-fifteen before she realized she'd forgotten to call her mother when she got home. Dottie had expected her around six. She was going to catch hell.

Dottie answered on the first ring, saying dourly, "It's about time you called."

"How did you know it was me?" Laura asked.

"My *friends* wouldn't disturb me after nine o'clock. They know I turn in early sometimes."

Yup, Laura thought. Her mother was really fried. She tried to slip away from Dottie's wrath as quickly as she could. "I'm sorry I bothered you. I just wanted to let you know—"

"You're my daughter. I expect you to bother me." Kids! Dottie's tone said. They were so inconsiderate, so irresponsible.

"I'm sorry I didn't call you right away. I just wanted you to know I'd gotten home safely. I'll let you get back to whatever you were doing."

"Why the big hurry? You don't even have five minutes to talk to me?"

Laura sighed. "Of course I do, Mom. I thought you were busy with something else."

"Yes," Dottie replied. "Busy sitting by my phone for the past three hours, waiting for you to tell me you were still alive."

"If you were so worried," Laura said with a mixture of guilt and exasperation, "why didn't you call me?"

"What for? I never imagined you were home."

Laura chalked one up for Dottie. She was the Annie Oakley of the Jewish mother set, the deadliest shot in town. "I'm sorry," Laura said yet again.

"Umm. So. You sound tired, Laura. You must have had a hard weekend."

"Not hard. Just busy. We skied both days."

"And now? Allan's still there?" Dottie said his name with dismissive scorn.

"Actually, I haven't seen him yet. He's at his office, working. I expect him back any time now."

"He was working this morning, too, when I stopped by to see how things were. I took the kids to Sunday school, but why not? I was going there anyway, to substitute for Mrs. Goldfarb. Her gall bladder is acting up again. We had lunch at Vic's. Allan was still working when we got home. Still, better work than a woman, since you insist on giving him another chance." Dottie paused. "I'll tell you, Laura, I wish you wouldn't do it. I met the most wonderful man at services Friday night. He was with his mother. You should see how he spoils her. You know what they say—a man treats his wife the same way he treats his mother."

Dr. Lefkowitz, the short, cadaverous dentist, had fallen out of favor awfully quickly. "A member of the temple?" Laura asked, relieved by the change of subject.

"No. That was the thing, sweetie. I'd never seen him before in my life, or his mother, either, so I went over to say hello." Dottie was a lot more cheerful suddenly. Matchmaking brought out the best in her. "You know me. I like to make people feel welcome."

And find out all about them. Laura came by her curiosity honestly. "New in town, then?"

"No. She had a goyish husband. Took the children to his church after her parents died, but she never converted and the family wasn't religious, so it's not as bad as it sounds. Then her husband passed away and she decided to go back to her roots. To find herself, she said. She's a nice woman, but very confused. Her son is a lovely boy, though. He was circumcised, thank God."

"What did you do? Follow him into the men's room and peek?"

"No. I waited till the rabbi's sermon put everyone to sleep, then unzipped his pants and pulled it out. What do you think I did? I asked his mother. He looks a little like that Jewish comedian, the one with the long hair who's always making those awful jokes about his relatives. Richard something."

Laura suddenly recalled that Alice Albright, unlike her late husband, was Jewish. "Was his name Arthur Albright?" she asked. There couldn't be two half-orphaned, half-Jewish men who looked like Richard Lewis running around town.

"Yes. You mean you know him already?"

"Sort of. We met at a party."

"Well, that's odd," Dottie murmured. "He didn't say a thing when I gave him your name and number."

"It was last fall. He's probably forgotten me."

"That explains it. You weren't at your best then. You know, dear, my friend Ethel's daughter met her husband three different times before he invited her out. Nothing. *Gor nisht.* And then, just like that, they fell in love. So if Arthur calls, you should give him a try."

"I'll do that," Laura said. It wasn't so much a matter of taking the path of least resistance with her mother as of being angry with Allan. She hadn't planned to date while they were in counseling because she figured she could work on only one relationship at a time, but if this was all the effort *he* was going to put into it . . .

He showed up at a quarter of ten, full of excuses and apologies. If Ned Brown hadn't been such a pain in the ass, he said, he never would have fallen so far behind that he was forced to work through all of Sunday to catch up. It wouldn't happen often, the way it always used to. He'd changed.

He stayed at the house till eleven-thirty, hunched over paperwork at the dinette table. Laura sat across from him with the Sunday paper, skimming the news and help-wanted columns, and then, at his request, checking the real estate section for promising apartments. He'd free up his evenings, he said, and they would look together. She agreed to make the necessary appointments. As he so correctly pointed out, he was much busier than she was.

In the meantime, he was staying with his friend Phil, whose duplex was a few miles away. His belongings were in Phil's guest room now, having been delivered to Laura's house by Carolyn late the night before. According to Allan, she'd arrived without notice or animosity, then waited calmly while he'd loaded everything into his car. The kids had slept through the whole thing.

Laura tried to picture the scene—this silent, amicable transfer of Allan and his possessions from his girlfriend back to his wife—but couldn't. Allan had been the one who'd walked out. WASP sang froid or not, Carolyn should have been angry, or at least stung. But Allan insisted she was too sensible for all that emotion. She'd seen things weren't working, realized neither of them would change, and calmly decided to get on with her life.

It didn't add up, but Laura didn't pursue the subject. She didn't have the energy to dig for answers that Allan resisted giving. Or maybe, she thought as she walked him to the door, she was simply fed up with having to guess, interpret, and pull things out of him. With him gone, she'd been liberated from ninety percent of all that. It was the one area of her life that had gotten easier.

She got to work at nine the next morning, half an hour late. She'd run a few errands after dropping off the kids—stopped at the cleaner's, bought some groceries, and filled her tank with gas. Freddie seldom showed up before ten-thirty or eleven, so there'd been no need to rush.

A few of the agents had left items in her in basket to run in the agency's newsletter, but she couldn't start writing till more material came in. There was nothing else on her desk, so she edited her résumé, changing married to separated, dropping a pair of old jobs, and adding her current job with Freddie. Then she typed the new version on the computer and printed off some copies.

She pulled out the files on the Hollister insurance policies next, as a reminder to prod Freddie about filing the claims. A copy of Hollister's death certificate had arrived in Friday's mail, but Freddie hadn't given her any forms to type up. As she'd told Bonita, he could be slow about processing paperwork.

He hadn't been this time. In addition to the policies and supporting documents, each file contained photocopies of Hollister's death certificate and *Bee* obituary. A copy of a completed claim form, filled out by hand and dated with Saturday's date, was included in each file as well. Not only had Freddie taken care of this, he'd come in over the weekend to do it. He hadn't been this assiduous about filing a claim since Arthur Albright, Sr. had drowned, and he'd had to badger the company into paying despite the absence of a body.

She looked at the policies held by Maggie Hollister—a term policy for half a million dollars and a whole life policy for a million even. Hollister had added the extra five hundred grand two years before. She checked the paperwork for the policy held by Bonita, who was listed as Hollister's business partner on the relationship-to-insured line. The dates were the same.

It made a certain amount of sense. Freddie was a good salesman when he exerted himself to be, so he'd probably solicited one of these policies after the other had been requested, or even proposed both at the same time. As the insured, Hollister would have had to sign papers pertaining to each in Freddie's presence. He'd have had to submit to a brief medical exam, too—answer questions about his medical history and give a vial of blood. By processing the two policies at once, Freddie had saved both Hollister and himself some time and aggravation. She wondered about the sequence of events, though—what had prompted him to bestir himself to hustle the two sales in the first place.

Bored, she made a pot of coffee, then carried a cup into his office. A janitorial service emptied the trash every night and vacuumed and dusted once a week, but the place still looked messy. She straightened the desk and coffee table, throwing out old papers and magazines, then watered the plants and polished the furniture and glass.

She was putting away the cleaning supplies when Freddie strolled in. "Hey, the office looks real nice," he said, and sniffed appreciatively. "Smells like lemon. I always like that. Thanks a lot."

"You're welcome. So how was your weekend?"

"Great, just great. Did a little fishing on Sunday. Most relaxing sport in the world, Laura—cruising around on the ocean, fighting a huge fish and reeling 'im in. Smartest thing I ever did, buying poor Artie's boat."

He meant Albright's deep-sea fishing vessel, which he'd bought from Alice soon after her husband's death. "It sounds wonderful. I see you did some work, too."

He looked blank. "Work?"

"Filling out those claim forms on the judge. I pulled out the files to remind you to do it, then noticed you already had. It was nice of you to come in on a Saturday to take care of it. Bonita and Maggie will be very grateful."

"It was the least I could do," Freddie said gravely.

"For the judge, and for the devastated women he left behind. You see, Laura, that's what people don't understand about the insurance business. We protect them. Give 'em help at the hardest time in their lives. The commissions are nice, but it's the satisfaction that counts."

She nodded. "So how did you happen to think of it? Selling those two policies at the same time, I mean. Protecting both Bonita and Maggie."

"It's second nature after all my years in the business. Bonita phoned about some insurance, and I thought, Why not take better care of Maggie at the same time? The judge was a busy man. This way, we could do everything at once." He noticed the mailman strolling down the corridor, and waved.

Laura took the mail and returned to her desk. It was a day for relatives, something Freddie had in abundance. Most of them were customers who expected him to keep in touch, and he did.

She never opened their letters, they were personal, but she always saw them eventually when Freddie had her answer them. She knew all of his correspondents by now. The three he'd heard from today were regulars.

The first two lived in Ohio. His great aunt Edna Mae Phelps was the family historian, a wealthy spinster who'd bought millions' worth of insurance for her nieces and nephews. His uncle Tom Cassidy was a retired salesman who enjoyed spinning hunting and fishing yarns.

The third correspondent, his childhood friend and second cousin Marion Kirby, was an artist who lived in a commune in New Mexico. He'd started writing last fall, sending Freddie short, bizarre notes that sounded as if they'd been composed under the influence of mescaline. Laura always enjoyed them, even if she didn't have a clue as to what they meant.

This particular note was on a postcard, in plain and irresistible sight. She squinted at Marion's spidery script. "I am surrounded by cold," he'd written. "I am the essence of ice. The frigid deeps of the Pacific Ocean. The snowy peaks of the Mogollon Mountains. But soon the summer heat will come. Searching me out, searing me, destroying me and my art. Heat is death. Heat is resurrection. And yes! Death is resurrection. But what is resurrection without redemption? Beware, my friend. The great vacuum is closing in." The great vacuum—of space, presumably—was his favorite metaphor. It seemed to represent a vengeful God. "It will suck us all up. Whoosh! Into a dank cell in hell, forever."

Laura was shaking her head and laughing when Freddie walked out of his office. She held out the postcard. "It's from your nutty cousin Marion. I hope you don't mind, but I couldn't resist reading it. He still thinks the great vacuum is after him."

Freddie made a face. "I wouldn't mind writing to the guy if he'd only buy some insurance. Everyone else in the family does."

"So why *do* you?" Not that he literally did. He made a few suggestions, and then Laura composed chatty, innocuous responses designed to soothe Marion's paranoid fantasies.

"Suppose he goes off the deep end 'cause he doesn't hear from me?" Freddie demanded. "You think I want to be responsible for that?"

"I see your point." But she was surprised he cared, given the fact that he considered Marion a total fruitcake.

"Damn straight," he said. "So how about lunch today? I'll tell you what the Feds are up to."

She decided she could survive a one-hour meal, especially if it meant acquiring more information. After all, she'd only have to stall him for another couple of weeks.

They ate in a restaurant ten minutes away, a place where Freddie was well known and serviced to the hilt. He was at his funniest and most likable, believing, perhaps, that victory was close at hand. But as the meal progressed, and the waiter brought scotch after scotch, his gossip about the FBI and his stream of amusing stories gradually gave way to muddled meanderings and boozy non sequiturs.

She offered to drive back to the agency, and he agreed. For once, he seemed to realize he'd imbibed an amount that might have given pause even to Mike Clemente's friends in the liquor industry. Visibly woozy when they got back, he weaved into his office and collapsed onto the couch.

"Coffee," he groaned. "I need coffee."

"Coming right up," Laura said. The pot was on the bookcase behind her desk. If she took her time, he'd be asleep when she got back.

He wasn't, though. Not yet. Cupping the mug, he said in a slurred voice, "Y'know, you women don't understand us guys at all. Why we need a little nookie on the side. You think it's just the sex. But it's not." He sipped his coffee. "Don't get me wrong. I love Mary Beth. I'd never break up my family. But she spends all her time on the kids and her hospice, and a man needs someone to talk to. Someone who's interested in his problems. Someone who understands his work."

"Speaking of which," Laura said, "I should really get back to my desk." If Freddie was going into his windup, she didn't want to be at bat when the pitch arrived. There was a limit to how many she could foul off.

He didn't seem to notice she'd spoken. "The sex . . . I'm a great kisser, honey, but hell, once I send the ol' warrior into battle, why, he cocks and fires, just like that. *P'choo! P'choo! P'choo!* Never lasts more'n twenty seconds. Then he's out of ammo for hours."

Laura wondered why he was confiding all this. It didn't exactly leave a woman panting to invite the ol' warrior to storm her fort.

"So it's the relationship that counts," he went on. "The conversation. 'Cause Mary Beth . . . Don't get me wrong. She's a great little gal. Buy a little something for my girlfriend, always get one for ol' M.B. But she doesn't understand the pressure I'm under. Two houses, three cars, four kids, the boat, the trips to Europe, the clothes and jewelry . . ." He set down his mug and closed his eyes. "Always money. More money. Shit, she should've married a Rockefeller. The scams I have to run to keep her happy . . ."

Laura snapped to attention. "What scams, Freddie?"

"You know. Like with Jimmy." He yawned. "Bonita's policy. Our deal."

"What deal?"

But he didn't answer. He was fast asleep.

She tiptoed out of his office, quietly closing the door. He'd written the actual premium check, she remembered, supposedly in exchange for cash Bonita had given him, but maybe the money had only been Bonita's share. Maybe he'd contributed to the yearly cost of the policy too, in exchange for part of the payoff if the judge should die.

And taking it one step further . . . She sat down at her desk, lightheaded with excitement at the thought of where she was heading. Freddie wasn't the type to waste money on speculative ventures. He wouldn't have gambled on Hollister's death without good cause. He must have known the judge was in danger. Maybe he'd even arranged that danger.

She mulled it over. You needed guts to plug someone from a few yards away, or even to hire a hit man. Freddie was basically a wimp, the type who picked on the people beneath him and brownnosed the ones above.

Still, something was going on beyond a violent murder and a coincidental million-dollar insurance policy. Freddie hadn't been nearly as upset about Hollister's death as an intimate friend should have been. If he'd seen it coming, he hadn't agonized about it in advance. Why not?

Bonita might have the answer. Maybe it would even point her toward the murderer. She fished out Bonita's business card, then dialed her number. The phone was picked up on the third ring.

"Bonita Franks, *chanteuse et pianiste*," Bonita said brightly.

"It's Laura Miller, Bonita. I wanted to thank you again for Saturday night. Vicki and I had a wonderful time. It did me a world of good."

"I'm so glad," Bonita replied. "I hope you'll come again soon."

Laura assured her she would. "By the way, Freddie mailed in your claim on Saturday. I know you'd rather have the judge back than all the money in the world, but at least you should have your check soon."

"Oh, Laura!" Bonita said woefully. "You don't know how right you are! I'm going to make a big donation in Jimmy's memory, to that children's hospital he supported."

"That's lovely. He would have liked that." Laura paused. Now, she thought, give her a push. "I'm just glad I reminded Freddie to pay the premium. He almost forgot. Did he tell you that?"

"You're kidding!" Bonita sounded appalled.

"No. The late notice was sitting around the office and I happened to see it. I nagged him till he wrote out a check. Under the circumstances—I mean, given the agreement you two had about the policy—" Laura waited a beat. There was no objection from Bonita. "—you'd think he'd be more careful about paying the bill, but that's Freddie. He gets so wrapped up in family and charity things, he forgets he has a business to run."

"Well, I'm certainly glad you nagged him, not that you should have had to," Bonita said. "I gave him that bill in November. He was supposed to take care of it."

By collecting her share of the money, then writing out a check, or by paying the full amount? Laura considered Bonita's indignant response, then took her best shot. "To take care of the premium, you mean. To pay the three and a half grand every year. You think he'd remember an amount like that, wouldn't you! It's not exactly small."

"You certainly would! Really, I owe you another dinner for sitting on him. Probably a hundred dinners."

So he *had* paid the premium—the whole amount. It was only logical to assume he'd gotten something substantial in return.

"Of course you don't," Laura said. "It wasn't your fault, for heaven's sake. If anyone owes me a dinner, Freddie does." She sighed. "He's always going on about how broke he is, Bonita. With my divorce and all, it's a struggle to make ends meet, but he claims he can't afford to give me a raise because his wife spends money like water. Well, he can afford it now, can't he?"

"He should double your salary," Bonita said. "Really, what's another fifteen thousand or so when you've got five hundred? You tell him I said so, Laura. I mean it."

"I'll do that. Thanks." Jesus! Half a million bucks. What did she ask now? Bonita was no Einstein, but she was smart enough not to confess to murder.

But opportunism . . . That might be a different story.

"Still, it's just terrible about the judge," Laura continued. "I don't mean to be critical, but if you saw it coming . . . Couldn't you have warned him?"

"Oh, Laura, don't you think I tried?" Bonita cried. "He put himself in peril so often, sending all those horrible people to jail. I wanted him to resign. Really, I was always telling him to. But he wouldn't listen."

So she was sticking to her original story, that Hollister had been killed by a vengeful ex-con. "I see your point. Some people are reckless about their own safety, especially men. The judge was obviously one of them. If he wouldn't listen, what could you do?"

"Nothing, except love him while he was here."

"And protect yourself after he was gone?" Laura asked, goading Bonita a little.

"Yes." She paused. "So you knew the truth all along. Well, if your tone means you think I should have told him, maybe you're right, but I couldn't."

What truth? Told him what? "Actually, I did sort of think that," Laura said.

"But he would have had a fit!" Bonita wailed. "He was even angry about Maggie's second policy. Accused her of wanting him dead. But he didn't dare get on the wrong side of her and her fancy family, so he had to go along. But who was I?" Her voice quivered with apparent hurt. "Only his mistress. Only the girl who adored him. I couldn't bear the thought of fighting with him, so I made some arrangements behind his back, hoping against hope that nothing would come of them. I'm not going to apologize for that. I tried as hard as I could to save him."

Laura was astonished. Far from wanting to protect Bonita, as she'd claimed at the funeral, Hollister hadn't even known the policy existed. "I'm sorry," she said. "I was out of line." She took a quick breath. She wanted to be sure she had things straight. "Really, if telling the judge about the policy would have led to a terrible fight, you had to go behind his back." She waited a moment. No argument from Bonita. "I'm just glad

Freddie was in a position to help you. That you thought of going to him and making a fair arrangement." Again, there was no objection. "If you want the truth, I would have done the same thing in your position. It's hard being a woman in a man's world."

There were a couple of clicks on the line. "There's my call waiting," Bonita said, suddenly as perky as a cheerleader. "It's been lovely talking to you, Laura. Tell Freddie I'll send him his half of the money as soon as I get my check. And tell him I said to give you that raise."

"I will," Laura said, but Bonita had already rung off.

Laura hung up also, thinking about Friday's news report. Hollister must have angered the mob in some way—stonewalled or double-crossed them—and Bonita must have known it. You didn't take out a million in insurance on a healthy man who could have been expected to live for decades.

It was clear why she'd needed Freddie's help to slip the policy past the judge but not why she'd needed his money. Maybe her house payments and her weakness for antique jewelry had left her close to broke. Or maybe he'd insisted on a large cut of the proceeds rather than a smaller bribe up front, and her price had been his paying the yearly premiums.

In any event, they'd cut a deal, a deal that explained why Freddie had lied to Mike Clemente at the funeral. The more people who knew about Bonita's policy, the more likely it was that one of them would learn that he'd run a scam and owned fifty percent of it.

She frowned. If Freddie had told the FBI about that policy, as he'd claimed he had, she was the queen of Romania.

TEN

She tried to be logical instead of emotional. Looking at the situation objectively, what did she really have? Speculation. Theories. Drunken or orchestrated confessions without a shred of written proof. It was a little early to run triumphantly to the FBI.

In the meantime, real life hadn't stopped because she got off on playing detective. She had rental agents to call, letters to answer, and a newsletter to draft. Becoming a federal informant would have to wait its turn in line.

She got down to work. Freddie finally wobbled out of his office at ten of four. Seeing him put an unexpected lump in her throat. Even though he'd been drunk and half asleep, she suddenly realized, it was possible that he remembered what he'd admitted. Wimp or not, he was a crook. If he felt cornered, he might become dangerous.

He stopped by her desk. "You don't look too good," she said solicitously. "Don't you feel well?"

He winced. She knew that expression. He had a headache from hell.

"I'm a little tired," he replied. "I must be coming down with something. Some virus I picked up."

Only if a mammoth hangover was a communicable disease. "Why don't you go home, then? You can sign these tomorrow. I'll leave them on your desk."

"Yeah, thanks. You better cancel my appointments."

"Will do," she said, thinking he couldn't possibly remember their conversation. He was acting too normal. "Do you need anything else?"

"The newsletter . . . Write something nice about Jimmy. Tell everyone about my eulogy."

Laura nodded and jotted it down. She thought of Freddie behind the wheel of his Mercedes. If he cracked up the car and took anyone with him . . . "Listen, maybe you shouldn't drive. Do you want me to call Mary Beth to pick you up? Or get you a cab?"

He waved his hand. "No, no. I'll be fine."

"Well, be careful. Drive slowly. I hope you feel better."

He mumbled his thanks and walked off, slowly but in a reasonably straight line. Reassured, she went back to work.

She called Allan as soon as she got home, telling him she'd scheduled five appointments starting at seven-thirty. He showed up at seven and started rough-housing with the kids, which warmed her enough to offer him some leftover lasagna. He quickly accepted, saying he hadn't eaten since breakfast and was starved. It was a stupid macho affectation, she grumbled, this business of skipping meals, as if he were occupied with matters of such critical importance that he couldn't leave his desk even for five minutes to buy a snack. He smiled at her sniping, obviously interpreting it as wifely concern.

Vicki's daughter Karen arrived to babysit, and they left for their first appointment. To Laura's surprise, Allan asked what she'd done that day instead of droning about his work, then actually listened to her response, which was something innocuous about the letters she'd written to Freddie's relatives. He brought up Hollister's funeral next. He was trying to be less self-centered, she realized as she answered his questions. To draw her out.

Pleased by his newfound sensitivity, she told him about her interest in Hollister's murder, then described the sex toys in the N Street apartment and her run-ins with Mike Clemente and Joseph Cassani. She didn't mention her amateur detective work—unlike Vicki and her mother, Allan would probably have made light of it—but he didn't seem to notice the gaps in her story. He was too busy zeroing in on Mike Clemente, whom he knew from the Capital Athletic Club.

She didn't know whether to be amazed or amused. She hadn't even mentioned that Mike had asked her out, much less admitted she was attracted to him, but Allan was threatened by him. Allan, the man who six months before wouldn't have cared if she'd given herself to the entire string section of the Sacramento Symphony, both sexes and sexual persuasions, was actually jealous of another man.

She told him Clemente wasn't her type, then mentioned that she was looking for a new job, and why. He answered that it was about time, that she was much too bright and efficient to waste her talents on Freddie Phelps. They were walking through the final apartment by then. Laura suggested looking again on Tuesday— the places that weren't small or run-down were too expensive—but Allan said he was too busy. He signed a lease on the last apartment as of April first, which was on Wednesday, but he wouldn't be able to move in until he'd rented or bought furniture and had it delivered.

The apartment was in a nice neighborhood, a two-bedroom flat in a new garden-style complex. The high rent reflected that, but Allan said not to worry, that they could manage financially. He wasn't normally so casual about money, but she knew where he was coming from. He saw the apartment as temporary, a place where he could live comfortably till he moved back into the house.

They went out for coffee afterward, then drove home. There was a moment of awkward silence when he turned off the engine. Both of them simply sat there, neither talking nor moving. Then he opened his door, but she put her hand on his arm to stop him from getting out. If he came inside, he might expect to sleep with her—even feel obligated to. She didn't want to invite that.

"You don't have to walk me to the door," she said.

"Actually, I wanted to get my briefcase out of the trunk. I brought you a copy of my schedule—to set up an appointment for counseling."

"Oh," she said, feeling foolish.

"I've got to go back to the office." He smiled. "You'll probably accuse me of inflating my own importance, but there's some work there that has to be done by morning."

She smiled back. "And if it isn't? What will happen?"

"Civilization as we know it will collapse the world over. I was going to work at Phil's, but we always wind up talking baseball and drinking too much cheap wine."

They walked around to the back of the car. Allan got out his briefcase and handed her his schedule. Putting it in her purse, she said, "About Wednesday. I know you can't have the kids at Phil's overnight, and you probably won't be in your new place yet, so why don't you take them out to dinner and then spend some time with them at the house?"

He closed the trunk. "Okay. I'll come around six."

"I was just thinking . . . My mother still has her

extra furniture in storage. Maybe she'd let us—let you use it. It would save us some money. I'll ask her if you want."

"Thanks. Of course, given her low opinion of me, she'll probably call in the nearest orthodox rabbi after I return everything. To make it clean again, like pots that've been defiled by heathens."

Laura laughed. Allan's sense of humor had been one of the reasons she'd fallen in love with him. It still exerted a powerful pull. "No, she won't. She gave up keeping kosher when Dad died. She's a stalwart of our temple now, remember?"

"Ah, but the old ways always reassert themselves in matters of life, death, and villainous sons-in-law." He kissed her cheek. "I've gotta go. I'll spread the word that you're looking for a job. You can give me some résumés on Wednesday if you want."

Laura said she would do that and went inside. She hadn't expected those moments of emotional connection, of sharp enjoyment. She suddenly wished he'd stayed. But then she remembered the times tonight when he'd delivered his opinions like God handing down the Ten Commandments on Mount Sinai, and she was glad he hadn't.

It was almost ten by then. She'd missed the early news, so she clicked on the TV in her bedroom. She listened absently to several commercials as she changed for bed. Then a teaser came on that drew her attention to the screen: "Kings forward Royal Paine makes a statement about that payment to Judge James C. Hollister, and FBI chief Kevin McKennery responds to news leaks. We'll tell you what they had to say on the ten o'clock news, coming up next."

She sat down to watch. According to the station's story, two federal agents had questioned Paine early that morning about a sixty-thousand-dollar payment he'd made to Hollister. The FBI hadn't made the interview public; Paine had, apparently over the Bureau's stringent objections. Then, that afternoon, an FBI clerical employee had complained that she'd been dismissed unjustly from her job after her boyfriend, a TV reporter, had tricked her into revealing details of the Hollister investigation.

McKennery wasn't happy about all the publicity, that much was clear. The camera caught him walking briskly to his car after work, saying in a clipped voice that he had no comment beyond the statement he'd issued earlier. It had defended the FBI's personnel policies and confirmed what Paine's statement had already made plain: that the government had been investigating Hollister at the time of his death. It didn't take a genius to figure out that they must have subpoenaed his financial records, or that a sixty-thousand-dollar check must have been deposited into one of his accounts. Obviously they'd traced the money back to Paine.

Paine had made his statement at practice that day. He was afraid of another leak, he'd told reporters, and wanted to go on record with the details of the payment before anyone could accuse him of being tied to Hollister's alleged criminal activities. He and the judge had been friends, he'd explained, both alumni of Duke, both starters on the school's basketball team. Hollister had asked him for the money the previous November and he'd written out a check.

The judge had offered no explanation of why he'd needed the sixty grand other than to say it was personal, and Paine hadn't asked for one. Hollister, after all, had been a federal judge. He'd promised to repay the loan with interest in six months, and Paine had taken him at his word.

The matter had almost ended with Hollister's death, Paine insisted. He never would have caused the family distress by demanding repayment of a mysterious loan that he doubted they'd been aware of. But now that the FBI had gotten involved and dragged everything out in the open, there was no reason not to file a claim against the estate.

It was another matter entirely as to whether he'd be repaid. According to the station, rumors were floating around the capital that there wasn't much of an estate to sue. James C. Hollister, who'd made millions during his years as an attorney, had apparently died flat broke.

Freddie strode into the office the next morning looking downright overwrought. Laura was puzzled at first, then anxious. It was only nine-thirty. Did this departure from his normal routine mean that his memory had suddenly improved? Had he rushed in early to speak to her about what he'd said the day before?

Then he passed by her desk and closed himself into his office, and enlightenment dawned. Every few months he held an all-day sales meeting at a downtown hotel, gathering together the agents from his entire territory. They traded war stories, swapped business news, and shared sales techniques. But the absolute highlight, at least according to Freddie, was the inspirational speech he gave at lunch, exhorting everyone toward greater success. He wrote these talks himself, just as he'd written Hollister's eulogy, putting real effort into his public speaking because he loved the attention and admiration it brought him. The next sales meeting was tomorrow, on the first.

Laura felt a rush of relief. Freddie was wrapped up in his writing, that was all. With any luck, she'd barely see him for the next two days.

In a perfect world, she would have been employed

elsewhere by the time those two days were over, but none of the résumés she'd mailed on Monday resulted in an immediate interview. Vicki had taken some résumés, too, but if she'd handed any out, or if she or Allan had spoken with anyone, Laura didn't hear from them. She hadn't expected otherwise, not so soon, so she wasn't overly concerned. Two more weeks, she told herself. Then she would fly into a panic.

In the meantime, she finished the newsletter, wrote a reassuring letter to Marion Kirby, and handled as much of Freddie's work as she could. On the personal side, she asked around about a counselor, got glowing reports about someone named Tasha Horowitz from several coworkers, and made an appointment for Monday at four. She also heard from Dr. Saul Lefkowitz, who called her on Tuesday to ask her out to lunch the next day. They arranged to meet at the Firehouse at noon. It was a classy restaurant in Old Sacramento, the historical section of the city.

"It was a nightmare," she told Vicki Wednesday evening. They were sitting in Vicki's kitchen, having coffee and cake while Allan spent quality time with Seth and Sarah across the street. "Remember how my mother said he had a good head of hair for a man his age? He was wearing the silliest-looking toupee I've ever seen. Almost jet black, with bushy curls. I swear to God, Vick, you could have flown to Baghdad on that rug. And remember how she described him as 'not so tall'? He was five-foot-five, tops, and that was with lifts in his shoes. The man—"

"Lifts?" Vicki interrupted, laughing. "How do you know he was wearing lifts?"

"Because he took his shoes off during lunch. There was this unpleasant aroma, so I dropped my napkin and very nonchalantly looked under the table while I was picking it up. There were his feet in all their liberated glory, stinking up the place, and these shoes with three inches' worth of heels and platforms. You know what's really gross? When a guy's socks are too short, and you can see thin, hairy legs between the tops of his socks and the bottoms of his pants. He must have realized I'd noticed the smell. He didn't exactly apologize, but I got a detailed description of how sore his feet were. He has problems with his arches."

"Probably from all those years of standing and looking into people's mouths," Vicki said. "So other than the fact that he's short with a bad hairpiece, smelly feet, and thin, hairy legs, how was he?"

"Awful. The man is a health-food nut with a Napoleon complex. He ordered for me, Vicki, a salad when I wanted a club sandwich with extra bacon. He refused to let me have a glass of wine, and let me tell you, I needed one badly within thirty seconds. He even insisted on inspecting my teeth."

"Honestly, Laura—"

"It's true. We were in the parking lot, waiting to pay the attendant. He told me I should get a bonding job. He offered me a deal if I would get it from him."

Vicki looked more skeptical than ever. "He didn't. You're making that up."

"Okay," Laura admitted, "but only the part about the deal. It's true about the bonding job. He said it was a shame my teeth weren't whiter, because they were so straight." She grimaced. "Hell, they should be straight! Dad got a freebie from his pal the orthodontist, so I was always the last in line to see him. He was a busy man. It took him six years to do my teeth. I had braces in college. Do you know how embarrassing that was?"

"Mortifying, I'm sure," Vicki said, "but at least your teeth look nice now."

"I always thought so. I mean, I've never thought of them as yellow. Do you think they're yellow?"

"Absolutely not. You wouldn't want them any whiter than they are. It wouldn't look natural."

Laura took a bite of cake. "Maybe natural is out in L.A. Or maybe Dr. Lefkowitz doesn't have the taste to appreciate the concept. He had on a hideous tie, with dark, fuzzy squiggles on it."

"Maybe it was supposed to match his toupee," Vicki said. "Wasn't there anything good about him? Was he an interesting conversationalist or—"

"He talked about his kids. Nonstop."

"So he's proud of them. That's very nice."

Vicki was playing devil's advocate now. Laura could see the laughter in her eyes. "Not proud. Fed up. All he did was complain. They're lazy, freeloading bums. They'll never amount to anything and he'll be supporting them for the rest of his life."

"What could your mother have seen in him?"

"Other than the fact that he was ritually circumcised at eight days of age?" Laura thought for a moment. "Money, maybe. He had more gold around his neck than a drug dealer. I'll bet he keeps the old crowns he takes out of people's mouths and has them made into jewelry."

"I don't think the gold is pure enough. Did he pay for lunch, at least?"

"Yup, and left a big tip." Laura paused. "And made sure I noticed. 'The service was very good here,' he says. 'I'm going to leave a little something extra.' And then he peels a twenty from a money clip bloated with cash, even though he'd paid with a credit card, and tosses it on the table."

"So he's loaded." Vicki grinned at her. "When are you seeing him again?"

Laura burst out laughing. "Never, not even for a free bonding job. If Mom is so high on him, she can date him herself. Not that she is. She found me someone new the other night. He even seems relatively normal, which given Mom's history makes me worry that he'll go crazy someday and bludgeon his mother and sisters with an ax, and then all the neighbors will say, 'But he was such a quiet man. So polite and unassuming.' Arthur Albright Jr., of all people." Laura filled Vicki in, not only about Albright, but also about what she'd learned from Freddie and Bonita.

Vicki played her usual role, that of the unflappable listener and staunch supporter, right through to the end. Then she asked what Laura planned to do about the insurance policy.

Laura hesitated, then admitted she wasn't sure. "I've thought about it a lot. Maybe it's my duty to say something, but I'm afraid to. I mean, blow the whistle in this country and you lose your job and wind up an outcast. Nobody trusts you or wants to hire you. I can't afford that. I have the kids to think of. It would be one thing if I thought Freddie and Bonita were guilty of murder, but I don't."

"Just insurance fraud."

"Yes, but I have no proof. The papers are completely in order. I'd probably be sticking my neck out for nothing."

"If you went to the FBI, you mean."

"Yes. They'd probably write me off as a disgruntled former employee out to get my boss, but let's assume they believe me. I don't trust them, Vicki. I could ask them not to interview Freddie or Bonita, and they could even agree, but where else is a case going to come from? They'll do whatever they need to to further their investigation. So let's say they ask Freddie and Bonita about possible insurance fraud. Neither one is a candidate for Mensa, but they have brains enough to trace things back to me. Who else knew about the policy? Only some clerk in Ohio. So Bonita's in trouble now, and she's mad at me. Thanks, but no thanks. She has friends I'd rather not tangle with. Even an anonymous tip wouldn't work, because there's only one person it could come from. Me."

"Laura." Vicki hesitated. "I know how badly you've needed some adventure and escape in your life. And I understand what a kick you've gotten out of playing real-life Clue. It's fun. I enjoyed it too. But maybe it's time to let go. Before things get dangerous, I mean."

The same thought had occurred to Laura. The only problem was, something inside her kept pushing her to go on . . . hated the thought of giving the excitement up. She was either very gutsy, she told herself, or absolutely nuts.

"Maybe you're right," she said aloud.

ELEVEN

It was noon on Friday, and Freddie Phelps looked as if he were having a seizure. His face was flushed, his eyes were bulging, and one cheek was twitching convulsively. For once, though, liquor wasn't the cause of his symptoms. The FBI was.

Two agents had come by the agency this time, not just one, and they'd been clipped and intimidating when they'd asked Laura to buzz Freddie. They'd strode into his office the moment he'd opened his door, leaving him to close it and hurry after them, and stayed for nearly an hour. Every now and then, she'd caught a curt couple of words from one of the agents or a phrase full of forced affability from Freddie, but it hadn't been enough to tell her what was going on.

They were gone now, and he was leaning over her desk, glowering at her. "What in hell did you tell those guys?" he demanded. "When did you speak to them?"

Her heart started beating double-time, making her throat and chest feel tight. "Nothing. I didn't speak to anyone. Why? What did they ask?"

"Things that say you opened your mouth." He ges-

145

tured angrily toward his door. "I want to talk to you. Inside."

She followed him to the couch. They'd barely sat down before he started attacking her again. "The Feds knew about Bonita's policy. They knew—"

"Of course they did," Laura said quickly. "You told them."

He was apoplectic now. He hadn't, obviously, but he'd claimed otherwise after the funeral and now couldn't admit he'd lied. "Right. But that favor I did Bonita—getting Jimmy to sign it thinking it was for Maggie—they knew about that, too. I don't know how you found out about that, but—"

"You told me." She couldn't deny knowing what he'd done, not after what she'd said to Bonita. The two of them might compare notes eventually.

He straightened, looking confused. "I did?"

She took a deep breath. The very thing she'd worried about was happening, and she wasn't even the cause. She thought about all the hours she'd spent lately, holding imaginary conversations with everyone from the Feds to Joseph Cassani. They were about to come in handy.

"Don't you remember?" she asked. "It was about a month ago, just after Michelle walked out. You were upset about the way she'd left, without saying good-bye or thank you. You went to lunch with a friend to get her off your mind, and when you got back, you called me into your office. Just to talk, you know? Somehow Bonita's policy came up—I guess you were troubled about what you'd done and wanted my opinion—and you told me all about it. I said not to worry, that Jimmy had been unreasonable not to sign it and that you'd only been helping a friend. Bonita, I mean." She paused. "Is it coming back to you now?"

It couldn't, since the conversation had never taken

place. "Sort of," he said. "I was in bad shape back then. You know how it is. It must've slipped my mind."

In other words, when he got drunk and talked too freely, as he thought he had that day, he sometimes forgot the things he'd said. In view of Monday, Laura was relieved to hear it. "There's no proof you did anything unusual, right? So what's the problem? It's not against the law for a man's business partner to take out insurance on him."

"But they knew she was his mistress," Freddie said.

"So? A man can be in business with his mistress. She's an entertainer. Maybe he was bankrolling her career."

"Yeah. That's what I told them. But the premium payments—" He checked himself. "Somehow they got the idea I was paying the premiums in return for a share of the policy. I don't know. Maybe they saw that check I wrote. Remember? Back in January?"

"In return for Bonita's cash. Sure I do." But she couldn't go along with Freddie's lie. Once again, he and Bonita might talk at some point. "I have to level with you, though. You mentioned something about your arrangement with Bonita the day we talked, and I put two and two together. I figured it was none of my business, so I never brought it up. But I still say the Feds can't prove anything, not if you and Bonita deny it."

"Yeah, that's right."

"Still, if you're worried about it, I'll be glad to tell them you wrote the check in exchange for her cash."

"Maybe," he mumbled. "I'll think about it."

She was making progress. He'd gone from irate to confused to uncertain. "When you decide what you want, just let me know."

He nodded. "Yeah, right. The thing is, I thought they would question you, too. Then, when they didn't . . . " His expression hardened. "It looked suspicious, Laura.

Damn suspicious. Like they already knew what you'd say."

She didn't understand it any more than he did. "Maybe it's because I'm only a secretary. They figured I wouldn't know anything." That had certainly been Freddie's opinion up till now. "Believe me, Freddie, if I *were* their informant, I'd be the first one they'd talk to, to protect my identity."

"Yeah, maybe that's true. But if it wasn't you or me . . . " He frowned. "It must have been Bonita. She must have opened her mouth to the wrong person. Bragged to one of the government's snitches, maybe. There must be plenty of 'em hanging around the casinos."

"There are," Laura said. "I've read about that." The Feds developed paid informants whenever and wherever they could, and a gambling town like Tahoe would probably be a high-priority location.

Freddie leaned back on the couch and rubbed his eyes. "God, what a morning. I'm shot to hell and it's only noon. And just when I was relaxed from playing golf." He'd taken some of the out-of-town agents to his country club the day before. "I need a couple of scotches to fix me up, I can tell you that. Let's go out to eat."

She was about to plead cramps or a headache, then thought the better of it. She wanted him reassured, not suspicious. "Let me make a quick trip to the ladies' room first."

"Geez. Women! You broads *live* in the bathroom." He picked up a magazine. "Hurry it up. I want to get out of here."

"I won't be long." She walked briskly out of his office, thinking she wasn't out of hot water yet, not even if he'd bought her story. The Feds had probably questioned Bonita today, too. And if she were even half as furious as Freddie had just been . . .

The bathroom, mercifully, was unoccupied. Laura

locked the door and leaned against the wall. The situation would have been ironic if it weren't so dangerous. She hadn't said a word, but everyone would assume she had, including Bonita. A wave of nausea hit her. Suppose Bonita complained to Cassani?

She was grateful she'd kept her mouth shut. She was a good talker, but she couldn't have lied her way out of this one. She was scared now, and it would have shown. She had to stick to the truth as much as possible. Suggest plausible alternatives and hope one stuck. Call Bonita as soon as possible to find out if she'd been questioned by the FBI and suspected Laura was the informant. If so, she would have to convince Bonita that the blame lay elsewhere.

Calmer now, Laura returned to her desk and peeked around Freddie's door. He was thumbing through his magazine, looking irritated and impatient. She went inside, thinking the call would have to wait. He was in no mood for further delays.

They talked shop over lunch. Both of them were wound up so tightly that the conversation eventually dwindled to sporadic exchanges about the food. Freddie insisted on ordering her some wine "to relax her," but she barely touched it. He didn't seem to notice. He was too busy belting down scotch, quickly and without enjoyment, as if it were an anaesthesia.

She suddenly wished she could do the same. She could picture Cassani's thugs bursting in some night and doing excruciating, degrading things to her body, then killing her. The longer she sat there, the worse her anxiety got, till she couldn't stand it a moment longer. Getting to her feet, she mumbled something about her stomach acting up and hurried away.

There was a phone outside the ladies' room. It wasn't the most private place in the world, but that couldn't be helped. She called Bonita, putting the charge on her credit card.

Bonita answered with her usual chirpy greeting. "Bonita Franks, *chanteuse et pianiste*."

"It's Laura Miller. Has the FBI been by to talk to you, Bonita?"

"The FBI?" Bonita sounded tense now. "No. Why?"

"Because they questioned Freddie this morning. They know about your policy—about Freddie slipping it by the judge and about the deal the two of you made. Freddie denied everything, of course. The Feds don't have any proof. They can't, because the papers are completely in order. Still, you'd better expect them. I just want you to know—I didn't talk to them and I don't know who did. Is it possible *you* let something slip? To a friend who informed on you behind your back? That's what Freddie thinks."

"He's wrong," Bonita said flatly. "I didn't tell a soul. He has some nerve blaming me, what with the way he drinks himself into—" She cut herself off. "Oh, God! That talk we had on Monday. . . I'd better get off the line."

Laura didn't have to ask why. That possibility had occurred to her, too, but she'd quickly dismissed it. "It can't be a wiretap. If it were, they would have questioned me too, and they didn't. If you didn't let something slip, Freddie must have. He held a sales meeting on Wednesday and took some of the agents to his country club yesterday. He probably got tanked at both. He's been drinking even more than usual lately."

"Yes. You tell him for me—" Bonita gulped for air. "You tell him to watch himself. To keep his big, drunken mouth shut. Remind him I have friends."

She sounded angry and very scared, and that scared the hell out of Laura. Bonita might start brooding and begin doubting her version of events. She had to calm her down, convince her once and for all that they were on the same side.

"Okay, I will, but don't worry. No real harm has been done. The Feds know about your relationship with Jimmy, but you could have been his business partner, too, just the way the paperwork said. Deny everything but that, and you'll be fine. I'm sure they'll believe you. You're a good actress."

"I'm a lousy actress and both of us know it," Bonita snapped. "I'd be on Broadway otherwise." Without another word, she hung up the phone.

Laura replaced the handset and walked slowly into the ladies' room, shaking with reaction.

Her dessert had arrived by the time she returned to the table, a slice of cherry cheesecake she had no desire to eat. Freddie was toying with his chocolate mousse, stirring and sculpting it like a kid. He stopped and looked up. His eyes were glazed with alcohol. "Where the hell you been? You been gone forever."

"In the ladies' room."

"You broads camp in there for hours at a time," he grumbled. "What is it, some kinda second home?"

She'd been gone for fifteen minutes. "There was a line. I had to wait."

She'd have to tell him she'd talked to Bonita, of course, to cover her own behind. Everything she did got her in deeper and deeper. She no sooner stuck her finger into one leak in the dike than she created others to plug up.

"I called Bonita, too," she added. "I thought I should warn her about the FBI. They hadn't shown up yet, but she knows what to say when they do. Everything should be okay."

Freddie grunted. "Umm. I was going to tell you to do that. O' course, you're so damn efficient, who needs to tell you anything?"

He was upset, angry, and drunk—and taking it out on her. "Great minds think alike," she said with a smile.

"Yeah. Great minds. Jimmy had a great mind. Not great enough, though. Didn't have the brains to keep away from the lake. . . ." His voice trailed off.

The lake, as in Bonita? Laura wondered, but for once she didn't ask. The game had lost its zest. It was probably better not to know.

He took a long swallow of scotch, emptying a glass that had been three-fourths full. "He was a great guy once. A guy's guy. Hell of a lot of fun." He shook his head. "Him and his damned hunches. They ruined his life. Just ruined his life. Let that be a lesson to you, honey. Luck is a bitch, not a lady. A bitch just like you. You're good at teasing, but you don't put out."

He was spoiling for a fight, but she wasn't about to let an alcoholic lecher provoke her into a public scene. "Personally, I'd say luck is an illusion, not a bitch. I was at Tahoe last weekend. I lost a few hundred playing blackjack."

"Blackjack!" He was contemptuous. "That's a pussy game. You got balls, you play poker. Poker against the pros, for real money. Damn Jimmy, anyway. Didn't know when to quit. Should've stayed away." He threw some bills on the table and got up. "Let's get out of here."

He was drunker than she'd ever seen him, so drunk he could barely walk. He lurched forward and reeled precariously through the door, then grabbed her arm for support. He groped for his keys when they got to the car, rooting around in his pocket for several seconds before he found them. He protested when she took them away, fondling her hip and thigh as she unlocked his door, but then settled into the passenger seat without further complaint.

She figured he would pass out as soon as they started moving, but he was too agitated. "Damn Jimmy, anyway," he mumbled. "Shoulda stayed away. Minded his own business. Bleedin' me. Bleedin' Artie. And Paine . . . A loan, he says." He laughed, a short, harsh bark of a sound. "Wonder what Jimmy caught him snorting."

Laura glanced at him. His eyes were closed, his body limp with liquor and apparent exhaustion.

He shifted in his seat. "Bastard deserved it. Had it comin'. *Boom! Boom!* One less lawyer." He belched. "Owed me, dammit. Owed me every last buck."

She was so thrown that she almost went straight through a red light. Relieved she hadn't hit anyone, she slowed down and moved into the right-hand lane.

Freddie snorted loudly, and she realized he'd finally fallen asleep. All that talk about hunches ruining Jimmy's life . . . It was the lake, as in gambling, not as in Bonita. The lake, as in poker, evidently, though Hollister wouldn't have played in public. He'd had an image to uphold, that of the respected judge who opposed gambling vehemently. He must have stuck to high-stakes private sessions against the pros, the type where you could win or lose a fortune. Freddie had all but said so.

She frowned. What was it he'd mentioned in his eulogy? That Hollister had never ignored a hunch? After Saturday night, she knew how that felt. You went on and on, disregarding logic and common sense, sure your gut instincts were too strong to steer you wrong. With her, it had happened once. With Hollister, it must have been a regular occurrence.

He hadn't been a hypocrite, then, but an addict. On some level he must have known it and tried to cover it up, or maybe even to warn people against the compulsion that was destroying his life, but he hadn't been able to follow his own advice. He'd trusted his hunches again and again, losing until he'd run out of money.

Everything made sense now. *Bleeding me and Artie,* Freddie had said. Hollister must have hit the two men up for money to pay his gambling debts. The sixty grand from Paine had obviously gone for the same thing. But whether it had been borrowed or extorted . . .

Her thoughts returned to Freddie's eulogy. *Jimmy knew everything that was happening in this town. He noticed things everyone else missed. Remembered things everyone else forgot.*

A man like that could do a great deal of damage to friends who were less than honest, especially if he was a judge and had the ear of government prosecutors. Maybe Hollister had been blackmailing those three men and others—the couple on that tape Bonita had wanted, for example. Hollister's tape, perhaps, hidden in plain sight in Tomlinson's apartment rather than kept in Jimmy's home or chambers. He wouldn't have had to threaten to make it public, just to play it for the lovers' spouses, who might recognize the voices where others couldn't.

As for his alleged ties to organized crime, he might have borrowed money from loan sharks and paid them back with favors, or owed the mob the money in the first place because they'd controlled the poker games he'd played in. Had he reached bottom, finally, and threatened to confess to the authorities if Cassani and company didn't back off? Had he tried blackmail once too often in an effort to pay his debts? Either way, he must have made some dangerous enemies—and at least one deadly one.

She pulled into the agency's parking lot and drove around to the back. Nobody she'd called about the tape had had the expertise to amplify it, so she'd stashed it in her safety deposit box temporarily. She didn't know what to do with it now. Throw it out, maybe. Keeping it might be dangerous. Or mail it to the FBI as a possible clue, except that they didn't need it, at least not enough for her to risk her neck on an anonymous tip that Bonita and her friends might trace straight back to her. The Feds had another informant. They probably knew more than she did by now.

Freddie groaned like a sick seal as she parked the car. He jerked open his door as Laura turned off the engine, then put his head outside and retched repeatedly. She knew that dry, hacking sound. She had two children.

Nothing came out of him but moans. "My stomach," he gasped. "Go buy me something. Some Alka-Seltzer. Oh, Jesus." He retched again.

Without a word, she started the car and began to back out. Once she would have sympathized, or pretended to, but not any more.

"Stop, dammit, the motion . . . " Not just sick, Laura thought as she braked, but trapped and snarling. "Let me out, you stupid cunt." He tumbled out of the car and stumbled to the door, presumably heading for the bathroom.

The office was miles from a supermarket or drugstore, but she wasn't about to rush. So she was a stupid cunt, was she? Someone to paw and proposition? Someone to patronize when he felt inferior and abuse because she wouldn't put out? She hoped he puked his guts out.

She was stunned by the intensity of her anger. It wasn't only what he'd said, but how he'd said it—the malicious contempt in his voice, the lack of any provocation other than her failure to sleep with him. And it was when he'd said it—after she'd spent hours trying to keep a suddenly perilous world from crashing down on top of her. The danger had probably passed, but her body was still primed to fight.

She started thinking about revenge—how sweet it would be, how satisfying. Given enough time and patience, she could probably even get it.

Freddie had spoken of scams on Monday. They

must have involved insurance payoffs, big ones from which he'd taken a healthy cut. She could search his inactive files to see who had died within a few years of buying a large policy. She could look for more cases like Bonita's, two or more policies issued on the same person on the same date, but with different beneficiaries. She could check, in short, for convenient coincidences.

It would have to be late at night, though, when the office was deserted. She'd need keys to the building for that, and she didn't have them. She looked at the ignition. Not yet, she thought. Not yet.

TWELVE

Freddie was snoring so loudly when she got back that she heard him from out in the hall, through his closed door. A secretary passed by, stopped to listen, and laughed. Freddie had spent twenty minutes losing his lunch in the men's room, she told Laura. The place had smelled like a frat house after a beer bust when he'd finally staggered out.

That had been almost an hour ago. Laura walked into his office, locking the door behind her. He was sprawled on the couch, his jacket off and his tie unknotted. She set the Alka-Seltzer on his coffee table, then crossed to his desk. He kept a petty-cash box in the bottom right drawer, using the money to repay her when she got him fast food and do-it-yourself knickknacks or bought cards and gifts for his family and friends. He took his time about reimbursing her, though, always managing to be "right in the middle of something" till she'd asked repeatedly. This time, she wasn't going to wait.

As usual, the drawer was locked. He'd once muttered something about keeping important papers inside, but all she'd noticed besides the cash box were some cardboard boxes of the type office supplies came in.

She took out the copy she'd made of his desk key to check how well it worked. It slid in easily and turned without a problem. She only hoped the key to the outside alarm box worked equally well, because Violet Snipson, the bookkeeper, was always grumbling that the least extra jiggle could trip the thing accidentally.

Laura paid herself for the Alka-Seltzer and slipped the receipt into the stack of sales slips on top of the cash. At the end of each quarter, Violet counted the money, totaled the receipts and reconciled the two. Now that Laura thought about it, Freddie probably charged all these expenses to the agency—listed Burger King as a business meal, a putter as customer service and drill bits as office supplies.

She stood up. He was moaning and grinding his teeth now, perspiring heavily. If the past was any guide, he'd be out for hours. She glanced inside the drawer, then shrugged. Why not? It would be interesting to see what he defined as important.

She knelt down again. The drawer held three boxes in all, stacked in a pile. She removed the first, which exuded a light, floral scent. It contained letters from Michelle, handwritten on expensive ivory stationery.

They hadn't been mailed; the envelopes were blank except for M.B. in the upper left-hand corner and the pet name Babycakes in the center. She rolled her eyes. Babycakes. It was more than the human brain could assimilate.

She closed the box and set it on the floor. The box below, a larger one, contained letters as well. She checked the handwriting and signatures, finding five more mistresses dating back thirteen years. Dear Freddie-pie. Papa Bear. Freddsie-love. Tiger Thighs. Ramjet. The warrior hadn't always been old and hasty to fire, it seemed.

She opened the third and final box, expecting to see

letters from even earlier mistresses inside. Instead, she found a gun nestled in tissue paper. Even more startling, she'd seen the gun before, or one very much like it. It was a small silver Lady Smith like the one in Tomlinson's apartment.

There was a tiny card in the box of the type one enclosed in a baby gift. "Freddie-pie," it read. "I'll treasure the lovely jewelry and miss you dearly, but I don't dare keep this. I'd be tempted to use it on myself. Maybe M.B. wants it. Love, Andi."

Andi was Andrea Furillo, Freddie's previous secretary and mistress. She'd developed breast cancer and moved to Boston to live with her parents, dying eight months later. As for M.B., it wasn't Michelle. She hadn't come on the scene until after Andrea had left.

Laura closed the box and put it back. M.B. was probably Mary Beth, Freddie's wife. Maybe he gave this sort of gun to all his women, for their own protection. One of them might have left hers in Tomlinson's apartment. Or maybe this model of gun was especially popular, and the two she'd happened to see were unconnected.

She was about to return the other two boxes to the drawer when Freddie snorted violently and called her name. She froze. He couldn't see her as long as he was prone on the couch—the desk, several chairs, and the coffee table were in the way. But if he sat up . . .

The couch springs creaked as he shifted positions. He called her again, more insistently this time. She waited, not moving, scarcely breathing, hoping he was mumbling in his sleep. Several more seconds went by. Finally, he began snoring heavily again.

She peeked around the edge of the desk. He was on his side, facing the back of the couch, motionless except for his breathing. Shaking a little, she arranged the boxes the way she'd found them and closed and locked the drawer.

The idea of sneaking in here late at night and searching through his files suddenly seemed totally screwy. It was one thing to ask a few questions, but to collect keys, tapes, and phone numbers, to shoot up excitement the way a junkie shoots dope was crazy. Reckless and irresponsible. It had to stop before her kids wound up visiting her in a hospital, jail, or cemetery.

But, God help her, it had been one hell of a trip at times, and even now a part of her was sorry to give it up. She'd never felt more alive than when danger threatened and fear raced through her blood, making every thought and action seem like a matter of life and death. Maybe if she hadn't had a family . . . She shook her head. The fact was, she did.

She tiptoed to the coffee table. Freddie was out cold again. She set his keys next to the Alka-Seltzer and returned to her desk. Two messages were tucked under her phone, one from Vicki and one from someone named Rita.

She typed letters till she'd settled down, then called both women back. Rita was the personnel director of a high-tech company in Rocklin, a northern suburb. She'd gotten Laura's résumé on Wednesday and wanted her to come for an interview as soon as possible. Vicki had two more possibilities, a medical group in the suburb of Carmichael that needed a new office manager, and Senator Ken Carlsen, who was looking for a secretary to replace a staffer who'd left his capitol office to take a full-time job with his campaign.

Laura scheduled all three interviews for Monday. She'd never called in sick when she wasn't, but there was a first time for everything.

Tasha Horowitz was fortyish and a little frumpy, an earth-mother type who put Laura at ease from the moment they first met. Allan hadn't arrived by five past four, when their appointment was supposed to begin, or even by four-fifteen, so she went into Tasha's office and asked to begin without him. The room contained a couch and several armchairs for clients, and in the opposite corner, a chair for Tasha.

Laura sat down on the couch and gave Tasha some background, explaining that she'd insisted on counseling because she was afraid Allan wouldn't, or couldn't, change, and was thus ambivalent about a reconciliation. It was four-forty by then and he still hadn't arrived, but she was more annoyed than angry. Tasha needed this information, and it felt good to talk. Besides, she'd had too good a day to let anything ruin it.

She kept going, explaining about her decision to leave Freddie, mentioning that she'd had promising interviews at firms in Rocklin and Carmichael. Carlsen's chief of staff had been interested in her too, scheduling her to see the senator himself at five-thirty the next afternoon.

Allan finally showed up at ten of five, when the session was all but over. He was sorry, he said, but he'd gotten tied up at work. "It was an emergency, a planning meeting for a possible teachers' strike," he explained. "I couldn't get away."

"So the meeting was more important than our future," Laura said.

He frowned. "Look, Laurie, the superintendent called a meeting. What was I supposed to do? It's my job."

"Tell him you couldn't come?" she suggested.

"He needed me there."

"Why? You're a labor negotiator. When did you become responsible for what happens inside the schools if the teachers walk out?"

"Okay. I'm not. I wanted to be there, that's all. I thought it was important."

"Then why didn't you ask him to reschedule it for some other time?"

"He's very busy. If he decides three o'clock on Monday is convenient for him, I'm not going to argue."

Her annoyance flared out of control. "Then at least you could have called. Told us you couldn't come."

"I kept thinking the meeting would end. That I'd get here in time for most of our session."

"And by four-twenty or four-thirty it didn't occur to you that you wouldn't?" she asked in disbelief.

"I didn't want to leave, to miss anything important."

That was when she lost it. "It would have taken you less than a minute to make a call, but fine. You didn't want to leave, even though both of us know that people say the same things over and over in these stupid meetings. If—"

"How the hell would you know what people say?"

"I mean, if it was more important to you to hear every word about a subject that didn't even directly concern you, even though it had been said five times before, than to show me some consideration—"

"So I was thoughtless. Selfish. I screwed up." He turned away from her. "Hell, what else is new."

Tasha had simply listened till then, her face showing no trace of what she thought, but now she said to Allan, "If you have some time, we can continue the session past five. I had a cancellation. I'm free till six."

"I can't. I'm meeting someone for dinner at—" He stopped and looked at Laura. She glared back. "Okay. I guess I have a few minutes."

"How many minutes?" she asked curtly.

"Ten or fif—" He stopped again and sighed. "Half an hour. I can be a little late."

"Fine." She reached for the phone on the end table. "I'll call Mrs. Fujimoto and let her know."

Allan took off his jacket and sat down, settling into a chair diagonally across from the couch. "So why are you here?" Tasha asked him once Laura had hung up.

"What do you hope to accomplish?"

"You want the truth?" He was pugnacious, antagonistic. "I'm here because Laura insisted. Personally, I think it's a waste of my time. I don't see why I need a stranger in the room just to talk to my own wife."

"Maybe you don't. Each case is different." Tasha paused. "Laura told me about Carolyn—that you'd planned to marry her. She says you've changed your mind. That you want to withdraw the divorce action before it becomes final and come home. Why?"

"Because it's stupid to let a meaningless affair break up a twelve-year marriage. I went crazy for a while. Made a bad mistake. I know it was hard on Laura, but it's over now, and I still love her." Actually, he looked as if he wanted to slap her.

"You say the affair was meaningless, but for a long time, you saw it as the most important thing in your life," Tasha pointed out. "Tell me about Carolyn. What was she like? What did you see in her?"

Allan was reluctant to talk, almost uncommunicative at first, but Tasha gradually loosened him up, so completely that Laura began to think he'd never shut up. It had been painful enough to hear about Carolyn's virtues in July and August; she didn't enjoy listening to them again, especially when Tasha seemed so understanding. Allan came to life when he described Carolyn—how sensual and exciting she'd been, how creative and intelligent.

Still, Laura kept her mouth shut. It was Allan's turn to talk, no matter how much she disliked what he was saying. And then he must have realized how he sounded, because he began listing Carolyn's faults. It was the same story he'd given Laura ten days before.

Tasha neither questioned his intentions nor took his version of what had happened as gospel. Surely Carolyn must have had some complaints, too, she said, other than the fact that he spent too much time with his kids and wasn't spontaneous enough. What were they?

Laura began to wonder why her counselor was going on and on about Allan and Carolyn when they'd come here to discuss Allan and her. And then he answered, muttering that they'd fought over money, and she realized that Tasha had caught something she'd missed. Tasha kept probing, and the picture became clearer. Carolyn had gotten tired of giving what she considered a financial free ride—all the expenses on the house plus more than half of everything else—to a man who ignored her in favor of his work, his kids, and even his ex-wife. Allan hadn't just left. Carolyn had stood there pushing.

Laura couldn't contain herself. "So she threw you out. That's why you showed up at the house last Friday night."

He did what he usually did when he felt cornered. He attacked. "No. We realized we were wrong for each other. We decided to split up. How many times do I have to repeat that?"

"But if she hadn't told you to leave that night—"

"I still would have walked out. I was there. I should know."

Laura ignored that. "And that's why she was so calm when she brought your stuff over on Saturday. Because she made the actual decision. Not you."

"No, Laurie." His jaw was so clenched it looked as if rigor mortis had set in. "She was calm because the decision was mutual. If you would listen to me for once, you might understand that."

The finances of the situation suddenly struck her. "If Carolyn was paying most of the bills, where did all your money go? You've been generous, but not that generous."

He stood up. "I don't see any point in continuing if you're going to jump all over me whenever I say something you don't like."

"I didn't, and you haven't answered my question. Where did all the money go?"

He avoided her eyes. "I was saving for a car. I got a CD player. A few suits. I don't know. It just went. Does it matter? Anyway, I took the savings and—"

"Of course it matters. I've been watching every dollar while you were buying suits and stereo equipment."

"You think I don't feel guilty as hell about that? I was trying to tell you. About a month ago, I took the car money and set up college funds for the kids. The important thing is, Carolyn and I are finished. It's over. Now can we put it behind us and get on with our lives?"

"No," Laura said. "Nothing's been resolved. I'm glad about the college funds, but don't you see? You never even thought to consult me. You don't take me into account. You're the same as you always were."

He grabbed his jacket and pulled it on. "The hell I am! I've been a terrific father—"

"But will it last? You dumped the kids on Mom and Becky last Sunday—"

"Because I had to work. Once the teachers have a new contract—"

"You'll find another emergency to throw yourself into. You always do, fifty-two weeks a year."

He started out of the room. "This is hopeless. You won't listen. Nothing I could do would satisfy you."

"At least I was here on time," Laura said coldly. "I cared enough to make it my first priority, even though it meant I had to cut a job interview short. Talk about being a sucker! I turned down two dates to try to patch things up with you."

"*Mazel tov,*" he grumbled. "Some of us are just natural martyrs."

Tasha got up and walked over to him. "Reconciling is much harder for Laura than it is for you, Allan. She needs you to be open and honest. She needs to come first in your life. Once love and trust are lost, it takes a lot of time and effort to rebuild them. Maybe you should think about that a bit."

"Sure," he muttered. "I'll do that."

Tasha turned to Laura. "And Laura, I know you've been hurt, and that you're angry and afraid, but it won't help to ascribe the worst possible motives to everything Allan does. Try to give him the benefit of the doubt, all right?"

"Yes," she mumbled. "All right."

"Next week at four, then?"

"I'll have to check my schedule," Allan said. "I'm pretty booked up."

Laura hoped his schedule wouldn't be as meaningless in the future as it had been today. "I'll call you, Tasha," she said.

Seth and Sarah understood Laura had been hurt and sympathized to a touching extent, but they still wanted Allan home. It was obvious to her that their expectations had been raised when he'd left Carolyn's, and that they assumed he would leave his new apartment soon and move back into the house. If he didn't, they would know she'd refused to let him and start thinking of her as the bad guy.

She couldn't have stood that. She'd tried to say and do the right things, never attacking him or putting the kids in the middle, but the truth was, she wanted them on her side. Still, she'd planned to wait till a decision had been made before she mentioned going through counseling.

Then, in the car on the way home from Mrs. Fujimoto's, Seth asked why she'd been so late, and she had to come up with an answer. She hesitated, then decided to level with him. It wasn't to her credit, but she needed the kids to know that she was trying as hard as she could.

"Dad wants to come home," she said. "To try living with us again. I didn't think it would work—that I'd be happy. I've changed in the past few years and I need him to change, too. To communicate better. To do more around the house and spend more time with us. He thinks he will, but I'm not so sure. Anyway, we went to a counselor today. I was very impressed with her. Her name is Tasha Horowitz."

Seth looked at his sister. He was a great one for explaining things to her. "Like the guy on 'Growing Pains,' Sarah. They talk to you about your problems and help you solve them. Married people go, too. Even whole families."

Sarah nodded. "I know. Amy goes with her parents sometimes. She hates it. They scream too much."

"Well, we didn't scream." Not too much, anyway. "We just talked."

Seth looked dubious. "No, Mom?"

"Maybe a little," Laura admitted. "Look, I'd like to tell you it went great, but it didn't. Dad was almost an hour late—"

"He got tied up at work." Seth spoke with the knowing cynicism of someone twice his age.

"Yes. So I got angry, and then he got angry. Tasha gave us some extra time, which is why I was late, but it wasn't the best start." She pulled the car into the garage. "How about some tacos for dinner?"

"Sure, Mom," Seth said. "We'll help you make them."

Laura smiled gratefully at him, aware that he'd dropped the subject and offered to help because he knew she was upset. She hoped that would be the end of it, but Sarah trailed her over to the cupboard just one step behind Sam, who was nagging to be fed. "If Daddy's moving back home, why does he need his own apartment?" she asked. Allan had picked up the kids from Sunday school the day before, taken them to lunch, and showed them his new place.

"'Cause maybe he's not," Seth said. "Mom won't let him unless he cleans up his act. Weren't you listening?"

Sarah's eyes filled with tears. Feeling tense, guilty, and very tired, Laura bent down to comfort her. For perhaps the twentieth time, she gave her the even-though-we've-separated-it's-not-your-fault-and-we-both-love-you speech.

Sarah nodded as if she understood, but according to all the best books, her feelings would be quite different. Trying to reassure her, Laura promised that she and Allan would try as hard as they could to work things out. At times like this, she felt like a monster for even considering her own happiness. Mothers, after all, were by definition self-sacrificing. Hadn't Dottie told her that more times than she could count?

She turned on Sarah's favorite TV show and asked her to grate some cheese, hoping the job would distract her into a happier mood. Sarah worked slowly and solemnly, but whether she was upset or simply concentrating, Laura couldn't tell. As for Seth, he'd opened the ground meat and was feeding morsels to Sam. Laura snatched away the package and told him to fix the lettuce.

"But the hamburger would make him happy," Sarah piped up, finally smiling a little. "Tina says so. He told her." Tina spoke feline and every other language Sarah could think of.

"Would it make *you* happy?" Laura asked. "Happy enough to give me a big hug and an even bigger smile?"

Sarah nodded, smiled, and gave Laura her hug. Sam got his ground round. And Seth, his eye forever on the main chance, sensed Laura was in a soft mood and talked her into going to Vic's for sundaes after dinner.

She read to them when they got back, a few chapters from *Charlotte's Web,* and then put them to bed. Despite the bad beginning, the evening was a good one, the kind that made her want to hug the children close and never let them go. The kind that made her wish there were a husband and father to share it with—and a friend and lover to talk to and snuggle with after the kids were in bed. The marriage she imagined had never existed, not even before Carolyn, but she yearned for it badly enough that the anger she'd felt at Tasha's started to seep away.

She'd just begun to unwind when her mother called, asking why she'd declined Art Albright's invitation to go out Saturday night. It cut no ice with Dottie that Laura had turned down Mike Clemente, as well. Dottie and Alice had gotten downright chummy during the past week, Alice was miffed that Laura had refused her son, and Dottie was upset that Alice was unhappy. Laura promised to reconsider. Anything to keep the peace.

She hung up, stared at the phone for a minute, and then called Allan. She didn't want to discuss anything momentous, just put things on a civil footing by asking about his schedule and finding out what time he planned to pick up the kids Wednesday evening. He answered with a harried hello, but that was nothing unusual. Allan considered himself the center of the known universe, involved, like the Hebraic God, in everything that went on. Even a minor crisis in some elementary school made him harried.

"It's Laura," she said. "I just wanted you to know . . . I'm sorry things went so badly this afternoon. I hope we'll do better next time."

"Yeah, me too. Uh, listen, Laura, I'm in the middle of something right now. Can I call you back?"

"Sure. Not after eleven, though. I—"

"I meant tomorrow. Tomorrow night. Okay?"

He wasn't only harried, she realized, but nervous. "Okay. It wasn't anything important. I just wanted to check on your schedule—"

"Right, right. I'll have that for you tomorrow night."

She heard a voice in the background—a feminine voice—but it was too muffled to make anything out. Something inside her snapped, filling her with a gut-wrenching anxiety. It was a feeling she'd experienced far too many times in the past.

"You've got company?" she asked in a thin voice.

"Just a neighbor. She came over to introduce herself." He laughed, but the sound was forced. "Don't worry, Laurie. She's your mother's age. I'll talk to you tomorrow, okay?"

"Yes. Sure." She hung up without saying good-bye.

Within seconds, she was making another call, to Vicki this time. Karen answered the phone. If Vicki had been home, Laura might have been able to control the driving compulsion she felt to see for herself, to know for sure, but Vicki was out at a meeting. Hating what she'd been reduced to but unable to stop herself, she asked Karen to come over for twenty or thirty minutes while she ran an errand.

Five minutes later she was in her car, driving to Allan's apartment. Carolyn's dark blue Mercedes was parked outside, not far from Allan's Toyota. Laura wanted to smash their windows, to write angry obscenities on their windshields with lipstick. Back in August, when Allan had bounced between her and Carolyn like a Ping-Pong ball and she'd seen his car in the neighborhood around Carolyn's house, she'd never done either. Instead, she'd driven back home to ache and tremble in private. The explosions had always come later, and they'd always been verbal.

This time, she took a pen and notepad out of her purse. "4/6," she wrote. "9:45 P.M. You sounded so upset that I came over to see if you wanted to talk. I never imagined the goyish goddess had beaten me to it. Was she your dinner date, too? L."

She unlocked the Toyota and left the note on the dashboard. Then, angry with Allan, herself, and the whole damn world, she drove home.

THIRTEEN

Her phone rang at seven-thirty the next morning while she was in the bathroom gulping down aspirins. Her head was throbbing like something out of a Roger Corman horror film and her corneas felt like they'd been scoured with crushed glass. There was no limit, it seemed, to the things that could keep her awake nights. Even the knowledge that she had the brains of a sprinkler head would do it.

She returned to her bedroom and picked up the phone. As she'd expected, it was Allan.

"I read your note," he said. "Maybe I should have been straighter with you, but I didn't want to upset you. Until last night, I hadn't seen or spoken with Carolyn since the night she brought my things over. I swear, Laurie, dinner yesterday was business—a meeting with someone from the state department of education. Carolyn showed up at my door with no warning at all, ten minutes before you called. I didn't know what to do."

Laura sat down on the bed. "Told her to leave?" she asked caustically.

"She was too upset. All hyped up. She's still my friend. I couldn't just—"

172

"Your friend! So that's what one calls a tramp who's given him his walking papers."

"Dammit, if you're going to be sarcastic—"

"Don't curse at me, Allan." Her voice was cold and hard, like Dottie's when she was angry and offended. Laura didn't know whether to be gratified by the effect or worried she was turning into her mother.

"All right. I'm sorry." He sighed heavily. "Try to understand. She was moving in fast forward, like she was on speed or coke. She went on and on, jumping from subject to subject. The teachers' strike, Hollister's death, her father's health . . . Drew's been having chest pains. They ran some tests last Tuesday. He wound up having an angioplasty. Carolyn's been in Palm Springs all week. They're very close. Maybe all the worrying sent her over the edge."

Laura couldn't imagine why Allan thought she'd be interested in Drew Seeley's medical problems unless it was because *he* so obviously was. "No wonder you haven't seen her. She wasn't even in town. But the moment she got back, you were right in there consoling her, weren't you? And you say nothing happened!"

"Nothing physical. I listened to her. Talked to her. That's all." He paused. "I didn't even know she'd been gone till she mentioned it, but frankly, I don't understand your problem with my seeing her. It's pretty sexist to assume a man and woman can't be platonic friends."

"It's pretty naive to assume that a man who's been thrown out of the house by his girlfriend and wouldn't have left otherwise won't want to go to bed with her again if he gets the chance," Laura retorted.

There was dead silence on the other end. She could tell herself from now till next New Year's that she didn't care what Allan felt or did, but her gut twisted a little at the obvious implication. His split from Carolyn hadn't been mutual at all. "So you didn't want to leave. You did want to sleep with her last night. You don't deny any of that."

"No," he mumbled, "but the night I left . . . We weren't getting along. Neither of us was going to change, and I could see it as well as she could. So to that extent, it really was mutual." He cleared his throat. "And, uh, last night . . . She offered, but I said no. I think I deserve some credit for that. Some credit for making up my mind and sticking to it."

Maybe back in July or August, Laura thought. Not now. "So you still want Carolyn, but you've decided to make the supreme sacrifice and stay faithful to me."

"You know something, Laura? I can't win with you. You say you want me to be honest, but when I am, you *still* beat up on me. The point is, I told her to leave last night. I wanted you more."

"Me and the house and the kids," Laura corrected. "Your old, comfortable life back, but with Carolyn as your good buddy, since you can't have her as your mistress and can't bear to give her up. That's what you really want."

"Look, if the idea of my seeing her bothers you so much, I won't have anything more to do with her. And if you're saying you're part of a package, what's so wrong with that? So is Carolyn and everyone else in the world. I don't make decisions in a vacuum any more than you do, and if I want the Laura package more than the Carolyn package— Uh, wait a moment, Laura." Some people had come into his office. She could hear talking in the background. "I've got to go now, honey. Ned Brown's on the other line. He wants to set up another meeting. I'll see you tomorrow night. I'll pick up the kids around seven."

Laura said good-bye and hung up. The Carolyn package and the Laura package! God! It was analytical enough to make her heave, and this from the man who'd gone on about his emotions for years now, babbling about true love and *carpe diem* like an adolescent who'd just discovered Life.

She trudged to the shower. The hell of it was, a part of her said to listen. A part of her said it made sense. A part of her said to accept a deal that could have been a whole lot worse and get on with raising her children. What did it really matter? What she wanted was a fairy tale, as far beyond her reach as Kevin Costner in a peek-aboo jumpsuit. Even the best counselor in the world couldn't change that. Nothing could.

She began to cry. Thirty-four years old, and she was ready to give up. To surrender and settle. To stop asking for happiness from life, and content herself with merely giving it. How had things gone so wrong? She leaned against the slick tile wall and let the hot water beat soothingly against her shoulders and back. God, she was tired.

She dressed for work and got the kids off to school, but when it came to actually going to the office, her willpower ran out. She returned to the house, and, for the second day in a row, called in sick. Then she changed into sweats, took the phone off the hook, and went back to bed.

When she woke a few hours later, she was only somber and listless, not wallowing in self-pity. The truth was, Allan brought out the worst in her. Tasha had been right on Monday. When she saw him, listened to him, all the old hurts and resentments kicked in. The things that had merely annoyed her before he'd left—his obsession with his work, his inflated self-importance, his assumption that he was smarter, wiser, and more savvy than she was—drove her crazy now. So she swung before she listened, and that was pointless and unfair, or at least self-defeating. If she couldn't love him anymore, if she wanted something he could never be, she should have the guts to get out.

She shook her head in self-disgust. Maybe Allan had been right on Monday, too. Maybe she hadn't gotten out because she preferred to be a martyr, to act the role of the perfect wife and mother while she gloried in the depths of her own suffering. St. Laura the Self-righteous.

She sighed and rubbed her eyes. *If* this, *maybe* that . . . Where were the goddamn certainties in this world? And how could you rip your children's lives apart when you weren't sure of anything?

Laura had seen stills of Ken Carlsen in the television commercials he'd recently started running, but they hadn't prepared her for the mesmerizing reality of the man. It was only fitting that he represented Beverly Hills, because his looks came straight out of the movies. Magnetic blue eyes; blond hair streaked lightly with gray; strong, even features in a face dignified by the first lines of maturity. If Central Casting had selected governors, Carlsen would have had a lock on the job.

A secretary, still hard at work despite the fact that it was well past five, had let her into his locked suite of offices, checked his schedule for her name, and ushered her into his presence. She'd sat in a chair across from his desk and they'd talked about her previous trips to the capitol—a tour she'd taken with Seth's first-grade class and four or five visits to attend rallies. He had the knack most good politicians did for putting people at ease and then charming their socks off, something Laura appreciated. Coming here today, she'd felt as if she'd patched herself together with twist ties and bubble gum.

"So tell me about yourself," he finally said. "Are you as liberal as my good friend Vicki Stonehouse is?"

"At the risk of blowing my chances—no. Actually, I don't think anyone's as liberal as Vicki. Not in her tax bracket, anyway."

He smiled. "I don't know about that. We've got some friends in Hollywood who've been very generous to our campaign, even though they consider me suspiciously conservative. For a Democrat, that is."

"Personally, I think you're just about right," Laura said, meaning it, "and not just because Vicki keeps saying so. It'll be nice to vote *for* somebody for a change, not just choose the lesser of several evils."

"Thanks, but it's not a prerequisite, Ms. Miller. We're equal opportunity employers around here." He drank some Coke from a can on his desk. "I should warn you—this isn't a job for someone who gets rattled easily. We've got three incoming phone lines that ring off the hook, and most of the callers are either angry or want something. Vicki said you were good with difficult people. You'll have to be, because this place is full of them."

"Your fellow legislators, you mean?"

"And their staffers. People in the governor's office, high-level bureaucrats, corporate types throwing their weight around, reporters, lobbyists . . . They'll nag, whine, and even yell to get what they want, both over the phone and in person. I expect my staff to stay polite—and to shield me from the people I don't want to see or speak with."

"That won't be a problem. I've dealt with everything from busy phone lines to abusive customers in my previous jobs. I never lose my temper, not even with my mother or my kids." She paused. "I should make that 'almost never.' I've been known to yell at my ex-husband now and then."

"Then I hope he never comes to the capitol," Carlsen said with a laugh.

"He doesn't. He works for the Sacramento Unified School District. He's negotiating with the teachers' union right now, trying to avoid a strike. The superintendent does the lobbying personally. He comes to the capitol—"

"Sure. Luis Mendez. A solid guy. He calls or comes by whenever major education bills are under consideration."

Laura reddened. "Of course. You're on Senate Education, and very supportive of the schools, according to Allan. My ex-husband. I'm sorry—I wasn't thinking."

"Listen, if you know which committees I'm on, that puts you one up on most of the people I meet with." He drank some more Coke, then asked her how Allan's negotiations were going. They talked about education after that, then discussed transportation issues, another particular concern of Carlsen's.

He leaned back in his chair afterward. "So what do you think? You want to come to work for me?"

Laura was a little bemused. "That's it? No questions about my résumé? No other people to see?"

"I've already seen them. Besides, Vicki said I'd never find anyone better than you, and I trust her judgment. And Jack Waltzer, my chief of staff, was impressed with you. So am I."

"In that case, Senator, I'd love to come to work for you."

"Everyone calls me Ken. When can you—"

He was interrupted by a knock on the door. Before he could ask who it was, a beautiful young woman swept into his office. Her blond hair was pinned up and she was wearing a dressy navy sheath, so it took Laura a moment to recognize Heather Martin, Carlsen's stepdaughter.

She was holding a Snickers bar that she finished in

one large bite as she walked around his desk to the back of his chair. She dropped the empty wrapper in the wastebasket, then massaged his shoulders. "Tight for a change, I see. Another hard day at the zoo, huh, Ken?"

"Is there any other kind?" He was a little stiffer suddenly, as if he were uncomfortable with such familial informality in front of a stranger. "Uh, Heather, I was about to—"

"Pack up for the day and take me to Frank Fat's for dinner. I missed lunch. I'm starved. And *you* need to relax for a while before you go mining for money in Davis." She looked at Laura and smiled. "Hello again. Did Mrs. Stonehouse talk you into working on Ken's campaign?"

"Only indirectly," Laura said. "She recommended me for a job here."

"I was in the process of hiring her when you came in," Ken said. "Where do you two know each other from?"

Heather picked up his attaché case from the credenza behind his desk, set it in front of him, and opened it up. "The steps of our apartment house. I was leaving the building when Ms. Miller and Mrs. Stonehouse showed up. You were in Orange County with Mom at the time." She walked around to the side of Ken's desk and dropped into a chair. "Congratulations on coming to work for the next governor of California, Ms. Miller. The main things you need to know are, he works too hard and should be spoiled as much as possible, and when I call him, you should put me through immediately."

"Unless I tell you not to. She can be a pest at times, Laura. She worries about me too much." He looked at Heather with a fond exasperation that Laura found touching. It was nice to know that step relationships could work out so well. "I guess I can manage a quick dinner, Hettie. Grab us a table and order me something with chicken. I'll be along in a few minutes."

"Will do, Governor. I'll see you again soon, Ms. Miller. Try to get him to drink water once in a while instead of Coke, okay?"

Laura said she would do her best, and Heather breezed out of the office. "What's so wrong with Coke?" Laura asked.

"Too much sugar and caffeine. She says it hypes up my system. Imbalances my biochemistry."

Laura burst out laughing. "This, from a woman who was eating a Snickers bar when she first came in?"

"Since when are kids logical? Anyway, she claims she can get away with it because she's twenty-five and exercises for an hour or two a day, whereas *I* have one foot in the grave and barely have time for tennis once a week." He tossed some papers into his attaché case. "I'd like you to start as soon as possible. You're coming at a good time. The Easter break begins when Thursday's session ends and runs through the following Sunday, so I'll be out of the office all week and things will be quieter than usual. It'll give you a chance to learn the ropes without the customary pandemonium going on."

"You'll be campaigning?"

"Right. Mining for money, Heather calls it. Begging for bucks. It's either that, or spend Heather's inheritance."

"She obviously idolizes you. I doubt she'd mind."

Carlsen flashed a dazzling smile. "Not until she wanted to buy a house or a fancy car, she wouldn't. So when can you start? Is Monday okay?"

Laura generally gave two weeks' notice before she left a job, but Freddie didn't deserve even the two days he was about to get. "Monday's fine," she said.

"You mentioned your kids. They must be out of school next week. If that presents a problem . . . "

"It doesn't." She would have liked to spend some extra time with them, but she couldn't afford the loss in pay and didn't want to start off on the wrong foot by asking for special favors. "They stay with their after-school sitter during vacations."

"Come in from eight-thirty to two next week. Full pay but no time off for lunch. Sandy will train you. I want you to take your kids to the zoo one afternoon. See a couple of movies with them. That way, maybe they won't resent it so much when Mom comes home exhausted and cranky every day. The next couple of months are going to be tough."

Laura thanked him for the time off, thinking he was as terrific as Vicki had said, wondering if there were any more like him out there.

She decided to do the prudent thing with Freddie and play the job-hopping game according to the conventional good-ol'-boy rules. He was a sleaze and a crook, but he was also well-connected in Sacramento. It would have been stupid to antagonize him, at least until that happy day when he was finally indicted, if indeed he ever was.

Having been away from the office for two days, she found a small stack of work on her desk. She set it aside, writing herself a letter of recommendation first. It never hurt to have a glowing reference from a previous employer in one's files, assuming he wasn't making license plates in Folsom Prison.

She'd printed off the recommendation and was working on the weekly newsletter when Freddie sauntered in looking downright chipper. Obviously there hadn't been any further interrogations by the FBI.

He stopped by her desk. "So what happened, honey? You party too hard over the weekend and need some time to recover?"

She ignored the way he was leering at her. "My life's not that exciting, Freddie."

"But it could be. Come on inside. I want to show you something."

She picked up the letter of recommendation and followed him into his office. He sat down on the couch and patted the cushion next to him, but she settled into an armchair instead. He didn't look so chipper after that.

There were some brochures on the coffee table from a cruise-ship line. He picked one up and waved it around. "You see this? It's gonna be this year's trip. A seven-day cruise to Mexico, first-cabin all the way. The guys went nuts when I told them."

He treated his top agents and their wives to a vacation every year, a modest payback for the commissions he received on their sales. Last year's trip had been to a plush resort in San Diego. "Sounds fabulous," she said in a bored tone.

"Mary Beth hates ships. Gets sick as hell in them, even with those little patches the doctors give you. So I thought, why not take Laura along instead? You deserve it, honey. You're a hard little worker."

She didn't have to ask whose stateroom he'd expect her to sleep in. This was it—the bald proposition she couldn't refuse. The say-yes-or-you're-fired ultimatum.

It felt good to be able to reject him. To deny him the satisfaction of firing her. No matter how politely she couched it, he wasn't so dense that he'd fail to understand why she was leaving or wouldn't realize she'd been job-hunting behind his back.

She smiled sweetly. "Gee, Freddie, it's nice of you to say so, and to offer to take me along, but I won't be able to go. I have some great news of my own."

"Great news?" he repeated. "Jesus, you're not pregnant, are you?"

"No, no, it's nothing like that. It's just that the most wonderful opportunity came along and I grabbed it. I knew you'd want me to. You're such a great believer in people getting ahead if they can."

He looked confused. "Sure, honey. Of course I am. Everyone knows that. So, uh, what's this big opportunity you got?"

"It's at the capitol, working for a state senator. I hate to leave before you can replace me, but he needs me to start on Monday."

"This coming Monday? That's all the notice I get?"

It was more notice than *she* would have gotten if she'd turned him down on the cruise without quitting at the same time, but she let it pass. "I'm really sorry, but Ken is just so busy. . . . That's Ken Carlsen, the one who's running for governor. But I'm sure you knew all about him even before he became so prominent, since he has so much influence over your business. As a member of the Senate Insurance Committee, I mean." It was a bluff. Carlsen didn't sit on Senate Insurance.

Freddie dropped the cruise-ship brochure on the table. She could see the gears grinding slowly in his head. She'd gotten a job with someone important. Someone with power over his life. It would be foolish to make an issue of when she left.

"Hey, don't worry about it," he said. "I'll call Ted at Camellia Personnel. He'll find me a gal real quick. That Ken Carlsen, he's a great guy. I might even vote for him if he wins the primary."

It seemed unlikely; Freddie measured politicians against the glorious conservative standard set by Ronald Reagan. "Really? Even though he's a Democrat?"

"Why not? He's not one of those wacko liberals who never met a tax they didn't like. Does a good job on that insurance committee, too."

"Oh, absolutely." Laura held out the letter of recommendation. "I figured I should have something from you in my files. I didn't want to bother you about writing it, so I drafted it myself. Of course, if you don't agree with what I said, or if you want to make changes . . . "

He took it, glancing at it for much too short a time to read more than a few words. "No, no, this is fine." He scrawled his name. "So you're working for Ken Carlsen. I have to congratulate you, honey. There's a guy I'd really like to meet. Never hurts to know the heavy hitters in this town, you know what I mean? Think you could put in a few good words for me? Introduce me if I come around?"

Laura stared at him. Talk about chutzpah. He was lucky she didn't introduce him to the sort of government official who carried a badge and a gun. "Actually, Ken's heard all about you. You know how open I am at job interviews. I told him everything, Freddie, absolutely everything. I'm sure—"

"What do you mean, everything?" His neck and face got red. "What did you tell him?"

She'd been talking about the way he'd harassed her, not about his insurance scams, but her meaning had gone right over his head. When would she ever learn? Hitting on one's secretary wasn't a crime to a man like him, just standard operating procedure. She would have laughed if it hadn't been the sort of misunderstanding it was best to avoid.

"Well, not *that*," she said, as though she was amazed he could think such a thing. "I'm not stupid, for God's sake. After all, I knew about Bonita's policy but didn't say a word. That makes me an accessory."

"Then what?" he demanded. "What did you tell him?"

"Everything else, of course. All about what I did for you here." She paused, unable to resist one final dart at his bloated male ego. "And refused to do, but you had no business asking me in the first place. I'm sure the senator would be fascinated to meet you. He's horribly busy, though. Give me a call sometime and I'll see what

I can do." The Messiah would have to drop by Carlsen's office before Freddie got in.

He looked puzzled for a moment, maybe because her true feelings had finally penetrated but didn't jibe with her casual tone. Then he shook it off. "Great, great. Listen, you have a couple of vacation days coming, so finish up the newsletter and get on out of here. Take some time off. Kick back for a few days. I'll mail you your check."

She'd used up every vacation day she'd earned, but Freddie knew that as well as she did. He kept track of details like that. The truth was, she'd gone from sexual object to symbol of sexual defeat the moment she'd turned him down, and now he wanted her gone as soon as possible.

That gave her a certain amount of leverage. "Sounds fine, except for the part about the check. I'm a little short right now. I'll need it when I leave this afternoon." She could wait for weeks otherwise.

"I can't do it," he said. "Payday's on the fifteenth."

In other words, he still called the shots around here. She stood, telling herself she didn't have to take it. She didn't work for him anymore.

"Oh. Well, we certainly wouldn't want to mess up Violet's bookkeeping, would we? I'll tell you what. I'll come in on the fifteenth to say good-bye. Bring some homemade brownies, have a little party, and pick up my check. I'm sure you'll have a new secretary by then. We'll invite Mary Beth. The three of us can have an interesting chat about what a devoted husband you are."

She'd backed him into a corner, and he didn't care for that at all. His anger swelled and surged, but he controlled it. His thoughts were crystal clear to her—that no stupid cunt was going to force him to change his mind, no matter how much she threatened to embarrass him.

Then he crumbled and snapped, "You're a fucking bitch, Laura. Your husband was a jerk to stay as long as he did. Tell Violet I said to write you a check. Then get out of here and don't come back."

She smiled. "It's been nice knowing you too, Freddie."

FOURTEEN

Another Wednesday evening, another session in Vicki's kitchen. Allan had taken Seth and Sarah for the night, congratulating Laura on her job with Carlsen as they'd packed the kids' suitcases. Then, so honest it was almost painful, he'd admitted to being so preoccupied with the negotiations that he'd forgotten about her résumés until after their fight. Then he'd handed them all out, but too late, obviously, to have done her any good.

"I was hardly even annoyed," Laura told Vicki. "At least he was straight with me for once."

"Umm. It's a nice change. So what did you decide about Art Albright? Are you going out with him Saturday night?"

Laura nodded. "Talk about the Jewish grapevine. I called him at eight last night to accept, and my mother called me forty minutes later, just thrilled to death. She's shepherding Alice Albright back to the fold by phone these days, and she sees Art as part of her flock. She says it's the first time I've been enthusiastic about one of her finds. She figures it means I'm finally over Allan. I very diplomatically refrained from suggesting that her previous finds might have had certain shortcomings."

"What diplomacy? She'd want specifics, and then what would you do? Tell her that her sweet little neighbor's son is a sexual pervert, or that her doctor's wife's beloved cousin picked his nose all through dinner?"

"Good point. Listen, about the party . . . Art said casual, but I got the impression it's going to be an upscale crowd. Could I borrow your new fuchsia and gold outfit?"

"Sure. Take the fuchsia shoes, too. They're a little big on me, so they'll probably fit you perfectly."

Laura loved those shoes, which were made of a buttery suede. Vicki's devotion to animal rights didn't extend to wearing vinyl. "Thanks." She sipped her coffee. "Listen, you haven't heard the lead item of the day yet. Freddie and I reached a parting of the ways this morning." She gave Vicki the details, then added, "It was probably stupid to go after him—he could tell all his friends what a bitch I am, and he has some very important friends—but it felt so good that I don't much care how angry I made him."

"And it doesn't worry you that he knows what you really think of him now?" Vicki asked. "After all, you have damaging information about him. A decent lawyer could probably get you immunity from prosecution for testifying against him. That might be enough of a threat for him to want to shut you up for good."

"But he knows there's no proof of what he did. I wasn't a witness to anything fraudulent, so it's my word against his and Bonita's about what each of them said. They'd need a lot more evidence than that to even try him, much less convict him. Besides, he's not a brooder. If a week or two goes by without the FBI showing up, he'll forget the whole thing."

But deep down, Laura wasn't so sure. Even though a logical man would have no grounds for concern, and

even though Freddie, as limited as he was, had the
sense to reason things out the same way she had, she
couldn't help picturing him going ballistic some night
and coming after her with a meat cleaver in one hand
and a grenade in the other. Her imagination was
almost as lurid as Seth's these days.

The union settled with the district late Thursday
afternoon, which was sooner than Allan or anyone else
had expected. Laura, who'd spent the day cleaning and
gardening, learned about the agreement when she
switched on the evening news and saw live coverage of
Ned Brown and Luis Mendez smiling and shaking
hands while Allan stood behind them looking exhausted but very pleased.

He called her an hour later. He was taking Friday
off, he said. If she didn't mind, he would pick up the
kids from school and keep them till Sunday evening.
He offered to call Mrs. Fujimoto to let her know they
wouldn't be coming the next day, then volunteered to
stop by the house after school and pack them up.

He added that he hoped she'd be able to talk when
he brought them home. Now that the crisis at work
was over, he could see how difficult he'd been. He
wanted to concentrate on their relationship now, to
work with her and Tasha to build a loving and satisfying marriage.

Laura had wondered how she would feel if Allan
suddenly did everything right. Now, it seemed, she was
about to find out.

Art Albright was a little late picking her up on
Saturday, which was just as well, because she'd noticed
at the last minute that she had almost no money in her

wallet and had zipped to the automatic teller machine for some cash. According to the receipt, she had ten extra grand in her account, obviously some sort of computer glitch. Dealing with banks, even when the error was in your favor, was like dealing with the federal bureaucracy. She didn't look forward to trying to straighten the problem out.

Art pulled up in a BMW, wearing a leather bomber jacket, dark wool slacks, and a cotton sweater with an abstract design in brown, black, and beige. A hundred fifty for the sweater, Laura estimated, and even more for the jacket. Obviously, he was doing well. One look and her mother would have fantasized about calling around to caterers.

She was glad she'd borrowed Vicki's silk separates. She was single now, but her wardrobe was still married to Allan Miller. It was conservative and ladylike, suitable for weddings and bar mitzvahs, dinners at the homes of Allan's colleagues, and PTA and temple fundraisers. Hardly the stuff of *Vogue* and *Cosmo*.

She asked Art about his work as they drove to the party. He was on the quiet side, something she put down to shyness, but once she got him going he didn't stop, and his story turned out to be more interesting than she'd expected.

An accountant by training, he'd gone on to a successful career as a financial planner in San Francisco. Then, the previous spring, his father had asked him to join Albright Investments as a partner. The request was out of character for a one-man show like Art Sr., but then, he'd been acting strange for months, withdrawing from his family, avoiding his friends, and rambling incoherently about abstract problems in philosophy.

Art Jr. had liked his life the way it was and doubted he and his father would get along. They'd clashed repeatedly during his youth and adolescence. Their

philosophies about investing were very different, too—
the father, a high flyer, the son, more conservative. Art
Jr. had declined the offer, but Art Sr. had pressed him,
saying they would run the business however he chose.
Art had known his father too well to believe it.

Several months had gone by. Art Sr. had become
increasingly agitated and unstable, mentioning suicide
at times. His wife Alice, aware that he was making less
money, had begun to worry that he would destroy the
business completely. She'd begged Art Jr. to reconsider,
saying Art Sr. was in no shape to run anything and had
decided to sell out. Art had agreed at that point, coming on board in July, just a month before the accident
that had taken his father's life.

He hadn't been on the boat that day, he told Laura,
but he sometimes wondered if it had truly been an accident, as all the witnesses had claimed, or a suicide. The
calm and confident man who'd made money even
when most of his rivals were losing it had disappeared
almost completely in the month before his death. In
any event, in the seven months since the accident, Art
Jr. had taken his clients, and the Albright family, out of
such speculative ventures as a gold mine and a computer research firm and concentrated on more conservative
investments like blue chip stocks, highly rated bonds,
and certain types of real estate. The profits were lower,
but there was less chance of a major loss.

Listening to the story, Laura wondered how many
of Art Sr.'s emotional and financial problems had
stemmed from the fact that Jimmy Hollister was
"bleeding him dry" at the time, at least according to
Freddie. She also wondered what crime or indiscretion
Art Sr. had committed in the first place, to leave himself vulnerable to blackmail. Unfortunately, those
weren't the sorts of questions one asked a new
acquaintance, not that Art Jr. could necessarily have

provided the answers. Maybe his father had managed to keep his problems a secret. Besides, if Art and his mother had known about Hollister's activities, would they have attended his funeral? Publicly mourned a man who'd contributed to a loved one's decline and possibly his death?

The funeral, of course, had been just two weeks before, so Laura was startled when Art turned onto 45th Street and passed by the judge's house. All the lights were on, both inside and out, and several couples were gathered by the front door. Obviously that was where the party was.

She glanced over her shoulder as Art parked the car. Someone opened the door and everyone trooped inside. "Isn't it a little soon?" she asked.

"I thought so, but Charlie says it'll be therapeutic for him, like an Irish wake. And he does throw great parties. Still, I kind of wonder. . . . " His voice trailed off.

"Yes? Wonder what?"

"About—about him and his father. Their relationship. They were always competing. To the day he died, the judge liked to brag that he could beat Charlie at Ping-Pong, one-on-one, and most everything else." Art looked down for a moment. "And, uh, there was a fight about money, too. The judge wouldn't pay for law school. Charlie took six years to get through Berkeley and the judge figured he'd supported him for long enough."

Or maybe he'd been too broke from gambling to pay for much of anything and had used the Berkeley complaint as an excuse. "But Charlie's in his last year at McGeorge now, right? So what happened? Who's paying his tuition?"

"Maggie's brother. He's loaded—runs a bank in L.A." They got out of the car and started toward the house. "When Charlie got into McGeorge, the judge told him he could move back into the house and use their cars if he paid the rest of his expenses from his savings. He'd been working for a few years by then. It sounded like a good deal to me, but Charlie resented it—resented the time he'd lost and how little the judge was contributing to his education. The way he saw it, his father was rich and he was broke. It wasn't fair."

"But at the funeral—that beautiful speech he gave . . . He seemed so grief-stricken."

"I know. I figured they'd patched things up before the judge died. Or that Hollister was as broke as everyone says, and Charlie found out about it and realized his father had done the best he could. But now I'm not so sure. I sure as hell wasn't giving parties two weeks after *my* father died."

"Neither was I. I don't care what sort of trouble Hollister was in. Charlie was his son. He should show more respect for his memory, at least in public. I'm surprised Maggie permitted this."

"I doubt she knows," Art said. "Charlie mentioned that she was in San Francisco, visiting her cousin."

"But she's bound to find out. Won't she be angry?"

"Even if she is, she won't stay that way. Charlie's her favorite child. She's never had money of her own, but it hasn't stopped her from getting him most everything he wants. Who do you think talked his Uncle Clayton into paying for law school?"

They were at the door now. Laura took Art's arm. "You know something? You're the first man I've met since my divorce who's spoken to me this way. Like a friend. It's very comfortable. I like it."

He rang the bell, looking pleased but embarrassed. "There's something about you. . . . I usually keep things to myself. You have to in my line of work. But you're so easy to talk to. I mean, nothing I've said about Charlie is a huge secret, but I still wouldn't want it spread around."

"I won't, believe me."

"I knew you wouldn't. That's the whole point." He paused. "Your mother told my mother that we'd met at a party last fall. I've been trying to figure out why I don't remember you. Why I didn't ask for your number that night. I probably shouldn't admit this, but my mother had to nag me into asking you out. I'll have to thank her."

Laura smiled. "That makes two of us. *My* mother nagged me into accepting. The two of them are probably—"

The door opened, cutting her off. The redhead who let them in was dressed in a designer sweater and a leather miniskirt and held a bottle of imported beer in her hand. From the look of her, it wasn't her first.

"Hi," she said. "There're movies in the den, food in the dining room, drinks in the sun room, and pool and poker in the basement. The upstairs is off-limits." She took a swig of beer. "I'm Jennifer Harris."

"Laura Miller and Art Albright," Art said. "I used to live down the street."

"And I know Charlie from law school, but there are people here who never saw him before tonight. It's that kind of party. Lots of friends of friends. Have fun." She finished her beer and walked away.

Laura looked around. The living room and glassed-in sun room were to her left and the dining room was to her right. The den was straight ahead, as were the stairs to the basement and second floor. The house was furnished with Oriental carpets, oil paintings, and Chinese and European antiques.

"Nice place," she said to Art.

"Maggie's parents used to own it. The Hollisters bought it from Maggie's mother after Maggie's father died—the furniture, the paintings, the whole nine yards. Mrs. Davies told my mother she was sick of old things. She moved to Beverly Hills to be nearer to Clayton, married a guy ten years younger, and began collecting modern art."

"How long ago did she leave?" Laura asked.

Art thought for a moment. "I was still a kid at the time. Hollister wasn't even a judge yet. Maybe twenty years ago."

Even back then, the house and furnishings would have cost a bundle. She wondered whether Hollister had gambled in those days. If so, he must have earned enough to cover his losses, because Freddie had liked him once, thought he was a "great guy." He wouldn't have felt that way about someone who'd blackmailed him from the earliest days of their friendship.

They went into the dining room. A lavish buffet had been set up on the table—piles of caviar and smoked salmon; various pâtés, mousses, and salads; cracked crab and giant prawns; beautifully arranged plates of cold cuts. Laura hadn't seen a spread this fancy since her cousin Melvin, the Long Island plastic surgeon, had married one of his rich patients and commissioned an ice-sculpture bust of his bride, new nose, new chin and all, as a centerpiece for the hors d'oeuvre table.

She moved closer to Art. "This must have cost a fortune. I thought you said Charlie is always broke."

"He is. Maybe he sold some of Maggie's antiques after she left town." He grabbed a couple of plates and handed her one. "Except that's something she *wouldn't* forgive. She's crazy about all this stuff. My mother always said she liked it better than the judge."

They walked slowly around the table, taking a little of everything. "Then they weren't especially happy together?"

Art shrugged. "Who knows about anyone else's life? I thought the judge was as straight as they came. A pillar of the community. Now I hear he was being investigated by the FBI. That someone he was doing business with in the mob might have shot him."

"And you? Do you think that's what happened?"

"Actually, I never had much to do with him, even when I was a kid and Charlie and I were best friends. After I moved to San Francisco, I saw him maybe three times a year. His death didn't really touch me. I have my own problems to deal with."

"Like getting your business back on track?"

"Yes." He reddened. "I shouldn't have said that about Judge Hollister. It makes me look callous and selfish."

"Not really," Laura said. "I used to worry about everyone I knew, but lately . . . Unless it's someone I'm close to, I don't have the time or energy."

They went into the living room. There were only two empty seats, a pair of matching antique armchairs between the doorway and the baby grand in the corner. The chairs were isolated from the other furniture in the room and seemed to be more decorative than functional, but Laura sat down anyway, putting her purse on the second chair while Art got them some drinks.

He returned with some wine for her and a beer for himself and asked her about her divorce. She'd learned the hard way to skip the gory details. Men seemed to prefer funny, superficial anecdotes—the sitcom version of her life.

Art was different. He asked thoughtful questions and seemed to want honest answers. He knew the other two sides of the triangle personally, so he was easy to talk to.

He'd met Carolyn back in July at a cocktail party at the Hyatt Hotel. The host had been Craig Tomlinson, who held the affair every year for the people he did business with and the public officials he dealt with. Carolyn had arranged the party on behalf of Seeley and Associates and was very much in evidence that evening, making sure there was enough food and liquor and that her client spoke with everyone who mattered.

Art and his father hadn't done more than say hello, though, because Tomlinson had been an Albright client for years and saw Art Sr. or spoke to him at least once a week. It was a relationship, Art said, that had ended with his father's death. Although he didn't explain why, Laura got the feeling that he disapproved of Tomlinson, or at least felt uncomfortable doing business with him.

Art Jr. had run into Carolyn fairly often after that at the Capital Athletic Club. He'd met Allan there as well, and heard gossip about his affair with Carolyn, but Miller was such a common last name that he didn't realize Laura was Allan's ex-wife until she'd mentioned Carolyn and him by name.

They finished trading life stories, then began speculating about Hollister's murder. They were so absorbed in their conversation that they barely noticed anyone else around them. And then a tall blond in a black velvet catsuit walked in.

Laura froze. In the past few months, she'd seen Carolyn only once, in a supermarket, and she'd wound up feeling totally humiliated.

She'd wanted to say a cool hello that day, to act like Queen Elizabeth addressing one of her chambermaids. Instead, she'd ducked down an aisle before they could pass each other, left her half-loaded cart by a soft-drink display, and fled the store. After that, she'd always checked parking lots for a dark blue Mercedes with license plates reading PR STAR before she entered any of the shops in the neighborhood.

Carolyn looked fabulous. She'd accessorized the catsuit with a sterling silver belt, a silver choker, and dangling silver earrings. The man by her side was nearly a foot taller than she was, dressed resplendently in purple leather pants, a gold silk shirt, and a purple and gold sweater tied casually around his neck. Royal Paine.

The Kings usually had games on Saturday nights, so Laura was surprised to see him. Then she remembered that they'd played that afternoon.

Carolyn spotted Laura and smiled, taking Paine's arm in a gesture she interpreted as meaning, "I'm interested in someone new now, so there's no reason not to be civil."

Laura smiled back, but her heart was beating a mile a minute. There was no reason for it, not when neither of them still loved the man they'd once fought over so fiercely, but to her body, Carolyn was still the enemy.

She walked over, still clutching Paine's arm, looking thrilled she'd run into them. "Laura! Art! Hi! You look wonderful, Laura. I love your outfit. Where did you get it?"

"From my neighbor's closet." *We don't all make six figures a year like you do, Carolyn.* "She got it at Macy's in San Francisco. Your catsuit is wonderful, too. They're so hard to look really good in." *You have to be tall and skinny, with no discernible figure.* "You do, though. Just fabulous."

"Thanks, but if you want the truth, I'd trade my shape in a minute for some decent curves like yours." Carolyn laughed. "God knows I heard enough about them from Allan. He was always after me to gain weight, but all that ever gets me is chipmunk cheeks and a pot belly."

Laura was flabbergasted. She'd expected polite chitchat, not straight-from-the-hip shooting, but oddly enough, she liked Carolyn better for it. "And he used to tell me how perfect *you* were. If you want a list of your virtues, you've come to the right place."

"As of six months ago, maybe. I've deteriorated rapidly since then. Just ask him."

Paine draped his arm around Carolyn's shoulders. "The man is blind. You get better every day."

"I'll have to keep you around," Carolyn said. "This is Laura Miller and Art Albright, honey. Royal Paine, but I'm sure both of you know that. He had a great game today—a triple double. The Kings won by three."

Paine shook hands with Laura and then Art, telling Art he looked familiar. "Wait a minute. I've got it. The Capital Athletic Club, right?"

"Right."

"His home away from home," Carolyn said. "He's so addicted to basketball, he'll even play one-on-one with *me*."

"Can't guard her close, can't block her shots, can only shoot lefty from the outside, and she's allowed to push me, trip me, and hang all over me. Dirtiest player I ever met."

They seemed so comfortable with each other that Laura doubted they'd just met. "Is that where you two got to know each other?" she asked. "At the Capital Athletic Club?"

"Yup. Best pickup place in town," Paine answered.

"Actually, we met last fall when I did a workshop for the Kings on how to handle public appearances," Carolyn said. "Royal thought I was a skinny white chick who hated men."

"Who, me? I never said that."

"But you thought it."

"Maybe at first, baby, but not after the Celtics game."

Laura had gone to that game with Vicki. She remembered it because the Kings had actually won, with a dramatic, come-from-behind run during the last few minutes of play. "That was the best game of the year," she said. "And that's when you and Royal first got together? After the game?"

"March eleventh," Royal said. "Exactly one month ago tonight, at a restaurant. Don't remember much about the game except winning it with a three-point shot at the buzzer, and don't remember what we had for dinner, but when we got to my house . . . That part is clear as a bell."

Carolyn never even blinked. "Royal was in a mood to celebrate. We did. So how's business, Art? Are things getting sorted out?"

"Slowly, but yes, they are."

"And you, Laura? Still answering personal letters for Freddie Phelps?"

"Not anymore." Allan had apparently discussed her with Carolyn as much as the other way around. No wonder she'd thrown him out. "I quit a few days ago. I'll be working at the capitol for Ken Carlsen starting on Monday."

"Really? How fabulous!" Carolyn took Laura's arm. "You know, there are some things I've been meaning to tell you. Excuse us, fellas. We won't be long."

Laura allowed herself to be led away, wondering what Carolyn wanted.

FIFTEEN

"First stop, the bar," Carolyn said, starting toward the sun room. "We just came from dinner at that new Indian place across from Pavilions, and my mouth is still burning. The food was delicious, though. You should try it some time."

That was social sophistication for you. The soon-to-be ex-wife and the former mistress, discussing the local dining scene. Laura checked the urge to say something sarcastic. If circumlocution was the name of the game, she could play it as well as Carolyn.

"Speaking of delicious food, did you look in the dining room yet?" she asked, and then used the line about Cousin Melvin and the ice sculpture. Carolyn smiled, and she continued, "According to my Aunt Rose, the sculptor acted like Picasso and charged the same way."

"If you want great art, I suppose you have to pay for it," Carolyn said. The crowd at the bar was three to four deep. "I'll brave the mob. What are you drinking?"

"White wine." Laura had nursed a single glass through dinner; if she was going to talk to Carolyn, a second would definitely help.

She people watched while Carolyn got the drinks, recognizing some of the guests from Freddie's parties and others because they were local celebrities—a model from Carmichael who'd made it big in Europe, a television anchor team, several politicians, a developer and his wife . . . It was almost a who's who of Sacramento.

Charlie was walking around with Jennifer, working the room like a politician. In fact, if it hadn't been for the top-40 rock music the tuxedoed pianist was playing, the party would have resembled nothing so much as a political fund-raiser.

She waited till he was free, then approached him. "Hi, Charlie. I just—"

"Hey, s'nice to see you again, Laura. You came with Art Albright, right? Hope you're havin' fun."

"We are. To tell you the truth, I've been gawking a little. The whole world seems to be here. You have some very prominent friends."

"Yeah, a few, but word got around about the party and people just showed up. Y'know how it is."

"Yes," she said, not knowing at all. She could have thrown a party a week for the next ten years and never attracted such a high class of gate-crashers. "Listen, I wanted to thank you for dinner. The food was terrific."

"My pleasure, Laura. D'ja meet Jennifer yet?"

"At the door." The two women smiled at each other.

"So how's Freddie these days?" Charlie asked. "He looked at li'l wasted at Pop's funeral."

And judging by Charlie's slurred speech, he was well on his way to the exact same state. "Actually, I don't work for him anymore," Laura said. "I resigned last week to take a different job."

"Yeah, I can imagine. Michelle walked out and Freddie got the ol' itch again, right? Started comin' on to you, wantin' you to scratch it, but you weren't interested."

"Something like that." She could do the proper thing and drop the subject, but why worry about propriety when Charlie so obviously wasn't? "So you know about Freddie and his girlfriends. I guess I'm not surprised. He wasn't especially discreet."

"Unlike my father, but what the hell, you only go 'round once in this life." He patted her shoulder. "Be good to my friend Artie, okay? He's had it rough lately. Damn tough thing, bein' an orphan." He cackled, then waved to some people nearby and walked over to greet them.

Carolyn showed up with their drinks a minute later, carrying a glass of wine and what looked to be plain ice water. Allan had once mentioned that she was prone to ulcers and steered clear of alcohol. Laura had replied that if her life was so complicated and stressful, maybe she would have done better to steer clear of married men.

She handed the wine to Laura. "It's too crowded in here to talk. Let's find someplace more private."

Laura nodded, her thoughts returning to Charlie Hollister. He'd obviously known about his father's affair with Bonita. What else had he known? That the judge was a compulsive gambler? A blackmailer with ties to the mob? That cold little cackle he'd given . . . Had he held this party to make a preemptive strike before the full truth came out? To announce to everyone who mattered that he hadn't loved his father and felt only contempt for his memory?

They crossed into the dining room. Several dozen people were milling around while the caterers set out dessert. Once again, a lot of the faces were familiar—a public-interest lobbyist, a pro quarterback from Davis with one of Royal's teammates, a woman legislator with her arm hooked through Mike Clemente's . . .

Laura was so startled that she almost tripped over the fringe of the carpet. It wasn't that Clemente was here; given all the big shots around, she wasn't sur-

prised he'd heard about the party and decided to come.
It was the way he was looking at her—intently, as if
he'd watched her from the moment she'd walked in. He
smiled at her. Nothing had changed between Tahoe
and tonight. He still attracted her. She still wondered
why he was so interested in her. And he still made her
damned uneasy.

Carolyn walked up to him. "Mimi . . . Mike . . . "
She and Mimi pecked the air by each other's cheeks.
"It's so nice to see you both. How are you?"

"Fine," Mike answered, kissing Carolyn's cheek.
"Eating too much but enjoying every bite. Working
hard but enjoying that, too."

"All the same, I'm glad we have next week off,"
Mimi said, "if you can call nonstop fund-raising time
off."

"Speaking of campaigning, this is Laura Miller,
Mimi. She just got a job with Ken Carlsen—at the capi-
tol, though, not with the campaign. Laura,
Assemblywoman Mimi Bradley. And you know Mike
Clemente, of course."

Of course? Laura thought, and then realized Allan
must have said something Monday night, when
Carolyn had turned up uninvited at his door and they'd
wound up discussing everything from the teachers'
union to Hollister's murder.

Mike kissed her on the mouth like an old and dear
friend. It happened too fast for her to flinch or stiffen,
but she felt wired afterward—jumpy and flushed. She
couldn't see him without thinking of Joseph Cassani,
but he affected her like a sexual stun gun.

"So you're working for Ken Carlsen now," he said.
"Congratulations."

"Thanks." She turned to Mimi. "It's nice to meet
you. I've heard so much about you." She was strong on
women's issues, but also a player around the capitol,

the type who sponsored legislation for Clemente's sort of client, then denied that campaign contributions had a thing to do with it.

Mimi smiled. "And you'll be hearing a lot more, I hope. Carolyn, how is your father doing?"

The two women chatted about Drew Seeley while Laura watched them and Mike watched her. She found it unnerving, almost menacing, and was relieved when Carolyn murmured something about letting him and Mimi get their dessert.

She was about to turn away when he put his hand on her shoulder. "I need to talk to you," he said, "but I'll catch you later, when you're not in the middle of something."

"Sure. Enjoy your dessert." She wondered what he was after, but her desire to give him the widest berth possible was a whole lot stronger.

She and Carolyn walked into the kitchen, found half a dozen guests standing and talking while the catering staff bustled around, and continued outside. The backyard was taken up largely by a flagstone patio and a big pool with a wide deck. Laura picked up the scent of marijuana as they passed through the crowd on the patio. She wasn't surprised. According to Vicki, there were plenty of movers and shakers in town who were fighting the war on drugs from the wrong side.

They walked to the far end of the pool and sat down at a wrought-iron table. Nobody else was around; it was private and very quiet. Laura set down her glass and wrapped her hands around her arms, but more due to discomfort than coldness. She'd never been alone with Carolyn before, never even talked to her except for brief exchanges on the phone about arrangements for the kids. She was so beautiful and self-assured that it was hard not to feel inferior, even when one occupied the moral high ground.

"I was surprised to see you with Art Albright," Carolyn began. "I thought you and Allan were getting back together."

Laura wasn't about to discuss the matter with his former mistress. "We might and we might not."

"Laura . . . I saw your note on his car the other night. The fact that I stopped by his apartment . . . I wouldn't want you to take that the wrong way. Nothing happened."

"Oh," Laura said. Propositions obviously didn't count.

"No, really. I was upset that night. I'd just gotten back from Palm Springs and I was worried about my father. Things welled up inside me and I went a little crazy." Carolyn sighed. "Old habits die hard, I guess. Royal was out of town with the team, so I went to Allan's. Please don't hold that against him. It wasn't his fault."

Laura didn't reply. There was no point to it.

Unfortunately, Carolyn wasn't the least bit discouraged. "I know you dislike me. You have every reason to. I'm not going to insult your intelligence by claiming to be something I'm not, like an angel who slipped just this once. When I see something I want I go after it, and in the past, I never cared about the consequences. The harder it was to get, the more I enjoyed having it. I guess I'm spoiled. Selfish."

An antisocial man-eater on a sexual power trip, Laura thought, but kept her mouth shut.

Carolyn leaned closer. "I wanted Allan, and I went after him, but all I got was his body. That was enough at first—both of us know how good he is in bed—but I wanted more after a while. To come first in his life and his thoughts. But I never did. You and the kids were too entrenched. Really, none of this was his fault. It was mine. Men are so vulnerable and naive. . . . I've always been able to manipulate them sexually. Allan couldn't help himself. He'd never met a woman like me before."

Laura rolled her eyes. Enough was enough. "Don't flatter yourself, Carolyn. You can call it a midlife crisis or plain old fashioned lust, but you didn't lure him into anything he wasn't charging at full speed. Have a good time with Royal and forget about me and Allan. One way or another, we'll manage without your help."

"But that's the whole point. I can't forget you. I feel too badly about everything."

Laura waited silently, skeptically. Carolyn wasn't into soul-searching. She must have a hidden agenda.

"Maybe I'm finally developing a conscience," she finally murmured, "but I'm sorry I messed up your marriage. I'd like to make things right for you again."

She obviously considered herself the cause and remedy of everything she chanced to touch, no matter how fleetingly. It was incredible, really, a monumental ego trip, but at least it explained where she was coming from.

"You didn't mess up my marriage," Laura said. "Things just happen sometimes, okay? If Allan had been happier with me, he wouldn't have left me, and if I'd been happier with him, I would have taken him back by now. If you're really so hot to atone, volunteer at a battered women's shelter or a rape crisis center. Help someone who really needs it, because I'm doing just fine without you."

"Actually, I already do," Carolyn said, sounding a great deal less earnest and regretful. "Volunteer, that is." She studied Laura for several seconds. "Allan said you were tough. He was right. I can see why I lost."

Laura thawed a little. Just when you thought you had Carolyn pegged, she surprised you. "I'm not tough. I just talk a good game. Muddle through the best I can, just like everyone else does." She sipped her wine. "So who do you volunteer for?"

Carolyn listed several groups that worked with needy or abused women. "I do publicity and fund-raising, not direct social service. I'd be lousy at holding people's hands and giving them strength."

"All the same, I bet you'd have some useful things to say about how to pick yourself up and get what you want. Of course, you'd have to cut the crap and talk to them straight." She paused. "So what's this all about? Why did you *really* drag me out here?"

"Part of it was you and Allan. Honestly it was. That scare with my father . . . It made me look at myself more closely. I didn't like what I saw." She hesitated. "Allan was so good to me last Monday. I knew it was over between him and me, and I felt the least I could do—"

"Was sleep with him one final time," Laura interrupted, "for auld lang syne." Did the woman never stop?

"God, is there anything he doesn't tell you?" she grumbled, finally dropping the repentant sinner routine. "Look, he was nice to me that night. I was grateful, maybe even a little nostalgic, so I offered. We all have our weak moments. I'm sorry, okay? Sorry for everything."

"Fine. Your apology is accepted." Laura shivered. She wasn't only wasting her time out here, but freezing her tail off. "I'm getting cold, so if you've said what you wanted to say—"

"Give me a few more minutes, Laura. Please. That night . . . Somehow Allan and I got on the subject of Hollister's murder, and he told me what you'd said about Bonita Franks—about how you'd been in the apartment she used to stay in." Carolyn moved her chair closer and lowered her voice. "It wasn't Hollister's. It belongs to one of my clients, Craig Tomlinson. He's got millions—runs a big conglomerate and owns part of a casino and racetrack. That apartment—I've heard all kinds of rumors about what goes on in there, and that box you found in the closet confirms them. But the thing that really spooked me—" She stopped abruptly.

Laura was hooked now. "Yes?"

Carolyn looked around, evidently to assure herself she wouldn't be overheard. "I'd better back up a step. About Tomlinson . . . I do business with him, but I don't know much about him personally. Allan told me you'd met Clemente a few times, so maybe you know that Tomlinson uses his lobbying firm. They have a good track record, almost too good. Sometimes I wonder how far they would go to get what they want. So when I heard about that Mafia don you met . . . Racetracks and casinos aren't exactly church thrift shops, Laura. Who knows what Tomlinson and Clemente are mixed up in? All those guns you saw . . . Who knows what they might have been used for?"

"You think one of them was used to kill Hollister? Is that what you're saying?"

"I think it's possible."

Laura disagreed. "Personally, if I'd murdered someone, I'd throw the gun into the nearest river, not stash it in a downtown apartment used by a parade of priapic men. Why risk somebody finding it, getting suspicious, and turning it in?"

"But a man is dead," Carolyn said. "A man who used that apartment all the time. Maybe he saw something he wasn't supposed to. Maybe it got him killed." She paused. "It sounds like you had a pretty thorough look around. Frankly, if the company Tomlinson keeps is as questionable as I'm beginning to think, I'd rather not have him as a client. Did you find anything unusual in there? Anything that would link him to something unsavory?"

Unsavory, no. Unusual, yes—an answering machine with an enigmatic outgoing phone message and special security features, and a computer with the same sort of precaution.

Laura started to say as much, then checked herself. Carolyn was far too sharp not to know exactly what sort of man she was dealing with. If Tomlinson made her uncomfortable, if she doubted his honesty, why not resign the account? Her sudden reservations didn't ring true.

Laura added in how profitable Tomlinson must be to Seeley and Associates and how determined Carolyn had been to dissolve her own defenses and get her talking. Then she asked herself why Carolyn was so interested in what she'd seen. The answer had nothing to do with doubting Tomlinson's integrity. It was that Carolyn wanted to protect him—that she knew there was something shady in his apartment and wanted to find out if Laura had seen it.

"Nothing I can think of," she said, "but now that I know the apartment is actually Tomlinson's, it explains the high-tech equipment in the office. I mean, I wondered why a judge would need it." Her voice trailed off. She'd spoken too quickly. Backed herself into a corner. Tomlinson might have known from Bonita that she'd been in his apartment—that she'd had the means to unlock his office, look in his portfolio, and put two and two together. She shouldn't have acted surprised about the place being his. He and Carolyn might have talked.

She shivered again. Tomlinson might even have put Carolyn up to this. She could be doing a favor for a valued client who was nervous about his apartment having been searched, finding out exactly what Laura had seen. Thanks to Allan, Carolyn already knew where she'd looked: everywhere. Playing dumb had been a mistake. It could arouse Tomlinson's suspicions, and God knew she was no more eager to have him for an enemy than Bonita or Joseph Cassani.

"Laura?" Carolyn said. "Are you okay?"

She sipped her wine, stalling for time. She couldn't suddenly mention the portfolio—admit to knowing all along whose apartment it was. "Yes. Sorry. I was just trying to think. . . . You asked whether there was anything unsavory. To be honest, I was checking for kinky sexual stuff, because Freddie used to talk about all the action that apartment saw. If there were damning papers around, I didn't come across them. There was nothing out in the open, certainly."

"Mmm." Carolyn paused. "Of course, like you said, Craig is very high-tech. He'd probably keep records and correspondence on a computer."

"There *was* a computer there," Laura said. "Also the most complicated answering machine I ever saw."

"Did you try them out?"

"Me?" She smiled and shook her head. "I don't get along with machines. I can't even figure out my microwave oven, much less program my VCR."

"Allan mentioned that your friend Vicki was with you. Is she any better with machines than you are?"

"Probably," Laura answered, "but she didn't want anything to do with them. She thought I was crazy to poke around. Kept trying to drag me away. I'm sorry I can't be more helpful, but the place just wasn't that mysterious."

"Well, that's reassuring," Carolyn said. "I was probably worried over nothing. I can be wildly over-imaginative at times."

It was a surprisingly fast about-face, but welcome all the same. Laura stood up. "We should get back to Art and Royal now. They must be ready to send out a search party."

Carolyn didn't argue. Laura couldn't tell whether she was suspicious, satisfied, or thinking about a completely different subject. Her face revealed nothing.

SIXTEEN

Laura stayed with Carolyn even after they'd returned to the house, the two of them searching for Art and Royal. Unless the men were holding hands in the powder room, they were nowhere on the ground floor. The second floor was supposedly off-limits, so that left the basement.

The room was large, as wide as the entire first floor and about half as deep. Paneled in oak and carpeted in a wall-to-wall beige Berber, it was furnished with chairs, couches, and an entertainment center on one side, a poker table and a pool table on the other, and a makeshift bar in between on a long folding table by the stairs. A large group, mostly male, was clustered around the entertainment center, talking and joking while a ball-game played on a big-screen TV. A second group was watching Royal Paine play pool against Mimi Bradley, who made what looked to Laura like a difficult shot and then teasingly asked Royal if he had his wallet handy.

Art was lounging against the back wall, sipping a beer as he watched the pool match, but Mike Clemente was nowhere in sight. Laura realized she hadn't seen him anywhere lately, either in the house or the yard.

Wondering where he'd disappeared to, she walked over to Art. "So Mimi's a shark, huh?"

"Yup. Nobody can beat her. Of course, she hasn't played *me* yet."

"You're really that good?"

"Good enough to take care of my pocket money when I was in college. I play the winner of this match."

She smiled. "In that case, good luck and go to it."

"Thanks." He put his arm around her, apparently more at ease now that he'd had a couple of beers. "So how did it go with Carolyn? You were gone for a long time. I was beginning to worry about you."

"Really? Did you think she'd slipped me a poisoned prawn or pushed me into the pool?"

"No. That she'd trapped you into having a conversation you didn't want to have. Another ten minutes and I was going to go rescue you."

She moved closer to him, resting her head lightly against his shoulder. "That's sweet, but I was fine. I'll tell you about it later, after you play."

They turned their attention back to the game. Mimi finished Royal off, then excused herself to go to the bathroom. Laura watched absently as she disappeared through a door opposite the entertainment center. A man on one of the couches was lifting a tiny spoon to his nostril; he inhaled sharply a moment later. She frowned and looked away, telling herself that the stupidity of strangers was none of her business.

Royal handed Mimi several bills when she returned, then went upstairs with Carolyn. If the sixty grand he'd given Hollister was blackmail money, it must have been for something other than substance abuse. Judging by tonight, he didn't even drink, much less use illegal drugs.

Art gave Laura his half-empty beer mug, then racked the balls. He and Mimi were playing a three-game match. A hundred bucks, winner take all.

The word had obviously spread that two good players were battling it out, because as the match progressed, more and more people drifted over to watch. Art won the first game, Mimi the second. Art had finished his beer by then, so Laura took his empty mug to the bar.

Art and Mimi had started the deciding game of the match by the time she returned. She didn't want to disturb anyone, so she watched from the edge of the crowd, her back to the bar and the stairs.

She was on tiptoes, craning her neck to follow one of Art's shots, when someone's hands came down on her shoulders. She started, then jerked around. Mike Clemente was only inches away, staring at her with a hard look that left her confused and anxious.

Her heart rate soared and her face got warm. She would have backed away if there had been anywhere to go, but the crowd was in the way.

"We seem to have been abandoned in favor of pool," he said. "Why don't we have that conversation now?"

She hesitated. She didn't know what game he was playing, only that she didn't like it and didn't want to join in. "I'm watching Mimi and Art. Maybe some other time."

"Like next year, hmm?" He smiled, but it was nothing like the warm looks he'd given her before. "I do know where you live, Laura. It's listed in the phone book, remember? You can talk to me here, or you can talk to me tonight at your house, but one way or another, you're going to talk to me. Which will it be?"

It was the first time she'd ever been furious with someone and scared of him at the same time. She wanted to threaten him back, to say she'd call the cops if he came anywhere near her, but parking on her street and waiting till she got home wasn't a criminal offense, and neither was tracking her down at her office. Sooner or later, he was going to catch her alone and say what he wanted to say. Besides, if something she'd done had bent him out of shape, it was better to hear him out and calm him down than to put him off and get him even madder.

She nodded, her eyes on a spot somewhere to the right of his ear. "Right now is fine. Go ahead."

"I had someplace more private in mind," he said, taking her arm in a firm grip. "There's a laundry room opposite the bathroom. We'll go in there."

He started across the room. She resented the Gestapo tactics but didn't resist. The sooner this was over with, the better, and the laundry room was as safe a place as any. There was always murder by agitation or excessive tumble drying, of course, but she'd be close enough to be heard if she screamed for help.

All the same, she was relieved when someone called to him as they approached the entertainment center. "Hey, Mike! I've got some great stuff here. You interested?"

He stopped. "No, but thanks anyway. Who's winning the game?"

"The A's. Nine to two or maybe four. Or one." The man giggled. "You sure you don't want to try some of this stuff? It's primo, man."

"Nope. You know me and my allergies. Coke and antihistamines don't mix."

Mike started walking again, but Laura dug in her heels. "Aren't you going to introduce me to your friend?"

"Sure." He smiled in a slow, lazy way that said he knew why she'd asked and found it funny, even absurd. The tension between them eased a little. "Laura Miller, Bob Kennedy."

It wasn't the sort of name one forgot. In fact, Laura remembered seeing it next to a door in the capitol and assumed this was the same man. He was the consultant to some committee, someone Clemente probably lobbied regularly.

"That's Laura Miller," she repeated slowly. "Remember the name, Bob. Your friend Mike insists on going into the laundry room to chat. He has a clean-clothes fetish. The smell of Bounce and Clorox drives him wild. Did you know that?"

Kennedy looked at her vacantly. "Uh, right."

Either he thought she was a total wacko or he was too spaced out to absorb what she'd said, but somebody else probably would.

Still holding her arm, Mike pulled her into the laundry room and closed the door. The room was about six feet by eight, with a washer, a dryer, and a large sink taking up most of the floor space. He leaned against the door, watching her with cool amusement in his eyes. She got as far from him as she could, standing in front of the sink, which was opposite the door.

"A clean-clothes fetish, huh?" he said with a grin. "You know, you make it hard for a guy to put the fear of God into you. You're too damned appealing."

The boyish smile, the burst of charm, the admiring gaze . . . It wasn't what she'd expected, and it left her confused and suspicious. Either he was toying with her or trying to reassure her, but she had no idea which one.

She looked at him warily. "That's what you brought me in here for? To put the fear of God into me?"

"Yup."

"Might I ask why?"

His grin got wider. When he smiled that way, so easily and winningly, it was hard to remember that his native habitat was a swamp. Her uneasiness diminished a little.

"You can ask," he replied. "You won't get an answer."

He crossed his arms in front of his chest, apparently in no great hurry to proceed. She told herself to wait for him to switch to his ax-murderer mode and have at her. To hear him out, then answer whatever questions he chose to ask as politely as possible—that was the sensible thing to do.

But the less frightened she became, the more irate she got. Where did he get off pushing her around? And what was this all about, anyway? Was she his first victim of the night, or had there been others? Because if that's what he'd been doing for the past hour, dragging people into pantries and laundry rooms and grilling them like Torquemada, someone needed to tell him this was twentieth-century America, not fifteenth-century Spain.

"I haven't seen you around lately," she finally said. "Where were you?"

"It was stuffy inside. I went for a walk."

She remembered the feel of his hands on her shoulders. "Really? I'm surprised to hear that. It was cool outside, but your hands were very warm."

"I had them in my pockets."

"You went outside even though your allergies were acting up? That wasn't very smart."

"They don't bother me as long as I take antihistamines."

If he minded her questions, it didn't show. He wasn't exactly friendly, but he wasn't hostile, either, just distant and matter-of-fact. Unless this was an exceptionally bizarre pickup attempt, it didn't make a lick of sense.

"But cocaine would have bothered you. Mixing it with antihistamines, that is."

"That's right," he said blandly.

"How do you know? Did you ever combine them?"

"Just once. It was a bad trip."

She doubted his story about going for a stroll, but

not that he did coke when his allergies weren't acting up. His casual attitude toward illegal drugs reminded her all over again of what questionable circles he moved in. What dangerous ones, too.

She looked at the floor. The room suddenly felt warmer and smaller. She couldn't think of another thing to ask except, What do you want? and Why don't you get on with it?

"What's wrong?" he asked. "Did you run out of questions?"

He was needling her, mocking her. The feelings she'd had before returned with a vengeance. Resentment and anger, fear and confusion.

She looked up. "You're the one who wanted to talk, not me. So talk."

"Talk is the wrong word. I'm going to ask you some questions. Give me straight answers and we won't have a problem." He paused. "I was surprised to see you with Carolyn Seeley tonight. Isn't she your ex-husband's girlfriend?"

"She was. She's seeing Royal Paine now."

"Do you and Paine know each other?"

"No. I never met him before tonight."

"He was at Hollister's funeral. You didn't meet him that day, or even before?"

"No."

"You and Carolyn—what did you discuss outside?"

He was using a crisp, cold tone, firing questions at her nonstop, and she resented each of them a little more. "I don't see what business it is—"

"You don't have to see. Just answer the question. What did you and Carolyn discuss?"

"My ex-husband," she said curtly. Her stomach had begun to churn.

"And that's all."

"Yes." Clemente was mixed up with Tomlinson. She

wasn't going to admit the truth and risk additional slips.

"Not anything else. Not her work, for example."

Laura felt panic setting in. What did he know? What did he suspect? "I told you—it was about Allan. She wanted—she felt guilty about the affair. She wanted to help me patch things up."

To her relief, he moved to a different topic. "Tell me something, Laura. Why is it that whenever I ask you out, you turn me down, then wind up the same place I do?"

It was a good question, but if there was an answer other than coincidence, she was in no fit state to find it. "I don't know, but if you think I'm following you around—"

"Hardly. You got here first. Same with the Alpine Room. Let's just say that your curiosity seems to coincide with my professional interests a little too often for your own good." He straightened. "You came with Art Albright tonight. How do you know him?"

"My mother met him and his mother at temple. She gave him my phone number."

"And when was that?"

This was intolerable. "You have no right to question me. I'm not going to answer you anymore."

"Better me than Cassani, Laura. It would inconvenience him to make a special trip to Sacramento just to talk to you, and Mr. Cassani doesn't enjoy being inconvenienced. He'd probably bring some of his friends along. Have them hold you down while he played etch-a-sketch on your body with his knife till you'd learned to be more cooperative."

If he'd brought up Cassani's name in order to terrify her into submission, it worked. She began to shake.

Obviously he noticed. "Your mother and Mrs. Albright—when did they meet?"

"A few weeks ago. The night of Hollister's funeral."

"And you've been seeing him ever since?"

"No. Tonight is our first date. Look, Art is a nice person. He's—"

"If I want your opinion, I'll ask for it. Have you seen Bonita Franks in the past two weeks?"

"No."

"Talked to her on the phone?"

"No." The lie was automatic, instinctive. She could barely think by now.

"That's not the way I heard it from her."

The shaking got worse. Clemente could have talked to any of the people he'd asked about. All of them, for all she knew. "Why did you bother asking if you already—"

"To see if I'd get the truth. Stick to the facts from now on, Laura. You'll live longer. What did you and Bonita talk about?"

She was paralyzed now, afraid even to answer. If Clemente caught her in a lie . . . But if she ratted on Bonita and Bonita found out . . .

"I repeat," he said. "You can tell me or you can tell Cassani. Take your pick."

"It—it was business," she finally managed. "Bonita—she had an insurance policy on Hollister. She wanted to know when she'd get her check."

"And that's all you discussed. Nothing else."

She stared straight ahead, seeing nothing, desperately trying to decide if it was safer to lie or tell the truth. No answer would come. "I don't know. I can't remember."

"Then think about it a little harder," he said harshly.

"I can't. I've had a terrible week. My divorce . . . And changing jobs . . . " She felt dizzy and short of breath, almost shell-shocked. "It's—a lot of it's hazy. I just don't remember. I swear I don't."

"Oh? And how about driving by Bonita's house two weeks ago? Do you remember that?"

He sounded so angry that she swayed in terror. She

grabbed the edge of the sink for support. God help her, but he'd spotted the Bronco that night and somehow found out it was Vicki's. He knew she'd seen his Porsche, knew she could place him in the house. Obviously that worried him—a lot.

"Yes," she said hoarsely.

"What were you doing there?"

"Just—driving by. That's all. I was curious about where she lived."

"Why?"

"There was no reason. Just—all the money she was going to get. I wondered how she lived. How much her life would change." Any more of this and she'd lose it completely—burst into tears or fly at him and try to claw her way out. "I want to leave now. Let me out of here."

He started forward. She pressed herself against the front of the sink. There was no escaping him, nowhere to run to. He kept going till their bodies were almost touching, then stopped. She wanted to turn around but was afraid to let him out of her sight. She knew that was irrational—he wouldn't try to hurt her with so many people nearby, and even if he did, it wouldn't matter which way she was facing—but instinct was in charge now, not logic.

He cupped her chin and asked softly, "Do you remember what I told you when we first came in?"

She could barely remember what he'd said ten seconds ago. His touch made her so queasy she almost gagged. "No. Please—"

"Does the phrase 'fear of God' ring a bell?"

It did. He had. "Yes. Can I please just go now?"

"In a moment. First I'm going to give you some advice. Don't ask questions about Hollister's murder. Keep your nose out of my personal business. And don't discuss this conversation with your friends. All right?"

"Yes," she said. "All right."

He released her and stepped aside. She ran out of

the laundry room and fled into the bathroom, locking the door behind her. Then she stood over the sink, panting and shaking, and vomited repeatedly.

Most of Charlie Hollister's expensive food went right down the drain, but mercifully, the bathroom was well equipped for common social disasters like losing one's most recent meal. She found a bottle of Scope in the medicine chest and a can of Lysol under the sink and used them both, then fixed her makeup as best she could.

She wasn't queasy after that, and both her looks and her breath were probably socially acceptable, but she still felt like hell. Shaky, sweaty, and scared out of her wits. For her entire life, she'd analyzed things to death, but she couldn't have reasoned her way out of a Skinner box just then.

What did she do now? Keep her mouth shut and pray she'd be left alone? Go to the Feds and beg for protection? Had she put her children in danger, too, or only herself? Why had Clemente come after her in the first place? What did he think she knew, or worry she might find out? Could Tomlinson's apparent interest mean she'd seen more than she realized, if only she could put everything together?

She didn't have a single conclusive answer to a single one of those questions. The past few weeks were a jumble, a mass of disconnected incidents and details. She needed to talk to Vicki. Vicki was calm and logical. She would see things Laura had missed.

Then, with a frightening flash of insight, she realized that talking to Vicki was the last thing she should do. She was dangerous to other people's health. If they knew what she knew, they might find themselves in the same sort of trouble she was in. She'd never felt so alone in her life.

*   *   *

Someone rattled the doorknob, startling her so badly she flinched. She was lost in thought, so absorbed in berating herself for the mess she was in that it was several seconds before her head cleared and everyday reality returned. The person outside was yelling by then, asking if anyone was in the bathroom.

"Yes. I'm sorry." Her voice was thin and raspy. "I'll be out in a moment."

She drank some water, then opened the door. She was roiling and churning inside, a few short steps from hysterics. She couldn't stay at the party. It was an effort even to talk coherently.

More people than ever were in the basement, blocking her view of the pool table. She stared at them, seeing little more than a mass of undifferentiated bodies. The thought that Clemente was somewhere in the room—that she might literally run into him—gave her the chills.

Still, standing in the hallway wasn't going to get her home. She edged her way through the crowd, searching for Art and trying to avoid Clemente, looking at people in that oblique way you use when you're pretending you're not looking at them at all. One of them was Freddie Phelps, who glared at her with such drunken hostility that she paled.

She finally reached the pool table. Art had beaten Mimi and taken on the next challenger. He was holding a cue in his hand, watching his opponent line up a shot. Mimi and Clemente were nowhere in sight.

Art noticed her after a moment and walked over. He looked concerned, even a little guilty. "You're mad at me. You have a right to be. I should have stopped after the match with Mimi and tracked you down, but Ralph's such a good player . . . It was a challenge. It won't take much longer. I promise."

She wanted to be reasonable. He shouldn't have to

quit in the middle of a match. "It's okay," she said. "Go ahead and finish. I don't mind."

She meant it, too, or truly wanted to, but there were tears only inches beneath the good-sport surface. Some people yelled or smashed things when they reached their emotional limit; she cried or threw up.

"Hey, you're really upset," Art said, looking more concerned than ever. "What's wrong?"

Her eyes welled up. Sensitivity from a male—a date, no less!—was more than she could handle just then. "It's, uh, it's nothing. Go on. I'll be fine."

Two billiard balls collided sharply, making her jump. Art walked over to Ralph, spoke to him for a minute, and then set down his cue. He didn't say anything when he returned, just put his arm around her and led her away.

She felt a pang of guilt. The way she'd been raised, women were supposed to make the best of things, to keep men happy at any reasonable cost even when they silently resented doing it. Art was a terrific guy, and she'd ruined his game. Spoiled his evening.

She didn't say a word, though, just followed him to the car and let him help her inside. She was too shaken to mumble protests she didn't mean.

He didn't ask questions, just drove to her house and parked in her driveway. The ride took fifteen minutes, which was long enough for her to get her emotions under some sort of control. She was sorry that the evening had ended so soon—and so badly—and wanted him to know it. She even considered inviting him in for coffee. But her mind was mostly elsewhere, and her composure was very precarious, so she figured she'd be lousy company.

She was about to apologize for ruining his evening when he switched on the light and asked her how she was doing. "A little better," she said. "Thanks for being so nice."

"Listen, nice would have been sticking by your side so that whatever happened while I was playing pool wouldn't have happened. I feel terrible about it."

"It's not your fault. Really, there was nothing you could have done, because if it hadn't been tonight—" She stopped in midsentence. She was saying too much. Still, she owed him an explanation, or as much of one as she could safely provide. "I'm mixed up in—in something that's causing me some problems. I'm sure it'll blow over eventually, but I got reminded of it tonight, and it upset me. I'll be fine, though. Really."

"Was it Carolyn? Did she say something to hurt you?"

He sounded ready to break out the tar and feathers. "No. It's just—I was in the wrong place at the wrong time a while ago. Some people aren't too happy with me now, and one of them spoke to me tonight. It's my own fault, really. I got involved in something I should have stayed out of."

"And someone threatened you because of it?"

"Sort of, but—"

"Dammit, Laura, that's nothing to fool around with. You should go to the police."

The conversation wasn't going the way she'd expected it to. The thought of talking to the police—to the FBI—made her shake all over again. "Maybe I'll do that."

"Maybe?" he repeated, looking appalled. "Only *maybe*?"

"It's not that simple, Art. Really, I can't talk about it. I'm sorry about the way things turned out, okay? I was having a good time. It was a great party." And she was going to start bawling if she tried to keep talking.

He took her in his arms and held her, gently massaging her neck. She was so touched that she wound up sniffling against his shoulder.

"Look, I understand better than you think," he said

softly. "Sometimes you find yourself where you'd rather not be and the choices aren't so easy. Believe me, I know that as well as anyone. And the way I've handled my own problems . . . I'm the last guy who should tell you what to do. Why don't we have dinner on Wednesday? You can think things over in the meantime. Maybe you'll feel more like talking by then."

"Okay," Laura said, but she knew she wouldn't confide in him. The only possible help was in the federal building on Cottage Way, but it was a toss-up as to which was more dangerous, talking to the authorities or going it alone.

SEVENTEEN

Dottie Greenbaum wasn't the buffer type, especially when it came to Laura and Allan. Put them all in the same room and she turned into a heat-seeking missile. Whatever was on her mind flew straight out of her mouth toward the psyche of her sinning son-in-law.

"So, Allan, are you still breaking your sacred marriage vows with that skinny blond tramp?" she'd asked him back in September. "You do realize you're scarring the children for life," she'd said a few months later, "but lucky for them, if they go crazy someday and burn down a forest or shoot at the president, God will understand and forgive them. *You* won't get off so easy, believe me."

Normally, Laura shuddered whenever Allan and her mother got within shouting distance of each other. But twelve hours after her conversation with Mike Clemente, she still got queasy when she thought about the threats he'd made. She couldn't have committed herself to chairing the third-grade bake sale, much less made decisions about the rest of her life, so it was like a gift from the gods when Dottie called to invite herself

to dinner and offered to bring the meal. One look at
Dottie's car and Allan would want to hustle the kids to
the doorstep and run like hell, not that his ego would
actually let him.

Dottie was right on time, marching into the kitchen
at six with a stack of aluminum pans. "So where's the
famous labor negotiator today?" she asked as she set
them on the counter. "I spent the afternoon with my
friend Celia, the one who lives right near Allan. I
stopped by his place to see if he wanted me to take the
kids for a few hours, but no one was even home."

"I don't know where they went," Laura said, "but I'm
sure he didn't kidnap them and take them to a different
jurisdiction, if that's what you're worried about."

"Listen, don't be such a wiseguy." Dottie turned on
the oven. "Allan wants you back. You're seeing another man. Who can say what crazy things that could drive
him to?"

"Even if he were tempted, he'd never leave his job,"
Laura said. "He's sure they couldn't survive without
him."

"He's good at it, I'll give him that, but really, he
should tell you where he's taking the children. You can
never be too careful about things like that."

Laura took some plates out of the cupboard. "I'll tell
you what, Mom. He's supposed to be here at seven. If
he's not, you can call the cops."

"Cops, shmops, you'd tie me to a chair before you'd
let me near the phone." Dottie took the plates and got
out some flatware. "I'll set the table, darling. You sit.
After all, you had such a bad night last night."

Laura was startled, but only for a moment. Dottie's
spy network could have given the Mossad a run for its
money. "Let me guess. Art said something to Alice and
Alice said something to you." She sat down, grumbling,
"The Greenbaum grapevine strikes again."

"If anyone should be annoyed, it's me," Dottie said. "I'm your mother, and you don't tell me a thing! I have to hear it the next morning from Alice Albright. Really, Laura, to leave a party early because someone was unpleasant . . . I was very concerned, and so was Alice. Who spoke to you? What did he say?"

At least Art hadn't told Alice the whole story, or maybe Alice hadn't told Dottie. "It was nothing. You're making a mountain out of a molehill. If that's why you decided to come over—because you figured you'd get more out of me in person than on the phone—"

"You're my daughter. Don't I have the right to see you once in a while?" Dottie began to set the table. "If it's such a molehill, you won't mind telling me about the mole. What happened, Laura?"

The right to privacy was guaranteed by the California Constitution, but when it came to Laura, Dottie didn't recognize its existence. Her mother either nagged her into submission or gave her so much guilt that she wound up spilling her guts the way the Exxon *Valdez* had spilled oil. That left only one practical alternative: to lie.

"You know how I get when I'm expecting my period, Mom. I should have ignored the whole thing, but I was too PMS-y." In other words, she was still working on a plausible story.

"Less than two weeks ago, you told me you had cramps and felt lousy," Dottie replied. "If you're getting your period again so soon, you should go to Dr. Schwartz. It's nothing to fool around with."

"Okay, so I'm not. You're sixty-six, for God's sake. Didn't anyone ever tell you you're supposed to be losing your memory, not recalling every little thing I tell you?"

"I'm sorry, but I'm too busy right now to get senile. Maybe next week." Dottie sat down. "So, Laura? What happened at the party?"

"It was nothing. Really."

Dottie sighed. "How your father and I produced such an evasive child, I'll never know. We were always so open and aboveboard."

"Right. That's why you spoke Yiddish to each other when you didn't want me to understand something. Because you were so open and aboveboard."

"That was different. You were only a child. We didn't want to traumatize you."

"I happen to remember how you were with your *own* parents. You never told them a thing. You claimed you didn't want to worry them with every little problem."

"They were born in another country. In a different century. They didn't understand American life."

Laura stood up. "The oven is ready. I'll put in the food."

"Fine. Don't tell me. So what if I'm sick from worry? It's a mother's job. I'm used to it by now."

"All right, since you insist . . . " Laura uncovered the pans—there were brownies and an apple cake in addition to a carrot *tsimmes*, short ribs, and a *kugel*—and put in the dinner. "It was Freddie Phelps. He cornered me while Art was playing pool and accused me of stealing some money from his petty-cash box. He threatened to call the police or complain to my new boss. I told him one of the cleaning people must have taken it, but he wouldn't listen, he was too drunk. I was afraid he'd start yelling at me in public. That people would believe him and think I was a thief."

"Who would listen to a *plosher* like Phelps? Who would believe a man who drinks too much and pesters respectable women?"

Only most of the white, privileged men Freddie knew, but Laura didn't say so. Asking indignant questions was part of the Greenbaum style. They were invariably rhetorical.

"Nobody!" Dottie declared a moment later. "Only morons! You should have stood up to him, Laura. Stayed put. Running doesn't accomplish a thing. It only makes you look guilty."

"But the police chief was at the party. He and Freddie are fishing buddies. Freddie might have talked him into arresting me on the spot."

"Friends, shmends, the police chief isn't a dope. You think he wants to get himself sued for false arrest? You have to stand up for yourself, Laura. You can't let bums like Phelps push you around."

"I know that, Mom."

"You lie down on the floor like a carpet, and people are going to walk all over you. How many times have I told you that?"

About the same number of times she'd insisted that honey caught more flies than vinegar, but she'd bought the story about Freddie and that was all that mattered. "So what do you think? If he bothers me again, should I threaten to sue him for slander? Or should I just hang up on him?"

Dottie thought it over. "Why wait for a next time? I'll talk to my friend Ed Roseman, the lawyer. He'll send a letter to Freddie and warn him to leave you alone. It's always more impressive, coming from a lawyer. I'll get you a good rate."

"Thanks but I'd rather not rake things up again. Freddie was very drunk last night. He's probably forgotten the whole thing by now." Laura opened the cupboard. "You want a little sherry before dinner? I have a new bottle of Harvey's."

"Fine. Change the subject. You're making a big mistake about Freddie, but what do I know? I don't have a degree from a fancy college like some people. I never even went to business. I'm only an ignorant old lady who should have lost my mind by now, according to you."

Laura laughed. "Come off it, Mom. I never said you weren't smart about things like this, just that I need to handle it my own way. If Freddie threatens me again, I'll talk to Ed Roseman. I promise."

Dottie smiled and shrugged. "You're all grown up now. If you want to make mistakes, who am I to stop you? I'll have that sherry now, and we'll talk. Tell me, are you finally finished with Allan?"

Laura got out the sherry. It was going to be a long night.

Allan showed up at seven-thirty, by which time Dottie had set a record for the most pointed stares at a clock and conspicuous checks of a watch by an antagonistic mother-in-law during a thirty-minute period. Laura had been worried, too, but she'd tried not to show it. Her mother was already irritated because she'd refused to state unequivocally that Allan Louis Miller would be her ex-husband come the end of May. The last thing she wanted to do was throw fuel on a smoldering fire.

The kids ran in ahead of Allan and started chattering about whales and dolphins, which would have told her where they'd been even if their new Marine World sweatshirts hadn't. Dottie listened to them for ten minutes, then shooed them over to the brownies and turned to Allan. "You're looking well," she said coolly. "It's a good thing, I suppose. Children should have at least one healthy parent."

Dottie's attacks made Allan feel guilty and callow, unfairly so, he thought. Still, he'd learned not to argue. She was the verbal equivalent of Ali in his prime. Try to defeat her with facts and logic, and she dodged, hedged, or bluffed her way back on the offensive.

He smiled weakly, looking a little like an abused dog eyeing a stick in its master's hand. "Thanks, Dottie.

You're looking well yourself. And thanks for the furniture. Everything fit very well."

"I got your note. You don't have to thank me again. You have very nice manners, though. At least you didn't forget *everything* your mother taught you, like promptness. You're very late. Laura was worried sick."

Allan glanced at Laura, obviously hoping for some support. She didn't provide it. The fact was, there was no shortage of phones between Vallejo and Sacramento.

"I'm sorry about that," he said after a moment. "We stopped at The Nut Tree for dinner. The kids wanted to look in the toy store afterward. By the time I realized how late it was, we were already back in the car."

"Of course. You're a busy man. You had too much on your mind to remember to make a phone call." Dottie smiled at him. "All the same, it's very impressive, the way you handled those teachers. Your mother must be very proud."

Allan looked warier than ever, a sort of conditioned response. When it came to Dottie and him, compliment was a synonym for setup. "Uh, actually, I haven't told her about it yet. I was going to call her tomorrow morning. She's doing very well, though. She'll be going up north for the summer in a few weeks."

"Just like every year, but in my opinion she's not doing so well at all. Only yesterday, she told me her arthritis was acting up. She was pleased about your success, though. Naturally, I gave her the details. You're her only child, Allan. You should call her more often. Talk her into visiting you. She misses Seth and Sarah."

Laura finally took pity on him. There was a limit to what a man should have to endure, and being attacked by Ned Brown and Dottie Greenbaum within the space of a single week surpassed it. Besides, the kids were paying an unhealthy amount of attention to the conversation.

"Allan's always asking her to come to Sacramento,"

she said. "He's a good son, just like he's a good father. It's just, she has such a busy life that it's hard for her to find the time." She walked to the counter. "How about some dessert and coffee, Allan? Mom brought some of that apple cake you like so much."

He shook his head. "Thanks, but I need to get going. Walk me to the car, okay?"

"Sure." She went into the hall for her coat while Allan said good-bye to the kids. Her defense of him would have seemed pretty hollow if she'd refused to spend even a few minutes alone with him.

He was carrying a small foil package when he walked out of the kitchen. "I'll never figure your mother out," he said as they went outside. "One minute she beats the shit out of me and the next she wants to feed me. She insisted I should take home some cake."

"She thinks you're a bad husband, but that doesn't mean she considers you a bad person." Laura hesitated, then blurted, "She'll probably be very nice to you once we're actually divorced."

Adrenaline surged through her at the sound of her own words—fight-rather-than-flight words, get-him-before-he-gets-you words. She didn't know why she'd said them, or even if she'd really meant them, only that the need to move—somewhere, anywhere—had suddenly been overpowering. All she ever did was react. It was making her crazy.

"Once we're divorced," he repeated slowly. "When did you decide that? Tonight? Did your mother just talk you into it?"

"She tried. I refused to let her pin me down." Laura leaned against Allan's car and stared into the front yard. Maybe it was having her life threatened. Being confronted with her own mortality. It made her want to grab for as much as she could. "I went out with someone I liked Saturday night. Art Albright. You've met him at the club. I'm seeing him again on Wednesday. I don't know what will come of it, only that I need to find out what else is out there. What else my life can be. I don't want to commit myself to staying in our marriage or even to working on our relationship. Not right now. The feelings just aren't there."

"I don't believe that." If she'd fazed him even a little, it didn't show. "You're thinking about the past few years, not the ten years before that. We had a good marriage, Laurie. A good life together."

"In some ways, but they're not enough anymore. Besides, there are some things you don't know about. Some things I haven't told you."

"What things? What are you talking about?"

"It's nothing to do with our marriage. Just—some career problems I've been preoccupied with. I need to stop thinking and planning and worrying, and just live for a change."

"I won't argue with that one. You should have done it a long time ago. But I have the right to wait for you if I want to, and I do. Counseling would help us find out what we want. So would seeing each other a few times a week."

It was a reasonable suggestion, but the idea put such a large knot in the pit of her stomach that she checked the urge to say yes. Allan wasn't Gummie or Sam. He would take time and emotional energy. The bottom line was, she didn't want to give him either right now.

"Maybe, but I feel like I need a break from all that." She forced herself to smile. "A little benign neglect between the two of us couldn't hurt, you know?"

"I disagree. We're not going to learn anything new by staying apart." He put his hand on her shoulder. She resented the sense of ownership the gesture implied. "I love you, Laurie. I'm not going to give up on us. I'm not going to walk out of your life."

She wanted to leave, to escape both him and the whole subject, but he would have followed her and kept arguing. She closed her eyes for a moment. After last night, she didn't have the strength for a confrontation.

"I'll be getting the kids early all week," she finally said. "Around two-thirty. What time do you want to come for them on Wednesday?"

"I'm shooting for five-thirty. I thought I'd take them to dinner and a movie. You want to come along?"

"I can't. I told you, I'm having dinner with Art Albright."

"Oh. Right. The capitalists' tool. He's not your type, Laurie."

"I'll tell him you said so, Allan."

He smiled. "*I'm* your type, but I guess I'll have to let you find that out." He pecked her on the cheek. "Good night, honey. See you Wednesday." He got into the car, and she walked slowly back to the house.

Marine World had exhausted the kids more than they wanted to admit. Laura read them a story, got them bathed and into their pajamas, and shepherded them into the kitchen to say good night to her mother. The room was spotless by then, even the floor, which was still damp from the mopping Dottie had given it.

Laura thanked her and hugged her, gently at first, then harder. Her mother hugged her back, stroking her hair the way she had when Laura was a child. This wasn't about cooking or cleaning, and both of them knew it.

The kids begged Dottie to play cards with them—anything to delay bedtime—and she agreed, taking them into Sarah's room while Laura went into the family room with the Sunday paper. An article about global warming put her to sleep in less than three paragraphs. When she woke an hour later, the lights were out, the house was quiet, and she was covered by the throw from her bedroom.

She tried to go back to sleep, but couldn't. Lying there and doing nothing became a torment all its own. She tossed aside the blanket and went into the kitchen. There was a note on the counter from her mother saying she'd left the extra food in the fridge and would call the next evening to see how Laura's first day on the job had gone.

But it wasn't her job that had her worried. It was what she would do afterward. Walk to her car at two o'clock and drive directly to Mrs. Fujimoto's? Or go to Cottage Way first, and talk to the FBI?

She returned to the family room and turned on the TV, flicking restlessly from channel to channel. *Topper*, which she'd loved as a teenager but hadn't seen since, was playing on American Movie Classics. Between watching TV and finishing the paper, she slowly settled down.

She turned on the news when the movie ended, listening with half an ear while she worked a crossword puzzle. It was the usual parade of disasters, politicking, and heartbreak—flooding in the Midwest, mudslinging in California, a child in critical need of a transplant in nearby Lodi. . . .

"And up at South Lake Tahoe," the anchor was saying, "the body of entertainer Bonita Franks was discovered just a few hours ago by a co-worker who became alarmed when Miss Franks failed to come to work earlier this evening and decided to check up on her."

Laura looked at the screen, the blood draining from her face. "Miss Franks, who sang at the Monte Carlo Hotel, was a favorite at the lake for her interpretations of Hollywood and Broadway hits. According to police, her body was found in the hallway of her Heavenly Valley-area house. There were bullet wounds in her head and chest, apparently made by a .38-caliber revolver that was found beside her body. Nothing valuable appeared to have been taken and there was no sign of a struggle or forced entry. At this point, police believe she was murdered by someone she knew—someone she invited into her home." The anchor turned to her colleague. "I saw her just a few weeks ago, Ted. She was a wonderful singer. She'll be missed."

Laura's stomach began to heave. As the newscast cut to a commercial, she ran into the kitchen and headed for the sink. She was crying and retching at the same time, her emotions a seething mass of shock, grief, and horror.

Whoever had come for Bonita could come for her next. He had to be stopped.

EIGHTEEN

The FBI office was easy to find, just down the hall from the main entrance into the federal building, but Laura almost wished it had been tucked away in some obscure back corner. She'd had a hectic day at work, running errands, working at the computer, and taking phone calls, too many of which she'd misdirected or disconnected because she was busy picturing herself dead and dismembered. She hadn't gotten out till three-thirty, and then an accident on Business 80 had delayed her even more. A long hike through the sprawling, mazelike halls here would have given her time to calm down, not to mention delaying a conversation that scared her senseless. Unfortunately, Cassani, Clemente, and Tomlinson scared her even more. She wanted this over and done with.

She opened the door. The reception room was standard government issue, small, bland, and comfortingly nondescript except for one feature: The left half of the room, the area containing the inevitable bureaucratic counter, was protected by what she assumed was bulletproof glass. There were no windows in the room, and only one interior door was accessible to the public. It was closed now, and, given the other security precautions here, probably locked. The only visible employee, a woman, was speaking on the phone. She noticed Laura come in but didn't acknowledge her.

Laura walked over to her. The violent pounding in her chest and the swollen sensation in her throat made it hard even to breathe, much less speak. The woman hung up, smiled, and asked if she could help. The smile made it easier to answer.

"I have information about the Hollister murder," Laura said. "I'd like to talk to someone about it."

She might have asked where the ladies' room was for all the reaction she got. "Why don't you have a seat? Someone will be out in a minute." The receptionist picked up the phone.

A middle-aged man with thinning hair opened the door a minute later and gave her an easy smile. He was wearing a plaid shirt, brown pants, and reptilian cowboy boots. He was so far from the lockjawed, somber-suited types she'd seen in Freddie's office that she wondered if he was even an agent.

"I'm Clint Osman." He spoke with a Western twang. "You wanted to talk to someone about Judge Hollister?"

Laura swallowed hard. At least he was friendly. "Yes. I'm sorry it's so late in the day. I'll try to be as quick as I can."

"No problem. We work a lot of overtime around here. Come on inside."

She followed him into a short hallway. There wasn't much to see, just closed doors to the right and left and an open one straight ahead. He led her into the room beyond and closed the door. There were no windows and not much furniture, only a large table and a dozen or so chairs. A phone and a clipboard holding a yellow legal pad sat on the table.

They sat down, Laura at the end of the table and Osman diagonally across from her. He picked up the clipboard and took out a pen. "Relax and take your time. We can stay here as long as we want."

"Okay. Thanks." She took a deep breath. "My name is Laura Miller. I used to work for Freddie Phelps, as his secretary. He was Judge Hollister's insurance agent."

Osman put the clipboard back on the table. He hadn't written a word yet, not even her name. "Would you excuse me for a minute, Ms. Miller?"

"Yes, of course."

He smiled and stood up. "I'll be right back."

Laura stayed in her chair. She didn't want to be caught nosing around. Maybe it was this spare, claustrophobic room, but she felt like a criminal. God knew she'd rehearsed her story like one.

Osman returned within minutes, walking in behind a man who fit the tough G-man stereotype perfectly. "This is Special Agent McKennery," Osman said. "He's going to sit in on our conversation."

He was also the boss, the Special Agent in Charge. He nodded at her and took a seat halfway down the table. He seemed so cool and unapproachable that she directed her response to Osman. "I know who Mr. McKennery is. I saw him on TV after the leak about Royal Paine."

Osman sat down and picked up his clipboard. "You've got a good memory. That's a good sign. We've got everyone from the media to the politicians breathing down our necks on this one, and we've been making about as much progress lately as a bunch of snails. I hope you'll be able to help us."

"Then you've been working on this case since the murder? Personally, I mean?"

"If you're asking whether I'll be able to follow whatever you tell me, the answer is yes. You were saying you were Mr. Phelps's secretary."

He hadn't answered her question, but at least he was pleasant, which was more than she could say for McKennery. The guy looked like he was sucking aspirins.

"That's right. I work for Ken Carlsen now, the state senator. I think you already know that Hollister's widow wasn't the only one who had a policy on his life. That Bonita Franks did, too." Laura paled a little. "She's the singer who was murdered yesterday at the lake. The gun they found . . . Could it be the same one that was used to kill Hollister?"

Osman shrugged. "Maybe, maybe not. Either way, we'll find out. Go on, ma'am."

"Yes. All right. Bonita—she wasn't really Hollister's business partner, just his mistress, but I guess you know that too, right?"

"Now, don't you worry about what we know and what we don't," Osman said, oozing folksy reassurance. "Just tell us your story. Believe me, it'll be more helpful to us that way. More complete."

Laura nodded, thinking that something was going on here besides a routine interview. McKennery wouldn't have come in otherwise. "Okay. I did wonder, though . . . Your agents came by Phelps's office twice, but they never spoke to me. Why not?"

Osman laughed. "Listen, Ms. Miller, if we screwed up on that one, I'd just as soon you didn't say so in front of the boss. Tell us about Bonita Franks and her policy."

"You mean you overlooked me then, but I'm important enough now for Mr. McKennery to be here? For you to have gone to his office to get him when you realized who I was?"

Osman glanced at McKennery, then shrugged good-naturedly. "We would have gotten to you before too long."

"So what happened between then and now?"

"I can't answer that."

"Can't or won't?"

McKennery handled the question. "Won't. This is a sensitive investigation, Ms. Miller. The details are confidential. If you have information to impart, we'd be glad to listen, but we're not going to satisfy your curiosity about our motives, our theories, or our actions. You were talking about Bonita Franks. Please go on."

She might have gotten something out of Osman eventually, but McKennery was pure flint. She hesitated, intimidated by his presence. She'd assumed she'd be talking into a vacuum, to some colorless, poker-faced agent who barely knew who she was.

She'd been wrong. They knew, all right, and the implications of that unnerved her. Maybe they thought she was mixed up in this. After all, they'd seen her with Bonita at the funeral. She'd worked for Freddie Phelps, a possible suspect. Still, if they thought she was involved, why hadn't they questioned her at Freddie's?

"Look, whatever I've found out, it was accidental," she said. "People just—told me things. Or made slips when I was around. Okay?"

Osman looked at McKennery again. "I never should have let you in here, Kevin. You're spooking the lady. Why don't you take a walk around the block?"

McKennery lazed back in his chair. "You can be transferred very easily, Clint. To someplace very cold, very remote, and very boring. Go on, Ms. Miller."

If he was joking, he had the most deadpan delivery she'd ever heard, but Osman simply laughed. "Don't worry, ma'am, his bark's worse than his bite. Just take it slow and stick to the facts. We'll try not to interrupt you."

Skip the questions and bullshit, Laura silently translated, and we'll get along fine. "Maybe I should start with the funeral," she said, and explained how she'd

come to attend. She described her relationship with
Freddie next, then told Osman about meeting Mike
Clemente in the church parking lot. Finally, she
explained how she'd wound up sitting with Bonita at
the funeral and agreeing to pick up some things she'd
left in an apartment near the capitol.

Her account of the two weeks that had followed was
accurate insofar as it went, which was about halfway to
the full truth. She was on shaky ground here, her actions
ranging from the unethical to the prosecutable. It was
one thing to tell the Feds that Freddie had babbled about
insurance scams when he was drunk, another to admit
that she knew the details of his deal with Bonita and had
even phoned Bonita to offer advice on handling a possible interrogation. It was one thing to have looked
around the apartment on N Street, to have checked
inside a portfolio, fiddled with an answering machine
and sorted through some sex toys, and even to have listened to a tape that in retrospect might well be important
evidence, and another to admit to swiping the original of
that tape and substituting a copy. With Bonita dead, the
cops would find the copy. Let them listen to *that*. She
didn't mention her fantasies about revenge against
Freddie, either; employees weren't supposed to copy keys
and open locked drawers. And since people with any loyalty or integrity didn't incriminate their friends, she
deliberately gave the impression that she'd been alone
both in the N Street apartment and up at the lake.

McKennery never said a word, just watched her as if
he could see straight through her. Although Osman was
more responsive, making comments of the I-see and
What-did-you-do-next? variety, his main concern
seemed to be taking a voluminous quantity of notes. All
in all, it was one of the less pleasant experiences of
Laura's life, right up there with childbirth and having
her husband walk out on her.

"How are you doing?" Osman asked afterward. "Are you okay?"

She nodded. "Yes. I'm just scared."

"That's understandable. Clemente threatened you and you don't know why. Seeley was interested in you and you don't know why. Now Bonita Franks is dead, and you think there's a connection between her murder and Hollister's. You think you could be next. If I were you, I'd be scared, too. I'd like to ask you some questions. See if we can make some sense of all this."

Laura glanced at McKennery. He was making some notes, writing with quick, hard strokes that were audible above Osman's voice. "Okay, but I need to call my babysitter first—to tell her I'll be later than I expected."

Osman handed her the phone. It was just past five; she allowed herself another hour here and said she'd be back by six-thirty. Then she wished she'd said six, because another hour of this and she'd be flirting with a nervous breakdown.

"Let's start with Phelps," Osman said as she put the phone back on the table. "He told you Hollister was blackmailing him, but he didn't give you details. You think Hollister had an expensive gambling habit. Phelps admitted to running insurance scams, either to pay off Hollister or to support an extravagant lifestyle, but again, he didn't provide details. You mentioned that you kept track of his important clients. That you answered his personal correspondence. Did you come across anything odd in the course of your work? Anything suspicious?"

He'd begun with the most dangerous area of all, one she'd tried her best to gloss over. "No. Not really," she said.

"How about the policy held by Bonita Franks? Was there anything unusual about it?"

He already knew the answer, damn him. He was about as friendly and folksy as a cobra. "There was one thing. Last January I reminded Freddie that the premium was overdue. He wrote out a personal check for it. He said Bonita had given him the cash for it over Christmas, when he saw her at the lake. I thought that was strange."

"Oh? Why?"

"Because nothing like that had ever happened before."

"Why would he lie about Bonita giving him cash?"

"I don't know."

"But you've got your suspicions. Tell me about them."

She hesitated, then decided she'd only be confirming what he already suspected. "He could have paid part of the premium and shared in the profits. Bonita felt the judge was in danger. She could have mentioned it to Freddie at some point. Maybe they made a deal. But I have no evidence of that. I don't want to make charges I can't back up."

"You're speculating, not accusing," Osman said with a smile. "I do understand the difference, ma'am. Let's move on. You suspected the apartment on N Street was Tomlinson's, and Carolyn Seeley confirmed that. Visualize the bedroom. A videotaping system can be almost as small as a standard videocassette. Was there anything that could conceal one? A mirror, a wall vent, even a hutch or bookcase?"

So they were interested in Tomlinson. She'd mentioned he'd probably used the apartment to curry favor in the legislature, but that was all. Did they think he'd used it for something more, like eavesdropping and extortion?

"The vent was in the floor," she replied. "The only mirror was the one on the dressing table, resting in a wooden stand. There were two dressers in the room, but they were mostly empty."

"Was there a lighting fixture in the ceiling?"

"Yes. A brass chandelier. There could have been a camera above that." A camera that had recorded her searching the bedroom. Except that if it had, it would have picked up Vicki as well, and nobody had questioned or threatened *her*. Or had they? Carolyn had specifically asked about Vicki only two days before.

"You've told me about everything you saw in the apartment," Osman said. "There's nothing else you can think of."

"No." It was the truth.

"And you have no idea what you might know or have seen that would cause Seeley and Clemente to question you."

"No."

"Let's talk about that. You think Seeley was fishing for information and that Clemente wanted to scare you off. You think he was involved in Hollister's death, or that a client he wants to protect was. Tomlinson, perhaps."

Laura nodded. "Yes. And the way he kept mentioning Cassani . . . Maybe it was just to frighten me, but the two of them—they *connected* the night they met. You could tell. I think Cassani's involved in this, too."

"Involved how? Speculate. Give me a scenario."

"I can't, except that they're tied together by the casino. Tomlinson owns it and Cassani is probably a silent partner. Seeley polishes up their public image and Clemente fixes things with the politicians and runs whatever errands they tell him to. Hollister probably gambled there. Maybe he saw something he shouldn't have, demanded hush money, and got killed for it."

"You say you saw Clemente at Bonita Franks's house while you were up at the lake. He was angry you'd spotted him. Do you have any idea why?"

It put her on edge, this habit Osman had of jumping from subject to subject with no outward reaction to what she'd said. "No, except . . . Bonita is dead now. Maybe they were closer than he claimed. He wouldn't want that to come out, not if he knew she was about to be killed." Especially if he'd been the one with the gun, she thought.

Osman looked at McKennery, who walked to the door and leaned against it. Laura felt trapped, as if a vital escape route had been blocked off. "Let's talk about Arthur Albright and his parents," McKennery said. "Whatever contact you've had with any of them, whatever conversations you've had, I'd like to hear about them."

The question came out of left field. She'd mentioned Art only once, saying he was a friend and former neighbor of Charlie Hollister's who'd gotten her number from her mother and invited her to Charlie's party Saturday night. As for his parents, they'd never come up at all.

"But why?" she asked. "Do you think they're involved in this in some way?"

Osman laughed. "He's not going to answer you, ma'am. You should know that by now."

Maybe not, but unless he did, she wasn't going to tell them about Art's business problems or repeat things her mother had told her about Alice. Her friends' personal lives were none of their business. Art Sr. was dead, though, so there was no harm in talking about him, and no reason not to mention facts that were public knowledge.

"Art Albright, Sr. drowned last August while he was deep-sea fishing," she began. "He was a friend and client of Freddie Phelps's. His widow moved to Pollock Pines a few months later. Freddie once said something about Hollister blackmailing Albright, but I have no idea what Hollister might have had on him. Art Jr. told me his father was anxious and erratic before his death, and maybe that was why—because he was being black-mailed. Art owns his father's investment company now. He was a financial planner in San Francisco before that. He bought the firm last July, about a month before his father's death."

A mysterious death. A questionable death. Laura stared at the table, thinking it might have been a prof-itable one, as well. "Art Sr.'s body was never recov-ered," she continued after a stunned couple of seconds. "Freddie had to push a little to get Alice—his widow—her insurance money, but Columbia did pay the claim eventually. Freddie wound up with Art Sr.'s boat. He told me he'd bought it from Alice, but maybe it was actually a payoff. The death could have been a suicide that the policy didn't cover." And Alice or Art could have been involved. She should have kept her mouth shut. "Still, that's just conjecture. Art Jr. wasn't on board that day, but he told me that all the witnesses felt it was an accident. And maybe suicide was covered by the policy. I've never read it, so I don't know."

McKennery nodded. "I see. Go on, Ms. Miller."

"That's it. There's nothing more to tell."

"How well do you know Alice Albright?"

"Not well at all. I met her a few times at the Phelpses, and I wrote notes to her now and then for Freddie."

"How did she react to her husband's death?"

"Other than by moving, I have no idea."

"Did she refer to him in her letters to Phelps? Mention missing him?"

"Not that I can recall. The letters were impersonal, even cool. She never discussed her feelings. She wrote about her problems with her house and her various jobs. She's gone from bookkeeping to banking to sales, then back the other way. Nothing seems to satisfy her."

"She was Freddie's friend, then? Not his wife's?"

Laura resented McKennery's clipped, almost adversarial tone, but she tried to be responsive. He wasn't someone she wanted to offend. "More his wife's, I think. At the funeral, Freddie mentioned that he found her at his house whenever she was in town, talking to his wife Mary Beth. I got the impression that she and Alice were fairly close."

"And Art Jr.? How did he react to losing his father?"

Laura wasn't about to mention that Art and his father had fought about most everything. "I've only gone out with him once, Mr. McKennery. It didn't come up."

McKennery smiled. "So they didn't get along, hmm?"

She flushed. "I told you, Art wasn't even on the boat. I don't see what this has to do with Hollister's murder—"

"Nothing, probably," Osman said smoothly. "Just take it easy, Ms. Miller. Nobody's attacking you. We're just trying to be thorough." He looked at McKennery, a long, questioning stare.

Silence filled the room. The tension went straight to Laura's stomach. Finally McKennery said, "Special Agent Osman seems to think we should put your mind at ease. I can tell you this much—we have questions about Albright's death. If it makes you feel any better, you haven't told us anything we didn't already know." He paused, then added in a conversational tone, "You know, Ms. Miller, it's no great secret that there are certain kinds of people the Bureau tries to keep an eye on. People like Joseph Cassani, for example. Somewhere in my files, there's a routine report that includes an evening he spent in the Alpine Room a few weeks ago.

He went there with a female companion and spoke to a lot of different people. Bonita Franks, Mike Clemente, two women who were dining with Clemente that night . . . One of those women was obviously you. Who was the other? And why didn't you mention that she was present?"

Laura was rigid with dislike by then. The man was a bastard, bullying her when he wasn't trying to trap her. Offer him some information, ask for a little help, and he treated you like a graduate of the FBI's Ten-Most-Wanted list. "Because she was keeping me company that weekend, and that's all she was doing. You don't need to know about her. She's not involved in this. Just leave her out of it."

"You said you were staying in a friend's vacation home. Was she that friend?"

McKennery stared at her, waiting for her to answer, but she didn't say a word. Coming here had been a mistake. It had gotten her in deeper than ever, maybe even partway to an indictment. She wasn't about to take Vicki along with her.

McKennery walked closer. "You associate with some very questionable people, Ms. Miller. You say it's a coincidence that you know them, that you're an innocent citizen who's stumbled into something dangerous, but you haven't convinced me that either of those things is true. Maybe they're your former friends. Maybe you had a falling-out. Maybe you have good reason to be afraid of them now. The fact is, you haven't been straight with me. You haven't given me a single reason to believe you or try to protect you. If you want my help, you'll leave the evasions and omissions at home next time and tell me what I want to know. Clint, finish up in here." McKennery left the room, closing the door so forcefully that Laura flinched.

Osman sighed heavily. "Sorry about that. I'm afraid

that patience isn't Kevin's strong suit. He's under a lot of pressure from Washington on this case, and it's made him even more ornery than usual." He slid his clipboard onto the table. "You're a sharp lady, Ms. Miller, so I'm sure you realize that this is a lot more complicated than a simple murder case. But remember, we have pieces of the puzzle that you don't. If we hear something important, we'll recognize it. But first we have to hear it, and we haven't, not from you. Personally, I understand your loyalty to your friends. If it were up to me, I'd do whatever I could to ensure your safety. But McKennery's the boss here, and he doesn't trust you. If you want him on your side, you'll have to tell us what you know."

Good cop, bad cop, Laura thought. If they could, they'd manipulate her into talking and then arrest her without a qualm. "I already have. There isn't anything else."

"And if you're threatened again? Will your memory suddenly improve? I'd stop playing games if I were you, because this particular league is too damn dangerous for amateurs."

"I know. That's why I came here. I thought you guys were the umpires." She got up. "Obviously I was wrong. You're more like security goons."

He winced, then grabbed his clipboard and stood up. "Vicki Stonehouse," he said evenly.

Laura stiffened. "What?"

"Your friend with the place at the lake. Our agent recognized her. Hell, she's been leading protests since she was in college, including a few against the Bureau, so he damn well should have."

"You have a file on her?"

He smiled. "If we did, it's probably been tossed into a shredder by now. The Evil Empire is history, Ms. Miller. We don't waste our time on liberal Girl Scouts like Mrs. Stonehouse anymore."

"You might have told me that before. You deliberately gave me the impression that naming her could get her pulled in for questioning."

"McKennery did, not me, and we don't volunteer information. Remember?"

"You just did."

"Sometimes you have to give a little to get a little. I'd like to tell you more, but I've gone as far as I can. Nobody's out to nail you. We'd just like to know whatever *you* know. Think it over, Ms. Miller, and if your memory suddenly gets better, drop by the office or give me a call."

Laura agreed, but nothing short of additional threats would get her back in this room. You couldn't believe a word these people said. The only way you could trust them was if you had a lawyer along to protect your legal rights.

Still, the interview hadn't been a total waste of her time. She'd learned that the Bureau was interested in Cassani, Clemente, and Tomlinson—that they were probably keeping an eye on all three. That was scant reassurance when people kept dying, but it was better than nothing.

NINETEEN

Seth and Sarah were full of complaints when Laura picked them up. She'd promised to come early, they said, then showed up later than ever. They'd been bored to death, doing nothing all day at Mrs. Fujimoto's. It wasn't fair, and where had she been all this time, anyway?

She mumbled something about problems in the office, then drove to the bank to straighten out the mistake in her account. But when she checked her balance on the ATM before going inside, it was exactly what it should have been. When ten grand was at stake, banks apparently caught and corrected their errors without your help. Procrastination had its benefits.

The kids were more restless than ever, so she swung by the drive-up window at Burger King and let them order whatever they wanted. Her attempt to placate them with fast food didn't work. They grumbled all through dinner, wanting to know if the rest of their vacation was going to be this bad.

She was out of sympathy and strength by then, so caught up in anxiety and fatigue that their complaints barely registered. They finally realized something was wrong when Seth said their vacation totally sucked—a forbidden use of the verb—and she didn't react. They didn't say a word after that, just went into the family room and watched TV. They knew by now that if they pushed her over the edge, she would either send them to their rooms or withdraw completely. They hated both.

She poured herself a glass of wine, then sat down with the phone. Vicki had called the day before to ask about the party, but Laura had put her off, saying she didn't have time to talk. She would have to level with her now, at least to some extent, in order to find out if anyone had threatened her.

"I went to the FBI today," she began. "Bonita's death was a big part of the reason, but there was something else, too. I wish I could tell you about it, but—"

"Something that happened at the party? Is that why you got rid of me so fast yesterday? Because you were upset and knew I'd ask why?"

There was no point denying it. "Yes. I'll explain as much as I can, but first I need you to answer some questions. Has anyone asked you about Hollister's murder? Questioned you about anyone or anything even remotely connected to it?"

"No, not unless you count Frank and the kids," Vicki said, sounding puzzled. "They thought Bonita killed him for the insurance money, but it looks like they were wrong. Why? Did someone question *you*? Someone at the party?"

"Yes, but never mind who. You're better off not knowing. If you knew what I know, it could land you in the same sort of trouble I'm in, and I'd never forgive myself."

"Jesus. You mean real trouble, don't you? Not just potential trouble, the way it was before." Vicki paused. "Who was it, Laura? Someone I've met? Did he threaten you in some way? Warn you off?"

Laura massaged her temples. "Vicki, please. For your own safety, just drop the subject."

Vicki sighed, a long, dramatic expression of disapproval. "Okay. You win—for now. So how did things go at the FBI? Did they believe you? Did you find out anything about the direction of their investigation?"

"I wasn't going to sit there and incriminate myself, so there were things I didn't tell them. They're sharp. They know when they're being stonewalled. They listened, fired questions at me like I was Lee Harvey Oswald, and then gave me hell for holding out on them. The boss there—McKennery—all he cares about is clearing the case. He's not going to help me unless I spill my guts, and maybe not even then. He thinks I'm one of the bad guys."

"So go back there with a lawyer," Vicki said. "Tell them you'll talk if they give you immunity and some physical protection."

Lawyer or no lawyer, the idea of returning to the Bureau wasn't any more appealing now than it had been that afternoon. To sit in that awful room again, to be doubted and lectured and interrogated . . . There was no way, not unless great bodily harm loomed on the horizon.

Laura's desk at work was in the front reception room, wedged in along with a coffee table and a pair of chairs for visitors, a bookcase and file cabinet, both crammed full, and a desk belonging to Sandy Donnelly, the woman who'd formerly held Laura's job and was now Carlsen's receptionist and scheduling secretary. The room was busy and somewhat noisy, even with the legislature out of session, but Laura liked it that way. She enjoyed being in the thick of things, watching people come and go and listening to the small talk they made with Sandy.

Sandy was training her as they went along, so that she never learned how to do anything till she was smack in the middle of it, and, as a result, had felt lost through most of Monday. Sandy hadn't left at all that day; she'd been too busy correcting the mistakes Laura had made. But halfway through Tuesday, when Laura hadn't sabotaged any phone calls or disabled any office machines, Sandy decided it was safe to go out. There was a baby shower on Friday for one of the secretaries, and Jack Waltzer, Carlsen's chief of staff, had asked her to help him pick out a present.

Laura told them to take their time. With Carlsen out of the office, she said, there was nothing she couldn't handle. And then, as she was eating lunch at her desk, Mike Clemente walked in, and she wasn't so sure. If was here on business, she could survive a brief conversation, but if it was personal . . . She didn't want to think about that.

He strolled to her desk. "What have you got there? Ah, chicken salad on an onion roll." He picked up the untouched half of her sandwich and took a large bite. "This is good. Homemade, right?"

She stared at him in disbelief, her heart pounding like a pile driver. Only a few days before, he'd threatened to have Joey the Bowie Cassani engrave postmodern doodles on her body. Was she supposed to forget the things he'd said? To act as if he were just another lobbyist?

She ignored his question about the sandwich. "What can I do for you, Mr. Clemente?"

"Nothing, Ms. Miller, except give me half your sandwich. I didn't have a chance to eat."

"Sure. Take it." One look at him and she'd lost her appetite.

"Thanks." He took another bite, then glanced at Carlsen's door. It was slightly ajar. "The senator's not here yet?"

Yet. As if he had an appointment. He couldn't have, though, because Carlsen was in Berkeley. "He's campaigning this week. He'll be back on Monday."

"Obviously he didn't mention he was coming in to see me. He was shooting for one o'clock. Probably got stuck in traffic." Clemente finished her sandwich, then peered into her lunch bag. "Got any dessert in there?"

He'd be asking her to fetch him a cup of coffee next. "Yes. Some apple cake. You can have that, too, if you want." She certainly didn't, not anymore.

He thanked her and fished it out of the bag. The fact that she was afraid of him didn't stop her from wondering why he was here—or being protective of her new boss. How had he gotten Ken to come in today? By making an urgent appeal . . . or by exerting heavy pressure? And if it was pressure, what had made Ken vulnerable to it?

She screwed up her courage, then murmured, "The senator seems to have changed his plans in order to accommodate you. Why all the hurry? Nothing's going on here this week."

"That's what makes it such a good time to see him." Clemente smiled, a chilling, almost feral sort of look. Laura reddened and shrank back in her seat. "Tell your friend Vicki that Carlsen's more pragmatic than she thought. We're meeting about AB 2962."

"You mean the betting bill? *That's* why he's coming in to see you?"

Clemente unwrapped the apple cake and took a bite. "Don't be so surprised. Politics and budget shortfalls make strange bedfellows."

But not this strange. Not to the point where an ethical man like Carlsen threw his principles out the window. If Clemente and his pals could get to Ken, they could get to anyone.

The phone rang, and, relieved by the interruption,

Laura turned to answer it. "If you say so, Mr. Clemente. If you'll excuse me, I have to get back to work."

He watched her while she talked to a constituent who was having problems with the secretary of state's office. She transferred him to one of Carlsen's administrative assistants, then picked up a letter from the stack of mail she'd been working on.

Clemente leaned across her desk. His face was so close that her forehead began to tingle. "I hear you were up at the federal building yesterday," he said softly.

The envelope fell to her desk, the letter still inside. She didn't even look up, much less answer. Had someone put a tail on her? Had she been followed to the FBI?

Clemente put his hand on her shoulder. She wanted to retch. "What were you doing there, Laura?"

Apparently he didn't know. Maybe she'd been spotted by a crony of his, someone who'd gone to Cottage Way to lobby a federal agency—a case of pure but horrifying coincidence. So far as she knew, there was nothing to connect her presence there with the FBI. There hadn't been anyone in the hallway either when she'd gone in or when she'd come out.

"I was shopping at Nordstrom," she said. "I offered to pick up some material for one of the AA's while I was out there—from the U.S.G.S." The Geological Survey was the first agency that came to mind. "In, uh, in connection with a bill in Agriculture and Water Resources."

"Oh? Which bill is that?"

"It hasn't been introduced yet. It's something about building a dam."

"That doesn't sound familiar. What dam? Where?"

He was doing it again, grilling her into a state of abject terror, but this time, she wasn't cornered in some stranger's laundry room. She looked up, her hand moving to the panic button under her desk. "I have no idea, Mr. Clemente. If you don't leave me alone, I'll get the state police up here and have them throw you out."

He straightened. "If I've made you uncomfortable, I'm sorry. I didn't mean to. I was just curious."

But it was more than curiosity, and both of them knew it. Intimidation was a way of life to Mike Clemente. Show any weakness and he went straight for your throat.

She picked up the envelope and took out the letter. He stood and watched for a moment, then sat down.

Carlsen arrived a few minutes later. He addressed Clemente as Mike and shook his hand, but his manner was cool, almost curt. It was obvious that he didn't want to be here, but whether the reason was his heavy schedule or his distaste for AB 2962, Laura couldn't tell.

Then he noticed her at her desk, and smiled. "Laura, how are you doing? Ready to check into the psych ward yet?"

"It's not *that* bad. I'm getting the hang of things. Can I get you anything? Some coffee or something to eat?"

"No, thanks. I'll grab a Coke." He kept them in a refrigerator by his desk. "No calls except from the A list. Sandy gave you a copy, right?"

Laura nodded, pulling it out of her drawer as Carlsen led Clemente into his office. The phone rang, some reporter for Jack Waltzer. She took a message, then stared blankly into space, brooding about what to do.

Whom Carlsen met and what bills he supported were none of her business, but the situation stank of coercion or at least influence peddling clear to the top of the rotunda. She couldn't just ignore that. Still, she was brand new here. It wasn't her place to approach Carlsen directly.

She was thinking about speaking to Vicki or even Heather Martin when Waltzer came back with Sandy. He was perfect, she suddenly realized, easy to talk to and closer to Carlsen than anyone else in the office.

She picked up his messages and walked over to him. "The boss is here, meeting with Mike Clemente. I wondered—"

"You mean they're in his office?" Waltzer glanced at Carlsen's closed door. "He's not in Berkeley?"

"No. They've been in there for about fifteen minutes. I thought you'd want to know—they're talking about AB 2962. The off-track betting bill."

He frowned. "What makes you think that?"

"Clemente told me they were. He knows I'm interested in the bill. Vicki Stonehouse and I ran into him a few weeks ago and they got into a huge argument about it."

Waltzer shook his head. "He must have been kidding you, Laura. Pulling your chain a bit. I've handled that issue for years."

"I know. Vicki mentioned that. That's why I thought I should pass on what Clemente said." That was it—she couldn't push any harder or go over Waltzer's head.

Waltzer thanked her, took his messages, and started to walk away. Then he changed his mind and turned around. "Let me know when Mike is gone, Laura. I'll check into it."

She smiled. "I'll do that, Jack. And thanks."

Sandy watched him disappear around the corner. "What you told him—it doesn't make sense. Mimi Bradley has a track in her district. Gets big bucks from the racing industry. She sponsors a version of that bill every session, trying to help them out. Jack always deals with it."

"And Ken always blocks it?"

"Yes. I'm not saying it would pass if he supported it—there's other opposition—but he's certainly a key obstacle." Sandy added that if Ken had decided to handle that area himself, he would have told her. Scheduling appointments with lobbyists was part of her job.

The two of them got back to work. No more than five minutes later, Clemente walked briskly out of Carlsen's office and straight out of the suite. That was unusual, Sandy said. He generally stopped to flirt and schmooze.

Laura immediately buzzed Jack, who strode into the reception room, knocked perfunctorily on Carlsen's door, and went into his office without waiting to be invited. Five minutes went by, then ten. Laura couldn't hear a thing. And then she caught the first unmistakable sign of discord—two muffled voices overlapping in rapid-fire bursts of unintelligible speech. The volume quickly increased till she could have been wearing earmuffs and made out every word.

"You don't even mention it—not a word—and I'm not supposed to mind? Is that what you're saying?"

"You know as much as you need to."

"Dammit, if you're not going to be straight with me—"

"You work for me, not the other way around, and anytime you don't want to be here—"

"Don't push me, Ken. I'm liable to take you up on it."

"Why wait? Why don't you get the fuck out of here if that's how you feel?"

"That's what you want? Fine! You've got it!"

Waltzer stomped out of Carlsen's office a moment later, slamming the door and stalking down the hall. Laura was afraid that Carlsen would storm out and fire her for sticking her nose where it didn't belong, but he remained in his office. "Is Jack really going to leave?" she whispered to Sandy.

"I don't know. He's practically Ken's alter ego, but I've never heard them yell that way before." Sandy leaned across her desk. "I can't believe he'd blow up over a policy difference, though. He's much too pragmatic. He's furious that Ken's holding out on him, that's all."

"Then Ken usually tells Jack everything?"

"Are you kidding? He didn't even propose to Jane till he'd talked it over with Jack."

Sandy looked bewildered, as if she couldn't imagine what was so important, or so sensitive, that Ken refused to share it with his chief of staff. Laura couldn't, either, but whatever it was, Clemente knew it, too. That was obviously what had gotten him an appointment in the first place.

She left at two-fifteen, picked up the kids from Mrs. Fujimoto's, and took them to a movie in the suburbs. They went to the park afterward, where she struck up a conversation about dieting with one of the other mothers while their children played. She'd heard women complain about afternoons like this, saying they turned one's brains to Play-Doh, but after the craziness of the past few days, adjectives like monotonous, prosaic, and banal had taken on whole new meanings, all of them positive.

It didn't last. Her first clue that the runaway train was still accelerating and that she was still on board came when she glanced through her mail. Amid the requests for money, offers of credit, and advertising leaflets, she found a letter from Edward Roseman, the attorney. He was enclosing a copy of the letter he'd written to Freddie Phelps on her behalf, he informed her, to put in her files.

"I have been engaged to represent your former secretary, Mrs. Laura Greenbaum Miller," it stated. "Please be advised that the defamation of her character, her reputation or her good name, or the making of slanderous or libelous accusations about her activities while she was in your employ, or before or after that time, by you or anyone acting in your behalf, will result in her taking immediate legal action against you."

Laura groaned and shook her head. Her mother hadn't said a word about this when she'd called the night before, but maybe it was inevitable. Dottie, after all, had wanted to testify in court about Allan's adultery despite the fact that California was a no-fault state. Laura winced at the thought of how Freddie must have reacted, but it could have been worse. Dottie could have marched into his office and ordered him to give up scotch, bimbos, and besmirching Laura's character. And if she'd known the truth . . . Laura pictured her lecturing Joseph Cassani about playing with knives, and shuddered. It conjured up images of being sliced up like sushi and tossed into Lake Tahoe.

She shoved Roseman's letter in her purse, then went into the bedroom and checked her machine. There were three messages on the tape. The first was from someone at the temple, asking her to bring a cake to services in three weeks. The second was from Allan, saying he was taking Wednesday off and would probably take the kids to San Francisco for the day. He wanted to pick them up at eight this evening and keep them till Thursday morning. And the third . . .

The third was from Freddie Phelps, who sounded as angry as he did drunk. "Listen, you li'l bitch, I dunno what your problem is, but I'll tell you this. If I get any more letters from your fuckin' hymie lawyer . . . if you tell any more fuckin' lies about me or mess around in my personal business . . . it'll be your fat ass that gets taken to court, not mine. You better keep your mouth shut if you wanna stay healthy. I got influence. I got friends. You better remember that, babe."

Laura removed the cassette, replaced it with a new

one, and tossed the original in the trash. Seth had been known to play back the tape and mimic the messages; she didn't want him imitating this one. Afterward, totally drained, she dragged herself into the kitchen.

Seth helped her make dinner while Sarah called Allan, to tell him that eight would be fine. They tiptoed around her after that, exchanging anxious looks every now and then, probably glad to be going to their father's. She didn't blame them. She was so tense that even the cat avoided her, as if she were a human fault line emitting invisible but deadly waves, telling him that an earthquake could strike at any moment.

Allan noticed, of course. Self-centered or not, he'd known her for sixteen years and could tell when she was upset. They hadn't exchanged more than a dozen words when he sent the kids to Seth's room, telling them to stay there till he gave them permission to come out. They didn't argue.

He took Laura's hand and led her to the living room couch. She didn't argue, either. Who had the energy?

He put his arm around her and cupped the back of her head. She was stiff and resistant at first, not wanting his comfort, but then he slipped his hand under his shirt and rubbed her back, and she relaxed and let him hold her. He could see something was wrong, he murmured, and he wanted to help. If she didn't want to talk about it, that was fine. This wasn't about marriage or the future, but about friendship. They'd spent half their lives together. She was the mother of his children. He wanted her to know that he would always be there for her.

The human contact felt nice. Comfortable and safe. He continued the massage for a long time, saying nothing. She snuggled against his chest, grateful for his understanding.

Then he stopped and pecked her on the forehead.

"It's bad to keep things bottled up inside you, Laurie. Take it from someone who knows."

She pulled away. "People talk when they're ready to. I'm not. Let's just leave it at that."

"But I'm worried about you. You've been edgy for weeks. I thought it was us at first, or maybe a problem with Freddie Phelps, but obviously it's more than that. I want to help."

She sighed. At least he meant well. "Then do what you just said. Be there for me. Take the kids if I ask you to. Listen to me if I need you to. But don't push me. Don't ask questions."

"What is it? Something with your mother? With your new job? With—"

"Allan—"

"With your health? For God's sake, Laurie, you can't not tell me! I'm your husband. Don't you trust me?"

The answer was no. Give him all the facts and he'd do what he thought was best, whether she agreed with him or not and whether she gave him permission or not. And that, she realized, was probably the central problem with their relationship. "It's not any of those things. It's a legal problem. If it gets any worse, I'll call a lawyer."

"What sort of legal problem? Were you in an auto accident?"

"No." She stood up. "I have some grocery shopping to do. Have a good time in San Francisco."

He jumped to his feet. "You're not going to tell me? You're going to let me go crazy worrying? If that's your way of punishing me for Carolyn—"

"She has nothing to do with this. I'm sorry if you're worried, but I have to handle things my own way."

He took her arm. "I love you, Laurie. Don't do this to me. Don't shut me out."

He saw this in terms of himself, not her. What *he* wanted. What *he* needed. She felt like an echo. A wraith. Like the pool of water to his Narcissus.

Something inside her clicked. If Allan could have, he would have turned back time. Deep down, he preferred what she'd once been. And if she could have, she would have lived in fast forward, until she'd become who she wanted to be.

Things had fallen apart. The center was gone forever.

TWENTY

I t was always easier for Laura when the kids spent the night at Allan's. She didn't have to nag them to get up the next morning or prod them to dress and eat. She could read the paper over a quiet cup of coffee and ease into the day ahead. On Wednesday, she really needed that. She was tense from the moment she woke up, almost primed for additional blows.

None came. Mike Clemente burrowed back into the mud of whatever sinkhole he'd sprung from, while Ken stayed in the state's heartland where he belonged, paying homage to the soil and its bounties and harvesting as many agribucks as he could. Jack strolled in at the same time he always did and acted as if nothing had happened, so presumably he and Ken had kissed and made up. The morning passed quickly, with no crises at all, and Laura slipped into vocational cruise control—confident, efficient, feeling as if she'd done her job for years.

Her most immediate worry, that Freddie would show up blitzed and make a scene, never materialized. He didn't phone her, either, not even at home; she called her answering machine to check. Knowing Freddie, he'd decided that he'd put her in her place and didn't need to bother with her again.

She wanted to keep things that way, so, in one of the best telephone performances of her career, she tackled her mother head-on. Not only did she thank Dottie profusely for her help, she claimed Freddie had apologized that very morning after finding the missing money in one of his suits.

Dottie was triumphant. Laura was relieved to the point of giddiness. When things kept going wrong in your life, having them go right was the greatest upper in the world.

She stayed late, working at the computer till four, and then walked to Macy's to get a present for Friday's shower. She window-shopped after that, working her way back to her car along the downtown mall. Art wasn't coming till six, so there was no reason to rush.

When she got home, she opened her garage with the remote and drove straight in. She was reaching for her package when she picked up the hard slap of shoes against concrete, coming rapidly closer. Alarmed, she jerked around in her seat. Vicki was running up her driveway. Frank—the calm one, the brick in an emergency—was right behind her, and he looked grim. Her stomach lurched. Something was very wrong.

Shaking, she got out of the car and closed the door. Frank put his arm around her, comforting her in advance. Panic slashed through her. The traffic on Highway 80 . . . The drug-crazed lunatics in San Francisco . . .

"Oh, my God. The kids. Frank—"

"It's nothing like that. Someone broke into your house this afternoon. It's a mess in there. We didn't want you to go inside till we'd warned you."

"They hit us, too," Vicki said, "but nothing was taken. That's what made me check your place. We think they were looking for something specific. That tape you took from Tomlinson's apartment, maybe. They got in through the sliding-glass door in your living room. Forced the lock. Same with us. We've got a locksmith coming tomorrow morning to make repairs."

Laura began to laugh. This wasn't real life, it was theater of the absurd. "This morning—when I got up— I wondered what else could possibly happen. And after all my brooding . . . It's really funny. Because getting my house ripped apart is nothing. Absolutely nothing."

Frank and Vicki exchanged a look, the kind that said her Crayola box was missing a few key colors. "I think she needs a good, stiff drink," Vicki murmured.

"Really, I'm fine," Laura said. "As long as the kids are okay. That's all I care about."

"All the same, we'll go inside with you."

"You don't have to, Vick. Believe me, this just doesn't bother me."

Vicki and Frank exchanged another look, then followed her into the kitchen. Every drawer and cabinet was open. Groceries, cookware, glasses and dishes, a few broken, lay scattered on the floor and counters. The file drawer in her desk had been emptied. There was even food from the refrigerator on the floor.

Stunned, she looked into the dinette and family room. The breakfront was open and half its contents were strewn around. The bookcase was empty, the books piled in careless heaps on the rug. Even the sectional couch had been searched, the cushions tossed haphazardly back on the frame.

No, it hadn't been the kids. And yes, that was the most important thing in the world. But this—this was an intimate invasion of her world. A rape of her privacy. "I don't think I want to see anymore," she mumbled. "Not just yet."

"You'll have to decide whether you want the police to come over," Frank said gently, "but personally, I don't see the point. The damage is probably less than your deductible, so there's no point filing a claim and risking a rate increase. If the crooks were careless enough to leave evidence behind, the cops would probably have found something at our house—not that I think they were. They weren't your average thieves."

Vicki took over, saying that she and the girls had left at ten to go shopping and returned around three to what they'd assumed was a routine burglary. She'd immediately called Frank, who'd come straight home, and then the police. But by the time the cops had arrived, they'd realized nothing was missing.

"The police were baffled. They know Frank is a pharmacist, so at first they thought the burglars might have been after drugs, but it didn't make sense that they'd leave expensive stereo equipment behind when they could take it and fence it. They finally decided it was personal—that someone had trashed the house for revenge, to get back at us for something we'd done. I didn't argue, just followed them around while they dusted for prints and questioned the neighbors. Nobody saw a thing. As soon as they left, I came over here." She had the keys to Laura's house, not that keys had been necessary. "I saw exactly what I expected. I tried your office, but you'd left for the day, so I stayed by my window and waited for you to come home."

"And here I am." Laura was still dazed. "God. What a mess."

"We'll help you clean up," Frank said. "The girls'll pitch in, too." He paused. "Vicki told me the whole story, or at least as much of it as you told her. I want to hear the rest of it, Laura. It's not just you now. It's us. For everyone's protection, you have to notify the FBI. I know you've got some potential legal problems, so I'll ask around about lawyers if you'd like."

"Yes. Thank you." There was no choice, not anymore.

"Good. I want you to pick up that tape as soon as you can get to your vault and—" The doorbell rang, interrupting him. "I'll get it. It's probably Becky and Karen."

Laura looked at the clock. It was five past six. "No, let me. It might be Art Albright. We were supposed to go out tonight."

"I'd be glad to get rid of him—"

"No, Frank. I'll handle it." She'd plead illness or a family emergency.

She walked down the hall, passing Seth's and Sarah's rooms on the way. She knew she'd begun to recover when it struck her that they weren't that much messier than on an average Friday. The major difference was, the clothes all over the floor were clean rather than dirty.

She opened the door. Art was on the front step, holding a bouquet of yellow roses. Becky and Karen were a few yards behind him, making their way up the walk. She introduced everyone, then sent the girls to the kitchen so she and Art could talk privately.

He handed her the flowers. She was flattered, touched. "Thanks. They're beautiful. Listen, things are a little crazy around here. Someone broke into my house. I just got back and found out. My neighbors are here, giving me moral support."

He hugged her. "What a bummer. Will your insurance cover what was stolen?"

She rested her head against his shoulder for a moment, then eased away. "Actually, from what I could see, nothing was stolen. You remember that problem I had? It seems to have followed me home. My best guess is, they were after something of theirs I took."

"Jesus. You've got to give it back to them, Laura. Mail it if you don't want to hand it over directly. And please. Call the police."

"I plan to, but I need some good legal advice first."
And given the things Art had said on Saturday, he
might know exactly who could provide it. "Know any
well-connected lawyers?"

He smiled weakly. "As a matter of fact, I do. Bruce
Bailey. He's got first-rate contacts with the Feds, but I
don't know about the local cops. You'd have to ask
him."

"You're in trouble with the Feds?"

"I didn't say that."

"But you are." It was a small world. "How come,
Art?"

"It's nothing I did personally, believe me. I didn't
even know it was going on. It traces back to when my
father was still alive." He grimaced. "Remember how I
mentioned he was a high flyer?"

"Umm."

"Let's just say he pushed the envelope till it broke,
and I inherited the consequences. I won't be indicted if
I can convince them I wasn't involved, but it's a tough
cell."

"The evidence is that damning?"

"Yeah, I'm afraid it is. Listen, I'd appreciate your
keeping this to yourself. It won't do my business much
good if it gets around."

"Of course." Fragments of previous conversations
drifted through her mind—about Art Sr.'s mysterious
death, and about his problems with blackmail and
declining profits—but she couldn't focus on them just
then. She had a more pressing concern to deal with.
"That is, I will if you will. You can't repeat anything
I've said to your mother, because if you do, she'll tell
my mother and my mother will go nuts. I saw her on
Sunday and she cross-examined me about Saturday
night. I don't want that to happen again."

He reddened. "Hell, I'm sorry, Laura. I didn't even

think about that. You probably wanted to kill me. If I could just explain . . . "

It was hard to stay annoyed with a man who looked so guilty. "Sure. Go ahead."

His mother was trying to make him a substitute for his father, he said, always pushing for more intimacy than he wanted to give, getting depressed and angry when he tried to draw away. He'd given in repeatedly, thinking it would keep her on an even keel, but he realized now that he'd only made things worse. He promised Laura he would keep his mouth shut from now on, and she believed him. After all, Alice had shown some discretion about what she'd passed on, so no permanent harm had been done.

"I know you're probably not hungry after all this," he said afterward, "but you should try to eat. Come on. It'll do you good to get out."

Laura shook her head. Her house was a wreck, she explained. Straightening it would take hours, even with her neighbors' help, and it had to be done tonight so the kids wouldn't see it when they got home tomorrow afternoon. The divorce was bad enough. They didn't need any additional trauma in their lives.

Art replied that well-fed labor was the most efficient and offered to pick up dinner. He returned half an hour later with pizzas and the fixings for sundaes, restoring Laura's appetite and destroying her hope that the silver lining to this whole mess would be rapid weight loss. With six people working, the cleanup went fairly quickly. The actual damage was minimal, just some broken kitchenware and the ruined lock.

The girls went home eventually, leaving the adults to talk. Half an hour later, the phone rang. It was Becky, saying she'd turned on the computer to work on a term paper that was due when school resumed, but couldn't get it to boot up. All she got on the screen was gibberish. She wanted Frank or Vicki to come and help.

Neither was a computer expert, so both decided to go. Laura wound up alone with Art, a situation she would have preferred to avoid. He made a gentle pass; she kissed him for a while, then cut things off. He was a nice guy, sweet and endearingly tentative, but the earth didn't move when he touched her, not even a tiny bit. She figured that had more to do with circumstances than a lack of chemistry and told him so, thinking that the way things had gone lately, Costner could have done a strip in her bedroom and her blood pressure wouldn't have budged.

"It's okay," he said. "I understand." He was the most easy-going male she'd ever encountered. "Let's go over to Vicki and Frank's. I know a lot about computers. If there's still a problem, maybe I can help."

She smiled at that. "Oh? How come you didn't mention that right away?"

He smiled back. "You know why."

They walked across the street. Frank was up in the office with the girls and the comatose PC, Vicki told them, poring over computer and software manuals. The three of them trooped upstairs to join him.

After a minute of rapid typing, Art announced that the hard disk had been erased. "Wiped clean, even the operating system." He looked at the girls. "Either of you have a friend who's a hacker with a warped sense of humor?"

Both said no.

"Do you back everything up on diskettes?"

Everyone said yes, even Vicki, who used the computer for her personal correspondence and organizational work.

"Well then, no harm done. If you want, I'll reformat your fixed disk and reinstall your software. Then you can copy your files back on."

Frank opened a drawer and took out a teak storage box. It should have contained dozens of diskettes, including the software to reinstall the operating system, but it was completely empty. When Laura added that to the fact that two houses had been turned upside down . . .

"Maybe they weren't after the tape," she said to Vicki. "Maybe it was something on the computer." Carolyn had specifically asked about that, she realized—about whether they'd checked Tomlinson's computer files.

Art looked puzzled. "What tape? What computer?"

She hesitated, wondering if she'd said too much. But given the things he'd confessed to her . . . "Remember I told you that I took something that didn't belong to me? It was an audiotape. Vicki was with me that morning. Her house was searched today, too. There was a computer in the apartment where the tape was. We couldn't get access, but maybe they think we did. That we copied a file containing—I don't know—something incriminating—and took it with us."

"So they came in here and stole all the diskettes. Probably copied the files from the fixed disk before they erased it, to check through later on." He nodded to himself. "That was smart. It eliminated the need to carry the computer out of the house."

Becky looked glum. "Now I'm going to have to type the dumb thing from scratch. What a pain." There were about a dozen sheets of paper sitting face-down in the printer; she picked them up and absently riffled through them. "Oh, well. It could be worse. At least I have my hard copy to work—" She frowned. "Daddy. Look at this." She handed him the final page.

"What happened to Hollister and Bonita Franks could happen to you," it read. "Don't make the mistake of sticking your nose where it doesn't belong."

Laura recognized the wording. "Maggie Hollister got a letter a few days after the judge died. It read almost the same way."

Art looked appalled. "You're saying the people who wrote this are the same ones who killed Hollister and Bonita Franks? *That's* whose tape you took? Why? What in hell was on it?"

"I'd rather not say. I thought it was Bonita's. At least, that's what she told me."

He put his arm around her. "I don't care what you tell me as long as you talk to the FBI. These people are murderers. They want to know who copied their file. When they find out Vicki didn't have it, they're going to keep searching. And next time—"

Vicki let out a gasp. "Oh, my God," she said to Frank. "The business files."

The files she meant were kept on a computer at the Del Rio Pharmacy, which was less than a mile away. The men went to the drugstore while the women stayed home, wondering whether they wouldn't have been safer if the positions had been reversed. Frank called within minutes, though, saying that the pharmacy hadn't been touched.

Maybe it was due to the drugstore's alarm system, maybe it was because the market next door stayed open till midnight, and maybe it was a simple oversight, but Frank didn't take any chances. He arranged for a private security guard to patrol for the rest of the night, then made additional backups of the prescription and financial records and brought them home.

Laura was thoroughly spooked by then. With the lock on her sliding-glass door broken, she was afraid to be alone in her house. Art offered to spend the night with her, but she turned him down in favor of Vicki's guest room, where she tossed, turned, and awoke at every rustle and flutter.

There were no more visitors, though, and only one complication: Allan phoned her at work the next morning demanding to know where she'd been. He'd called at ten and gotten no answer, he said, then kept trying for the next three hours. He'd been frantic with worry.

She couldn't tell him why she'd stayed at Vicki's. "I'm sorry you were worried," she said, "but where I spend my nights when you have the kids isn't any of your business anymore."

"Oh. I see." It was obvious what he thought. "Next time you're going to be out, maybe you could leave me a number. The kids wanted to tell you about San Francisco. They were disappointed when I couldn't reach you."

She agreed, feeling guilty now. She'd never asked the same of him, but there was a reason for that. When Daddy wasn't reachable, it meant he'd gone out. If Mommy wasn't, the kids' precarious sense of security began to crumble.

Meanwhile, on the plea-bargain front, Frank called around about lawyers and gave Laura the names of the top three. None could see her at the times she was free till the week after next, but she didn't mind waiting. Busy probably meant better.

Still, she was a nervous wreck. The people who'd searched her house had been after something other than Bonita's tape—something she didn't have. Carolyn and Clemente might have been after the same thing. And if it hadn't turned up yet, if the file was still out there, the person who'd taken it might try to make use of it, and she might get the blame. So whenever the phone rang unexpectedly, or she heard a sudden noise late at night, her body kicked into defensive overdrive, like a radar system that saw a swarm of missiles in the most harmless flock of birds.

TWENTY-ONE

It was Saturday morning, and Laura was cleaning her house. She always did it in the same order, starting at the back, in the living room, and working her way down one side, to the kitchen, dinette and family room, and up the other, to the kids' bedrooms and bath and then the master suite. She and the kids had an agreement. If they picked up their rooms without complaint and fed themselves without making a mess, they could watch TV all morning. If they didn't bug her while she was cleaning, she wouldn't bug them about turning down the sound.

She'd worked quickly, wanting to finish early so they could take a drive that afternoon, probably up to the foothills. They could picnic there. She'd feel safe for a few hours.

She dragged the vacuum into her bedroom. Her bath was on the right, a few yards inside the door. She always used the outlet by the sink, at the far end, because she could reach everywhere from there without leaving wheel marks on the carpet.

She walked into the bathroom and plugged in the vacuum. A door closed, very softly. Her bedroom door.

She froze, fear rising in her throat. And then she shook her head impatiently, because it was only Seth or Sarah with some imagined emergency. The house was locked. Nobody could get inside.

She called out their names. There was no answer. Frightened all over again, she tiptoed to the door, peeked outside . . . and almost jumped out of her skin. Mike Clemente was standing by the bedroom door, blocking it off.

There was only one reason she didn't scream, and it was standing right beside him—a boy of twelve or thirteen, tall, gangly, and very cute. The kid, a future ladykiller, looked a lot like Clemente. Both had jeans and T-shirts on, Clemente's from Rutgers, the kid's from Georgetown. He grinned so winningly that she blinked in confusion. He had braces on his teeth. He looked about as menacing as a New Kid on the Block.

"Hi." He pointed to Clemente, who walked farther into the room, stopping directly across from her. "I'm supposed to tell you. . . . My dad's a Fed. Undercover FBI. He's not going to hurt you. He just wants to talk to you."

She took a step backward, retreating into the bathroom. She was barefoot, dressed only in shorts and a tank top, and felt exposed and vulnerable. She looked from one to the other, trying to take in what the kid had said, wondering if she should believe him when she wouldn't have believed his father in a hundred years. She'd read books about undercover agents. They didn't drag their families into their work—except for the guy who'd taken his wife to a dinner with his targets in the mob. He'd passed her off as his girlfriend so they would stop trying to fix him up with their female relatives.

"If you're really a federal agent, let me see your ID," she said to Clemente. Not that she'd be able to tell if it were real or forged. And not that she'd talk to him even if he convinced her he was the genuine article.

He looked amused. "I don't have it on me, Laura. It's not something you keep around when you're undercover. You could be searched. Or your car could be searched. Or even your house or office."

"So get it from wherever you keep it and bring it back here. Show it to me. Then maybe I'll believe you're what you say you are."

"Actually, I don't know where it is. The last time I saw it, it was in my dresser in Seattle. I was a supervisor up there. Hated every minute of it." Frowning, he looked at his son. "You have any idea if it's still there?"

The kid walked over to join him. "No way, Dad. Stan uses that dresser now. He hates finding your stuff around."

"So? You know where Mom put it?"

"She mailed some stuff to your parents last year. Your commendations and junk. Maybe it was in there. Or maybe she stuck it where Stan couldn't find it, like in her desk at work." He peered into the bedroom, then added to Laura, "If I could use your phone, I could call my mom and ask. Would that help any?"

"Hardly, since I'd have no way of knowing who you're really talking to."

He considered that for a moment. "You could watch me dial. You'd see it was a Seattle number."

"And the person on the other end could be the local godfather's sister, for all I know." She wasn't so much frightened now as incredulous. "You can't not know where your own badge is," she said to Clemente. "Your ex-wife wouldn't send it somewhere without telling you."

"You don't know my mother," the kid said mournfully. "She hates the FBI. Maybe she even threw it away."

"It's not something I've needed lately," Clemente remarked. "I haven't thought about it in years. The fact that I don't have it—does that present a serious problem?"

Laura gaped at him. "Well, what do *you* think?"

"That it does." He paused. "Couldn't you just take my word for it? Or Rob's? I mean, who would make up a story like that?"

"*You* would. Whether you're lying or telling the truth right now, you've obviously made up tons of them in the past."

"Yeah, I guess you have a point." He put his hand on his son's shoulder. "We seem to be at an impasse here. Maybe you could tell her what a fine human being I am."

"Sure, Dad, but it'll cost you another twenty bucks."

Clemente rolled his eyes. "Well, hell, Rob, now she's never going to believe us. That's the last time I ask *you* for help." He looked at Laura again. "I didn't pay him to come here. Honestly. He just likes to stick it to me. Give me a hard time. That's what happens when they hit adolescence. Wait a few years. You'll see."

He thought this was funny. Both of them did. For all she knew, she was in grave danger here, and the enemy was doing a vaudeville routine. "How did you get in here, anyway? I thought the FBI gave up breaking and entering back in Jimmy Carter's day."

"Your back door was unlocked. The one in here."

"The hell it was. Not after—" She stopped, appalled by what she'd almost told him.

"Not after what?"

"Nothing. The door was definitely locked, that's all."

"Okay. You're right. It was." He smiled. "I'm good with locks."

"You mean you picked them?" There were two locks in that door, including a one-inch deadbolt.

"Yeah, but don't worry. I didn't damage anything. Listen, I really do need to talk to you. Is it okay if Rob hangs out with your kids for a while? He knows who I work for because I had a desk job in Seattle, and he knows what my cover is because he visits me fairly often and he sees the way I live, but that's as far as it goes. He doesn't know what I'm investigating. Or why I'm here. Or how you're involved. I can't let him listen to our conversation."

The man had terrorized her repeatedly and broken into her home, and he expected her to stand there and chat? "Forget it. I'm not going to talk to you. I don't want anything to do with you. I want you out of my house."

"Look, I understand that you're angry and I don't blame you. I know I scared you, and I'm sorry about that." He ran his hand through his hair. "We thought it was the best way to proceed. Believe me, I didn't enjoy it."

"*You* didn't enjoy it? Jesus, I don't believe this! Am I supposed to feel sorry for you?"

"You're not making much progress," the kid observed. "She's seriously pissed at you, Dad."

"I noticed." Clemente handed the boy some keys. "Wait for me in the car. You can listen to the radio. Be sure to lock it after you get inside."

"Can I drive it a little? Just up and down the street?"

"In your dreams, Rob. Go on now, get out of here. And don't slam the gate on your way out. I don't want you scaring Laura's kids."

"Yeah. Okay." He started toward the back door.

"Hold it, Rob," Laura said crisply.

He turned around, unsure of what to do. "Huh?"

"Just wait right there." She felt safer with the kid in the room. "The last time I checked, Mr. Clemente—or whatever your real name is—American citizens still had Miranda rights. I'm declining to talk to you. If you're really an FBI agent, you'll respect that and leave my house."

"Wrong," he said evenly. "I'll do whatever I have to

in order to do my job. Rob! Out of here."

The kid glanced at his father, then looked at Laura. "If he says to go, I have to go. But he's a good guy. Really brave. Really tough. And uh—" He glanced at his father again, red-faced now. "He totally likes you. Per—"

"Shut up, Rob."

"Personally, I mean. Give him a break." The kid darted to the back door, unlocked it, and slipped outside.

Laura was even redder than the kid by then. It was one thing not to know whether someone wanted to kill you or take you to bed, but what really unnerved her was, she wasn't sure which she wanted to do to *him*.

He lazed against the wall, his face revealing nothing. "It really is Clemente. I'm using my real name on this case. I hope I can tell you about it eventually."

"I'm really not interested." But she was, or at least intensely curious.

"So you won't talk to me. Even though people have been murdered. Even though you're scared out of your mind half the time."

"Because of you. You're the one who threatened me. You're the one who scared me."

"To find out as much as I could. And to push you into going to the Bureau and telling us the rest. But you didn't. Or haven't yet."

"And that's why you did it? It never occurred to you people to admit you needed help and ask me to cooperate?"

"I'm asking you right now."

She glared at him. "Go to hell."

"Look, we didn't ask because it wouldn't have worked. You were too involved. Too afraid of what might happen to you if you talked. You would have closed up tighter than a vestal virgin and we'd never have found out what you know."

He was right, but she wasn't going to say so. Even if

he was really a Fed, she didn't trust him. After Monday, she didn't trust any of them.

"No comment, hmm?" He sighed. "Okay, if that's the way we have to play it." He took a few steps forward. She backed farther into the bathroom. "You have some serious legal problems, Ms. Miller." His voice was FBI clipped now, like McKennery's. "Let's start with your phone conversations with Bonita Franks on March 30th and April 3rd. Her line was tapped. We have you on tape. You knew about her arrangement with Freddie Phelps in regard to her policy on Hollister's life. You made it clear that you expected a piece of Phelps's profit in the form of a raise in return for reminding him to pay the premium. You helped her fabricate a convincing story in case she was questioned, which she was. Advised her on how to lie to federal officers. At a minimum, that's conspiracy, insurance fraud, and obstruction of justice. And while we're talking about lying to federal officers, there's your conversation with Special Agents Osman and McKennery this past Monday. We've got a videotape of that one. You told so many lies, both explicit or implicit, that even I was amazed, and I was used to you by then. If you want a long stretch in prison, you're well on your way to making your dreams come true. Cooperate with me, and I'll do what I can to keep you home with your kids."

Wiretaps and videotape. God. He was a Fed, all right. Given the things he knew and the tone he'd used, he had to be. A versatile one, too, to give him his due—the charming good cop and the arrogant bad cop all wrapped up in a single, noxious package. Trained to lie like a world-class con man, manipulate like Machiavelli, and intimidate when he couldn't persuade. The sooner she got a lawyer, the better.

She shrugged, pretending to be unimpressed, just

angered enough by his tactics to pull it off reasonably well. "You know something, Mr. Clemente? I think I liked you better when you were a sleazy lobbyist."

"You didn't like me at all when I was a sleazy lobbyist," he shot back. "If you had, you'd have told me what you knew and we wouldn't have to go through this right now. As it is, you're in serious trouble. If I were you, I'd start talking."

"Not a chance." She held out her wrists. "Slap on the cuffs, Special Agent Clemente. Haul me off to the slammer. You can't have a vicious criminal like me walking the streets of the town, terrorizing innocent citizens."

"You think this is funny." He was stiff now, offended.

"No. I think you're trying to intimidate me. And I think that stinks." She dropped her hands. "I told you people on Monday, I'm an honest person who's caught up in something I don't understand and can't control. You wouldn't listen. You treated me like a criminal. Believe me, if I ever go back to your office, I'll have a lawyer with me every step of the way."

He closed his eyes for a moment in what she interpreted as utter disgust, or maybe despair. "Oh, hell, Laura, don't do that. No lawyers. Please."

"Oh, right. God forbid I should even up my odds against you people."

"Dammit, there's no 'people' here. There's just me. Can't you try to trust me? Help me out a little here?"

"Sure. If my lawyer says I should."

He stared at her for several seconds, then sighed and walked away, farther into her room. She followed, hoping he'd given up, that he was on his way to the door. Instead, he kicked off his shoes, lay down on her freshly made bed, and gazed at the ceiling, his hands behind his head. It had been bad enough when he'd taken over her lunch; now he was taking over her whole damn room.

She stopped a few feet away from him. "Do you mind? That happens to be my bed. I didn't invite you to use it."

"Damn shame, too." He looked at her. "Think about what I've told you. About me. About who I am. You could blow me out of the water if you wanted to. Tell everyone from Jerry Burke to Craig Tomlinson who I am."

She stared at him, horrified by the idea. "Don't be ridiculous. I wouldn't do that."

"No? Why not?"

"Why the hell do you think? Because I don't want to screw up your investigation. Or put you in any danger. I happen to be a loyal American, Mr. Clemente."

"I believe that. And I'm grateful for it." He paused. "I shouldn't have come here. Shouldn't have spoken to you. You do realize that."

Now that she thought about it . . . "Because you're working undercover."

"Yes."

"So why did you?"

"Because you can help me. Because you know more than you've said—maybe even more than you realize. And because I tried to get you to open up in every way I could think of short of this, but nothing worked. If you didn't cave in after Tuesday, you never will." He sat up, bracing himself against the headboard. "You're too damn curious for your own good and you lie as much as some sociopaths I've known, but not nearly as well. I'm sure you're straight. McKennery isn't. He doesn't trust you. It's nothing personal, just the company you keep. Believe me, he'd feed my favorite body parts to his pet Doberman if he knew I was here. You don't tell anyone that you're working undercover, not even the local cops, and especially not someone your boss considers a possible coconspirator. Keep that in mind, okay?"

She frowned. "What for?"

"I'm your insurance. If McKennery hassles you, you can tell him you know who I am. Believe me, it's more important to him to keep me on the job than to go after you. Of course, I hope you won't have to do that. And I hope you won't drag a lawyer into this, either, because he'd probably advise you to say as little as possible and then we'd never get anywhere."

Laura walked around the bed and sat down cross-legged on the other side. He was treating her like someone with intelligence as well as information now, so maybe there was something to discuss. The fact that he was sitting there in a T-shirt and tight jeans, looking sexy as hell, didn't exactly hurt his cause, either.

"After you got through with me Saturday night, I ran into the bathroom and threw up," she said.

"Yeah, I figured." He grimaced. "I'm sorry, Laura."

"The last few weeks have been hell. You've been a big part of the reason. I thought you were swamp muck. I was afraid of you and I despised you. I'm still pretty angry with you."

"That's understandable."

"You've been trying to manipulate me from almost the moment we met, right up through this morning. I resent it."

"I don't blame you. I'd feel the same way if I were you."

"But the end justifies the means. Is that it?"

"It wasn't something I planned in advance. McKennery wanted to question you after he heard the tape of your first phone call to Bonita. I knew you well enough by then to realize it would be counterproductive. I passed on a message saying so and he passed one back that he'd hold off, but I needed to get to you however I could. I would have succeeded, too, except that you don't like cops any more than you like lobbyists. And Kevin came on too strong last Monday. He should have stayed in his office and let Clint handle you, but he's supervising this case himself and nothing could have kept him away. In fairness to him, most people would have cracked after the amount of pressure we put on you. You were tough. Very tough."

"You're talking as if . . . I don't know. As if I'm some sort of puppet. As if it's all a game."

"I'm trying to explain what happened. I'm sorry if it sounded as if I didn't regret frightening you. I do."

"Do you? From what I've seen, you'll say whatever you need to to get what you want. When it comes to lying, I'm as far out of your league as a bat boy is from Jose Canseco."

"I'd better be. If I weren't good at lying, I would have been killed a long time ago." He leaned forward. Everything about him softened—his tone, the look in his eyes, even the way he carried himself. "But I never confuse the role I'm playing with real life, Laura, and you're real life. *My* real life. I won't always be able to tell you what you want to know, but I won't ever lie to you again. Or try to manipulate you. That's a promise."

He moved closer and put his hand on her knee, stroking it in a gentle but sexual way. Her theory that circumstances could short-circuit chemistry went up in flames. Flustered, she pushed away his hand and scooted toward the foot of the bed.

He smiled, so tenderly that she flushed like a kid. "Before, you wouldn't go out with me because you disapproved of what you thought I did for a living. What's the problem now? That you disapprove of what I really do? Or that you're too damn angry to let me near you?"

"You have an awfully high opinion of yourself."

And saw more than she wanted him to know. "Didn't anyone ever tell you that women dislike that in a man?"

"Then you're not attracted to me. You don't like me."

"I think we should talk about something else."

"Okay." He was grinning now. "Your nipples are erect. You've got goose bumps on your arms. And you're blushing."

"Ah, the eagle eyes of the ace agent," she answered tartly. "I'm impressed."

He laughed, then said in a husky voice that sent chills down her spine, "In other words, I'm going too fast for you. You want me to back off. Give you some time."

"That might be nice."

"Okay. I can fake patience." He swung off the bed. "Tell me about your phone calls to Bonita Franks. What were they all about?"

It was amazing how welcome those questions were. Context was everything. "What did you say you were investigating? Political corruption? And how did you say you got involved with the Hollister murder case?"

"No way, honey. The way it works is, I ask the questions and you answer them. No trades."

She looked at him ingenuously. "If I give you the names of the attorneys I'm considering hiring, will you tell me which one is best?"

"Oh, hell." He groaned. "Don't start that again, Laura."

"Look at it this way. The more I know, the more help I'll be. There are things I might never think to mention because I have no idea they're important."

"No, there aren't. I'm incredibly thorough. I'll cover all the bases. Trust me on that."

"You saw the videotape, Mike. You know what an erratic memory I have. For example, my house was broken into and searched on Wednesday. I used to know what they were after, but I've forgotten. They left a note behind, but I don't remember what it said. And then there's the tape I told Osman about. It was only a copy. I still have the original, but I don't recall where I put it."

"McKennery was right," he muttered. "We should have dragged you into a small room with a bare lightbulb in the ceiling and tortured you till you cracked."

She smiled. "About those lawyers . . . "

"The best in the business is a guy named Clemente." He strode over, lifted her into his arms and kissed her on the mouth. "You win. We'll talk."

They wound up at the zoo, talking quietly and discreetly while Rob and the animals diverted Seth and Sarah. Mike wouldn't say what he'd been doing in Los Angeles or how he'd wound up at Burke/Maravich, only that he was part of a wide-ranging investigation into money laundering, mob ties to legal gambling, and extortion and influence peddling in state government. After a year, he was close enough to his bosses to be entrusted with some of their more questionable errands, but he hadn't reached their inner circle yet.

As a result, a lot of the time he operated blind. His meeting with Carlsen was a case in point. He'd been told to request an appointment, that Carlsen would bargain on AB 2962, which the senator had. He'd been angry but controlled that day, agreeing to remain neutral on the bill but not to support it, saying that no amount of pressure would change his mind. Mike had no idea what had moved him even that far.

As for Hollister, he'd gone to the funeral aware of the Bureau's investigation, but more to massage the dead man's influential friends than to find out who had killed him. That investigation had begun the previous fall, when Hollister had been recorded on an FBI wiretap offering a judicial favor in return for the reduction of his gambling debts. Similar conversations had followed. In the months since, the FBI had examined everything from his spending habits to his rulings from the bench. Mike had looked around his house the night of Charlie's party, but hadn't found anything of interest.

In any event, his primary concern wasn't Hollister, but the judge's pal Tomlinson and some of Tomlinson's racing and casino cronies. His own investigation had begun to focus on their activities by then. That was why he'd pursued Bonita Franks, because he'd just been briefed on the Hollister investigation and had heard a great deal about her.

Not only was she Hollister's mistress, she was close to Tomlinson and had ties to the mob. Like Hollister, she'd shown up regularly on the FBI's wiretaps. The bug on her phone dated to about a week before Hollister's death.

The judge had fallen for her when he'd first seen her sing, Mike explained, about three years before, when his gambling was starting to spiral out of control. The mob had targeted him by then as someone they might be able to corrupt and use. They'd asked Bonita to respond to his advances and she had, embroiling him more deeply with the mob, earning some antique jewelry whenever she was especially helpful.

The judge had dragged his heels at times about delivering on the favors or information he'd promised, but there was no indication that his stalling had gotten him killed. Still, Bonita must have thought it would eventually, and had covered herself with insurance. Even so, she'd apparently been genuinely fond of him. He'd treated her like a lady and tried to educate her about history and politics, and in return, she'd satisfied his craving for masochistic, homoerotically tinged sex.

Mike had gone to the lake the day after the funeral to talk to a fellow agent, he told Laura, and stayed there to check out Bonita. Later that night, he'd swung by her house to learn the identity of the friend she was so eagerly expecting, found Charlie Hollister there, and talked his way inside. Bonita had returned a short time later. It was obvious that she was crazy about Charlie, full of fantasies about marrying a lawyer, but he didn't return her feelings. He'd made a sarcastic comment before she arrived indicating that his main pleasure in the relationship had been to cuckold his father, intimating that if Mike wanted her sexually, he was welcome to her.

"And did you?" Laura asked. They were standing outside the reptile house, waiting for the kids. Snakes gave her the willies. She never went inside.

"No." He smiled. "I prefer difficult brunettes."

It was the first personal comment he'd made all afternoon. "You're supposed to be giving me time, remember?"

"An hour and a half isn't long enough?"

"No. Do you have any idea who killed her? Could it have been Charlie?" She suggested a possible scenario—Bonita killing the judge for the insurance money, then arguing violently with Charlie about marriage and being shot with her own gun.

Mike shook his head. "He's got an alibi. He was with Jennifer Harris all day. It's not airtight—they were alone most of the afternoon—but he told us Bonita had given him whatever he asked for, including ten grand to pay for the party Saturday night, and insisted he never would have killed his own gravy train. He didn't know how she'd gotten the money, but he thought she might have sold some jewelry. The revolver by the body *was* the murder weapon, though. It was used to kill Hollister, too."

"And left behind the second time but not the first. Do you have any idea why?"

He shrugged. "We don't even know if the same person killed both of them."

"Did you trace the gun? Find out who it belonged to?"

"We're working on it. We got into a hassle with the local cops about jurisdiction, so we didn't get it back to Washington till Wednesday. The ballistics matched, but there were no prints on it and the serial number was filed off. The lab guys managed to bring it up. It was registered to a woman in Sacramento, but she moved a few years ago and didn't leave a forwarding address. None of the neighbors had ever heard of her. We're in the process of tracking her down."

"Was her name on any of your wiretap tapes? Did anyone recognize it?"

"Nope. Andrea Furillo. Ring any bells?"

Laura suddenly felt dizzy. "That gun you found . . . Was it silver with a wooden handle? A Smith & Wesson Lady Smith?"

Mike looked stunned. "Yes. How the hell—"

"Because I've seen it. I know who Andrea Furillo is. Or was. Freddie Phelps's former secretary. His former mistress, too. She died of breast cancer about a year ago."

Mike folded his arms across his chest, looking every bit as formidable as McKennery ever had. "It's time you started talking." He ran his finger down her cheek in a gesture that was half tender, half stern. "I expect to hear everything, Laura. *Everything.*"

TWENTY-TWO

The kids walked out of the reptile house, straight to Laura and Mike. She'd introduced him as someone from work she had to talk to, but kids could sense intimacy the way Sam sensed ground round. Seth said he was hungry and Sarah claimed she was tired, but the truth was, they'd had their fill of staying out of the way while some stranger monopolized their mother's attention. She bought them ice cream, promising them pizza for dinner if they would go to Fairytale Town and amuse themselves for a while longer. It was across the street, a small theme park featuring mazes and sets based on children's stories.

Thanks to the Bureau's videotape, Mike knew everything Osman and McKennery did, which was almost everything that had happened. Laura sketched out the rest as they trailed after the kids—how she'd copied Bonita's tape and kept the original, then pried information out of Bonita and Freddie about the Hollister insurance policies; how she'd snooped through Freddie's desk and seen Andrea's gun and note; how she'd come home on Wednesday to a pair of ransacked houses and a threatening letter.

He was pleased about the tape, especially since a thorough search of Bonita's house had failed to turn up the copy Laura had made. He wanted the original, to send to Washington for amplification. The information about Andrea Furillo was helpful, too. There was no question that Freddie had had motives for both murders—to end Hollister's blackmail and to silence Bonita about the insurance policy—so if the gun Laura had seen in his drawer turned up missing, he was going to have some lengthy explaining to do. Finally, the idea that Tomlinson was worried about stolen computer data dovetailed with the rest of Mike's investigation, although he wouldn't say how or why.

As for the letter on Vicki's printer, it could have been written by anyone with knowledge of the letter to Maggie Hollister. Since she'd talked quite freely and Charlie might have too, the similarity in the wording didn't prove a thing. That first letter had proved worthless, a laser-generated page and envelope devoid of fingerprints, but Mike still wanted to pass along the second one to Washington.

"There's just one area you haven't covered," he said as the kids ran onto a model pirate ship. "I understand your reluctance, but I'm going to have to insist that you talk about it. Art Albright. What do you know about him?"

"That he's a nice guy with a clingy mother and some serious business problems." And that the Bureau was obsessed with him. "I like him, Mike. He told me he was an honest person trying to straighten out the mess his father had left behind, and I believe him. He mentioned being investigated by the FBI, but he didn't say why."

"Actually, our involvement is fairly recent. Customs is the lead agency on the investigation. There's been some DEA involvement, too. In view of that, maybe you should ask yourself now nice and how honest Albright really is."

"Look, I've told you as much as I can. If I've missed something . . . You can't keep pulling your close-mouthed-federal-agent routine and expect me to come up with sparkling insights. What is Art supposed to have done, anyway? Why is half the government after him?"

Mike stared at the three kids as they tore around the ship. "Yeah, okay. It was originally a money-laundering case. Drug money from Mexico, mob money from rackets in California, cash skimmed at casinos and racetracks. We think Art Sr. controlled a number of businesses that he recommended to certain clients as highly speculative but potentially lucrative investments. There was everything from a gold mine to a genetics research firm, but the businesses existed mostly on paper. The mine was old, played out. The cutting-edge genetics company was an ordinary lab. And so on. Clients put dirty money in, then got it back as large gains on supposedly small investments, or as reimbursements for goods and services that were never actually provided."

Laura hated to believe it, but it rang too true not to. It explained how Art Sr. had made money even when times were tough—crime was recessionproof—and why he'd been vulnerable to blackmail. Still, it didn't prove anything about Art Jr.

"Art told me he'd taken his family and his clients out of speculative ventures like the mine," she said. "Look at it from his side, Mike. He only bought the firm because his parents nagged him into it, and then he must have found out what was going on. He refused to go along, but getting out of the money-laundering business wasn't that simple. He didn't want to attract attention or get his parents in trouble, so he had to do it tactfully and quietly. Naturally it seems suspicious now, but what choice did he really have?"

"None, if it happened the way you say, but look at

the timing. Art Jr. bought Albright Investments just six weeks before the government seized the firm's records. Four weeks later—two weeks before we went in with our warrant—Art Sr. fell out of a boat during a storm and drowned. I think he got nervous. That he'd known for months that we were after him. Informants have been known to work both sides of the street. And if he was paying hush money to Hollister, that would have given him an additional motive to get out. So he pretended he was cracking up, brought Art Jr. in to clean up his mess, and conveniently died. We couldn't indict a missing body, and unless we could prove Art Jr. did more than get out of the money-laundering business— that he committed criminal acts—we couldn't indict him, either. The bottom line is that Albright Investments can't be seized under the RICO statute, which it otherwise might be. I'd say that's very tidy. Very convenient."

"You're saying Art Sr. is still alive? That he faked his mental breakdown and his death, then retired to Rio?"

"Not Rio, Tahiti, but to tell you the truth, the guy might have been a genuine nut case. We've been told he could seem completely rational one minute and totally unhinged the next. He was fixated on painting. Thought he was the next Gauguin. He used to babble about running off to the tropics and devoting himself to his art. Maybe he's living out his dreams, because he hasn't contacted his family—" Mike cut himself off. "What's wrong? You look like you've seen a ghost."

Laura felt as if she had. "Marion Kirby," she said, reeling at the thought.

"Marian Kirby. Right. Who the hell is she?"

"It just hit me. Marian Kirby, from the old *Topper* stories. She and her husband George were the ghosts, but the Marion I mean is a he." It was crazy—surreal— but that didn't mean it was impossible. "A few months ago, someone named Marion Kirby started writing to Freddie from New Mexico. Freddie said Kirby was his cousin. That he was an eccentric artist. He was a total paranoid, always going on about how the great vacuum was going to suck him up and deposit him in the lowest pit of hell. I thought he meant outer space. That it was a metaphor for suffocation. For death and eternal suffering. But maybe it was vacuum as in Hoover. J. Edgar Hoover."

Mike nodded calmly, but Laura could see he was excited. "It's possible. Kirby's letters . . . Did you save them?"

"Yes. I never threw anything out."

"And the original paperwork from Albright's life insurance policy? Is it still in Phelps's office?"

"It should be."

"Then I want to borrow those keys you copied."

It was obvious why. He was going to search Freddie's office. Compare the handwriting in Kirby's letters to the signature on Albright's insurance forms. Check on Andrea's gun.

She smiled slyly. "Gee, Mike, why don't you pick the locks?"

"Because you mentioned there was a finicky alarm system, and I'd rather not have to deal with it. Are you going to give me the keys or aren't you?"

"You're asking me to abet an illegal act?"

"With the number you've already committed, what's one more?" He put his arm around her. "We're juggling four or five different balls in the air with this investigation. If we go in with a warrant, it's going to tip people off all over the West. Paper shredders everywhere will start working overtime. If Kirby really is Albright, he might leave New Mexico before we can find him and pick him up. Anyway, I won't get caught, and if I'm not caught, it never happened."

Laura watched absently as the kids ran off the pirate ship and raced into a castle. "You have the soul of a con man." And she did, too, just a little. "You don't know where to find things. I do. I'll have to come along."

He shook his head. "Nice try, honey, but forget it. That's why God made diagrams."

"You're incredibly bossy, you know that? As bad as Allan. I hate bossy men."

"You don't have to marry me, Laura. You just have to cooperate with my investigation."

She walked toward the castle, thinking she was beginning to understand why his ex-wife had hated the FBI.

They'd come in separate cars and returned the same way, Mike parking several blocks from her house as he had that morning, then slipping into the back with Rob. Vicki knew both him and his Porsche. He didn't want her to see either.

Laura was on the phone when he knocked, talking to Vicki's daughter while the kids squabbled a few feet away. Cradling the handset between her ear and shoulder, she opened the door. "Actually, Karen, I'm glad he canceled. I wasn't in the mood to go out. Naturally I'll pay you anyway."

Karen refused the money and excused herself to pick up another call. Mike, meanwhile, had ordered the kids to the family room to watch TV. Laura expected Seth, at least, to balk, but he didn't, maybe because Rob was something of a glamorous figure to him, and *he* hustled out like a recruit obeying a drill sergeant. The younger kids followed.

Mike closed the door behind them. "What was that all about?"

"I was supposed to go to a play with Art Albright tonight, but he can't make it. Vicki's older daughter and her boyfriend are going to use the tickets." Laura tapped the playback button on her machine. "It was a strange message. Why don't you listen?"

Art's voice was soft, almost furtive. "Uh, Laura, it's Art. I'll have to ask for a raincheck on the theater. My mother is here. She's all upset. I don't know what's gotten into her. That is, when I told her we were going out . . . I thought she liked you—I mean, I know she does, but she gets in these moods . . . I've got to calm her down. Don't be angry, okay? I'll call you tomorrow. Maybe you could save Wednesday for me. We could go to dinner."

She switched off the machine. "The odd part is, Alice is the one who nagged him into asking me out in the first place. She and my mother started matchmaking the moment they met. But maybe she feels threatened now. Like I said, she's really clingy. She wants to keep Art neurotically close. And if I got too important to him—"

"I get the drift. So he really likes you, hmm?"

"I guess so." She saw the glint in Mike's eye and shook her head. "No way, Mike. Art is my friend. I'm not going to wear a wire and try to trick him into incriminating himself while the damn thing transmits every word."

He took her refusal with good grace, merely asking for the keys, the tape, and the letter, remarking that the sooner he got the tape and letter to his contact agent, the sooner they could be sent to Washington—probably today, by Federal Express. She hadn't hidden any of the three, not after what had happened on Wednesday. If someone wanted them badly enough to break in, he was welcome to them.

She took them out of her night table and handed

them over. Mike's plans suddenly seemed real in a way they hadn't previously. "When are you going to Freddie's office?" she asked.

"Tonight around two. I figure the area will be dead."

He was right. The businesses in the vicinity were closed on weekends. "Well, if you can't be good, be careful. What about Rob? Does he need a place to stay?"

"He's sleeping at my neighbors' house tonight. He's friends with their son."

"Will you tell him? About leaving, I mean?"

"I'll have to mention it, in case anything happens. He's smart enough to realize it's business."

"Won't he get upset? Won't he worry?"

Mike put his hands on her waist. "Why? Will you?"

"Yes." She felt jumpy, unsettled. "Mike . . . Do you think you could come by after you're done? Tell me how things went?"

He looked pleased. "Yeah, I think I could do that." He kissed her, a slow nuzzle that packed the erotic punch of a howitzer blast. "I'll knock on your back door. Sleep in something sexy tonight." He dropped his hands. "Draw me that diagram, and then I'll get out of here."

She fished out a piece of paper and began to sketch. The truth was, she didn't own any sexy nightgowns. She couldn't decide whether that was good or bad.

His knock woke her out of the restless sleep she'd fallen into around one A.M., after a movie on cable had ended. She was startled at first, then relieved. She looked at the clock as she got out of bed. It was two-thirty. He'd been awfully quick.

She turned on a lamp and opened the back door.

Sam, who was sleeping in his usual spot at the foot of her bed, roused himself for long enough to look around, then buried his nose in his tail. Mike was dressed in black, carrying a flashlight and a manila envelope. She didn't think, just flung herself against his chest and hugged him. He dropped the flash and envelope. Within seconds, he was kissing her neck, his hands moving to her hips to pull her close.

She jerked away. Like the hug, it was pure instinct. "Please, Mike. Don't."

"Sorry. It was the nightgown. I couldn't help myself."

She was wearing a Lanz flannel that covered her from neck to wrists to toes. "It's just—I've never been with anyone but Allan, and the kids are right down the hall, and I barely know you—"

"You don't have to explain." He picked up the flash and envelope, sat down on the bed, and petted Sam, who ignored him completely. "Your cat . . . Are you sure it's alive?"

"He only moves for food."

"Oh. Neutered, obviously." He patted the bed. "Come on. Take a look at what I've got."

She sat down beside him. He took a sheaf of papers out of the envelope—a note to someone named Betsy and photocopies of the Albright insurance forms and the Kirby letters. She flipped through the insurance forms, looking for Albright's signature. The spidery script all but jumped out at her.

"Jesus," she murmured. "He really is alive."

"It looks that way. We'll fax this stuff to the lab so the handwriting guys can make sure. I assume we've got Albright's writing on some of his business papers, too, so that should provide an additional check."

"What about the letter and tape? Did your contact agent get them off to Washington?"

He nodded. "I told her what I was doing. She

chewed my butt about talking to you, but the truth is, she's used to me by now."

"And the gun?"

"It was still in the drawer. I wrote down the serial number. We'll trace the ownership." He put the papers back in the envelope and sealed it, then tossed it aside. "You said you saw that same model of revolver in Tomlinson's apartment. That's an interesting coincidence. I'd like to check it out—check out the computer, too. You didn't by any chance copy *those* keys, too, did you?"

"No," Laura said. "I was only too curious for my own good, back then. I wasn't a career criminal yet. But don't worry. There's no alarm system."

"I'd prefer to enter the place legally, in case I have to testify about it." He paused. "Actually, I heard about that apartment months ago. I started working on getting in there as soon as I got Tomlinson's account— told him I have a taste for S&M but can't keep whips and chains around because Rob visits me all the time and gets into everything. He put me off—he's selective about who he gives the keys to—but I'll keep trying. Claim I have a hot date who likes to be tied up and tortured."

He curled a strand of her hair around his finger and then smoothed it out. Every time he touched her, the whole damn room caught fire. "Interested in coming along? Playing the part of the hot babe?"

She was *very* interested, especially if they could get into Tomlinson's computer and find out why her house had been searched. "That depends. What would I have to do?"

"Nothing too complicated." His voice was federal-agent bland. "Let me tie you to the bed. Pretend it turns you on when I whip you. In case there's a camera, that is."

She started to edge away, but he laughed and pulled

her back. "I was joking, Laura. We won't even be alone. I'll need to get a computer expert up there. I asked you to come so you could tell me if anything's changed." He massaged the back of her neck. "I'm very conventional when it comes to sex. Boring, even. You could probably teach me a lot. Open up whole new worlds for me."

She blushed. "I doubt it. About the apartment . . . Suppose the place is bugged? Suppose there really is a camera? Won't they wonder why a third person is there?"

"I'll tell them you get off on servicing two guys at once."

"And if they recognize my voice or face?"

"I heard you might cause trouble. I took you out to find out what you know."

"Much like real life," she pointed out.

He smiled at that. "No comment. Tomlinson will be in town this week. I'll keep working on him. Contact you if I can bring him around. You can wear a hat with a veil if you want, but I'll sweep the place for bugs before you get there. Check around for cameras, too."

"Okay." An alarm bell suddenly went off. "Mike— what you said about bugs . . . What about in here? Suppose they bugged the house on Wednesday, when they—"

"Relax. I was here for over an hour before you came in this morning. I made sure the room was clean. In fact, I was thorough enough to hope you'd be wearing your black lace teddy tonight."

"Oh." She looked down. "Listen, I hate to kick you out, but I'm really tired. Thanks for coming over. I would have worried all night if I hadn't seen you."

He sighed. "It's pretty damn hard to leave when you say things like that."

"I'm sorry."

"I guess I'd rather hear it than not hear it." He lifted her chin and kissed her, then stood up. She resisted the urge to haul him back down. "I'll be in touch. You can call me if you need to, but watch what you say on the phone. No real names. You're my cousin Marie from New Jersey. If it's an emergency and you can't reach me, phone the Bureau and ask for Betsy Olmstead. She'll call my beeper for you."

"She's your contact agent?"

"Right." He scrawled his home phone number on a business card and handed it to her, then picked up his envelope and flashlight and let himself out of the house.

Laura locked the door and got back into bed. Of all the men in the world, she had to lust after an undercover cop who probably changed jobs and cities every year or two. A workaholic like Allan, who, instead of fielding zingers from the likes of Ned Brown, had to worry about dodging bullets from wiseguys like Cassani. She sure knew how to pick 'em.

She spoke to Art Albright the next day and agreed to have dinner with him Wednesday evening. It had taken a lot of talking, he said, but his mother had finally realized how possessive she'd become. Laura told herself that if a couple of friendly dates could send the lady over the edge, she didn't want to be around when Alice learned that Art Sr. had been arrested by the FBI.

She tried to separate the man she knew and liked from the one she'd discussed with Mike, but it was impossible. She felt like a snitch from the moment she let him in. Allan hadn't picked up the kids yet, so they went into the living room to talk. She realized Allan's lateness was deliberate when he showed up ten minutes later, helped himself to a beer, and stuck like glue for the next half hour, touching her repeatedly and making four references to when they'd been together.

She and Art talked about their respective legal problems over dinner. She stuck to her original story, that she was hiring a lawyer and would tell the FBI as much as he advised her to. It was the truth; she couldn't change her plans without arousing the Stonehouses' suspicions.

As for Art, he opened up a bit more, saying that, while he hadn't broken the law the way his father had, he'd known and done enough to be vulnerable to prosecution. The Feds were pressing him harder now, pointing out that a trial would cost him dearly even if he were acquitted. His lawyer had advised him to cut a deal, but if he talked in exchange for immunity, the people he'd fingered might realize who had named them. Then it would be witness-protection-program time, and he dreaded the idea of starting over again.

He said that if his father hadn't been dead already, he would have killed him himself—a joke, obviously, but a bitter one. Laura wondered if it was possible he didn't know the truth. Freddie obviously did, and Alice might too, but at the rate she was going, Laura half expected her to flip out completely, disappear in a Sierra snowstorm, and turn up in the Southwest calling herself Georgia Kirby.

Art came in for coffee after dinner, but that was all he wanted, just coffee and sympathy. He was too wrapped up in his problems to be interested in anything more. Laura felt he'd gotten a raw deal and hoped she could persuade Mike to help him. She told him to call or come by if he needed a friendly ear, and he said that he would.

After he left, she got into bed with her calculator, her checkbook, and her most recent bank statement, which had come in that day's mail. She opened the envelope. The statement listed deposits of nearly ten extra grand

and withdrawals of about the same amount. She thought about the error she'd caught the week before and checked the individual deposits and withdrawals. Five of each were mistakes, the deposits on April 10th and the withdrawals on the 13th, all involving just under two grand apiece. There was no indication of where they'd come from and gone, just the notations "Transferred to Account" and "Transferred from Account" followed by asterisks referring her to a string of long reference numbers. Still, everything balanced. What the computer had mistakenly given, it had apparently taken away.

The computer, she thought. Two ransacked houses, stolen computer files, numerous bank errors, businessmen who'd laundered money with a man who later "drowned." There were connections here—there had to be—and she had the feeling that two people were dead because of them.

TWENTY-THREE

It was ten-thirty Thursday evening, and, like some strapping, dark-haired Goldilocks, Mike was asleep on Laura's bed, sprawled out within kicking distance of an inert Sam. A briefcase, obviously his, was sitting on her night table. She stared at him, wondering how long he'd been there. She'd put the kids to bed at eight-thirty, then culled her mother and Vicki from the kitchen, trying to scoff convincingly when they'd complained, quite accurately, that she was being evasive about what was going on in her life. She'd read after that, but as many times as she'd passed by her room, she hadn't noticed Mike lying there till she'd turned on the light and walked inside. He looked amazingly angelic for a man in his line of work.

She shook his shoulder. "Mike. Wake up."

He opened his eyes and smiled groggily. "Hi."

"Hi, yourself. I should give you a set of keys. Save you the trouble of picking my locks."

"It's no trouble. Twenty seconds and I'm inside." He slowly sat up, then picked up the remote and turned on the TV. It was white noise, he said, in case the place had been bugged between Saturday and tonight.

He yawned. "It's been a long day. Got any coffee around?"

"No, but I'll make some. I've been wanting to call you, but I was afraid I'd say something wrong and get you in trouble."

"Why? What happened?"

"Something strange is going on with my checking account. I thought I should talk to you before I called the bank. I'll get the statement. It's in the desk in the kitchen."

He followed her down the hall, turning on the radio before he sat down with the statement. The transfers could have been errors, he said, but it was also possible that someone had washed money through her account, transferring it by computer from the source account through one or various others to his own—perhaps a numbered account in Switzerland. If computer theft had taken place, it would explain why her house had been searched. The victim might have traced the withdrawals to her account, then checked to see if she had the data necessary to have pulled the scam off—account information and access codes.

"I'd like to take this," he added. "Make a photocopy for Betsy and let her work with the bank to trace the path of the money. The source account probably belongs to Tomlinson, but it won't hurt to make sure."

"Whoever transferred the money would have needed my account number. Maybe I could figure out who had access to it and work back from there."

Mike looked amused. "The number is on every check you write or deposit. Besides, looking up your account number would have been child's play to someone who was expert enough with computers to get into the bank's system in the first place."

"Oh. Right." She joined him with their coffee. "What about you? What happened with the stuff you sent to Washington? Is Marion Kirby really Art Sr., and did they track him down yet?"

"Did you have dinner with Art Jr. last night?"

It took her a moment to realize why he'd asked. "Yes, and if I were going to open my mouth about his father, I would have done it by now. Besides, if you trusted me enough to tell me who you are, you should trust me with the details of your investigation."

"You think Art Jr. is a choir boy. You consider him a friend."

"Which is why I didn't ask him any questions last night." She smiled. "All the same, he volunteered some interesting information. Would you like to hear about it?"

Mike shook his head. "Sorry, Laura. I can't do it. It's too sensitive. What did he tell you?"

"It's slipped my mind."

"Then there's no point taking you to Tomlinson's apartment Saturday night." He sipped his coffee. "If you can't remember what you heard last night, you certainly won't recall what you saw nearly a month ago."

So he'd gotten the keys. Outflanked her again, because he knew she was dying to get back in that apartment. "God, you're aggravating. What about the tape and the gun? Can you talk about *them?*"

"The tape is why I'm here. Your so-called original was recorded from another tape or tapes, but the lab was able to bring a fair amount up. I want you to read the transcript. It might be a father and daughter. That would certainly jibe with your theory that it was used for blackmail."

They returned to the bedroom. The transcript was in his briefcase along with a flashlight and a battery-powered device the size of a vibrator, the latter with several drill- and bladelike attachments. "And I thought you used something the size of a nail file," Laura said. "This is cheating."

"It's harder than it looks, and you watch too many

private-eye shows." He tossed her bank statement into his briefcase, then handed her the transcript.

She started reading.

Segment #1

Woman: Oh, yeah. That's good. Hot . . . you're so hot. So slick and smooth and big. Oh, God. Yes. Yes! Harder, baby. Do it harder.

Man: Like this?

Woman: Yes. Oh, yes.

Man: You want more?

Woman: Please . . . Oh, God. I love you so much.

Next minute and thirty-eight seconds are unintelligible. Subjects appear to be having sexual intercourse. Twenty-six seconds of silence follows.

Man: This is no good. We have to stop. It's not fair to Jane.

Woman: What she doesn't know won't hurt her. (Laughter) Anyway, better me than someone else. At least it's all in the family, Pops.

Segment #2

Woman: But you asked me here, monsieur. And now I intend to have my way with you.

Man: No. Don't start in again, Hettie. It's not right. Baby, no . . . Don't . . . Oh, Jesus . . . That feels so good . . . (Note: Intermittent sucking noises. Female appears to be performing fellatio on the male.) You shouldn't . . . Oh, God, I can't stand it anymore . . .

Woman: If you don't like it—
Man: Yes. I do. Don't stop, baby. Please, don't stop. You make me so crazy. . . .
Woman: Of course I do. You love me.
Man: Yes. You're so beautiful. . . . Oh, God, don't stop again. . . .

Next three minutes and twenty seconds are unintelligible. Subjects appear to be engaged in fellatio. Thirty-nine seconds of silence follows.

Woman: Now it's my turn, Pops. I'm gonna get you nice and hard again. And then you're gonna make me feel real good. . . .

Next six minutes and seventeen seconds are unintelligible. Subjects appear to be having sexual intercourse.

End of tape.

Laura couldn't have been any more shocked if someone had found evidence that George Washington had molested the Custis children. "I think it's Ken Carlsen and his stepdaughter Heather Martin. He calls her Hettie sometimes. Jane is his wife. Heather's mother. They never had a father-daughter relationship. She was always away at school. She finished her master's last spring and came here to work. Moved into his apartment." Apartment 5C, she suddenly remembered. "It's directly above Tomlinson's. Hollister must have overheard them. Realized what was going on and taped them. Bonita must have known about it. It would explain why she wanted the tape after he died—to give to her boss. Earn herself some antique jewelry if it was useful. And it was, wasn't it? Tomlinson must have contacted Carlsen, alluded to the tape, and blackmailed him into meeting with you."

"Exactly." Mike paused. "We seem to have acquired another couple of murder suspects, although how they'd get Andrea Furillo's gun—"

"No. I don't believe that. Heather might be capable of murder, to protect Ken, but not Ken himself. He's one of the kindest, most decent men I know."

"For God's sake, Laura, he's sleeping with his wife's daughter."

"It's obvious who chased whom. And she's so beautiful, Mike, so madly in love with him. I'm not saying it's okay—I think it's tragic—but people are human. They have flaws. They make mistakes."

"Like Art Albright. He's just another weak but fundamentally decent human being in your opinion."

She raised her chin. "Yes. He got sucked into a no-win situation and handled it as best he could. I doubt he even knows his father is alive. Why can't you people ease up on him and give him some time? He'll probably decide to cooperate. He just doesn't want to die for it, or have to start all over again with a new identity."

"So he's close to cutting a deal, hmm?" Mike smiled. "Thanks for the information. I'll pass it along."

So the Bureau could squeeze Art till he cracked. It was always "we" with Mike, always "us." If you forgot that for a moment, your friends paid the price. Without a word, she tossed the transcript on the bed and turned around.

He wrapped his hands around her arms from behind. "Okay. I won't pass it along. Not yet. Do you want to hear about the gun?"

He knew she did. "No."

He nuzzled her neck. "How about Art Sr.? You want to hear about him?"

"I thought that was top secret."

He kept kissing her. "It is, but I'm desperate for forgiveness. You have any idea how much you turn me on?"

She had an excellent idea, because he did the same thing to her. "Mike, please. I told you before—"

"Yeah, right. I remember the whole list." He turned her around. "The gun was registered to Mary Beth Phelps."

"Really?" She was too startled to stay annoyed. "So the wife and the mistress had the same model of gun. And one of those guns—or a third one—was in a drawer in Tomlinson's apartment." She thought for a minute. "Freddie once told me that whenever he got something for his girlfriend, he got the same thing for Mary Beth. As if cheating was okay as long as he treated his wife and mistress the exact same way."

"You're saying he bought a gun for Andrea, so he got one for Mary Beth. And that somehow they got switched."

She nodded. "Yes. There's a waiting period, right? So maybe it happened when he picked them up."

"The registered owner is supposed to purchase and take possession of his gun in person, but I suppose the rules could have been bent along the way." Mike picked up the transcript and put it in his briefcase. "If Andrea's gun wound up in Mary Beth Hollister's hands . . . You've met Mary Beth. Suppose she found out Hollister was blackmailing her husband. Was she capable of killing him?"

Laura shrugged. "Maybe, but she was in Europe with her parents when Hollister died. And Freddie . . . He could have made the switch himself, because he'd decided to kill Hollister and he figured a dead woman's gun couldn't be connected to him, but I doubt he has the guts for murder. He cons and slithers his way out of tough situations. He doesn't confront them directly."

"We'll have to question both Mary Beth and him. Get search warrants for his house and office. First, though, I want a look in Tomlinson's apartment. I've got the place from four till midnight. Come around six. I'll check it out before you get there."

Mike grabbed his briefcase and slipped outside. Several seconds went by before she realized he hadn't told her a thing about Marion Kirby.

The automatic garage-door opener, she thought two nights later, was a major technological breakthrough. You could get in your car in a closed garage and escape your house and street without a soul getting a decent look at you. If you were dressed the way she was, in a skin-tight leopard-print Lycra outfit and a matching hairbow with a black veil, that was a real boon. Still, it was better to walk the streets in thrift-shop specials from the Madonna school of fashion than to be spotted and recognized in the vicinity of Tomlinson's apartment.

Mike didn't react at all when he first saw her, just closed the door and put on the chain. Then he traced the neckline of her top with his finger—it was a wide, deep V—and whispered, "Great outfit." He nuzzled her ear. "Is it a disguise or an invitation?"

"A disguise," she hissed back. To the extent she could still think coherently, she reasoned that he wouldn't have whispered without good cause. "Why? Are we being taped? Recorded?"

"See those books in the secretary? They're dummies. Big brother is watching, with an infrared-activated camera." He pushed up her veil. "I left it there. I figured it was safer to give it something to tape."

He backed her against the door and gave her a slow, thorough kiss. A movie kiss. Maybe clothes made the woman, but more likely, the man did. He radiated enough erotic heat to blister the usual erogenous zones and burn out Tomlinson's lens into the bargain. She put her arms around his neck and kissed him back, standing on tiptoes to fit herself to his body, slipping into his rhythm as if they'd been lovers for years, not giving a damn about the camera.

A minute or two went by. She'd never gotten so hot so fast in her life. But when she slid her hand between their bodies to unbutton his shirt, he loosened his hold and broke the kiss.

"I was working on the office," he mumbled, straightening away from her. "I need to finish up in there. . . ."

"What? Oh." She let him go. "Jimmying the lock, you mean."

"Sweeping the room for bugs before my computer expert shows up." He backed up a step. "He's at a family party. It was either me or his marriage, and he chose his marriage, but he's the best guy we have, so what could I do? He's calling before he leaves his in-laws'. I knew he'd be late, so I left the office till last. But the locks were tougher than I expected."

He'd spoken in a normal voice—a little strained, maybe, but not especially soft. Given the sensitive subject matter, that was odd. She glanced at the secretary, then stared at him suspiciously. "Those books . . . Should I bother taking a closer look?"

He smiled. "Probably not. There's nothing unusual about them."

"Then you made it all up. All that mumbo-jumbo about infrared sensors. There's no camera in here. No bugs." She repressed the urge to smile back. "You're a sociopath, Clemente. A menace to the values this country was built on."

"You're right. I'm scum, Laura—weak, amoral scum, with a sick fixation on animal prints. You're my only hope. You sympathize with human weakness. A woman like you could reform me overnight."

"Oh? Is that before or after I open up whole new sexual worlds for you?"

"Simultaneously. By the way, there's no way in hell I'm not making love to you tonight."

She was beginning to believe he was right. "You mean the real reason I'm here is to be seduced?"

"I can seduce you anywhere. You're here because you're smart and observant."

Smiling at him, she touched the top lock on the door. "I'm trying to be. This lock . . . It's new, Mike. A month ago, there were only two locks in this door."

"Good work. We'll trace the details of the installation." He pecked her on the lips. "Look around while I finish in the office. The only thing I noticed so far is that the Lady Smith is missing. I couldn't find it anywhere."

Laura searched the place methodically, but neither could she. In fact, nothing struck her as unusual until she joined Mike in the office. He was holding an instrument with all sorts of knobs and dials, still checking for bugs.

"There was only one lock in the office door before, the push-button kind," she whispered. There were two now, both much stronger. "And the door itself—it feels heavier now. Solid instead of hollow, like the other doors are."

He put down the machine, replying in a normal tone of voice. "The security's been beefed up since the last time you came here. The three new locks are high-security models made by a company in Germany." The phone rang, the line in the kitchen and bedroom. He went to answer it, and she continued looking around.

The improved security was the only change she noticed. The gun was still in the same drawer of the desk, the answering machine was still being put to the same dubious uses, and no interesting new books had appeared on the shelves. She went into the bedroom, glanced at Mike, and looked questioningly at the chandelier.

"Nope." He was stretched out on the bed. "The place is clean. That's disappointing—blackmail tapes would have helped our case—but maybe it's not surprising. Favors, sexual and otherwise, will get you a lot more in the long run than bugging and blackmail will." He got up, then grabbed the chair from the dressing table and put it in the closet. "Bring me my flashlight, then come over here." He pushed aside the clothes and hopped onto the chair. "I want to show you something."

The flashlight was on the dresser. She picked it up, kicking off her pumps before she joined him on the chair. They wound up nestled like spoons, her back to his chest, his arm around her waist to steady her. She could feel his erection against her buttocks.

"Is there really something in this closet," she asked, "or is this another of your highly creative passes?"

"You have a one-track mind, but you'll have to wait." He turned on the flash and pointed it at the ceiling. "See that hole in the corner? What do you want to bet that Carlsen's bedroom is directly above us? That the hole runs through to the floor of his closet? All Hollister had to do was drill the hole, then tape a wire with a miniature mike against it. Attach it to a voice-activated recorder that he left on the closet shelf." He paused. "Phelps was right. Hollister noticed things other people didn't. He must have had his suspicions about Carlsen and Heather and gone looking for proof to blackmail them with."

"And found it." She jumped off the chair and backed out of the closet. "How long before your computer expert gets here?"

Mike followed, putting the chair back under the dressing table and then returning to the closet to fix the clothes. "Fifteen or twenty minutes. I was wondering . . . " He pulled out the black jumpsuit. "Would it help if I put this on?"

Her eyes dropped to his crotch. It was instinctive, automatic, but he caught it and smiled. Blushing, she looked away.

"Is that a yes?" he asked.

She pictured him in the jumpsuit. She wasn't the least bit tempted to laugh. "I don't think I'm ready to answer that question. Do you want me to look around the bedroom?"

"Sure." He hung up the jumpsuit, then leaned against the wall and watched her.

His gaze packed almost as big a sexual wallop as his touch. She could guess what he was thinking, especially when she rummaged through the underwear and condoms, but she was a thirtysomething mother of two. A nice Jewish girl from Queens. She couldn't picture herself having frantic sex with some restless cloak-and-dagger type on red satin sheets in a shady apartment.

Then she finished checking the bathroom and saw the warm look in his eyes, and she wasn't so sure. "There's nothing new, Mike. Sorry I wasn't more help."

"You haven't checked through the playthings yet." He pulled down the box and set it on the floor.

She walked over and knelt down to look. Mike didn't do a damn thing but stand and watch, but she was still flustered and embarrassed. When she looked at the things in this box . . . If Mike could see the pictures in her mind . . .

She slowly stood up. "There might be some new gadgets in there. I'm not sure. I'll get out of your way now, before your friend shows up."

He stroked her hair. She tensed a little. "Relax,

Laura. I told you, I'm the most conventional guy in the world. If you're worried I'm going to lash you to the bed and attack you with a studded vibrator, don't be."

"I'm not. It's not you. It's me. First I want to, then I don't. I don't know why."

He put his arms around her. She didn't move, just stood quietly in his embrace, torn between staying and leaving. "You know what I think? You're not nervous about sex. You're scared of the future. But I'll tell you something. I'm as—" There was a loud buzz. "Hell. Fong always did have lousy timing. Wait right here. I'll be back in a minute."

"Really, Mike, I think I should go. You have business to take care of—"

There was another buzz, longer this time. He mumbled a curse and released her. She hesitated, then started toward the door.

She never knew what hit her. One moment she was walking, and the next he was grabbing her wrist, slapping on a handcuff, lifting her off her feet. "Forget it," he said as he strode to the bed. "You're not going anywhere till we talk." He put her down and cuffed her to the headboard. Then he left, closing the door behind him.

She looked at the cuffs, thinking irritably that one of the keys in the blasted box had better match the lock, picturing herself at a locksmith's with a brass headboard attached to her wrist if none did. And then she remembered who she was with—the Houdini of the special-agent set—and giggled. The man had a multitude of talents, she had to give him that. He could pick locks, charm you senseless, debug rooms, scare you half to death, and probably talk you out of your firstborn child. And he could kiss. Lord, could he ever.

She sat up straighter, trying to get more comfortable. He was right. She'd been scared of the future. She'd finally found a guy who made love as much to her mind as her body, and she'd been scared! She shook her head, thinking she was even crazier than Marion Kirby. You didn't turn down beluga in a Bugatti.

The front door opened and closed. She heard talking in the hallway, then the office door shutting. Mike came in a few seconds later, locking the door behind him. For the first time since she'd met him, he looked unsure of himself. She thought that was adorable.

He walked halfway into the room. "Can we talk?"

"Maybe," she said coolly. "Take off the cuffs and then we'll see."

"Yeah, okay. I'll, uh, I'll need to find the key. It's probably somewhere in the box."

"No. No key. You locked me up, Clemente. The least you can do is demonstrate how that vibrator thing works."

He looked confused. "You want me to pick the lock? It would make you less angry?"

"I'm not angry, just curious." She paused. "And resigned. If I have to sleep with you, I'll sleep with you. It won't be so bad." She smiled. "Kissing you sure wasn't."

He walked to the bed. He didn't look confused or uncertain anymore, just hot. On the verge of spontaneous combustion, in fact.

She laughed and held out her free hand. "Hey, wait a minute. Not here. I meant later, not now."

He caught her by the wrist and kissed her palm, then sat down. "Why not?"

"For one thing, your pal Fong is right across the hall, and for another—"

"You're afraid he'll feel left out? You want me to invite him in?" He took the bow out of her hair and dropped it on the floor. "Forget it, honey. No offense, but he'll take computers over group sex any day of the week."

"Very funny. Listen, this bed has been the site of all sorts of illicit and depraved activities. It's probably bad luck. It's probably even against my religion."

"So you'll convert." He took her in his arms and kissed her deeply. Pushed up her top and caressed her breasts. Fong stopped mattering. So did the history of the bed. She kissed him back, touching him every place she could reach. Things were moving so fast and felt so good that she was already looking ahead to the next time, because once would never be enough.

Then the problems began. She wanted to lie down beside him, to tease him a bit while most of their clothes were still on, but there was no way to do that without dislocating her shoulder. The headboard resembled a grid, and he'd cuffed her near the top center. They fumbled around on the bed, trying to get as close to each other as they could. She wound up on his lap with her legs wrapped around his waist, which would have been absolutely sensational except for one thing. Her arm was being yanked from its socket.

She pulled away, then collapsed against the headboard, laughing hysterically. "Oh, God, my arm . . . " She rubbed it with her free hand. "You may be a hotshot undercover agent, Clemente, but you don't know borscht about bondage. Get these damn things off me while I'm still in one piece."

Smiling, he nuzzled her breasts. "Sorry, but I doubt I can walk. We'll have to find a more workable position."

"You wouldn't say that if it were *your* arm. I'm not risking my most useful limb just to make love with you. I don't care if you have to crawl, hop, or slither like a snake, just get these off me."

"Without the key. You expect me to stagger into the office with an erection as big as Mount Whitney while Ryan Fong ogles me every tortured step of the way."

She hadn't, actually, but it had a certain twisted

appeal. "He won't even notice. He's busy with the computer. Anyway, there's not nearly as much to see as you obviously think there is."

He burst out laughing. "You're murder on my ego, but you're probably right. About Ryan, that is."

He left the room, returning several minutes later with his briefcase. She made a face at him. "I can't believe you stopped to chat. Even Allan wasn't that much of a workaholic."

He looked apologetic. "Believe me, I didn't want to, but Ryan needed some sympathy. He was mumbling to himself about the computer. He's having a problem getting in."

"Not nearly as much of a problem as you're about to have."

"Now where have I heard that before?" He took out his equipment, then sat down on the bed. The cuffs were off within seconds.

"I'm impressed," she murmured.

He started to undress her. "Not nearly as impressed as you're about to be," he said.

TWENTY-FOUR

Laura had read enough articles in women's magazines to know how the game was played. Coolly. Close to the vest. You didn't ask questions or make demands. You didn't bare your heart and soul unless the man did it first.

But she was lying naked in Mike's arms, and the sex between them had been an erotic maelstrom. He was absently rubbing her back now, looking utterly content. Forty years ago, he would have been smoking a cigarette.

She wriggled downward and folded her arms on his chest, resting her chin on her crossed wrists so she could look into his eyes. "The last time I had sex was a month ago, with Allan. It was good physically—it always was with him—but afterward, I felt empty inside. Like I'd made a terrible mistake." She looked down for a moment. "I don't feel that way now, but maybe I should. I'm getting more and more hung up on you, and the life that makes you happy isn't the life I want. I *was* scared before, because tonight—or a series of tonights—is all there will ever be, and it's hard for me to deal with that."

He smoothed her hair, very gently. "You think I'd blow my cover for a one-night stand? For a murder case that isn't my responsibility? Or even for a political corruption case that is? This was never about business, Laura. I told you that before. I was looking at three or four more months undercover, maybe even longer. And then I met you. Every time I saw you I fell a little more in love, but I did what I was supposed to. Tried to charm you, and when that didn't work, tried to scare you. But I kept thinking. . . . In three months, you could be back with your husband or living with someone else. In the end, I couldn't let that happen." He cupped her chin and kissed her. "Not when I could have this."

He hadn't promised a thing, but she enjoyed the words he'd spoken. "Oh? And did it ever occur to you that you couldn't have this?"

"Nope. The only reason it didn't happen sooner is that you're straighter than Highway 5 through the Valley. Even respectable corporate lobbyists are too corrupt for you. I told that to Kevin, but he wouldn't listen. Ordered me to get my brains out of my crotch and keep my hands to myself."

"Your brains or your ego?" she teased.

He smiled. "Facts are facts, honey. You had the hots for me from the first time we met."

"The first time was at Pavilions. Actually, it was the second time."

"The second time, then. It took me a little longer, but I was preoccupied at the funeral." He paused. "After five or six years in this business, you start having days when you tell yourself you're getting too old for it. I saw you at the lake, and I realized those days were coming more often. That I was tired of being around crooks all the time. Of leading a life that was nothing but work because normal friendships outside the Bureau are impossible. And then there's Rob. The longer I'm in California, the more I miss him. He doesn't have much use for Stan. Maybe you picked up on that."

She had, and also on the fact that he idolized Mike and got along with him unusually well. "A little, but how old is he now? Twelve? Thirteen?"

"Almost thirteen."

"So who doesn't rebel at that age?"

"Almost no one, but Nancy's expecting a baby in August, and between a tough pregnancy and her problems with Rob, she's getting more and more stressed out. She complains about him all the time, and he complains about her and Stan. I've tried to referee, but I've also started to suggest, very tactfully, that it might be better for everyone concerned if she sent him to live with me."

"But she'll never agree unless you're leading a more normal life. That's why you're thinking about settling down."

"That and you."

Those words changed everything, and she liked them even more, but still . . . "Mike—I feel the same way you do, but you're going so fast. I'm not even divorced yet."

"And I'm still undercover." He looked amused. "Don't worry—we'll be sneaking around for months. I've thought about taking a desk job when this is over, or doing private investigations, but I'll probably practice law. With college coming up for Rob, I'll need the money."

"Your salary from Burke/Maravich—you turn it in to the government?"

"Right. I get enough back in expense money to maintain a convincing lifestyle, but the clothes, the furniture, the car—technically, most of it belongs to Uncle Sam."

"He can have it. I'll take what's left." She traced a design around his nipple. "All those jobs—all that moving around. What were you really doing all that time?"

He laughed. "You want to seduce the answer out of me? Go right ahead."

"It was encouragement, not seduction. Come on. Tell me."

"I already have. I was an attorney in Chicago and L.A." He pulled her on top of him and put his arms around her. "I got bored with corporate law. I wanted to do something idealistic, so I joined the FBI. Spent the next the next few years as a street agent in Washington, Florida and New York, then took undercover jobs investigating the courts in Chicago, a survivalist hate group in Montana and organized crime in Texas."

He'd moved to Seattle next, taking a job as a supervisor in the local field office, hoping to revive a marriage that his work had all but killed. But a year later, his old boss in L.A. had contacted his parents to find out where he was, wanting to recommend him for a job with a financial services company the Bureau was interested in because of its alleged money-laundering activities. His marriage had devolved into a mass of old resentments and new recriminations by then. His desk job had bored him. When Nancy had given him an ultimatum—her or Los Angeles—he'd chosen Los Angeles. Burke/Maravich had lobbied for the firm, so he'd gotten to know the principals. He'd impressed them enough to be offered a job eventually, and the Bureau had ordered him to Sacramento.

"And here you are," Laura said.

He slid his hands to her buttocks and pressed her against his groin. He was hard again—had been for some time. "Yeah. Here I am."

She grabbed another condom from the night table and slid it on him. Then, straddling him, she eased him inside her and moved slowly up and down. He grasped her hips and smiled, looking as if life couldn't possibly have been more perfect than it was at that moment.

"Sweetheart," she murmured, "where's Marion Kirby?"

His smile got broader. "For information like that, you'll have to dress up in the black peekaboo underwear and do an erotic dance with the bullwhip and the Ruger Redhawk."

She ran her fingers down his chest to his pelvis. "Really, Mike. Where is he?"

He pulled her down to kiss her. "Later, Laura."

Kirby, alias Art Albright, Sr., was still in New Mexico, under close but clandestine government surveillance, Mike told her afterward. There were so many interdependent facets to the investigation, that, like a house of cards, if even one were removed or disturbed, the whole game could collapse. When the subpoenas were finally served and the warrants finally executed, it would be all at once.

"And when will that be?" Laura asked.

"Weeks or even months. The longer we investigate quietly, the stronger our case will be." Mike got out of bed and began to dress. "I should check on Ryan. See how he's doing."

"You never forget work for very long, do you?"

"The sooner we finish, the sooner we can go home. To my place, not yours. It's more private. Fewer nosy neighbors."

"Sounds good to me. I'll have to call Allan, though. He says it traumatizes the kids if they want to speak to me and he can't reach me. Is it okay to use this phone?"

"Yes." He gave her a quick kiss. "Come into the office when you're done."

"With you and Ryan Fong."

"Good point. Ryan's oblivious, but not *that* oblivious. You should probably get dressed first." He strode out of the room.

Allan and the kids were out, so she left a message—not that she'd be with Mike, because Allan would have had a cow if he'd known, but simply the number where she could be reached. Then, smiling as if she were tipsy on champagne, she pulled on her clothes and made up the bed. She was about to meet a total stranger—an officer of the law—dressed like a bimbo. Reeking of sex with one of his colleagues. And she was so damned happy, she scarcely even cared.

She walked into the office. There was a second computer on the desk now, bigger than a laptop but smaller than Tomlinson's PC. Fong had taken the latter apart, connecting part of its innards to the computer he'd brought along. He was skimming a spreadsheet on the portable's screen now.

Mike was sitting next to him, watching. "Laura Miller, Ryan Fong," he said, pulling her down on his lap.

Fong didn't look up, just grunted.

"The computer was locked up tight. Ryan had to access its hard drive through the portable. He's checking through the files, looking for financial information." Mike pointed to the microcassette recorder sitting by the answering machine. "We listened to the tape on 555-7711. It was nothing but letters and numbers. Messages like 'Cee. Five from four. In seven and thirteen.' Instructions of some sort, possibly."

Ten more minutes went by. Fong finished looking through the files. Nothing unusual had turned up.

"Maybe the data's in code," Mike said, "although if it is, God knows why Tomlinson thought Laura would be able to spot it and crack it. But go ahead and copy the files. I'll have them sent to Cryptology."

Fong picked up a floppy disk. "Or it's in a hidden file—a file the computer's been programmed to omit when it lists what's in a directory, either for security reasons or to guard against an accidental erasure." He inserted the diskette. "If it is, this should find it for me—let me access a complete list of the files on the hard disk."

He went to work, searching for a file whose name he didn't recognize. Suddenly he smiled. "Bingo. 'Eos,' last revised at 9:16 A.M. on April 14th." Today was the 25th. "Let's take a look."

He accessed the appropriate directory and retrieved the file. A list of words and phrases appeared on the screen, numbered from one to twenty-eight, each followed by several longer numbers.

"At least some of those are companies," Mike remarked. "Part of ACX Enterprises. The numbers from one to twenty-eight might correspond to numbers on the answering-machine tape. The other numbers look like account numbers and security codes. Make me a copy, Ryan. Then you can put the computer back together and get out of here."

Fong laughed. "Buddy, you're the one who's in a hurry to leave, not me, not that I blame you. But where there's one hidden file, there could be others."

He copied the Eos file onto a diskette, then resumed his search. "Hmm. 'Echo,' last revised a few minutes ago."

He retrieved the file. It contained a list of other files, each followed by a date, a time, and how it had been used. The final entry indicated that the Eos file had been retrieved and copied at 7:52 that evening. "It apparently lists all activity except for Echo itself," Fong said. "You see that, Laura? I've got all the brains, but when this is over, he'll get all the glory."

She nodded sympathetically. "True, Ryan. Life's unfair. Go back to March 28th, would you? That's the date Vicki and I were in the apartment. Maybe someone else was here that day, too, and we got the blame."

He scrolled backward. There was nothing on the 28th, but there was a long list of entries on April 6th. "I'll be damned," she murmured. "Starting at 5:20 A.M., someone checked through dozens of files on the disk."

"Checked but didn't copy or print." Mike pulled a datebook out of his pocket while Fong scrolled forward. "Look at Thursday, April 9th. Someone copied Eos at 9:23 A.M. The next day, ten grand wound up in your account. The money was withdrawn on Monday the 13th, the day before Eos was revised. On the 15th, your house was searched by someone looking for a computer file. What do you want to bet that the stolen money came from accounts in the Eos file?" Mike asked Fong to scroll backward again. "Interesting. Other than on April 6th, the only entry between March 28th and April 9th is on the evening of March 29th. 'CRT' was retrieved, revised, and printed. Tomlinson gave a speech to the Commercial Roundtable on Monday the 30th. I was there. Obviously he worked on it Sunday night. He left for L.A. straight from the speech and didn't return to Sacramento till April 13th. He called me that evening and told me to meet with Carlsen—that he would deal on AB 2962."

They checked the Eos entries again. The file had been retrieved on April 6th, retrieved and copied on April 9th, retrieved again on the 13th, and retrieved and revised the next day. "Tomlinson must have learned about the missing money almost immediately," Mike went on. "He suspected a computer breach, so he came to Sacramento on Monday the 13th to check the Echo file and saw that someone had copied Eos the previous Thursday. He probably had the bank change the security codes the next morning, then entered the new numbers into the computer. He must have known from Bonita that you'd been in the apartment on March 28th. You could have copied her keys and returned on April 6th and 9th. And if he'd traced the money to your account by then—"

"I'd be his prime suspect. The timing makes sense, but why would he think that Vicki or I could get into his computer when even an expert like Ryan had problems?"

"For all he knew, you were an expert, too, or had the help of one. You would have had to be, to get into the bank's computer system."

"Unless she worked there." Fong erased his activity from the Echo file. "Laura—back on March 28th . . . When you first saw the computer, what was on the screen?"

"A C-prompt. I tried to get into a directory—any directory—but you needed a password for everything but some computer games and DOS."

"Then Tomlinson tightened his computer security between then and now, because it was harder to get in tonight. Much harder."

"And before?" Mike asked. "What level of skill would have been required? What sort of equipment?"

"No equipment. If it was set up the way I think, the password would have been located in the programming. Anyone who knows computers well would have been able to go in and search for it."

"Like Art Albright," Mike said to Laura. "He knew what was wrong with Vicki's computer when the rest of you didn't. He even had a motive—a reason to have a grudge against Tomlinson. Doing business with Tomlinson and his pals could cost him his business. Send him to jail."

"But he doesn't do business with Tomlinson, at least not anymore," Laura pointed out. "He couldn't even have gotten the keys to the apartment."

"He might have told you he didn't, but that doesn't make it true. We have reason to believe otherwise."

"Fine. Even if you're right, why steal only ten grand? That's peanuts. And why run it through my account when he could have chosen some total stranger's?"

"Because you were the logical one to pin it on. You were in the apartment. You had access to the computer."

"But I never told that to Art." Laura hesitated, then admitted, "I guess he could have found out, though. I told my mother, and if she told Alice, Alice might have told him."

She stared at the screen, thinking about how sweet he'd been the Wednesday her house had been ransacked, how worried he'd seemed about her safety, how appalled he'd appeared at the tie to Hollister's murder. He was too transparent to have been acting that evening. He couldn't be behind this.

Mike's house was in Land Park, a rental about ten blocks from Carolyn Seeley's place. They drove there in separate cars, parking side by side in the garage. Laura wasn't sure who grabbed whom, only that they wound up naked on the living room rug, and that Mike was tender and passionate where Allan had only been skillful, and that they laughed together afterward about the floor being too hard, the house being too cold, and the two of them being too old to risk their backs and health that way.

They talked afterward, ordering in pizza and cokes and eating in bed. "What's McKennery going to say when he finds out you disregarded both his orders and the law?" Laura asked. "It's not the sort of thing you can keep secret."

"You're right," Mike admitted. "Between the Kirby letters and the mix-up with the guns, there was no way he wasn't going to find out that I'd been in Phelps's office, so Betsy leveled with him. He wasn't too happy. I believe the words reprimand and dismissal were used a few times. But his mood improved when he heard about the Furillo ID and the letter on Vicki's printer. Then the transcript of Bonita's tape came in, and he cheered up a little more. Anyway, nobody outside the Bureau will ever hear about my transgressions, so he can afford to let them pass."

"Nobody except me, and we all know how dangerous *I* am."

"He likes you better now that you've identified the voices on the transcript and helped with the guns. He told Betsy to stick strictly to her job, which is to stay in touch with me and keep me straight, and to give me a message: If I don't go by the book from now on, he'll nail my balls to the wall when this is over."

Laura winced. "I hope he doesn't find out about Tomlinson's computer."

"There's no reason he should. I needed some direction and Eos should provide it—tell me where to go next and what to look for." He put his glass on the night table. "Tomlinson and his pals—they make millions legally, but it isn't enough. They're probably skimming casino and track money and cutting in the mob. Laundering gambling and drug money, working financial scams, pushing off-track betting. If lives are destroyed and our institutions go to hell, that isn't their problem. These guys could give a clinic on greed. I want them as much as I've ever wanted anyone."

She snuggled closer to him. "I love it when you talk ethics. I'm a sucker for idealism in a man. Personally, I'm not nearly so noble. The one I want in jail is Freddie Phelps, and my reasons are entirely personal."

"We'll get him for you, Laura. On insurance fraud, if not murder."

"Then you don't think he killed Hollister?"

"He's a suspect, but so are plenty of other people." Maggie Hollister, he said, for the insurance money or because she was tired of being cheated on. Her son Charlie, because he'd hated his father and could count on the generosity of his mother. Heather Martin or Ken Carlsen, because Ken was being blackmailed. Bonita, who could have killed Hollister for the insurance money and then been murdered with the same gun. Craig Tomlinson, who'd been close to Hollister and had enough questionable business interests to make him a possible blackmail target. And finally, if Hollister had extorted money in return for his silence about Art Albright Sr.'s money-laundering business, any of the Albrights. Whether the murder weapon had been in Tomlinson's apartment or at the Phelps's house, most or all of those people had probably had access to it.

The phone rang and Mike picked it up. "Hello. Why? Who did you want? Yes. Just a moment." He put his hand over the mouthpiece. "Allan, I assume. He sounds unhappy."

He was. He asked if she was with Art—obviously they hadn't talked enough for him to know Art's voice—and she reminded him that it was none of his business. He didn't press her, just said tightly that he supposed he deserved this and hoped she'd come to her senses once it was out of her system. She didn't respond.

He mumbled that the kids wanted to talk to her and put on Seth, as if he and Sarah had been the reason for the call. Laura knew better. He'd called to check up on her.

Much later, lying awake while Mike slept quietly beside her, she thought about the couples who wound up fighting bitterly on battlefields created out of their own grievances and resentments, using their children as the pawns, either too blind or too obsessed to stop. She and Allan couldn't become one of them. They simply couldn't.

She saw Mike a few days later at work and treated him coolly, like the arm-twisting lobbyist everyone believed him to be, but her greeting Wednesday evening was considerably warmer. With the kids at Allan's, she'd more or less expected him, so she'd changed into her black teddy and waited for him in bed. Her efforts didn't go unappreciated.

"So how's it going with the lawyers?" Mike asked half an hour later. "Did you hire one yet?"

"I have one more to see, tomorrow after work, and you sound like Vicki. She calls me after every appointment." She caressed his stomach, then moved her hand lower. "Mike, couldn't I tell Frank and her the truth? It would be so much simpler."

"No." She took away her hand, and he laughed. "Hey, why did you stop?"

"Because it never gets me anywhere."

"Sure it does. You're dynamite. I'm just stalwart as hell." He kissed her nose. "Start again, then ask me if I've found out anything new. I swear I'll talk."

"You'll talk anyway."

"True, but I'll be a lot happier while I'm doing it." He grabbed his jeans and took a piece of paper out of his pocket. "I asked Betsy to look through the Franks wiretaps, to see if there was anything relating to the Carlsen tape. She came up with this."

It was the transcript of a conversation between Bonita and an unidentified male, recorded on Saturday, April 4th. The man, Laura realized almost immediately, was Craig Tomlinson.

He'd called to thank her for a package, obviously the Ken Carlsen-Heather Martin tape, then asked if it had belonged to Jimmy. She'd said yes, adding that she'd remembered it at the funeral and asked a friend to fetch it from the apartment and send it to the lake. She'd been running too late to go herself, she'd explained, and had wanted to enclose a transcript before sending it on.

Tomlinson had scolded her for giving her keys to a stranger, but she'd assured him that Laura was a good and reliable friend. Besides, she'd said, she'd asked for lots of different items, as camouflage, so there was no need to worry. Still, she promised to be more careful in the future.

The tape confirmed what Laura had suspected. "Two days later," she reminded Mike, "Carolyn showed up at Allan's and got him to tell her what I'd seen in Tomlinson's apartment. And the following Saturday, she waylaid me at Charlie's party and asked me the same thing. Obviously Tomlinson put her up to it. He was concerned that I'd been in his office."

"But not worried enough to make a special trip to Sacramento to check the Echo file, probably because a week had gone by without any problems. He did take precautions for the future, though. We found the locksmith who worked on his apartment. Tomlinson called him on Monday, April 6th and asked him to install the German-made locks and the new door. The locks had to be shipped from a distributor in San Francisco. They arrived on Wednesday the 8th and the work was done on Thursday the 9th. The locksmith mentioned that a woman was in the apartment when he got there. She said she'd forgotten some movies and was picking them up. She asked him what work he planned to do."

"Did he remember what she looked like?"

"Medium height with short blond hair, dark glasses, and a tan trenchcoat. On the thin side, probably around fifty." He paused. "That was around nine-thirty in the morning. She was the one who copied the Eos file, Laura."

And whoever had copied Eos had moved money through her account. "Did Betsy have any luck at the bank?"

He smiled. "Good question. What do I get if I answer?"

"A damn good cup of coffee tomorrow morning."

"You've got yourself a deal," he said with a laugh. "Someone in the electronic banking department noticed one of the withdrawals on Monday the 13th, decided it was unusual for that particular company's account, and phoned the firm's bookkeeper. That was a bad break for whoever took the money, because the bank normally ignores transactions under two grand. Five different accounts were hit, all belonging to ACX companies that were listed in the Eos file. The money went into your account first, then into five others. Those five accounts had two things in common. Like yours, they were in the Golden West Bank, all in different branches, and all of them belonged to clients of Albright Investments. Art Jr. had power of attorney for each one. He wired requests to the five branches to withdraw the funds in cash, saying an employee would make the pickups. The woman who showed up fits the description of one of his clerks. Short blond hair, average height, thin and fiftyish. She was wearing dark glasses and a tan trenchcoat."

That was as smoky a gun as you could find. Laura felt as if someone had punched her in the stomach. "Oh. So what happens now?"

"Tomlinson was close to Art Sr. We believe he's done business with Art Jr. I want to know more about those ties. Whatever Art Jr. may have done—assuming he's not guilty of murder—he's probably a minor crook compared to Tomlinson and his friends. If he helps *me*, I'll help *him*." Mike looked at her somberly. "Help me out, Laura. He likes you. Trusts you. Invite him over, give him some wine, and get him to talk about his dealings with Tomlinson. Please."

She couldn't bring herself to say yes, but she promised to think about it.

TWENTY-FIVE

T he third and final lawyer on Laura's list was Bruce Bailey, Art Albright's attorney. She talked to him for half an hour, told him she'd get back to him once she'd make a decision, and thought guiltily that Rodin's statue would be done thinking before she was.

She returned to his reception room to find Art and his mother sitting in adjacent chairs, Art looking preoccupied and Alice, dour. Art smiled at her. "Laura! Hi. I see you decided to talk to Bruce. How did it go?"

"Very well. Thanks for the recommendation. Alice, it's nice to see you again."

Alice nodded coolly, saying nothing.

"Mom was concerned about my situation," Art said quickly. "She has some questions for Bruce. He agreed to squeeze us in after his last appointment—you, obviously."

Laura joined them, telling Alice how sharp Bailey had seemed and how easy he'd been to talk to. She was making small talk, trying to smooth over an awkward situation, so what came out of her mouth next surprised even her.

341

"Still, it's a tough decision. The others were good, too. I've gotten myself into such a mess . . . " She bent closer to Art. "What I need is someone to talk to, someone to bounce things off of. I haven't told anyone the whole story, not even the lawyers, but I think I could tell you. Could you come for dinner on Saturday? It would really help."

"Sure, if you think—"

"You can't," Alice interrupted. "We're going to your sister's."

Art's jaw tightened. "Oh? That's news to me, Mother."

"Carol said to tell you. It slipped my mind. Your family should come first, Arthur."

"If Carol wants to invite me to dinner, she can call me herself. Laura, I'd be glad to come over, but don't bother cooking. I'll pick up some Chinese food. What time?"

"Six, and let's make it for drinks, instead. I have some hors d'oeuvres in the freezer." She smiled at Alice. "You have a wonderful son. He's been a good friend. I won't keep him for too long, I promise. I'm sure he'll be able to make it to Carol's dinner."

Alice looked at her balefully. "How thoughtful of you. Your mother taught you such nice manners."

Laura stifled a groan. Her mother. How could she have forgotten? "Alice, I'd appreciate it if you didn't say anything to Mom about my being here. You know how she worries, and if you tell her I'm seeing lawyers—"

"I'm her friend. I wouldn't add to her troubles."

"Thanks. You're very understanding—"

"It's for her. Not for you." Alice picked up a magazine and started reading.

Defeated, Laura told Art she'd see him on Saturday and left the office. Meeting him here had simply has-tened the inevitable, she supposed. She'd never been much good at saying no to a man she was in love with.

She called Mike at ten that evening—no name or explanation, just "I have to see you." He was there within minutes. One look at each other and they decided business could wait.

Later, she explained about running into Art and inviting him by for drinks. "You said that if he helped you, you'd help him, providing he isn't in too deep. I believe you, but you're not McKennery or the U.S. attorney. How do we know they'll honor your promise?"

"He's got a damn good lawyer. If he's worth enough as a witness, they'll deal. By the way, Betsy's been checking out the names in the Eos file. Remember Albright's money-laundering companies?"

Laura nodded. "Like the gold mine, you mean."

"Yes. All of them have been sold since last winter. We've been trying to track them down to find out who controls them now, but the transfers are such masterpieces of corporate obfuscation that it was close to impossible till we started with the ACX companies and worked the other way. Turns out that Tomlinson bought at least one of Albright's companies through a pyramid of firms he controls, then restructured and renamed it. It's listed in the Eos file as Jennex. They're still working on the others. My guess is, when Art Jr. went out of the money-laundering business, Tomlinson and his mob-connected cronies decided to do it on their own. The numbers on the phone tape might be instructions about moving funds around. Be sure to find out what Art knows about that."

Laura took out a pad and pencil, then asked what else she should be sure to find out.

*   *   *

It was one thing to wear a wire and ask some questions, another to expose one's children to it. Laura arranged for Seth and Sarah to spend Saturday night with their best friends, a girl Sarah's age and her ten-year-old brother. They had a music recital at two, their mother said, but the family would be home by six.

Mike was coming at five, so that left a spare hour to fill. Laura tried Becky first, asking her to take the kids to the mall to window-shop and eat, but it was Frank's birthday and Vicki was having his family over to celebrate. The Stonehouses gave Vicki fits, especially Frank's father and older sister, so Laura told Becky to pass along her condolences.

She called her mother next, but Dottie was busy, too. She had a movie date with Alice Albright, who'd obviously conjured up Carol's dinner out of thin air to keep Art out of Laura's clutches. Art's efforts to the contrary, she was as possessive as ever, but she'd apparently kept her mouth shut about meeting Laura in Bailey's office, and that was all that mattered.

That left Laura with two options—to feed the kids early and park them with other friends for an hour, or to call Allan. She thought back to Saturday night. Allan enjoyed doing her favors. It made him feel important and needed. In fact, sometimes she thought he wanted her approval even more than he wanted her, and that the more of it she gave him, the better they got along. Throwing herself on his mercy could only help.

It was a touchy request, asking him to take the kids so she could entertain another man, but she assured him that Art was coming to talk, nothing more. Allan couldn't have been nicer. Not only did he agree, he insisted on coming early and taking the kids to a movie, so she could get things ready without having them underfoot.

By Saturday at four-fifteen, when the three of them drove off, Laura had begun to empathize with McKennery and his juggling act. It had been bad enough when she'd had a house, a mother, two children, an adulterous ex-husband, and a lecherous boss to contend with. Now she had an adulterous boss who was also a murder suspect, a crooked ex-boss who'd become a bitter enemy, and a confused ex-husband who thought he wanted to drop the ex. Her lover was busy Elliott-Nessing bad guys, an operation that had turned her into a cross between a Nixon plumber and a suburban Mata Hari. And the guy she'd thought was her pal had probably played computer hopscotch through Golden West Bank and made her look like the hacker, getting her in trouble with the type of person whose business associates were named after weapons. The double shift had been a picnic by comparison.

It got worse. At four-thirty, Vicki called for moral support, sounding perilously close to total personality disintegration. Laura had barely finished shoring up that front when she heard from another—her mother, who announced that she and Alice were blowing in later to say hello.

That was all Laura needed. "Actually, Mom, it might be better if you didn't. Art and I have a lot to talk about, and—"

"I thought I was always welcome in your house," Dottie interrupted, "but if I'm not, even for half an hour, that's fine. We won't come."

"Of course you're always welcome, but tonight just isn't the best time." Mike walked in with a canvas tote bag and flashed his FBI ID at her. Laura raised her eyebrows, then mouthed, "My mother," and made an exasperated face. "I have to go now. There's someone at my door."

"Sure, and your kettle is boiling over, too. You

haven't been yourself lately, Laura. Don't think I haven't noticed. I love you. I'm very concerned."

"I love you, too, and don't be. I'm fine. I'll call you tomorrow, but I really do have to go now."

Dottie said the longest long-suffering good-bye in the annals of modern motherhood. Mike, meanwhile, was rearranging her closet, cramming ski boots and bags of old clothing onto the shelves in order to make room on the floor.

"So you found your ID," Laura said. "Where was it?"

"In New Jersey. Rob was right. Nancy sent it to my parents. It was in an unopened carton in their attic. I had them mail it to Betsy."

"And you brought it today for show and tell?" He couldn't use it, not without blowing his cover.

"You never know." He began to unpack his bag, setting a receiver/recorder and a set of headphones on the floor, then taking out a transmitter. The latter was about a quarter-inch thick and smaller than a playing card. A tiny microphone on a thin wire was plugged into one end.

Laura couldn't help noticing what else was in his bag. "Why the gun? You don't usually carry one, do you?"

"I don't usually need one. Remember, I'll only be able to hear you, not see you, so if Art does something threatening, like pull out a gun, you'll have to say so. I'll be there in seconds. Drop to the ground and get as far away as you can."

Art didn't seem like the type to wave a gun around, but he hadn't seemed like the type to steal ten grand, either. "Would you stop trying to scare me? I had enough of that in the Hollisters' laundry room."

"I want you a little scared. You'll be more careful that way." He took out some adhesive tape. "Take off your clothes. I want to test this out."

"You want me to strip so you can tape some gadget

to my body? Boy, the honeymoon sure was short."

"To a T-shirt or a tank top, and you can't imagine how much I'm looking forward to removing it."

Wearing a wire was a lot like having a pimple, she thought an hour later; you felt as though even a small one was glaringly obvious. It wasn't, not when it was tucked beneath a wide belt and a bulky sweater, but she was still acutely conscious of it.

She hugged Art hello at an awkward angle, her hip turned slightly inward, her body unnaturally stiff.

He assumed it was nerves. "For you," he said, handing her a bottle of wine. "You look like you could use some."

She microwaved the hors d'oeuvres while Art opened the wine, then took him into the living room to talk. "This whole mess started at Hollister's funeral," she began, "when I ran into Bonita Franks. She was the judge's mistress."

"The singer who was murdered? She and Hollister were sleeping together?"

He sounded astonished, convincingly so. "Yes. She and Hollister used to stop into Freddie's office every now and then to have lunch with him and his girlfriend. Anyway, Bonita asked me to pick up some things of hers from an apartment downtown. She used to stay there when she came to Sacramento. I thought the place was Hollister's—that's how they always referred to it—but it's actually Craig Tomlinson's. Maybe you know about it, since he was your father's client for so many years."

"The one in the building opposite the capitol? *That's* the apartment you mentioned the day your house was ransacked?"

"Yes. Have you ever been inside?"

"Sure. My father took me up there once, right after I moved to Sacramento. He pointed out the highlights."

Art drank some wine, looking embarrassed. "Or low-lights. What happened next?"

"Bonita gave me the keys to everything, even the office. The computer in there—it's the one I mentioned at Vicki's. Did you see it?"

Art hesitated, visibly uncomfortable now. "Uh, yes. An IBM, right?"

"Right. So your father had a key to the office, too, just like Bonita did?"

"I guess so. Why?"

Because it would be easy for you to get inside if you still had the keys, Laura thought. "Tomlinson apparently loans that apartment to people who can help him politically," she said, "but he keeps the office locked. I think it's off-limits to everyone but certain business associates. So if he gave your father the key . . . He wouldn't have done that unless your father had to go in there at times, Art. This is hard for me to say, but you pretty much told me he'd broken the law. I think Tomlinson might have, too. That some of the business they conducted out of that office wasn't legitimate. If I'm wrong, I'm sorry."

"You're not wrong," Art said grimly. "That's why my life is in the toilet right now, but it's not something I can talk about."

"Believe me, I understand." She didn't want to push him, not so soon. "Getting back to the computer—I'm almost sure that Tomlinson thinks I got into it and stole some data. That he's the one who had my house searched."

"But why?" Art looked totally confused now. "Even if he knew you were in his office, it's a big leap between that and computer theft. And that letter in Vicki's printer . . . I know the guy, Laura. He wouldn't kill anyone. There must be some other explanation for the whole incident."

If he didn't believe every word he'd said, he deserved

an Oscar for the caliber of his performance. "That night at Charlie's party, when I was so upset . . . It started with Carolyn Seeley. She asked me what I'd seen in the apartment, including whether I'd gotten into the computer. The truth is that I couldn't, but I lied and claimed I hadn't tried. Then, while you were playing pool, Mike Clemente cornered me in the laundry room and warned me to mind my own business. He threatened to get some Mafia don after me if I didn't. I was terrified. I had no idea what I was even supposed to have done till Vicki's files were erased. Then it began to make sense. Both Seeley and Clemente have close ties to Tomlinson, and I'd been in Tomlinson's office. Bonita worked for him. She must have mentioned that I'd picked up her things—said something that got him worried."

"Oh, God." Art looked sick, stunned. "It never occurred to me. If anything had happened to you . . . "

"What didn't occur to you?"

"The computer. I never even checked. That was stupid."

"Checked what? What are you talking about?"

"Our problems . . . They seem to be intimately connected. Life is sure as hell strange sometimes."

She suddenly remembered Mike. "You look awful, Art. Really upset. Please, tell me what's wrong. How are our problems connected?"

"Tomlinson's computer . . . He must have set up a hidden file to record when anyone used it, and how. A check on people like my father. I didn't look for that, but I should have."

"You mean *you* used his computer? You didn't return his keys after your father died?"

"Uh, no. That is, someone made an extra set. It's a long story." He drained his glass and quickly refilled it. "I really shouldn't talk about it."

"Of course not. I understand completely." She could

afford to be patient. She had alcohol on her side. "But when were you there? And why?"

"About a month ago. I looked through his files. Sort of a follow-up to my father's business dealings."

Laura gulped some wine, trying to seem rattled. "For God's sake, what did they do together that you felt you had to look through his files? That letter . . . People get killed for all sorts of reasons, Art, and—"

"I told you—it was nothing like that. Tomlinson's got ties to the mob—Clemente wasn't bluffing about that—but his personal operations are strictly white-collar stuff. Money laundering, tax evasion and financial manipulations."

"And you were trying to find out more about that by checking his files?"

"No. It was more like—insurance. I was looking for information, in case he caused me problems."

"Problems?" Laura repeated. "You mean he was after you, too?"

"No. I had as much on him as he did on me, but my mother is so damn paranoid. She had this delusion he was going to blackmail me. Destroy me. It calmed her down, knowing I could get into his computer. Seeing the notes I'd made on his files."

Laura was about to ask for details when the doorbell rang. She cursed silently and got up. "I'd better get that. I'll be right back."

She hurried down the hall, wanting to strangle whoever was there. It was Vicki, though, and she was steamed enough to power a turbine.

"His father can't take a bite without turning into a food critic," she muttered, stomping inside. "I've had to listen to one discourse after another about what's wrong with my seasoning and cooking techniques. And Frank's bitch of a sister—she goes on and on about how *normal* Becky and Karen are, meaning that they're boring dimwits, whereas *her* two brats, who are busy tearing up my house and assaulting their cousins, are exceptionally gifted and need to be challenged. I was afraid I'd belt one of them if I didn't get away. I told them I needed some things from the store, but I'd probably smash up the car if I tried to drive."

Laura put her arm around Vicki's shoulders. "Go on into the family room. There are some magazines on the coffee table. I'll get you a glass of wine."

"You're on, but bring it into your bedroom." She started down the hall. "I need to lie down. Turn out the lights and vegetate in front of the tube."

Laura stopped her. "Wait a minute. My bedroom—you can't go in there, but I could bring the TV into—"

"Why not? Is Art Albright in your bed, buck naked and panting?"

"Yes. That is, he's not naked, but we—"

With exquisite timing, Art chose exactly that moment to call out, quite obviously from the living room, "Is everything okay, Laura?"

"Just fine," she called back, then said to Vicki, "Actually, it's Sam. He's been sick all day, retching up everything he eats, and he's finally asleep on the bed. I don't want to disturb him."

Vicki looked dubious. "Sam? The cat with the cast-iron stomach? I'd better take a look. I've had more experience with that sort of thing than you have."

Laura gave up. She had her hands full with Art; she couldn't take on Vicki, too. "We have to talk. Go into Seth's room. I'll be there in a moment."

Vicki went, and Laura hurried back to the living room. "It's Vicki, Art. Her in-laws are over, driving her nuts. She needs to vent her frustrations. I shouldn't be much longer."

Art said he understood, but his tone was cool, almost ironic. Laura didn't stop to ask why, just raced into Seth's room and closed the door. "I'm really sorry," she murmured into her chest, "but enough is enough. Don't have a fit, okay?"

"If you're talking to Tina," Vicki said, "you're in the wrong child's room."

"I'm talking into a microphone that's taped to my chest," Laura murmured. "I've got an FBI agent in my closet, recording my conversation with Art, but don't worry, he's harmless. Please—don't ask questions. Just—"

"An FBI agent? You mean *Art* has the answers they need?" She paused. "I'm glad I came over. It's much more interesting here than it is at my place. I don't suppose I could pop into the bedroom and watch?"

"Absolutely not. Go into the family room."

Vicki bent close to Laura's chest. "Listen, if it were up to me, I'd keep you company. I want you to know that."

"Vicki. This happens to be a serious—"

"I know, I know. I'll sit on the couch and watch TV. I'll mind my own business. I'm not the sort of person who would knowingly obstruct justice." Grinning, Vicki left the bedroom. The TV went on a few moments later.

Laura was back in the living room by then. "Vicki's going to stay for a while," she told Art. "She'll be okay. She just needs a break."

"Sure. It's the least you can do for such a close friend." He handed Laura her glass. "In fact, I'm surprised you didn't talk to *her* about your problems."

In other words, he'd realized by now that he'd done all the talking so far. "I can't. Her husband is the straightest arrow around, and she tells him everything. If he knew what I'd done, it would end our friendship."

"What's to tell? From what I've heard, you haven't done a damn thing, at least not from the FBI's point of view."

"But I have. I was giving you some background first, that's all." She explained about Freddie and Bonita's insurance scam, claiming that she'd known the details but had lied to the Feds because she'd been afraid that telling the truth could be dangerous or even deadly. She reminded him about the audiotape, too—an apparent blackmail tape, she said, almost certainly evidence, that she'd stolen and ultimately destroyed.

His suspicions dissolved. She nibbled on a quiche, pretending she was too badly shaken to go on when she was actually racking her brains for what to ask next. Art had admitted to using the computer, presumably on April 6th, but he hadn't said exactly what he'd been after. She had to find out. And she had to find out if he'd used it again on April 9th, and why. He'd known that his father had helped Tomlinson launder money, but denied taking part. Was it the truth? And what about his mother? Alice had nagged Art to get damaging information on Tomlinson and insisted on meeting with Bailey, so she must have known about Art Sr.'s activities. Just how involved had she been?

Laura put down her plate, then topped off both their glasses. "About my house being searched . . . There's more. I was about to tell you about it when Vicki showed up. My last bank statement had ten grand in deposits and withdrawals that I never made, on April 10th and April 13th. Vicki's files were destroyed on the 15th. I think there's a connection, Art—that someone copied account information from Tomlinson's computer, stole money from him, and ran it through my account to pin the blame on me." She sighed. "Someone must really have it in for me."

He stared at her, a glazed look in his eyes. "Ten grand? That was the amount?"

"Yes. Why? Is there something significant about it?"

"Your account . . . Is it in a Golden West branch?"

"Yes. What have you figured out?"

He looked more dazed than ever. "That it's all my fault. Don't worry—I'll square things with Tomlinson. He won't bother you again."

"But how is it your fault? I don't understand."

"I talk too much. Give in too easily." He reached for his wine. "I don't think. Or maybe I'm just stupid as hell."

"Of course you're not. You're sweet and generous, and if someone took advantage of you, you're hardly to blame."

"Right. It's the story of my life, I'm just an innocent bystander." He wasn't just stunned now, but disgusted with himself.

Laura put her hand on his knee. "Art—when you bought your father's business and learned what was going on . . . You ended it, right? If you're down on yourself because it took you a while, you shouldn't be. Nobody can extricate himself from a mess like that overnight. Look at me. The harder I try to get out, the deeper I seem to get in."

"You don't understand. Those speculative companies I mentioned the night of the party . . . They were fronts. Not much more than money-laundering and expense-account machines. I could have dissolved them and gotten out clean, but I sold them to Tomlinson and his pals instead, so my family could make a final windfall off the sale. I didn't want to, but I was pressured to go along, and I caved in. That's the bottom line. I was scared and gutless, and I caved in. I designed a complicated series of transactions—supervised the whole operation. I convinced myself they would never be traced. That I'd been too clever." He hung his head. "I was wrong, Laura. Bailey got a call from the Feds yesterday morning. Sooner or later, they're going to figure it all out. Use RICO to seize my company. Send me to jail."

"But you talked about cutting a deal. Couldn't you still do it? Offer them information in exchange for immunity or at least probation?"

Art laughed, but despondently, almost bitterly. "They don't need me anymore. The stuff I took part in . . . They're going to trace it all without me. The guy who knows every scam Tomlinson ever pulled—who could name his own terms and have the Feds panting to accept them—is dead."

He really believed that. There wasn't a doubt in Laura's mind. "What about your mother, then? Maybe your father confided in her."

"My mother is an extremely troubled woman. Let's leave it at that." He gulped some wine, then blinked in confusion. "Are you expecting someone else? I think I heard your doorbell again."

He had. She wanted to throw something at the nearest wall. "Maybe it's Frank, looking for Vicki."

She should only have been so lucky. It was Allan, and he was looking for Art. "I want to talk to Albright," he said as he stalked inside. "Don't try to stop me. It's something I have to do."

The primeval male, she thought, defending his territory against intruders. "We're just friends now, but even if we were more . . . As much as I appreciate the way you helped tonight, Allan, I'll have to ask you to stay out of my private life."

"I can't. I love you. I'm still married to you. Albright wouldn't be here if he didn't want you. He needs to understand that we have a history together. That I'm not giving you up to him or anyone else without a fight."

"You hear that? Load up your Colt .45 and head for the O.K. Corral."

He frowned. "What did you say?"

"I was kidding. Do I have any say in this, or do you plan to hit me over the head with a club and drag me to the nearest cave?"

"I wish it were that simple. Where is he?"

There was obviously no stopping him, but at least he wasn't storming the bedroom. "In the living room, but believe me, you're totally off base. You're going to wind up feeling very foolish."

He ignored her and marched away. She followed, listening to his speech from the living room doorway. It was from the Fidel Castro school of oratory, impassioned and seemingly endless. She went to get Vicki after a while, telling her it was a performance not to be missed.

Art barely reacted. He was too dejected at first, then too astonished. But Allan's final pronouncement, "If you're looking for a fight, you've got one, and I don't intend to lose," finally snapped him out of his trance.

"Your need to be in control—it's not healthy, Allan," he said mildly. "No offense, but you should get some professional help." He looked at Laura. "How did you stay married to this guy for so long?"

"I don't know. The way I was raised, I guess. And he *is* great in bed." The doorbell rang again. She grimaced. "I don't believe this! I might as well buy airtime on TV and invite the whole city to tune in."

As she walked down the hall, she heard Vicki telling a story about her in-laws, dissolving the tension in the room. The situation was hopeless. The whole mood had changed. Art would never keep talking, not even if she sent everyone packing.

She opened the door. Her mother was standing outside with Alice Albright, holding a covered cake dish. There was a burst of laughter from the living room as they stepped inside. Dottie was bad enough, but Alice . . . An IRS auditor would have been only slightly less welcome.

"I made you a chocolate cake," Dottie said. "We were going to leave it and run, but since you're having a party, maybe you'll ask us to stay."

Laura kissed her and took the cake. "Thanks, Mom, but I'm not having a party. People showed up uninvited. Come sit down. I'll make some coffee. We'll have some of your cake."

Dottie said that sounded nice and started down the hall with Alice. Laura followed, noting absently that Alice was wearing a tan trenchcoat. So was her mother—half the world owned them—but Alice was thin. She didn't look a day over fifty. Laura paled a little. Put a blond wig and dark glasses on her, and maybe, just maybe . . .

They entered the living room. Laura introduced Alice to Allan and Vicki. Art mumbled hello, looking at his mother with such icy fury that "maybe" turned into "yes, definitely" with all the force of a bolt of lightning.

Laura took Alice's arm before she could sit down. "Why don't you help me with the coffee and cake? You've got the wrong idea about my relationship with Art, and I'd like to straighten things out."

Art started to get up. "Laura, my mother—"

"Really, Art, it'll be fine," Laura said, waving him back down. "Ten minutes and we'll clear everything up."

Alice glanced at Art and then Dottie, her expression bland. "I'm always interested in my son's friendships. If you want to talk, I'm willing to listen."

"I do." Laura led Alice into the kitchen and closed the door. "I don't know why you swiped ten grand from Craig Tomlinson," she said pleasantly, taking the coffee out of the freezer, "but there was no need to run it through my account and get me in all kinds of trouble. I'm not after Art. I'm seeing someone else."

"Really! And behind your mother's back, too." Alice clearly didn't believe her. "What's his name?"

"It's nobody you know. By the way, where are you working these days, Alice? At a branch of Golden West Bank?"

"In a dress shop, and what's all this nonsense about stealing money and working in a bank? I thought you wanted to talk about my son."

"You've worked in at least two of them. You wrote to Freddie about it. I used to read and answer his mail, you know." Laura measured the coffee and turned on the kettle. "There's not the slightest doubt in my mind that you were working in a Golden West branch during the middle of April, because you don't know enough about computers to break into a corporate system. If you did, you wouldn't have nagged Art to go to Tomlinson's apartment. You needed him to find out the password to get into the computer. To tell you which file contained the security codes for Tomlinson's accounts."

"You're a sick girl, Laura. I feel sorry for your mother. I'm going to warn my son about you, I can tell you that." Alice started to walk away.

"Why did you kill Hollister? Because he knew your husband was laundering money and blackmailed him into a nervous breakdown? Were you afraid he'd do the same thing to your son? Or did he find out your husband wasn't really dead and start blackmailing *you?*"

Alice had stopped at the word *kill*. She stood rigidly for several seconds, as if she couldn't decide whether to go or stay. "I have no idea what you're talking about," she finally said.

"Then I'll spell it out. Art Sr. writes to Freddie from New Mexico. He calls himself Marion Kirby. He says he's an artist. Freddie got drunk one day and told me the whole story—about who Kirby was and about the deal you made on the insurance."

Alice turned around, very slowly. "You say one word about that and you'll be sorry." Her tone was eerily cheerful, her expression, smiling. "I'll go after your children if I have to. And do stay away from Art, dear. You're not nearly good enough for him."

The woman was a homicidal fruitcake. Laura edged away from her. "If I say one word about it," she replied as evenly as she could, "*you'll* go to jail, but frankly, I have too many problems of my own to get involved in somebody else's vendetta. After all, it isn't as if Hollister's death was any great loss to the world. He was blackmailing Freddie, too, and cheating on Maggie with Bonita."

She picked up the kettle. "Besides, I'm fond of Art, and he'd be upset if I got you in trouble. Would you get down the dishes, Alice? They're in the cupboard above the microwave. The forks and cake server are in the top center drawer."

To Laura's astonishment, Alice opened the cupboard. She was still smiling, but the look in her eyes reminded Laura of Jack Nicholson in one of his weirdo roles. The smile, too, come to think of it.

"You want something, I suppose," she said. "What? Hush money? My son?"

"Neither, but I *am* curious about Bonita. I got to like her after a while, and she *was* talented. It's too bad she's dead. What did you have against her?"

"I barely knew the woman. All this talk about blackmail and murder . . . " Alice set down her purse and began taking out dishes. "Really, Laura, you have the most extraordinary imagination. The only thing I'm guilty of is helping my husband. Marion's a genius, a pure and innocent spirit, but he was trapped inside Art for years. The long confinement damaged him. Deformed his soul. I liberated him, but it's not enough. Genius needs to soar."

Alice kept talking as she got out the flatware, babbling about Marion and Art, getting more and more
incoherent as Laura made the coffee and tried to think.
Maybe Alice had killed Bonita because Bonita had
begun blackmailing her where the judge had left off.
The only flaw in the theory was that Bonita hadn't
seemed to need the money.

And then Laura remembered the ten grand she'd
given Charlie for his party. That amount—ten grand—
had struck a stunned chord in Art. Maybe Bonita
hadn't sold jewelry to raise the cash, after all.

"Really, I sympathize with your problems," Laura
said when Alice finally stopped talking. "In my opinion, it all goes back to Craig Tomlinson. He ruined
your husband and compromised your son. Left you vulnerable to Bonita's demand for ten thousand dollars. I
don't blame you for paying yourself back out of his
accounts. Most people would have taken far more. You
were very scrupulous, Alice."

She nodded. "Yes. I'm an honest person. I would
never take anything I wasn't entitled to."

"Nobody would have blamed you if you had.
Tomlinson's such scum. I can't give you the details, but
he's been blackmailing someone I care about very
much."

"And a loyal friend," Alice went on, as if Laura
hadn't spoken. Her eyes were glazed now, as if she
were somewhere far away. "I know who killed
Hollister. It was that cheating bastard Phelps. Mary
Beth told me her gun was missing. That's when I figured it all out. She was in Europe at the time, you
know. She'd never divorce him because of the children,
but they're bound to trace the gun's ownership eventually. Then he'll go to jail, and she'll finally be rid of
him."

So Alice had taken the gun during a visit to her

friend Mary Beth Phelps. She'd left it in Tomlinson's apartment afterward, hoping someone would find it and turn it in, and that Freddie would be arrested for Hollister's murder. When that hadn't happened, she'd retrieved it in order to kill Bonita. She hadn't put it back in the apartment because she couldn't; a third lock had been installed in the front door by then.

"That Freddie is a real creep," Laura agreed. "He would have fired me for not sleeping with him if I hadn't quit first. Do you think he killed Bonita, too?"

"He might have. Or someone might have found the gun in Tomlinson's apartment and decided to use it." Alice didn't seem to realize that the gun's location had never been mentioned. "The place was full of them, you know."

"Yes. I was there. There's only one thing I don't understand. The ten grand you picked up in cash from the five banks . . . Why didn't you just move it into an untraceable account? Why impersonate one of your son's employees?"

"She was after Art. Imagine, a woman who's old enough to be his mother! It was disgusting, but an anonymous little tip should take care of her." Alice picked up her purse. "It's all in the timing, dear. I let you go out with Art to find out what you knew about the accident. About Marion. But that was before. Who knew I would get more out of your mother than Art ever did from you? That we would become such good friends? She's a wonderful woman. It's shameful, the way you take her for granted."

Alice opened her purse. The skin prickled on the back of Laura's neck. Somehow she knew what was coming.

She yelled to Art to give them a hand, but Alice cut her off, calmly taking out a gun and pointing it at her. "Never mind, dear," she called to Art. "We can manage without you." She paused. "It's all in the timing. You'll leave Art alone from now on, won't you."

One mention of the G-word and Mike would charge out of the closet to the rescue. Laura couldn't let him do that—couldn't screw up two long years of work on the case. After all, as loony as Alice was, she'd concealed the two murders carefully. Laura only hoped she'd realize that a corpse in the kitchen would be a trifle hard to hide.

"Yes," she said. "There really is someone else, but even if there weren't, I know I'm not good enough for your—"

She was interrupted by Art, who opened the door, looked at his mother, and blanched. "What the hell—? Are you nuts? Put that thing away. Where did you get it, anyway?"

Alice raised the gun a fraction higher. "It's a dangerous world, Arthur. A woman has to protect herself."

"From Laura?" Art started forward. "Give me the gun, Mother. You don't know what you're doing."

"Just stay where you are," Laura said quickly, speaking to Mike. "I'm okay. Nothing's going to happen."

Alice glared at her. "How dare you give my son orders?"

Allan entered the room at a rapid trot. "Did I hear Art say— Oh, Jesus. Get back. Get out." He was talking to Dottie and Vicki, both of whom were right behind him. "Laura has to leave now, Mrs. Albright. She has to get our children. They're at a—"

"No! Nobody's leaving but me and my son." Alice fired a shot in the ceiling, then gestured at the doorway into the hall with the gun. "The rest of you. Into the bathroom."

The door from the garage flew open and Mike barreled through. He grabbed Alice from behind, wrenched down her arm, and tackled her to the ground, all in a single, fluid motion. He wound up on top of her, in sole possession of her gun, his own gun still tucked securely into his waist.

"Special Agent Michael Clemente, FBI," he said, pulling out his ID. "Allan, make sure Albright doesn't leave. And Laura, call 9ll. Get me some help here."

"Police brutality," Alice shrieked. "Get off me, you cretinous thug. I'll sue. I'll phone the media. I'll—"

"Oh, shut up, Mother," Art snapped. "And you— get out of my face," he said to Allan. "I'm not going anywhere." He closed his eyes and shook his head. "If insanity is genetic, I'm goddamn doomed."

"Mrs. Albright, you're under arrest for the murders of James Hollister and Bonita Frangelico," Mike said, rolling off her. "You have the right to remain silent. . . . "

Dottie sidled up to Laura, who was talking to a 911 dispatcher by then. Mike finished with Alice and walked over to Art, repeating his Miranda routine as Laura hung up the phone.

"So, Laura," Dottie said. "This secret agent of yours—Michael Clemente—that's an Italian name, *nu*? A Catholic, I suppose. Still, he's very nice looking, and a cop is probably better than a lobbyist. Exactly how close a relationship do you have?"

Laura figured the tape was still rolling, and that everyone from Kevin McKennery on up was going to listen to it eventually. "You just found out your good friend killed two people, and you're worried about my social life?"

"Sounds to me like her relationship with Mr. Clemente is very close indeed," Vicki said, strolling into the kitchen. "You should probably get used it, Dottie. Both of us know how stubborn Laura can be."

Dottie snorted. "That shows what you know. No offense, but you should stick to saving the world and let *me* worry about my family. Alice, when you get yourself a lawyer, have him call me. I'll be glad to testify that you're off your rocker." She marched up to Mike. "I'm an old lady. A very religious woman. Laura is my only child. I'm sure you're a good man, but you're all wrong for her. I'll die of a broken heart if she gets mixed up with you."

"It's a pleasure to finally meet you, Mrs. Greenbaum," Mike said. "I can see where your daughter gets her looks and spirit. By the way, my mother is half-Jewish."

Dottie cocked up an eyebrow. "Is that so, Mr. Clemente? On which side?"

"My grandmother's name was Pearl Klein. Laura tells me that your late husband was a wonderful man. If it's all right with you, I'd like to name our first child after him."

Allan looked from Laura to Mike to Dottie, his eyes bulging in disbelief. "Your first child? Dammit, Laura, you can't be serious about this guy! You've never liked cops. You barely even know him."

"And who asked your opinion?" Dottie demanded. She smiled at Mike. "You and Laura will come to dinner Friday night. I'll teach you a few blessings. Take you to temple. Then we'll talk."

EPILOGUE

Ken Carlsen became the governor of California. Bonita's blackmail tape mysteriously disappeared, but high FBI officials are known to salivate at the thought of Carlsen's bright future in national politics. Jane Martin Carlsen finally consented to move to Sacramento, but is often heard to complain, like Nancy Reagan, that nobody in town can "do hair."

Carlsen's chief of staff, Jack Waltzer, arranged for Heather Martin to take a job in Washington, D.C. as a staffer to Senator Sonny Bono. She married a middle-aged Supreme Court justice from New Hampshire two months later. The pair is often cited by Washington movers and shakers as one of the capital's top ten "fun couples."

Royal Paine became a free agent and signed with the Los Angeles Lakers. Liberated from the hapless Sacramento Kings, he went on to become a perennial NBA All-Star.

Freddie Phelps was convicted of two counts of insurance fraud and sent to a minimum security prison, where he became the unofficial inmate director of social activities. His inspirational book, *Triumphing over Adversity*, is now number three on the *New York Times* best-seller list. Numerous organizations have already booked him as a speaker in anticipation of his upcoming release.

Mary Beth Phelps stood gamely by Freddie through his trial, then divorced him and ran off with one of her hospice clients. He was cured two months later with a new gene therapy developed by a deranged Jennex scientist who was under the mistaken impression that he worked for a real genetics research firm.

Art Albright, Sr. was arrested in New Mexico. He was found by psychiatrists to be suffering from a split personality dominated by the artist Marion Kirby, who disavowed any knowledge of the activities of Arthur Albright. Judged incompetent to stand trial, he is now in a federal medical facility, where he spends his days at his easel. His abstract paintings, called brilliant by critics, sell for amounts in the middle five figures.

Alice Albright was convicted of larceny, insurance and bank fraud, and two counts of murder, and sentenced to life in prison without possibility of parole. Although shunned by her fellow inmates as dangerously paranoid due to her conviction that every single one of them is after her son, she is visited regularly by Maggie Hollister and Mary Beth Phelps, both of whom credit her with giving them a new lease on life.

Art Albright, Jr., became a federal informant, helping to convict Craig Tomlinson and others, and then, convinced that his genes were tainted, had himself vasectomized. He entered the Federal Witness Protection Program, relocated to a small town in South Dakota, and married a widow with six children. In between babysitting stints, he operates a worldwide computer consulting business out of an office in his basement.

Carolyn Seeley had an epiphany while swimming laps in the Capital Athletic Club pool, decided to devote herself to social service, and established a foundation to fund programs and shelters for battered women. Often called the Jane Addams of the nineties, she is married to Allan Miller, who got fed up with working for peanuts and is now a top executive with MTS Incorporated, the parent company of Tower Records.

Mike and Laura Clemente own a private detective agency in Sacramento. Their operatives include Dottie Greenbaum, who specializes in premarriage investigations. Their son was born within a year of their marriage, bringing the number of children in their home to four. Mike and Laura had planned to give the boy the Hebrew name Avraham, after his grandfather Abraham, and choose something more contemporary for his English name, but Dottie demanded the whole schmeer. It should be obvious who won.

Deborah Gordon is the award-winning, best-selling author of 23 books for Silhouette and Harlequin. She lives in Sacramento, California.